## CHAPTER 1

### Stairway to Heav

Forty-five minutes, three penalty points, and one speeding fine later, my trusty old Vauxhall Astra estate lurched to a grinding stop outside 12 Birkdale Avenue, our three-bedroom married quarter, perched precariously on the south side of Portsdown Hill, overlooking the island city of Portsmouth and the dark waters of the Solent. Peering through the evening darkness, I could just see the far lights of Chichester, then scanning back past Hayling Island my gaze came to rest on the vibrant, blue, and red glow that framed the arch of the Spinnaker Tower. I had always loved that brilliant neon blue colour but after being pulled over by a smug copper in an unmarked Sierra Cosworth, ten minutes ago, I'd gone right off it.

Snapping from my daydream; speeding fine or no speeding fine, I remembered that there were much more exciting matters afoot. Earlier I'd been enjoying a coffee, waiting to be called for my next stint in front of the radar, when my issued blue rucksack had started buzzing.

"BOYS R OFF TO THE CINEMA. YOR LUCKS IN!" Intrigued by the message, my interest had almost been outweighed by being irked at how it was written, knowing that Alice would have been chuckling to herself as she typed it; to simultaneously arouse me and exasperate my inner pedant. Shelving my grammar policing, I mentally erased the message and, fantasising about the imminent bedroom gymnastics, threw open the car door and went tearing down the concrete steps.

Bounding into the porch, I began rattling my key feverishly in the lock before flinging open the front door and exploding into the hall. Gypsy, my faithful beagle, stood waiting,

1

gazing expectantly with her one good eye, her tail wagging at the end of her trembling fat body, anticipating a welcome home fuss. *In a minute.*

"Hellooo?" I panted loudly into the hallway, rubbing the dog's head as I dropped my bag, before hanging my hat on the coat stand. My greeting was more of a question, trying to ascertain exactly where Alice was, although I had a pretty good idea.

"I'm up here," she sang. I thought her voice sounded playful, as it came drifting down the stairs from our bedroom.

Throwing my jacket on the floor, I kicked off my shoes, undid my belt, and hopped towards the stairs, yanking my feet as I stepped out of my trousers. Taking three steps at a time should have been quicker than one, but in my lust-fuelled excitement, my stockinged feet repeatedly slipped on the carpet and twice I fell, thudding into the creaking stairs, almost chinning myself. Undaunted, I scrambled up the last few steps and clawed my way onto the landing, just as my younger son Jack emerged from the bathroom.

"Er, hi Dad," he said awkwardly. "Okay… Sooo… I'm sure there's a perfectly good reason why you're kneeling at the top of the stairs in your saggy Calvin Kleins, puffing like you've just run a marathon but if you were desperate for the loo there is one *downstairs*," he suggested, shaking his head with a concerned scowl, "but it's all yours now. Your throne awaits," he scoffed with a welcoming sweep of his hand.

"I er… I thought the light was on downstairs… and um… someone was in there. But thank you," I mumbled, red-faced and breathless, still on all fours. I imagined Jack contemplating a Google search for 'what to do if you think your dad is having a mental breakdown.' Instead, tutting loudly, Jack turned away, easing his bedroom door open just far enough so that he could slip in sideways. As he slid into the dark interior, disappearing behind a closing door, I heard him talking to his brother, "Toby, I think Dad's finally lost

Shooting the Gap
By
Paul Griffin

For Alison, Toby, Flynn and Cloudy

it."

"Erm, what *are* you doing?" Alice asked from the bedroom doorway, a duster in one hand and a tin of spray polish in the other.

"One minute," I replied, grunting my way from kneeling to vertical, holding up a finger, and heading to the bathroom. Shutting the door, I stood waiting for what I thought would appear to be an average wee's length, before flushing the loo and running the tap. My performance was complete, so I retrieved my trousers from the hallway and walked back upstairs to find Alice sitting on the bed chuckling to herself.

"You thought they'd already gone to the cinema didn't you," she sniggered.

"Yes," I whispered through gritted teeth, "when you said *they're off* I thought you meant they were just leaving. Thank God I kept my pants on."

"Don't worry, if you had been *tackle out,* I think Jack would have just added it to his list of things to tell a shrink," she chortled. "Maybe if you'd been thinking with the organ in your head instead of *that* brain," she said, pointing to my saggy boxer shorts, "you'd have remembered I told you this morning that they're going *tonight.* Been a little absent-minded lately haven't you husband?" Alice jabbed, tapping her wedding ring finger.

"Um, you could say that," I admitted, bowing my head.

"Well keep your engine running Romeo. The boys need to be in Port Solent for six and I'll have a surprise for you when you get back," she winked.

"Okay," I panted excitedly like a border collie on speed.

"Right, I'll go and make some tea, see if the boys want one, would you?" Alice instructed stepping from the room and heading downstairs.

"Sure. Have you done much today?" I asked, unbuttoning my shirt, hoping that Toby and Jack would have spent some quality time with their mum.

"I've hardly seen them except for feeding time at the zoo," Alice warbled, trying, and failing to sound unhurt. "They've been in their room on that bloody PlayStation nearly all day." *That'll be my fault for buying it for them.*

"Right," I sighed, pulling my socks off, "I'm going to grab a shower, but I'll go have a word with them."

## CHAPTER 2

### Private Dancer

I slowly turned the handle, silently pushing open the door to the boys' room. Apart from Jack's thumb randomly pushing a button they were both motionless, frozen rigid like mannequins, transfixed by the image on the TV. Looking at the screen I could see why. A pair of very realistic computer-animated breasts swayed, bouncing in front of their intense gaze. I'd expected to walk in and be met with the normal scene of them each sitting wearing a headset, screaming animatedly, hollering instructions to their online teammates, as hordes of gun-toting soldiers frantically scampered across a digital battlespace. I didn't expect to see a young woman grinding rhythmically, jiggling a massive pair of tits.

Creeping silently up behind them, I stopped inches from the backs of their heads, still unnoticed, "*What are you doing?*"

"Jesus Dad!" shrieked Toby, as they both jumped, springing up like scalded cats.

"Why are you letting your little brother play this? Whatever *this* is," I asked, glowering at Toby.

Jack sat back down, quickly regaining his composure, and carried on playing.

"Chill out Dad, it's just a lap dance," he replied coolly.

4

I never thought I'd hear that phrase coming from the mouth of my thirteen-year-old son, and certainly not what he said next.

"But you can meet her in the car park behind the strip club and take her home for sex if you like."

"*W-what?* She's a prostitute?" I stammered.

"No Daaad," Jack answered, shaking his head in annoyance, "you *pay* for the lap dance, but she doesn't charge if you take her home and make her teeth rattle. She's only a stripper. Do keep up." *Make her teeth rattle. Where has he picked up that delightful expression?*

"She only takes her clothes off for money," Toby confirmed, joining in, "they'd never make a game with prostitutes. It's got carjackers, drug dealers, and pole dancers. Oh, and you can run people over too, but there are no hookers, that would be tasteless. Seriously, what's wrong with you Dad?" he asked with feigned disgust.

Sapphire, the shapely topless figure on the screen continued writhing and snaking her body, wearing nothing but a G-string made of purple dental floss. Momentarily, I caught myself glued to the screen. *Those look amazing.* The spell was broken by an unexpected sensation stirring under my towel. I noticed that it no longer hung straight down and had a slight unwelcome bulge. *Oh God not now.* This could take some explaining.

"Turn it off!" I demanded, in an attempt to remove the possibility of any further arousal by a computer-generated lap dancer's swaying boobs. The little minx.

"Whaaat? Are you joking?" Jack whined.

"Turn it off *now!*" I bellowed. Jack angrily began stabbing the buttons and flicking the joystick until the home screen appeared.

"Happy now?" he asked venomously, dropping the controller on the floor and throwing his hands in the air.

"No, I'm not! How long have you had this?"

"It was a joint Christmas present last year," Jack stated flatly, scrunching lines into his forehead.

My knuckles clenched and I started thinking about what I'd say to the irresponsible arsehole who'd thought it okay to buy my sons such a violent, vile, and inappropriate gift.

"And who the hell bought it for you?"

I was ill-prepared for the reply as Toby and Jack exchanged puzzled looks.

"*You did!*" they chimed in unison.

"Oh." *Bugger. I need to have a very serious chat with myself about responsible parenting.*

"Oh dear, Dad, losing your memory?" Jack mocked, handing me the game's thin plastic case. "Remember now?"

Immediately recognising the cartoon cover, I recalled driving after a night shift to West Quay Shopping Centre in Southampton to buy it.

"I thought this was car racing," I offered lamely. I hadn't paid much attention when I'd bought it and honestly believed it was a racing simulation game. *I must have had a busy night shift.*

"It is, sort of. You can steal cars and then you have to outrun the police or run over pedestrians," Toby explained.

"Or shoot them," Jack added gleefully.

"You can kill people?"

"*Yeah*," they both answered, a little too enthusiastically for my liking.

"... aaand you can play golf on it too," Jack added, seeing the horror on my face, intimating that this game might appeal to me.

"Nice try," I replied. "If it's so violent, why doesn't it have some sort of age rating?" I asked, turning the case over.

"What like that one there... and there... and there?" Toby countered, pointing to the red circled 18+ symbols on the front, spine, and back cover. *Double bugger.*

"Blimey, Dad. First, you lose your hair, then you forget that we've got a downstairs loo and now your eyesight's going. Should we just shoot you now and put you out of your misery?" Jack quipped. "I'll do it, I've had lots of practice!"

"I didn't *forget* we had two toilets. I thought someone was in there," I lied, keeping up the ruse.

"If you say so, Dad. *Cuckoo, cuckoo*," Jack sang, circling his index finger at the side of his temple.

Ignoring Jack's taunt, it suddenly struck me why my younger son's reaction had been so extreme on Christmas morning. "No way, I don't believe it!" he'd shouted as he'd torn off the wrapping paper. I realised now that it wasn't just excitement, he genuinely couldn't believe that I'd agreed to him having an 18+ game that clearly stated it contained drug references, swearing, nudity, violence, and sexual content.

"I used to be happy playing paddle tennis," I offered humbly.

"*Paddle tennis!* You mean *Pong*?" asked Toby.

"Yes, it was great," I replied, in defence of the innocent game from my childhood.

"Oh yeah, *amazing*, 2D table tennis in black and white. Bloop... Bloop... Bloop..." Jack mocked, moving his fingers up and down, mimicking the prehistoric video game. "Just how old are you Dad, ninety?"

They both started laughing, the little gits.

"Forty-four thank you. And I'll have less of your cheek son if *you* want to make it to fourteen?"

"So, can we play it or are you going to go off ranting on another one of your moral crusades?" Jack asked, bending down to retrieve the controller. "Oh, and just remember who bought it for us," he added cockily, pointing an accusatory finger directly at my face, "*Captain Underpants.*"

I'd scored a massive own goal, two if I included being caught trouserless at the top of the stairs. The boys had owned this game for almost a year and would definitely have discovered all of the inappropriate content. Twice. Taking it away now would only irritate them, giving them further grounds to accuse me of being Dickensian.

"Yes, I suppose so, but don't tell your mum," I conceded.

"*Whapeesh.*" They both made the sound effect and chuckled as they mimed me being whipped.

"Talking of your mum, she said she's hardly seen you." Their smiles instantly wilted as both their heads dropped, looking to the floor. "We've talked about this. She's a bit upset that you've been playing this *all* day. Come on boys, make the effort, and spend some time with her, you've only got one mum you know. Promise me," I pleaded.

"Sorry Dad, we got a bit carried away." *I bet you did; I came close myself just now.* "But yes, we will. I promise," Toby confirmed with a shamefaced grin.

"Jack?"

"Yeah, I promise. Sorry."

"That's okay. Right, Mum's making tea. If you want one go and ask her yourself. I'm going to grab a shower and then I'll give you a lift to the pictures."

"*The pictures!*" Jack chimed derisively. "Just how long will it take us to get to *the picture house dearest Papa*? You know, with one of us walking in front of our horseless carriage waving a red warning flag?" He chuckled while turning away, obviously keen to get back to the strip club.

"Do you want a lift or not you little pervert?"

"Yes, please Dad, and Mum says the reason I'm a little deviant is that I take after you." *Harsh but fair.*

"Right, the cinema then. Better?"

Jack popped his thumb up.

"And if you're going to carry on playing *that*," I said with half-hearted contempt, "try and keep the noise down. Okay?"

"*Okayyy, we'll keep the noise down*," Jack answered uncertainly, slowly turning around and shaking his head at me. *Try and keep the noise down! What was I talking about?* They'd been quieter than church mice when I sneaked in just now. I was so used to saying it because of the shouting and swearing that usually accompanied them playing online shoot-em-ups like Call of Duty. Although, in my defence, I absolutely did not want to hear the sort of noises they might make playing with a buxom stripper on Grand Theft Auto.

Their mystified expressions followed my retreat as I sidled out of the room, illuminated by the glowing TV screen that came flickering back to life as Jack reloaded the game. Closing the door I caught one final glimpse of Sapphire's curvaceous bottom, dancing provocatively. Shaking my head I walked to the bathroom, leaving my seventeen and thirteen-year-old sons lusting after a topless lap dancer.

## CHAPTER 3

### Joy and Pain

Standing in the bath with both hands against the cool tiled wall, leaning into the shower's hot flow, I dropped my head, letting the water pummel the back of my neck then run off my nose and mouth and trickle down my spine. I imagined washing away the impending speeding fine before my mind started playing a video of me at work in front of the radar screen.

Mid-morning I'd been controlling four Harrier GR7 jump jets from their home base of RAF Cottesmore. As the formation had gone screaming from Rutland towards Kent, Sussex, and the English Channel at 430 knots, I'd woven a safe path for them through the busy stream of commercial air traffic climbing and descending over the southeast of England. The formation of close air support jets, en route to bolster the International Security Assistance Force in Afghanistan, were planning to transit over France, the Swiss Alps, then hug the Italian Adriatic coast before dropping into Gioia del Colle Air Base located in Bari, sat in the arch of Italy's foot, before their next leg to Cyprus and ultimately Kandahar Air Base.

High above the deserted beachfront of Eastbourne, the screams of four Rolls-Royce Pegasus engines filled the air, as the jets whistled and whined their way out over the south coast. Midway across the Channel, I tried ringing French military ATC. There was a short delay when the French radar controller began refusing to take the handover, contesting that he "*wasn't expecting any 'Arriers zis weekend.*" He quickly surrendered when I informed him, robustly, that these were Royal Air Force mission jets, heading to support ISAF troops in Afghanistan and they were not stopping. In the spirit of *entente cordiale* and with inimitable Gallic charm, he begrudgingly accepted the formation.

The second session after lunch had been crazy. The ongoing major NATO training exercise had generated a demanding tanking sortie requiring two hours of non-stop controlling. I'd been part of a team of three, manoeuvring fast jets and two air-to-air refuelling tankers in a thin sliver of airspace east of the Isle of Man and high above the Irish Sea, surrounded by airways. Vectoring a constant stream of thirsty RAF Tornado bombers and American F-15 fighters on and off the back of two flying petrol stations going 300 knots was hard enough. But doing that while trying to keep them apart, avoiding passenger jets, and keeping all my aircraft safe inside a slim protective corridor had been draining and almost pushed me to my limit.

Grabbing the soap and Alice's pink shower puff, I furiously rubbed until it spewed into a rich frothing ball. Lathering myself from head to foot in velvet-soft, creamy foam, the memory of work faded as the vision of a thong appeared. A fine, gossamer strip of purple disappeared into the crack of a pert bottom, swaying hypnotically before my eyes. *Hmmm, maybe I should have had a cold shower.*

Cleansed, relaxed, and refreshed I stepped out of the bath. Before my foot hit the floor, a searing pain slashed across my ankle. Ripping back the shower curtain I wiped my eyes in time to catch the sight of a ginger tail whipping away through the open door. *Your days are so numbered you little shit.* Looking at the scarlet lines trickling down my foot I began wondering if Lucky's sole purpose in life was inflicting pain, misery, and suffering. That's about all he'd done from the moment I caved into Alice's cunning ultimatum and rescued the horrible little bastard.

# CHAPTER 4

## I Surrender

Alice kept talking about getting a dog when we first moved in together. It had been easy to dissuade her as newlyweds with little money and then the boys came along, plus we regularly moved house with each new posting. I managed to convince her that we didn't need the added stress of a pet. However, when the boys started boarding school, Alice's nest suddenly became empty and even I had to agree that our three-bedroomed house practically rattled with just two of us, so my excuses had started wearing a bit thin.

"You know, we *could* have another baby," Alice suggested plainly, dropping a conversational bomb during, what had been, a pleasant Sunday pub lunch. I almost choked on my beef and ale pie.

"What… you want… er… an… another what?" I eloquently replied.

"Baby! Small pink thing, two arms, two legs, food goes in one end, biohazard material comes out the other, remember?"

I couldn't tell if Alice was joking. We already had two growing boys, both rapidly approaching the stage where they could be classed as young men, and I didn't have a clue how to diplomatically articulate that Alice would be classed as one of the *older* mums. Not without getting filleted in The Red Lion with a steak knife. I giggled nervously, concentrating on my food. *Another baby!* Our firstborn, Toby, had been an absolute joy from the moment he arrived; gurgling, feeding, and sleeping as he grew. So, there hadn't been the slightest hesitation when we decided to try for a second. Suckers. Angry from the moment he fought his way out from between his mother's legs, Jack arrived kicking and screaming at the world. Having had one child who made Garfield look hyperactive, while the other displayed all the

12

charm and charisma of a furious wasp trapped in a jam jar, was she really prepared to roll the dice again? *Two Jacks, or worse, a female version.* It didn't bear thinking about. Sitting silently mulling over Alice's proposal, I decided that now might be a good time to give in and take her mind off a third child. Dog, cat, stick insect, although I'd have heartily welcomed the news that Alice was expecting triplets over the possibility of getting a bloody rabbit.

Emerging from the shade of the pub we found ourselves bathing in the warmth of a sunny English afternoon and set off up the narrow street. Alice began marching at a furious pace and a moment later I watched her lunging across the busy Portsdown Hill Road. Running to catch up with her, I started panting, as together we cut through the thick hedge on the far side. We headed for home, immersed in awkward silence, striding across lush open grassland. Well, I strode; Alice stomped. *Sorry grass, this is my fault.*

Nearing the stile we'd crossed earlier, Alice stopped.

"Can you hear that?" she asked.

"What, I can't hear anything?"

"Shhh," Alice ordered, holding up an angry finger while crouching down, cocking her head to one side. A weak mewling drifted from nearby.

"Hellooo?" Alice said softly. *"Puss, puss."*

Glad for the distraction, I bent down next to her, turning my head and straining my ears. A slight movement to my right caught my eye. Spotting the source of the pathetic noise I crouched closer. A tiny ginger and white kitten perched, looking out from the middle of the prickly hedge, mewing and vulnerable. Alice saw it too.

"Ahhh. You have to help it!"

The kitten's delicate bony frame wobbled, supported on painfully thin legs like ginger pipe cleaners. Bowing despondently, the poor little thing's scrawny neck appeared to be struggling to keep its head up. It continued watching me with pleading, sad, pitiful blue eyes, trapped inside its thorny prison. I reached in, "Ouch," scratching the back of my hand on the sharp sticks and barbed twigs. The kitten remained motionless, crying louder as my fingers neared. Cupping and closing my hands, I softly enveloped its fragile body. Slowly I began withdrawing my arms, maintaining the lightest pressure on my precious cargo, as if I'd trapped a butterfly and didn't want to damage its wings.

"Careful," Alice directed nervously, as I concentrated, squeezing my elbows and hands together slightly to fit through the narrow space, fearful of crushing the delicate creature.

"*Yaaarrrgh bastard!*" I screamed as the thing between my hands exploded into a spitting ball of hair and flailing claws. Dropping the small beast onto the grass, it landed with a barely audible thud.

"*Henry!* You frightened him," Alice chastised, kneeling to pick up the demonic fuzzball. It jumped, clawing up her jacket sleeve then froze, spreadeagled on her shoulder. Alice stood up.

"Hello, puss. Don't be scared baby," she clucked, turning her head to the kitten as it began unhooking its front claws and shakily sat up. Crouching on Alice's shoulder, it slowly turned its head towards me, baring its needle-like fangs as it hissed.

"Look at him, he needs his mummy. Don't you? Yes, you do," Alice cooed. "You're lucky we found you," she added, looking lovingly at the hostile, spitting gargoyle on her shoulder. I scoffed and began shaking my head.

"*Lucky*," she exclaimed, with an expression of gleeful certainty, "that's what we'll call him."

"*Call him! What!* Why on earth do you want to call that angry little fucker anything?" I asked, examining my throbbing, lacerated palms. "And Lucky," I scoffed, "he's more like Lucifer! Come on, let's call the RSPCA and dump it on them," I barked.

"You're not an angry little fucker, are you? *No*. He's an angry fucker," Alice said pointing towards me. "You're a scared baby, *aren't you*, and we are not *dumping* you. No, we're keeping you," Alice continued defiantly.

I couldn't believe my ears. My wife wanted to give a home to this vicious little ginger psycho that we'd just found, or rather I'd rescued. *Where had it come from?* The Defence Science and Technology Laboratory on top of Portsdown Hill, only a mile away? Maybe it had been set free after a botched research programme to create animal weapons. Although I had no intention of leaving it here, there was no way I'd be letting this horrible little bastard into my house. *No way.*

"*We are not keeping it!*" I said, taking a firm, authoritative stand, with a gulp.

"Okay then, Henry," Alice replied stoically, "we won't give this poor defenceless orphan a home, we'll take it to the RSPCA, and as you said, *dump it*. I won't rescue this sweet, sorry abandoned kitten and have a pet to love and nurture and cuddle who'll love me back." *Cuddle! That thing'll have your bloody eye out.* "We'll take it to the rescue centre and that will be the end of it. We'll never see it again."

"Good," I said nervously, feeling uneasy that Alice had capitulated without the slightest hint of a fight. *Strange.*

"It's fine, my boys are in boarding school, and you say we can't have any pets. After all darling, you're the boss, so I guess we'll just have another baby."

Forcing a smile I took a step towards Alice, wagging a playful bloodstained finger at the hissing satanic kitten.

"Hello, Lucky."

## CHAPTER 5

### Fast Car

The round trip dropping the boys at the cinema was proving to be mental torture. From the second we lurched away from the front of number 12, all the brain in my head and the much smaller one in my pants could think about was Alice and getting back as fast as possible, without getting another ticket of course.

Thankfully both the boys had been wearing seatbelts when the car came screeching to a sudden halt in a disabled parking bay opposite the steps of The Odeon.

"*Jesus Dad*," screamed Jack, "if you keep driving like that you will end up with a blue badge. If you survive the crash."

"Sorry, was I driving a bit fast?"

"Um, you could say that Dad," said Toby, "I think we left my insides on that mini roundabout back there," he said, pointing over his shoulder. "They should be arriving shortly. Why are you in such a mad hurry?"

"Erm, Mum said you had to be here for six."

"Yes, Dad *six* o'clock. *Look!*" Jack said, jabbing his finger at the dial above the radio cassette player. "When the big hand is on the ten and the little hand is nearly on the six what time is it?" Jack asked, imitating a Play School presenter.

"Ten to six," I muttered.

"Yes, ten to six, well done Dad, have a gold star. Tomorrow we'll try shapes and colours."

"Very funny."

"If this had been a DeLorean, we'd have gone back in time," Jack joked. "So, come on, what's the real reason you were driving like a loony?" He persisted, pressing me for the truth.

"What? Oh… that… I um… just need to get back to… to um…" I stumbled.

"*Oh no,*" exclaimed Jack, his face contorting in disgust, "I know why. Oh God, it's disgusting. It should be banned at your age. I've got a horrible vision of you with your trousers off again. Poor Mum."

"Have you got enough money for food?" I asked, appealing to their stomachs to quickly divert attention away from my groin.

"Yes, Mum gave us a bit extra thanks," Toby confirmed, resting a sympathetic hand on my shoulder.

"Well take this too," I said, handing him a tenner, hoping to buy their silence.

"Thanks, Dad."

17

"Yeah, thanks Dad," Jack echoed, climbing out of the car, "don't drive too fast *and try not to upset the neighbours*," he shouted with a wink. Jumping out of the car, he began running up the stairs with his fingers splayed over his face, theatrically screaming, "*my eyes, my eyes.*"

I lowered the window. "*Give us a ring when you want picking up*," I shouted, my face burning. Jack stopped, turning around to give me a thumbs up, then mimed poking two fingers down his throat until the shoulder-rocking figure of Toby caught him up and they walked off together laughing. My phone started buzzing.

"Hurry up IM WAITING 4 U!"

Reversing quickly, I graunched the gearstick into first and sped away, racing through the car park. If my old banger had been fitted with a flux capacitor, I would have been back in 1955 before the boys could smell the popcorn.

A juddering screech of tyres announced my arrival back outside number 12. Handbrake, lights, engine off, go! Leaping from the car, I sailed down the steps, jumping clear of the last three, breaking into a short sprint along the path before bouncing through the porch, bursting through the door, and scrambling up the stairs. I sprang into the bedroom, panting.

"*WHAT THE F...*" I yelped.

Meeting the terrifying sight of a six-foot bunny girl in towering five-inch, black patent leather stilettos, and brandishing a riding crop, the looming shadow of a deeply suppressed, dark fuzzy memory started forming in my mind.

# CHAPTER 6

## Welcome to the Jungle

On the morning of my fourth birthday, my mum announced that we were going to spend the day at Robin Hill.

"Oh wow, thank you, Mummy. Thank you so much, I am so *upcited... what's Robin Hill?*"

"It's a country park, darling. Daddy and I want to take you there as a birthday treat. Is that okay?" Mum asked with a loving smile.

"Of course, it's okay Mummy. Thank you, thank you a thousand million hundred Mummy, this is the best birthday *ever.*"

"You're very welcome, Henry," Mum beamed.

"*Mummy.*"

"Yes, darling."

"What's a country park?"

I'd have been on the verge of wetting my new, shiny red nylon, Six Million Dollar Man y-fronts if I'd heard the words 'chocolate' and 'milkshake' in the same sentence.

From our white-walled, red-roofed, hilltop home in the sleepy village of Carisbrooke, overlooking the historic motte-and-bailey castle, it took a hot, sticky, and perilous fifteen minutes to reach Robin Hill, nestled amongst the lush, rolling downs and stunning woodland of Downend, at the heart of the Isle of Wight. Seated in the back of my dad's lethally upholstered, bright yellow Ford Cortina Mk III, I spent the entire journey in a state of excited anticipation and fear, my chubby pink legs rigidly braced like a giant plastic doll. If they dropped more than a few inches, the backs of my calves would touch the seat's blisteringly hot black vinyl piping and I'd be branded for life.

The charmingly named park proved to be almost exactly as my overactive imagination had pictured it, except for the dinosaurs. What a disappointment. Not a single Brontosaurus roamed the grassy parkland, but I still loved it. Wide open spaces where I could run freely, the climbing frames, the Death Slide, treetop walkways, an amusement arcade, the Tarzan swing, the playground rides, the ice cream, and then there was the collection of weird animals.

Apart from the strong smell of ammonia and the interior's near pitch-blackness, I was captivated by the occupants of the Jungle House, with its assortment of lizards, snakes, bats, and huge exotic insects and spiders. Tottering through the darkness, amazed, I continued gawping while tightly clasping my mother's reassuring hand. Trembling with excitement, I paused at each exhibit, dividing my attention between the intriguing creatures, and keeping control of my Mr. Whippy. To balance the top-heavy ice cream in my podgy little hand, while trying to peer into the dimly lit, murky recesses of the terrariums and cages, required a great deal of concentration. Approaching the last few displays, I stopped in front of a large glass tank. My face glowed, painted with a creepy shade of green from the display's dim, ghostly backlight. I frowned, attempting to read the printed label placed above a faded colour Polaroid.

"Gol-ee… Golly-ah… what does it say, Daddy?" I asked eagerly.

"Goliath bird-eating spider," Dad answered helpfully.

"Huh, it eats birds. How does it fly Daddy?" It seemed like a perfectly logical question.

"No, son, it catches birds on the ground."

"Ohhh." That welcome bit of news went a long way to preventing some hellish nightmares and my need to constantly check the skies.

"Hello, Go-li-ath bird eating spider," I sang, tapping gently on the front of the tank and peering into the alien, shadowy interior. Raising myself on tiptoe, I tried stretching my neck to get a better view. At eye level lurked a dark, menacing, inert shape huddled in one corner.

"I think he's asleep, Mummy," I said disappointedly, turning around.

In the corner of my eye, I saw a mass of thick hairy legs spring to life, scuttle across the brown, fibrous floor, and jump. Snapping my head back I came face to face with the gigantic spider thudding against the glass, rearing up and baring its massive fangs just inches from my saucer-like eyes. I screamed, soaking Steve Austin, and ran, wrenching my sweaty palm from my mother's grip. My heart thumping, I sprinted, crashing through the exit, running headlong from the darkness into the brilliant summer sunshine.

Had I not been running for my life and temporarily blinded by the dazzle, I would have seen the low-fenced enclosure. The pen's solid wooden stakes had been pile driven into the ground and surrounded in tightly wound, thick metal wire. Tearing blindly across the grass, panting loudly, and letting out a low, strangled, panicked moan, I could feel my heart smashing against my ribcage. Fleeing as fast as my wet little legs would carry me, I ran for my life, clutching Mr. Whippy.

Slamming into the taut wire so hard it sang, everything below my hips stopped. Pivoting at the waist, I spun around like a miniature gymnast performing a high-speed forward roll on a horizontal bar. My legs went flying into the air heels first, flipping over my head. In a flash, my view of the world suddenly began whirling in a kaleidoscope of blue to green and brown and back to blue as my feet and back thudded into the patchy baked earth and the floor punched the air out of me. I lay motionless, wheezing, unable to fill my lungs. I was not the only victim. On impact, Mr. Whippy smacked me in the face and exploded. Spattered all over the pen, it looked like he'd been fed into a woodchipper.

Large shapes began stirring around me. Blinking, confused, I lay on my back, hungrily sucking at the air in ragged bursts, covered in bits of the broken wafer, and splattered with soft, sickly sweet, vanilla-flavoured goo.

If I'd been walking past the pen and had asked Dad to help me read the sign nailed to one of the posts, I would have discovered that it contained Flemish Giants. These freakishly big specimens looked to be half rabbit, half bear, and could have bested a Rottweiler. The first rabbit, a gigantic buck, made a tentative lop towards me. It bent down and I felt the tickle of its whiskers touching my leg. It hopped closer, the earth beneath me shaking as its massive paws landed, thumping the ground. It stopped at my shoulder, blocking out the Sun as it began licking at the pale yellow gloop on my face. Looking up, I became transfixed at the sight of a giant pair of furry, floppy ears outlined against the bright blue sky.

I didn't hear the attack signal, but others quickly appeared. Within seconds I could feel the ache and pressure of my tiny limbs being squashed as they jumped on me, the pain searing as they scratched, raking my exposed skin. I lay stricken, covered in ravenous, clawing, nibbling, colossal, long-eared bunnies, wanting to scream but unable to breathe. I was being licked to death or worse, eaten alive while staring at those massive furry ears. Just at the moment when I thought *I'm going to heaven*, something started sliding under my legs and back, followed by a wonderful sensation of weightlessness, of floating up and away from the ground and out of the pen and back into the light. Through a haze of tears, I recognised the familiar, comforting smile of my dad and gasped, burying my face in his thick chest.

"It's alright, son, I've got you."

"Th…the buh…hunny... ra… ra… rabbits. Th... hey… tried to e…e…eat m… m…

me," I rasped and blubbed.

"Shhh, you're safe now."

Wrapping myself around my rescuer's neck, I hugged him tightly, sobbing until I fell asleep in his strong protective arms.

## CHAPTER 7

### Weak in the Presence of Beauty

Almost forty years, one wife, two sons, a sadistic ginger tomcat, and a fat, half-blind beagle later, my descent back into that traumatic, terrifying episode had begun…

Frozen to the spot, the deafening whoosh of blood started pounding my eardrums as my heart began trying to beat its way out of my heaving chest. Gypsy excitedly came puffing up the stairs and wobbled into the room in front of me. She froze, crouching low on her forelegs spreading her paws, and began snarling at the thing in front of her with the massive ears. Her hackles rose, bristling as her lip curled, quivering, to reveal her pink, spotted gums and sharp, pointed canines.

Crack!

As the swishing, short whip, smacked into Alice's hand, Gypsy leapt up, bolted between my legs, and shot down the stairs whimpering.

Alice, meanwhile, continued staring hungrily at me as I stood, breathing heavily, my mouth wide, my eyes even wider, the sexual tension crackling like a threadbare electric blanket.

*Oh Lord no. Please no.* I quivered, utterly transfixed by those giant ears. Alice pointed the riding crop at me.

"I think *you've* been a naughty boy and bunny needs to punish you," she said

23

suggestively, spanking her palm with the crop's leather flap. I would normally have eagerly ogled and been physically aroused by my wife's large breasts, currently making a valiant attempt at breaking out of their black and red lace, corseted prison. Instead, I couldn't take my eyes off those large, pink-lined, black furry ears.

"Well, say something then, or bunny will get angry," she demanded.

"I can't. I'm too scared," I squeaked.

"Hopefully you'll be scared *stiff*," Alice snarled, smacking the crop into the palm of her fur-cuffed hand again.

"What's up Cock?" she asked in a sultry Bugs Bunnyesque voice, pointing the leather end at my crotch. The answer was nothing. Gulping, as if trying to swallow a thorn-coated ping pong ball, I just stood there, petrified, fixating on those huge furry ears.

"No... nooo... don't... don't eat... me," I whined, literally unable to move as my breathing came in short, frantic, panicked bursts. My vision started blurring, my head feeling light and woozy as the room began spinning. I could feel myself falling, tumbling, my arms flailing as the room went round and round and round. I was sinking, down... down... down... then weirdly, I was four years old again and laying on the floor of that rabbit pen.

## CHAPTER 8

### Embarrassment

"Henry? *Henryyy?*" Alice sang, leaning forward and clicking her fingers in front of my eyes.

"Leporiphobia. I... I'm leporiphobic," I muttered ashamedly to the now de-eared, unshod Alice whose face bore wrinkles of concern.

"Leporiwhat?" She'd clearly never heard of the word.

"Leporiphobia."

"What the hell's that?"

"It's the fear of rabbits," I murmured.

"Fear of *what*?" she asked curtly, sighing as she crossed her arms and began tapping her foot.

"Rabbits."

"Are you shitting me?"

"No," I mumbled, still unable to look her in the eye.

"Seriously?" Alice asked. I nodded shamefully.

"Oh Henry, I had no idea. Why didn't you ever say anything?" I don't know why but she didn't sound completely surprised or too sympathetic. Sitting on the bed I lifted my head from my hands, looking at her sideways.

"Well, I know I never actually told you outright, but I just assumed that you knew that I wasn't too keen on rabbits. Do you remember the Cadbury's Caramel advert?"

"Yes, now that you mention it, I do actually. I thought it was a bit weird and slightly pervy when you started twitching and got all sweaty when it came on. I just assumed that cartoon girl rabbit with the sexy West Country accent was some sort of creepy, kinky turn-on for you," she said, unfolding her arms and relaxing her shoulders.

"*A turn-on!* Good God no, she absolutely terrified me," I quavered, laying down and resting my head in Alice's lap.

"Is that why you used to get funny about reading Beatrix Potter to the boys?"

"*Yes.* I was fine with Jemima Puddle-Duck and Mrs. Tiggy-Winkle but Benjamin Bunny and Peter Rabbit could fuck right off."

Recounting the whole disturbing tale of my four-year-old near-death experience at Robin Hill, Alice kept smoothing my head. I'm sure she'd have understood the fear of sharks, snakes, or even dogs, but a fully-grown man afraid of rabbits… I *had* tried hiding my irrational fear but thought Alice would have guessed by some of my extreme reactions over the years, normally around Easter or on that Christmas Day when I leapt up from the sofa and grabbed a sand iron, disappearing into the garden to practice my chipping. I stayed out there in the cold for nearly two hours because Alice had insisted on letting the boys watch Watership Down. The BBC had chosen to show it, *again*. The bastards.

"Honestly, I didn't know," she cooed, making no attempt to hide her grin as she bent down, taking my face in her hands, and kissing me gently on the forehead. *Hmmm.* I still wasn't entirely convinced.

"Come here," she chuckled, pulling me up and pressing my ear against her soft, warm chest while continuing to stroke my head, "you poor little bunny."

## CHAPTER 9

### Killer Queen

Over dinner, Alice kept plying me with red wine, in an attempt to ease the awkwardness of the bedroom disaster no doubt, possibly for both of us. I'd been delighted when she said she would pick the boys up and continued quaffing, trying to drown my shame in Merlot. However, a whole case wouldn't have been enough to lessen the impact of the unappealing bombshell she was preparing to drop.

"Are you feeling alright now?" Alice asked softly.

"Yeah, I'm okay. This is certainly helping," I said, raising my glass, "and I had a pretty good day at work. Completely mental but in a good way."

"Good," Alice replied with a gentle smile.

"Best of all, being a weekend, there was no chance of bumping into you know who."

"Sounds perfect," Alice suggested. I nodded, sighing deeply, enjoying the wine's comforting warmth.

"So, how would you feel about a visitor?" Alice probed with a pleading grin.

"Who?" I asked, the Merlot's calming effects instantly draining from my brain as I tensed, steeling myself for the answer.

"Um, I think my mum wants to come and stay for a few days."

*Holy Mary Mother of God! Shoot me now.*

"Henry. *Henry!*"

I sat staring, my eyes glazing over again, shell-shocked, trying to think if I'd ever had a worse evening.

"Henry, did you hear me?"

"Oh yes, I heard you. I was just wondering how long it would take me to drive to Beachy Head."

"Oh, stop it, she's been a bit depressed." *Well, there's a surprise.* I believed that Alice's pro-IRA mother Eileen had been on a downward spiral since the signing of The Good Friday Agreement.

"What's wrong, has the price of Semtex gone up?"

"Oh, stop it, she's still not herself."

"You mean she's lost that vibrant sunny disposition that always lights up the room?" I asked with vino-induced bravery.

"Don't be mean, she's really miserable," Alice chided.

"I know, I *have* met her." My staunchly Catholic mother-in-law made me feel guilty every time I came close to smiling, and I believed her dislike for me, an Englishman and member of the Armed Forces, rivalled that of our psychopathic cat.

"*Henry!*" Alice snapped, "I know she's never exactly been a Butlins' Redcoat, but she's not been the same since Dad left."

"Neither has he. I've never seen a happier man."

Alice's meek and painfully humble dad, Dougal, had walked out seven months ago. Drunkenly stumbled to be more accurate, because it had taken a large amount of Dutch courage, but the gentle old soul had finally mustered the bravery to leave. The lucky sod now spent his days playing golf and cribbage and sampling the products of microbreweries. The thought of him striding down a fairway free and unfettered, or huddled by a crackling fireside enjoying several hands of crib with his friends, while slowly getting drunk, made me very happy and a little envious.

"Well, I've said it's okay if she stays for a few days. To try and cheer her up."

"Good luck with that!" I sneered, harbouring the thought that any attempt at lifting my mother-in-law's spirits would be a Sisyphean task. Only three things seemed to make her smile, UK Defence cuts, coming to visit, purely to make me miserable - that usually put a smirk on the sour old bat's face - and seeing the cat. Eileen and the sadistic Lucky got on famously. The normally aloof feline became unnervingly affectionate whenever she visited and, uncharacteristically, would happily curl up on her lap and allow himself to be stroked. The two appeared to have a strange affinity with a mutual interest in exacting misery on me.

They made the perfect couple, like Rosemary and Fred West.

"Maybe your mum could cheer me up for a change," I suggested.

"And how *exactly* would she manage that my love?" Alice scowled.

"Well, she could threaten to come and stay for a whole month and then cancel or maybe move back to Scotland, the Shetland Islands perhaps."

Seventeen years ago, the news of our elder son Toby's imminent arrival had been enough motivation for Eileen to shelve her aversion to all things English and move south of the border to be near her first grandson. I imagined that living in the enemy's territory would have caused her to wear out her rosary beads worrying about her father, a gunrunner for The Scottish Brigade, spinning in his grave.

"*Stop it!* She's no trouble, and it's not like she's active anymore."

"I'm glad to hear it, almost as much as SO15."

"Oh, *that's enough!* Don't be ridiculous, you know what I mean. I know Grandpa Angus had a bit of a chequered past but Mum! That nonsense my dad fed you is a load of horseshit."

I wasn't so sure. Having endured several passionate lectures and been forced to listen to Eileen's support for a united Ireland at my dinner table, I had absolutely no doubt where her loyalties lay and often wondered just how *active* she'd been in her younger days. Even at almost eighty, her presence was enough to force me into making a cursory check of the underside of my car and tremble when I started the engine.

The opening bars of Carl Orff's 'O Fortuna' caused us both to jump.

"That'll be number two son asking for a lift then," Alice said.

"Yep."

"I still don't understand why you've got the music from the '70s' Old Spice advert as Jack's ringtone."

"I just like it," I deflected with an affable shrug. I did like it but Alice's strong aversion to horror films meant that she had no idea it was also used in The Omen movies about Damien, the prophesied Antichrist.

Alice went to collect the boys, leaving me with instructions to clear the table and take Gypsy out. Having loaded the dishwasher, I sought solace in another healthy glass of red in the unlit lounge, the only light the feeble glimmer of streetlamps bleeding through the thin curtains. Sinking into the sofa's soft cushioning I smiled, peering into space, thinking about my sons and how they seemed to have gone from babies to young men in the blink of an eye.

I could never quite comprehend just how different two brothers could be. Admittedly they were four years apart but even so, physically they were almost different species. While Toby was stacked, Jack could be best described as strung together. Still, what he lacked in stature he made up for in sharp intellect, confidence, and a wickedly impish nature bordering on demonic. So fiendish, it often pushed his mother and me into the welcoming embrace of Oddbins. We really should have seen that the writing was on the wall from as far back as the point of his eventful conception or as a distraught, post-natal Alice had once drunkenly referred to it, The Curse of the Pharaohs.

## CHAPTER 10

### Walk Like an Egyptian

Inspired by a school trip to the British museum at the age of thirteen, Alice developed a burning passion and desire to learn about antiquities and the ancient world. In particular, she had been enticed by the mysteries of pharaonic history. So, reluctantly, I found myself agreeing to Alice's suggestion of a budget week-long Nile cruise. I had wanted a week at a resort in Tenerife that completely coincidentally, just happened to be on a golf course, but Alice had seen through my thinly veiled scheme and made an eye-watering promise. She assured me that if I planned on buggering off and playing golf every day, leaving her by the pool with our three-year-old, after I'd finished my very first round, I would need to find the Canary Islands' most gifted, colorectal surgeon to have my putter removed. After a short deliberation I warmly congratulated Alice on her excellent idea, a Nile cruise sounded perfect.

It turned out better than I'd anticipated, as it ended up being just the two of us. Apart from a disastrous weekend involving the unexpected appearance of a window cleaner and a defective adult toy at a North Wales B&B, that was reported in the news the following day as The Towyn Inferno, we hadn't been away together as a couple since before we'd started a family. We couldn't ask Alice's parents, they were planning a trip to Ireland for a long weekend in Donegal, which I assumed was code for my father-in-law Dougal playing golf while Eileen ran clandestine workshops in chemistry and advanced soldering. Luckily my parents said they were free and could be reached with just a short ferry trip across the Solent.

Our budget holiday began with a fairly uneventful EgyptAir flight to Luxor's International Airport. The painless five-hour journey preceded a terrifying, twenty-five-minute white-knuckle coach ride to the docks. We bounced along through a perpetual cloud of dust, at speeds that would have frightened me if I'd been driving a car with a seatbelt and airbags on a tarmacked highway and been able to see where I was going. The driver blindly hurled the whining coach left *and* right at the last minute to dodge oncoming lorries and taxis. Alarmingly he navigated two roundabouts by electing to drive around each one in different directions and narrowly missed an abandoned fruit cart in the middle of the road tethered to a terrified donkey. It was one of the few times I wished I still wore my St. Christopher.

I had repeatedly traipsed up and down the quayside searching for our ship, leaving Alice guarding our luggage in the shade of an orange seller's awning. After twenty fruitless minutes, I'd started melting under the blistering Egyptian midday Sun. According to the rep, who'd dismissively waved me away with a flick of the hand shouting "Yalla, yalla," the boat should have been right here.

The dockside writhed, swarming with porters, suppliers, dockers, traders, and boat crews, and standing, completely lost, in the middle of it all, I kept asking for help as the world continued buzzing and jostling around me.

"Nefertiti?... Nefertiti?" I pleaded to the sea of faces rushing past.

In desperation I threw my hand out, grabbing a startled boy in a white tunic.

"Nefertiti?" I asked despairingly.

The wide-eyed boy's slender arm shot up past my ear, pointing to the ship right behind me before he wriggled free and disappeared, dissolving back into the bustling throng.

The name on the bow had originally been spelled out in individual dark varnished wooden block letters but time and tide had stripped her of the letters N, R, and the last I. Walking to the top of the gangway I could see that the missing symbols had been roughly hand-painted back on but were only visible this close. I had been scanning the names of all of the boats as I'd sweltered, frantically hurrying back and forth along the dock, and remembered passing the EFE TIT six times. I thought it had been an odd name. *Idiot.*

I reckoned that the Two-Star Nefertiti must have been a shade under seventy-five feet long. She looked completely out of place, dwarfed in the dominant shadow of a gang of grand cruise ships twice her size, gleaming with the promise of water-borne luxury. Every rivet along the old girl's off-white sides had rusted and bled and on closer inspection, I could see that her wavy Plimsoll line wasn't a Plimsoll line at all, but a filthy brown, scum-encrusted tide mark. I thought the shabby crate could have been as old as her namesake and would not have looked out of place in a maritime museum. Although timeworn, and appearing a little unloved, the antiquated vessel proved to be more than adequate.

We were both pleasantly surprised when we walked into our cabin to find spotlessly clean towels and bedding and a gleaming toilet and shower. The smartly uniformed crew smiled at every encounter and the service and food could not be faulted either.

On our first morning, we stepped from our cabin into a sweet aromatic cloud of freshly baked pastries and warm bread. By night, we lounged, savouring the heavenly smell of tangy, exotic, spice-infused dishes with cous cous, tender chicken, rich goat meat, and slow-cooked tagine of lamb. Best of all our enthusiastic English-speaking tour guide Ayman proved to be a godsend.

Earning a degree in Egyptology from John Hopkins University, he had spent the last three years volunteering at the Faculty of Archaeology at the University of Cairo, while supporting himself as a tour guide. The four years he'd spent in Baltimore had sculpted his English almost as perfectly as the carvings of Komombo, Edfu, and Abu Simbel.

Alice and I spent hours gawping, stunned by the beauty and size of the temples, and enthralled by Ayman's detailed knowledge, hanging off his every word as he drew us into the ancient world, seducing us with the mysteries and hidden secrets of the pharaohs. I had to admit that, despite my initial misgivings, I was loving the whole experience as we cruised down the Nile; possibly not all of the smells but definitely all of the sights that we were encountering. Apart from the early hiccup of not being able to find the boat it had been plain sailing. That was, until four days into the trip and a disastrous evening in Aswan when Ayman offered to take a small group, including a slightly pissed Alice and a reasonably sober me, on a brief excursion to experience real Egyptian coffee.

As a heat haze drifted lazily from the harbour, the shimmering Sun melted towards the horizon creating another wonderfully balmy North African evening. We sauntered down the clanking, hemp-lined gangway to the dock, waiting at the bottom for the last few members of our party.

"Okay, everyone, please keep together and very soon you will be sat enjoying a most wonderful, sweet, and exotic cup of Joe or as we say in Arabic, *qahwa*," Ayman enthused.

"Ooh, *qahwa*, sounds so much more exciting than Maxwell House. Don't you think?" Alice said nothing, replying only with a thin, unenthusiastic smile.

The one-storey whitewashed building, topped with red corrugated sheets leaned at an alarming angle towards the river but luckily its sturdy wooden chairs and tables didn't. Ayman called a waiter over and began ordering coffee for everyone. Looking across the river, the edges of a huge palm tree's silhouette wavered, backlit by the glow of the sinking red disc as the darkening sky faded to hues of bluey purple. *What a perfect evening.*

"We need to go!" Alice barked. *What? We've only just got here.* We had literally been sat down for five minutes. Why did she want to go already? I couldn't believe that I wouldn't get the chance to see if the thick, strong, sweet Egyptian coffee that had just arrived would taste as good as it smelled.

"Really?" I asked, hopeful of sampling the enticing, ebony liquid.

She started giving me 'The Look', and when Alice gave me that look and said we had to go, I knew better than to argue.

"Okay, okay, I'll just try a sip," I conceded. Desperate to at least sample the delicious coffee I put the cup to my lips, briefly.

"*No, now!*" Alice snapped. To convey exactly how 'now' she meant, Alice looked like she would have picked me up by my bollocks and dragged me back to the boat if only she'd had the strength to. Luckily for me, she appeared to be using every ounce of concentration and energy in trying to keep her sphincter clamped tighter than a camel's in a sandstorm. She had gone deathly pale and when her stomach began gurgling loudly enough for me to hear, I knew I had to get her to a toilet and fast. Apologising profusely to Ayman and the rest of the onlooking group I jumped up, throwing two crumpled Egyptian £50 notes on the table.

As Alice began waddling away, I stopped, looking back at the café, and pointing.

"I could ask if there's a toilet in there," I shouted to her retreating back. I thought I was being helpful but the malevolent look in Alice's eyes, as she turned and glared at me, said otherwise.

The Nefertiti sat waiting less than half a mile away, at least a ten-minute arse-clenching shuffle. However, I knew this wasn't the moment to make an argument about my wife's potential imminent public humiliation versus, what I considered to be, an unreasonable aversion to public lavatories, although even I'd been shocked by the primitive drop, squat, and plop facilities.

"*Nooo!*" she seethed in a demonic growl. Suddenly looking like she'd taken a shower fully clothed, she started waddle-sprinting back towards the boat, having an uncanny resemblance to a clockwork goose that had been overwound.

"Oh God, oh God, oh God, please let me make it," I heard her murmuring, catching up to her. I could see panicked tears welling in her worried eyes. I had never seen her looking so scared. I didn't know what to do, feeling completely useless but tried some reassuring phrases.

"It's okay my love, we're nearly there. Don't panic. Not far now."

"We are not *nearly there,*" she snarled through gritted teeth, "and I can't believe that you let me come out in a fucking white dress." *What? How is this my fault?* I had never been brave enough to even think about suggesting what my wife wore and resisted the temptation of pointing out that 'fucking white' wasn't a real colour.

A few excruciatingly long minutes later, as we were nearing the quayside, the bow of the Nefertiti slid into view.

"Look, there's the boat!" I said encouragingly, pointing at the antique vessel. Alice looked up from the dusty road that she had been fixated on, whimpering gently as her tight shoulders relaxed slightly at the sight of the Nefertiti, tied up on the outside of two other cruise ships. Reaching the gangway of the first boat, we bounced up the creaking planks, rushing between a few couples sitting relaxing, enjoying sundowners. As Alice started crossing the highly polished floor of the pristine Nile Emperor her stomach began making a horribly violent and very loud gurgle.

"Please no, please, please, please," she sobbed, her whole body shaking, shrouded in the clinging wetness of her transparent 'fucking white' dress. She looked to be desperately clenching every muscle, trying to not decorate the Five-Star cruise ship's brilliant white decking with a Jackson Pollock in mocha.

"Good evening, madam." The Nefertiti's deck hand greeted Alice warmly, offering her a helping hand aboard. She didn't reply, instead skipping across the small gap separating the two boats before barrelling straight past him. Grabbing the handrail, she went thudding down the short flight of stairs.

"*Move!*" she roared, barging the startled receptionist out of the way, grabbing the room key from the hook behind his head, and ripping the small, flimsily mounted rack off the wall in the process. I watched her scuttle along the corridor, ramming the key into the lock before bursting into the cabin. Mouthing 'sorry,' I gave an apologetic smile as my eyes met the terrified, startled gaze of the young man cowering behind the reception desk, attempting to recover the broken rack and scattered keys.

The door slammed, followed immediately by loud, panicked shrieking and the wrenching sound of splintering wood. Trailing just a few paces behind, I stepped into the cabin, throwing myself back against the door in horror at the scene of devastation. It looked like someone had dropped a depth charge into a gravy boat. Some of the matter was up the walls and impressively she'd speckled one of the ceiling light fittings. My head dropped, following the racket coming from the loo.

I assumed Alice was trying to drown a duck in the toilet or possibly a whole flock. The gutsy little fellas were protesting loudly, clearly refusing to go down without a fight. The din began echoing around the cabin and I contorted my face, grimacing with every horrible quack. The noise was so deplorable I started sweating in sympathy as Alice continued passing an angry Donald and his three nephews through a blender.

"Are you okay?" I asked stupidly.

"Ughhh… Do I sound… Ughhh… Okay?" Alice moaned, battling on.

"No, my love," I replied weakly.

"I am far from okay, I think… Ughhh… I'm melting," she groaned.

A moment later the rancid stench hit me. I retched and stopped breathing. It smelled like Alice had died on the toilet and been decomposing for a week.

"*Gottagobackinaminute*," I gabbled, crashing out of the door, and rushing down the corridor holding my breath. I came skidding to a halt opposite Reception and began breathing in again.

"Huh, huh, huh," I panted, "sorry huh... about that just now...huh... my wife ..."

The young man behind the desk offered me a sympathetic smile, presenting an open palm.

"Here sir," he said, extending his hand. It held a small, paper cup containing a mottled brown pill about the size of an aspirin. I must have looked puzzled.

"For your good lady sir," he explained, "this make her good."

I held up my hand, declining politely. "How did you ...?" I began, then thought that the fact she'd barrelled past the poor lad moments earlier, sweating profusely and with the wide-eyed and panicked expression of someone desperately in need of the loo had probably given him a bit of a clue. If any doubt, as to the reason for Alice's abnormally bullish behaviour, had existed, it soon evaporated.

The receptionist and I turned towards our cabin as the sounds came echoing along the corridor indicating that one plucky little duck hadn't quite given up the fight. In its death throes, the duckling resurfaced making loud, angry, dribbly quacks mingled with Alice's sobs. Shocked by the clarity and volume of the noise I tried rapping my knuckles on the cabin wall to the right of the desk. A loud knocking filled the reception area. Unfortunately for Alice, the Nefertiti's acoustics appeared to be better than those of the Royal Albert Hall.

Having read about the dangers of Travellers' D&V in Egypt we thought ourselves well prepared to deal with a bout of Ramesses' Revenge. The UK FCO's travel advice pamphlet said not to trust local medicine, drink unbottled water, or have drinks with ice. Alice had packed what appeared to have been the booty from a ramraid on Boots the Chemists, having brought a separate washbag filled with an array of liquids, pills, and sachets. The home-bought medication had no effect. It was about as useful as a marshmallow dildo and after only two hours Alice's resolve broke.

"I don't care what's in it, please just go to Reception and get me one of those bloody pills?"

Whatever it comprised, possibly two parts sand and one part cement, Alice, although somewhat weakened, made a miraculous recovery. By lunchtime the next day she managed soup and a sandwich, without any hint of a return visit from Huey, Dewey, and Louie. She also got the barman to administer several doses of anti-malarial gin and tonic too, but this time *without* ice. I could not believe the speed of her recovery or that, for once, I'd got off scot-free.

"I still feel disgusting, and I can't even bear the thought of you touching me, I feel so unclean," Alice said the following day, sitting on the edge of the fresh bedding and new mattress.

"You poor thing. Should I go to a local market the next time we dock and see if I can get you a cloak and a bell?"

"Maybe. It was just, *ugh,*" she shuddered, "I'm sorry to be such a party pooper."

"Well, you can forget the party, you're definitely a pooper or more like a turbo muck spreader."

"Henry!" Alice barked.

"Sorry. Well don't worry, your virtue's quite safe."

"It's really knocked me sideways and it reeked! I'm sure I can still smell it," she grimaced.

Despite Alice's moratorium on nookie, the miracle pill allowed us to return to a state where we could continue enjoying the remainder of the holiday. We enjoyed it so much that

Jack's 'immaculate conception' occurred on the last night of the trip, as we were steaming back to Luxor.

While reclining on deck, the Nefertiti slipped gently past the sleeping riverbank, softly chugging as she cut through the warm night air and still, dark waters of the Nile. I lay resting on one elbow sporting a full-length, white cotton gallabiyah, my head wrapped in a traditional, red and white chequered shemagh. My mind continued gently floating, as I lay relaxing on a woven rug. smoking a sheesha pipe, giggling, and barefooted. The air bubbled with the sounds of music and laughter as we and the other guests, gathered in traditional costumes relaxed, embracing the sensory pleasures of the local food, drink, and hypnotic belly dancing.

Sadly, the revelry seemed to start winding down far too soon, and under the influence of some rather potent Lebanese marijuana, we drifted back to our cabin. At the time I had no idea that Alice had slipped a few Egyptian pounds to one of the waiters for some 'special tobacco.' Back in our cabin I'd still been peckish and felt like the world was a lovely fluffy place, right up to the point where a giggling Alice admitted to what she'd done. Despite my mellow, hedonistic state, I went absolutely ballistic when she casually dropped into the conversation that she'd knowingly bought and given me a Class C drug. The night's mood instantly changed.

"*You stupid, stupid cow, you've done what?*" I thundered.

"What's wrong? Why are you shouting?"

"Why am I shouting? *Why am I shouting?* Are you fucking kidding me?"

"Calm down."

"No, I will not calm down you silly bitch. One, I'm an officer in the RAF and two, an air traffic controller and now and again a bunch of people surprise us with a little visit and one of them watches me while I piss in a pot, and then do you know what happens?" I asked still raging.

"No," Alice answered sheepishly.

"Then they test it for drugs. You know, like mari-bloody-juana."

Alice looked at the floor, but I hadn't finished.

"I could be court-martialled, get kicked out, and lose my pension. Then we'd have no money and nowhere to live. And that stuff can stay in your system for months. *Get it now?*"

"Oh my God, I'm so sorry, I just didn't think."

*"No shit!"*

Alice had been so contrite and amenable from a combination of alcohol, severe guilt, and the carefree effects from some top-quality black leb, that when I finally calmed down, she temporarily erased all memory of her exploding bowel episode and revoked the sex ban. On our return, I spent countless fretful weeks in a state of perpetual fear, terrified that the Compulsory Drug Testing team would turn up. I anticipated diabolical consequences, our world being turned upside down, and our lives changing forever. Instead, it took nine months and only one person to achieve all of that. We named him Jack.

## CHAPTER 11

### Do You Really Want to Hurt Me

Sitting in the darkness, I continued dozing, picturing the relief on the midwife's face, as she offloaded a wriggling, angry pink baby, screaming blue murder. The memory faded as a paw began gently pressing on the back of my hand.

"Hello girl," I yawned, stretching. Gypsy bolted, performing her strange, pre-walk habit of running away.

"Come on then, let's get you out," I sighed to an empty room.

After coaxing Gypsy from her usual hiding spot, I bundled her out of the door and she happily trotted at my side, pootling around the block, snorting puffs of steam into the cold night air.

"Honestly girl, I don't blame you for running away earlier. I wish I could have. That thing you saw in the bedroom, it scared the crap out of me too. Why do you think she chose a bunny girl outfit though?" Gypsy stopped beneath a lamppost and cocked her head, her milky eye staring blankly past me, then resumed sniffing the cocktail of dog perfume at its base before squatting and adding her own 'eau de toilet.'

"I'm not sure but I reckon she might have done it on purpose. You know, after last weekend when I forgot what day it was and went and played golf. What do you reckon?" She answered by walking away from me stiff-legged, dropping a random string of steaming dog turds. Having collected and tied my sack of warm nuggets, we turned left and set off down the road, crossed over to dispose of the lumpy bag, and crossed back, taking the steep cut between the row of houses. Reaching the corner of a back garden we turned right, heading along the dimly lit path running along the back fences that merged with the start of our road.

"I'm not sure that inviting Eileen isn't some sort of punishment too. The only one who'll be glad to see her will be the bloody cat. Speaking of which," I said, giving the lead a gentle tug, "*you* girl, are meant to be man's best friend. My friend. That ginger thing is *our* enemy. You *and* me. He's a flipping nuisance, and *you,* my brave guardian, need to sort him out."

With her normal indifference, Gypsy walked on, sniffing the ground, obviously finding the smell and fishy crumbs inside a discarded Scampi Fries packet far more interesting than my monotonous drawl.

Ten minutes later we were back home with Gypsy resuming her position in front of the fire. I was still flicking through the Sky planner when I heard the car pull up, followed by the muffled, excited jabbering of voices that boomed, filling the house as the front door opened.

"Hi Dad," Toby chimed, poking his head into the lounge.

"Alright, how was the film?"

"Awesome," he grinned, giving me a thumbs up.

"Oh good. Did Jack like it?"

"Yeah, I think so," he shrugged.

"I can't remember the last time I went to the pictures," I confessed, trying to recall the last film I'd seen.

"Oh, it's brilliant now, Dad," Jack chipped in, stepping out from behind his brother's huge frame, "it's in colour these days, there's sound and everything, and they've got rid of the man at the front playing the piano."

"Oh good, you *are* back. For a second I thought your mum might have left you in the car park or was thinking that you might have been abducted."

The boys quickly disappeared, no doubt revisiting the sordid recesses of their video game bordello. I let Alice finish off the last of the wine, after which it took about two seconds for us to agree on having an early night. Not a euphemistic *early night* an *early* night; I was still feeling a bit odd about earlier and more importantly had to be up for work the following morning.

Gypsy appeared, tentatively putting her head around the bedroom door, presumably checking to see if the giant *whatever it was* from earlier had gone. Content that the coast was clear, she came plodding to my side of the bed, putting her front paws up on the edge of the mattress.

"Nooo. *Your* bed!" I ordered.

Rejected, she slumped to the floor, harrumphing, and head down went plodding towards her basket. Crestfallen, she collapsed into it as if she'd been shot, huffing loudly enough to ensure I heard her discontent.

Lying next to Alice, I began mulling over the evening's events. This would probably be our first and last attempt at any kind of role-playing. What a shame. Why, oh why, did she choose to be a bunny? *Of all the mammals in all the world...* I was thinking that I'd have preferred a Naked Mole-Rat Girl when a guilty thought struck me. Maybe I'd got it all wrong. Was this her attempt to overcome her lack of confidence in the bedroom? Had she needed to dig deep, summoning all her courage to get dressed up like a Playboy bunny? Had I ruined everything? Had *I* humiliated *her*?

All things considered, I couldn't quite understand how my childhood hadn't reduced me to being a total basket case. Alice had insisted she didn't know about the rabbit thing. *Or did she? Hmmm.* Looking across I saw her eyes were wilting as the Kindle in her outstretched hand started to droop. She'd be asleep soon. I tried reaching across.

"I'm readin', I'm readin'," she slurred, reasserting her grip. Waiting a few more minutes until the blinds were fully down, I gently prised the device from her grasp, sliding it under her pillow before leaning across to kiss her on the forehead.

I began fidgeting restlessly, haunted by the spectre of a visit from Eileen and that whole rabbit thing was unsettling. My eyelid twitched as I lay looking at the ceiling, again grappling with the thought that Alice might have known, and for some reason had chosen this moment to use it against me, or maybe just test her suspicions. Could it have been what I'd mentioned to Gypsy, something to do with our anniversary? It would certainly make sense.

Last Saturday, I'd stupidly chosen to celebrate eighteen years of marriage by playing thirty-six holes of golf on the unimaginatively titled Meon and Valley courses at Meon Valley Hotel and Country Club. Apparently, the traditional gift to mark eighteen years of marital bliss should have been porcelain and our special event could quite easily have been marked by me having a china vase smashed over my head. Okay, so I didn't deliberately choose to celebrate our anniversary by playing golf, I'd perpetrated one of the most heinous crimes a husband can commit in a marriage, I'd forgotten it. If I'd remembered I'd have bought Alice some nice flowers and only played eighteen. At least it would have been an appropriate number.

Was this dressing-up performance and inviting her mum some sort of revenge? I doubt, however, she expected to reduce me to a gibbering wreck. Then again, maybe she was delighted with the outcome. Points scored. Things levelled up. Balance restored. *Maybe I had it coming.*

It had been a taxing day. The bedroom drama aside, work had been stressful but at the same time rewarding. My civilian colleagues could almost set their watches by the airline traffic that called at the same time, point, and level each day, but as a military controller, no two days were ever the same, and what I needed was at least seven hours of restful sleep to be on my A-game tomorrow. Looking at the space where Alice had stood, I could still feel a prickle of discomfort and not wanting to run the risk of being prodded repeatedly by an angry wife disturbed by my Olympic-standard snoring, I lifted the covers, swinging my legs out. Gypsy stirred, looking over expectantly, then came creeping towards the blanket box at the foot of the bed, eager to occupy the warm spot I'd just vacated. Pointing a firm finger at her hopeful face as it popped up, I mouthed 'no,' before sneaking along the landing to the spare

room.

## CHAPTER 12

### Welcome to My Nightmare

The familiar trills of a harp announced the arrival of seven o'clock, gently plucking me from my restless slumber. To be fair, Alice had been quite supportive of our unsuccessful role-play. Well, eventually. My toes still hadn't fully uncurled when I'd gone to bed in the spare room, and I'd only been in there a few minutes when she appeared in the doorway.

"What do you think you're doing in here?" she asked, in the same tone as if she'd caught one of the boys trying to hide vegetables in their mashed potato when they were toddlers. "I felt you get up and I can't settle if you're not in bed with me," she admitted with a beckoning smile.

"Well, I just thought. You know," I offered weakly, "because of my snoring and what happened with the dressing up thing."

"Don't be silly. Come on, come back to bed," she said, turning towards the open door, her arm trailing behind her. Happily taking my wife's extended hand, I let her lead me back to our room where we talked briefly before drifting off.

What sleep I had managed clearly hadn't been restful. I felt wretched and my limbs were refusing to move like they were made of fatigued concrete. This morning's sluggishness must have been caused by my troubled dream. The most sickening part had been the image of my seventy-nine-year-old mother-in-law wearing a basque and bunny ears, seductively licking a 99 Flake through a black ski mask. *Do I need to see a therapist?* In my defence, I figured that whoever reckoned there'd be a thriving market for kinky pairs of giant floppy ears, priced at £19.99 and just a click away, really, really needed help. Sooner the better too. What was wrong with keeping it simple, like a Naughty Nurse, Slutty

Santa, or even Miss Whiplash?

I tried moving, my aching joints graunching as if someone had stolen my synovial fluid.

"Ughhh," I groaned, rolling over and slowly getting out of bed. I'm not sure who complained the loudest, me or my knees.

"Arrrgh," I screamed, leaping as a hot needle of pain jabbed me in the heel.

"Shurrup!" Alice grumbled.

I began scouring the ominous shadows beneath the bed, waiting for the menacing beast lurking there to show itself. Nothing. Then a lightning-fast flash of ginger and white appeared, flicking from the darkness towards my bleeding foot then disappeared. It swiped again, baring its gleaming black talons. *God, I really hate that cat.*

Grabbing a tissue, I began dabbing my throbbing heel then threw on my dressing gown. The disobedient, incompetent cat-botherer slipped out from under the covers, oblivious to the presence of my attacker, plopped off the bed, and followed me to the bathroom, waiting outside. Greeting me with a wagging tail as I came out, she eagerly thumped down the stairs, following me to the kitchen. I fed her first. She waited patiently, trembling next to her bowl.

"Go on then," I commanded, unable to stomach watching her slobber and slurp. Instead, trying to block out the sound of Gypsy's impression of a ravenous pig in a trough, I stood gazing out the kitchen window, letting the demands of the day settle into some semblance of order in my weary brain. It was Alice's turn to walk the dog today, so right now my chores extended to the banality of breakfast, showering, and getting ready for work. Another shift as guardian of the skies, keeping those aloft safe in their aluminium tubes as they wheeled, soared, and swung above the clouds. Oddly, the burden of responsibility had never weighed heavy. I was an old hand, with multiple controlling tours under my belt and a spotless record. Twisting the cold tap I filled a tumbler, drinking it down in a series of gulps, eyes closed. And there they were, those terrifying floppy ears dancing before my eyes. *Jesus!*

## CHAPTER 13

### Danger Zone

Shortly after joining the moderate flow of M27 motorway traffic, I gently accelerated, watching my speed like a hawk, never daring to venture above seventy, then flicked the lever to set cruise control; another speeding fine would be as welcome as a mariachi band the morning after. Despite the occasional interruption to my thoughts from the radio, I kept replaying the previous evening's events over and over. The sight of Alice with the giant furry ears, the childhood memory of lying helpless in the rabbit pen, and that horrible dream kept bothering me too. *Was Eileen really coming to stay?* I couldn't stop myself from thinking about it. Twenty minutes later, my tired, scrambled mind and my aching body were still yearning to be back in bed as I approached the solid steel security gates of the National Air Traffic Service Control Centre, Swanwick.

The enormous, modern, glass-fronted building, housing the nerve centre of the UK's Air Traffic Control services for civilian and military flights, lay hidden from prying eyes. Situated halfway between Southampton and Fareham, and only a few miles east of the River Hamble, the centre sat nestled in the bottom of a leafy bowl bordering a lake-lined nature reserve.

Every workday required the same routine, so before reporting for duty, I headed along the main corridor towards the ATC Briefing Room. Stepping inside, I avoided the return of the heavy double doors that thudded together, cocooning me in a vault of silence. Nothing I read gave me any cause for concern or reason to think it would be anything other than a routine day. Stepping from the silence, a flurry of bustle and chatter hit me in the face as I entered the Main Operations Area, heading straight to the Military Supervisor's desk at the heart of the buzzing control room.

Flight Lieutenant Stefan 'Vlad' Netsov, that morning's military air traffic supervisor, greeted me.

"Morning, Henry," he rasped.

My mate's nickname had come from the fact that his father was Romanian, and young Stefan had been plagued by chest complaints and mild asthma as a child. He'd grown out of it after emigrating to the UK as a teenager, but still had a permanent, faint, squeaky wheeze when he spoke and the slightest hint of an Eastern European accent. I often wondered how he'd passed his RAF entrance medical and got through the rigours of officer training. Anyway, he had, somehow, but it hadn't taken long before his sharp-witted flight commander noticed his unique rasping voice, dubbing him Vlad the Inhaler.

"Hi, Vlad, where do you want me?"

"Um, there's one track for Central shortly."

"Sure, no problem," I said assertively. Grabbing my controller's headset, just like I'd done over a hundred times before, I walked to the radar console and plugged in.

Scouring the screen, I continued listening intently while receiving a verbal handover from the off-going nightshift controller, allowing me to start building a mental 3D image of the Central sector.

"Okay, I've got it," I confirmed confidently and started looking for 'RCH915', my first customer.

Spotting the aircraft's radar data block approaching my airspace, I entered '235.875' into the radio frequency window. A few seconds later, the familiar tone of a mid-west American accent began filling my headset.

"Swanwick Military, good morning, Reach Nine One Five Heavy on handover, we're direct Land's End, maintaining flight level three four zero."

"Reach Nine One Five Heavy Swanwick Mil identified, continue own navigation direct Land's End, flight level three four zero, radar control," I answered.

"Roger sir, radar control, Reach Nine One Five Heavy."

Normally, I would have requested a cleared flight path through my civilian counterpart's airspace, but God knows why today I decided that 'taking five' would be a better idea. 'Taking five' was a bit like playing Frogger in 3D and meant that I could fly through pretty much any airspace without talking to another controller, provided I avoided all other air traffic by five miles laterally or five thousand feet vertically. To achieve this, I had to predict my aircraft's path and ensure that it remained at the centre of a ten-thousand-foot high, ten-mile-wide bubble that no other aircraft could burst. Even with a highly manoeuvrable and agile, high-performance fighter jet, it required a huge amount of attention, concentration, and planning. I should have known better, realising that my plan of doing it with a United States Air Force C-135 transporter had one major flaw.

A Boeing C-135 Stratolifter is a bulky, bumbling behemoth designed for carrying very heavy payloads, not to dodge things. Military forces around the world have small, fast, pointy planes to do that. However, in my defence, trying to avoid passenger airliners at this time on a Sunday morning with a C-135 wasn't complete lunacy. It wasn't like I was directing a fully fuelled truck the wrong way around the Monaco circuit on race day while trying to miss all the oncoming F1 racing cars. No, that would have been utter madness. I could only see a few airliners that were flying around at a similar level, so it was more like doing it during a Grand Prix practice session.

I sat gazing as the vision of Alice in towering black patent stilettoes, with her tightly corseted heaving boobs, and wearing those bloody giant furry ears drifted into my mind. If it hadn't, I might have noticed the two KLM Boeing 747s at flight level three four zero, converging on my aircraft. Luckily for me, the civilian London Airspace controller directing them spotted the potential problem.

"Swanwick Mil Central," I answered.

"Hi, it's London Upper Sector, I wondered what your plan was with the Reach?"

If London Upper was asking what my plan was there must be something in the way of my aircraft that I'd missed.

"I was going to watch it through and take five," I said, scouring the screen. Apart from the obvious perils of taking five, I also should have noted that Reach Nine One Five's callsign ended with the word 'heavy.' The pilot had deliberately included the word on his initial call to highlight that the aircraft was fully laden with fuel and cargo, making his normally slow and cumbersome aircraft, more sluggish and less manoeuvrable than a giant, flying concrete sloth.

"Okay, well I've got two KLMs to affect you at the same level," the civilian controller said with unbridled contempt. I wasn't sure, but in the background, I thought I heard the word 'dickhead.' The London Upper controller had seen the problem a mile off, well, about forty miles off, actually, and his tone said, 'well numbnuts if you don't do something we're going to have a major problem.'

My eyes scoured the radar intensely, looking for both aircraft. Two green radar blocks, 'KLM57' and 'KLM64' caught my attention, slowly tracking towards 'RCH915.'

The Royal Dutch Airline Jumbo Jets appeared to be following one another, about twenty miles apart, both showing 'FL340.' *Why hadn't I seen them?* Admittedly, if I was really busy with four or five aircraft under my control, I might not spot the occasional conflictor on an initial scan, but not two. Even worse, when I projected the KLMs' and RCH915's paths, blue lines appeared that clearly crossed. *Shit! What is wrong with me?*

"So, what's your plan then? Are you going to sequence between them?" he suggested irritably.

I looked at RCH915 while gauging the space between the two KLM airliners, as they continued down their projected paths. Edging closer to the point where they would meet, I continued assessing the three aircraft's positions and relative speeds. Somehow, I stupidly convinced myself that pointing my aircraft to fly between the two fast-moving passenger jets was an effective plan and a sound idea.

"Yes," I said boldly, "I'll shoot the gap!"

At no time in all my years as an air traffic controller had I ever been taught or even heard the phrase 'shoot the gap.' I also knew that no one else in the history of aviation had. Shooting the Gap could not be found in any Air Traffic Control manual, anywhere, because to be honest, it was about as sensible as playing hopscotch in a minefield.

As the radar images continued closing, I could see that the first KLM would comfortably pass well ahead of my aircraft, so all I had to do now was make sure that RCH915 shot the gap and passed at least five miles ahead of the second one. That was all. Simple.

Watching nervously, I waited, biting my lower lip as the radar returns of the C-135 and the second Jumbo Jet continued tracking towards each other. My vision became fixed on the ever-decreasing space and my heart started thudding as the realisation dawned that my initial plan might not be so much slightly flawed as totally and utterly shit. I could see that the two aircraft were converging towards the same point, closing in on one another with each passing second, both at FL340. I knew that I needed to do something about it quickly. My shirt collar suddenly felt two sizes too small and began tightening around my throat.

"Reach Nine One Five turn left heading one four zero degrees, traffic left ten o'clock, twelve miles, same level converging."

On any other day, I would have turned the Reach away to the right but for some reason, I thought that I had time to turn left and go behind. My 'brilliant' new plan was to pass behind the second Jumbo and get RCH915 back on track, once clear. If I'd been controlling something nimble and agile, like a Harrier or even four of them, that could turn on a sixpence, it would have worked. Regrettably, the lumbering C-135 displayed nimbleness and agility in the same way that early 20th-century, unsinkable transatlantic cruise ships did when it came to avoiding icebergs. My stomach knotted into a fist and despite my years of controlling experience, waves of fear and panic started washing over me.

"Roger, left heading one four zero degrees, Reach Nine One Five," the pilot acknowledged.

Watching, wide-eyed, RCH915 started turning slowly to the left. Very, very, very slowly. I gawped, willing it to turn faster and get behind the approaching Jumbo. Instinctively I knew this wasn't going to work. With horror, I saw the aircraft turning so slowly that he was aligning himself on a perfect collision course with the passenger-laden Jumbo Jet. I needed to react, but instead of responding, I froze momentarily. Like the winded four-year-old trapped in the rabbit pen, I felt completely powerless, and my dad wasn't there to save me.

"Reach Nine One Five, *avoiding action*, climb flight level three five zero, previously reported traffic now southeast seven miles converging same level." A voice had come from somewhere. My voice. Something instinctively triggered me into taking control. My racing mind decided that if I couldn't get behind the converging Jumbo in time then perhaps, I could try climbing over it.

The pilot's reply did nothing to allay my worst fears.

"Roger climbing flight level three five zero, Reach Nine One Five *Heavy*," he reiterated, "we're still in the turn here and pretty full today sir, but we'll give it our best."

The C-135's sickeningly slow rate of turn had revealed to me its pitiful lack of responsiveness. I should have known that its inability to climb rapidly with a full load would be as bad, possibly worse. I would have had more success if I'd been yelling at a partially deaf, asthmatic double amputee to run up a flight of stairs.

"Not good. Not good. *Fuck, fuck, FUUUCK!*" I thought I had only said the words in my head. A palpable absence of noise engulfed me as the normal thrum of the Ops Room ceased and rows of headset-wearing meerkats started bobbing up and down, looking in my direction, searching for the source of the loud profanity.

RCH915's height display obstinately remained at '340' and I could only sit, gawking at the perilous situation unfolding before my wide and desperate eyes. Two, three, four of my phone lines started ringing, lights blinking, alarms wailing. The cacophony of sounds became the soundtrack to the melee as the two radar images, still with matching height readouts, continued edging closer and closer. Suddenly, they started flashing red.

"God, nooo," I moaned loudly, forcing myself to watch, as the miles between the aircraft continued rapidly dissolving. Four, three, two... A second later the two aircraft, both at the same height, merged into an undecipherable mess of flashing red numbers and letters.

My forehead prickled with sweat as my heart started slamming against the wall of my chest. I wanted to scream, instead, holding my breath, I closed my eyes, and began praying. There was nothing else I could do.

Grimacing, I half opened one eye. Breathing out slowly, I watched, desperately relieved as the merged mess of radar blips and numbers separated. Sighing heavily, I continued staring intently as one scrambled block of flashing red numbers and letters broke into two, diverging before they stopped flashing. My rapid pulse continued throbbing in my head, my insides writhing like snakes in a pit, and my entire body felt hot, clammy, and wet with sweat. For a split second, the world around me dissolved. I imagined myself standing in an arcade playing Frogger, waiting for the words GAME OVER to materialise. Instead, Vlad appeared at my side and placed a quivering hand on my shoulder, his face deathly pale, sounding like he needed a nebuliser. I assumed he'd witnessed the near catastrophe on the radar screen at the Supervisor's Desk, but events had happened so quickly that by the time he'd reached me to try and help it had been too late.

Trembling, I turned to my ashen-faced friend, trying to quell my churning stomach's attempt to decorate the radar screen. "I think I might need to go and have a little lie-down," I said weakly.

"I think… you might need a lawyer," Vlad wheezed, "and Henry," he continued, his face taking on an even more grave look, "I'm sorry but I'll have to call the boss." *Take me now Lord, take me now, and make it quick.*

# CHAPTER 14

## If I Could Turn Back Time

Almost two angst-filled hours had trickled by since my attempt to turn a Royal Dutch Airlines Jumbo Jet and a United States Air Force C-135 into the world's first eight-engine Push Me Pull You. Having been swiftly relieved by a fellow controller, I'd gone plodding along the cold echoing corridor to the cafeteria, slumped into a comfy chair, and stayed there, staring out of the window. Sitting there stewing, I became vaguely aware of other people coming and going and had the feeling that they were all shunning me, deliberately avoiding conversation and eye contact. *I bet everyone knows.* Leaving me isolated on an island of ignominy, I felt that they had obviously chosen to sit as far away as possible and were probably silently judging me too. *I deserve it.*

Squirming restlessly, still in shock, my brain fizzed, struggling to reconcile exactly what I'd done and more importantly, why. *I'm such an idiot. What the hell was I thinking? A jumbo jet! That would have been hundreds of people. I know they were Dutch but still. Oh my God!* As another wave of utter wretchedness came washing over me, I put my head in my hands, my heart and insides crushing with the immense, sickening burden of shame. I was still trying to control my breathing and strangle the bubbling sobs in my tightening throat when Vlad appeared, his expression sombre. Looking like a black-capped judge about to pass sentence, even his eyes seemed blank and devoid of hope, their message, 'You're doomed.'

"Squadron Leader Koch's here and he's just watched it all in the radar replay room. He wants to see you in his office *now*."

"Okay," I nodded despairingly.

"I don't think he'll be putting you forward for October's controller of the month,"

Vlad rattled, with a thin, sympathetic smile.

Nodding to Vlad, slowly getting up out of my chair, I began walking the Green Mile to the squadron leader's office. *Bloody marvellous, he's going to absolutely love this.*

## CHAPTER 15

### You're the Devil in Disguise

The nameplate on my boss's door read, 'SQUADRON LEADER T N KOCH - BA (HONS) RAF.' The T stood for Timothy or Timbo to his friends, both of them. I had no idea what degree subject he'd studied, skulduggery probably, and every time I walked past his office, I couldn't help but mentally change (HONS) to read STARD.

Ludicrously, he claimed that his surname should be pronounced 'coach' and not 'cock.' Everyone else agreed on the alternative and his thoroughly deserved nickname, Isaac!

Stood waiting outside his office door, I could see Swanwick Mil's answer to Napoleon sitting at his desk through the tall, slender sidelight window. I had always thought that his greasy, slicked-back hair, sharp profile, and diminutive stature made him look like the result of a rendezvous between the nasty little French Emperor and a weasel. He sat rocking slowly back and forth like a Bond villain, his fingertips pressed together to form an arch. I knocked, expecting to be called in. Making a performance of appearing busy by rustling some paper in his In-tray, he then started playing with his mouse, staring intently at his computer screen, leaving me to brood outside. My knuckles thudded into the wood, rapping on the door a second time. The squadron leader made a theatrical jump in his chair, looking up with apparent surprise. Pointing his stubby index finger at me he smiled, hooking it twice. Clenching my jaw, I sucked air aggressively through my flaring nostrils, bracing myself. I looked at the pulsing veins branching across the back of my hand as I grasped the

58

icy steel door handle. Wondering if its frosty, insensitive touch was a portent for the cold-hearted creature and chilly reception awaiting me on the other side, I pushed the door open, stepping into his lair.

"Ah, Henry," Isaac purred, dispassionately, his piercing blue eyes glinting as, almost imperceptibly, the corners of his mouth turned up into the merest hint of a *screw-you* smirk, "do come in." As the door behind me clicked shut, I stopped in front of his desk, trying to calm my breathing and steady my shaking hands.

"So, I've watched the replay and it's obviously controller error. I can't begin to describe the damage you've done to the RAF's reputation and the impact it's going to have on our delicate relationship with the civvies. I'd call it a severe cognitive failure or in layman's terms *you,*" he spat, looking me squarely in the eye, pointing aggressively towards my face, "royally fucked up." I didn't answer, I was preoccupied, trying to control my breathing and bubbling anger.

"Anyway, you've been around long enough to know what happens in these circumstances." *No, not really, I've never been in this situation, but I imagine you're going get to take real pleasure in making me squirm because I messed up and ruined your weekend to boot.*

I settled for, "I don't know sir. Retraining I expect and some form of counselling."

"Counselling! Whatever for? *You* screwed up Flight Lieutenant, deal with it." *Wow, that'll be compassion with a small c then.* That wasn't the only word I was thinking of that started with a small c or in my cold-hearted boss's case, a massive one. His mouth contorted into a malicious sneer before quickly reforming back into a smug bastard grin.

"Obviously you're suspended from controlling until further notice and will of course be subject to a formal investigation. You'll need to complete an incident report first, but I strongly suggest, and by that, I mean *I'm telling you...*" He emphasised the point by tapping the rank slides on his epaulettes, "to take next week off as annual leave. God knows how long it will be before you'll be allowed back on console, if at all, and you're no good to me here if you can't control. We wouldn't want any more *fireworks.*"

Bristling, my nails dug into my palms. That last comment referred to an old festering wound that he liked to pick at and wouldn't allow time to heal. Not wanting to give him any more satisfaction or a reason to grin any wider, I ignored the provocative jibe. Taking a deep breath, I slowly unfurled my knotted fingers.

"Any questions?" *Yes, how did an uncaring, insensitive twat like you get promoted?*

"No sir."

"Good. Don't forget to submit a leave pass," he instructed, continuing to grin.

I felt that he was clearly revelling in my discomfort, and if he had grinned that infuriating, sanctimonious sickening smirk any wider his head would have split in two. I wished.

"Okay, sir," I said, weakly, "I'm about due some leave, anyway."

"Unless you've got any questions, I'll see you next Monday, and don't forget to file an incident report too. I *will* check."

"Oh, I know you will," I muttered defeatedly under my breath.

"*What was that?*" he snapped.

"Nothing, *sir,*" I answered, in a half-hearted attempt at respect.

"Just watch yourself *flight lieutenant.* After this morning's *fiasco*, you're already on thin ice and we wouldn't want it to ruin your *rocketing* career now, would we?" He sneered, pinning me with a cold, piercing stare. I could have sworn I heard the bastard chuckling.

My mouth pursed slightly preparing to form the 'w' of 'wanker,' but I knew I'd ultimately pay a high price and closed it again. After today's events and our previous run-ins, experience had taught me that the little shit would already be devising some unscrupulous scheme and plotting my downfall. I didn't need to give him any more ammunition. Instead, with my heart thumping, my ears ablaze, and hot tears of frustration starting to swell, I set my jaw, striding out of the office to head back down the corridor to the Crew Room.

Storming out, brooding about Isaac's callous snipes, I slammed the office door behind me. Glancing back, I caught sight of him through the sidelight. Leaning across his desk, I watched the little bastard grinning as he picked up his phone and start dialling.

## CHAPTER 16

### Don't Worry Be Happy

Sitting numbly, I continued staring at the computer screen. I tried biting my cheek to control my anger while attempting to muster sufficient enthusiasm to fill out the two forms that Isaac had demanded and kept chastising myself for expecting an ounce of sympathy from him. The slightest hint of concern for my welfare and fragile state of mind wouldn't have gone amiss, even from someone that I despised. Despite our mutual dislike for one another, if the tables had been turned, I know *I* would have instinctively been concerned for his mental well-being and shown some degree of kindness and empathy.

The air incident report template in front of me remained blank, unlike my whirling mind. *How stupid am I? A mid-air collision.* I shuddered. *I nearly wiped out hundreds of people and two aircraft.* My stomach tightened, lurching as I replayed the chilling sequence of events over and over, unable to stop the disturbing looping video in my head.

The click from the opening office door hit the stop button.

"Hi Henry, I thought you might need this, my friend," Vlad rasped, giving me a weak sympathetic smile as he walked in.

"Thanks, mate, you're a star," I replied, taking the steaming cup from his hand. "Look, I don't mean to be rude, I probably should talk to someone, but I just want to crack on with finishing this crap," I said, pointing to the monitor, "and then Foxtrot Oscar."

"Hey mate, it's fine. I understand. Isaac's already poked off and I wouldn't want to hang around either. If you feel like a chat though, just give me a call, any time. Seriously."

"Thanks for the coffee Vlad and just, well… thanks mate."

"Take it easy and don't beat yourself up about it too much.," Vlad said. I sighed, nodding slowly. "And if you want to talk just pick up the phone," he added, opening the door to leave. Vlad stopped halfway, turning back, giving me a wistful look as he offered the deep existential observation that life is full of unpredictable events; "Henry, my friend, shit happens," he wheezed.

I shouldn't have been surprised that Vlad would check on me and bring me a coffee, but I couldn't face it. I had zero appetite and I really wanted to be left alone. I felt far more comfortable worrying and beating myself up. *I am such an idiot.*

I chastised myself again for being naive and expecting some understanding from my appointed line manager and supposed leader. I knew my energy would be better spent completing these forms, then I'd have the rest of the week off. Toby and Jack had an inset day tomorrow but then they'd be back to boarding school and weren't due to come home until the following weekend. *I might even get some bunny-free, quality time with Alice. And a round of golf, possibly two.* I sighed, feeling the tightness in my neck easing slightly. *There could be an upside to this mess after all.*

Just as quickly as the flash of optimism sparked, it fizzled, popped, and died. *How could I have forgotten?* My fingers drummed on the desk as I sat gazing into nothingness, contemplating my separatist mother-in-law's potential visit. It might have been an unpleasant prospect, but I couldn't stop her from turning up. *No, but I can stop worrying about something beyond my control, get these reports filled out, and get the hell out of here.*

With a newfound determination, I turned my attention back to the computer in front of me, my fingers blurring with a rekindled sense of purpose. Fifteen minutes later I had finished the mandatory incident report and submitted a leave request. I emailed them, making doubly sure that I Cc'd Isaac then, grabbing my things, started heading for the car park.

*Surely, she won't be at home. Will she? For God's sake, stop it!* I turned the engine over, scolding myself for revisiting the unsavoury possibility, and tried dragging a squeegee across my mind as I put the car into gear and started driving home.

An uneventful thirty minutes later I parked opposite the moss-coated concrete steps jutting from the steep, grassy bank. Pulling on the handbrake, I turned the key, waiting until the engine coughed and died. Immersed in silence, I sat, staring blankly past the house's pale brick face, gazing through the windscreen towards Gosport, then the Solent, smiling nostalgically as my misty eyes settled upon my birthplace, the Isle of Wight.

12:23. I sighed, shaking my head at the realisation of how much my world had changed since I'd left for work a little over four hours ago. My stomach had managed to slowly uncoil itself on the drive home and even though my mind had insisted on replaying the harrowing radar images, I'd tried redirecting my thinking onto the endless possibilities of the days ahead.

Slinging my rucksack over my shoulder, I crunched onto the pavement as something ginger scooted from underneath the neighbour's car. *Not again Lucky, please, just leave me alone.* Despite feeling like my brain had been injected with novocaine, my heart warmed a little, lifting my sagging spirits an inch higher when I spotted Alice, with no sign of an elderly female paramilitary dementor hovering behind her.

## CHAPTER 17

### Cry Me a River

"Oh! Hello, part-timer," Alice joked with surprise as she met me in the hallway, a cup of tea in her hand, "you're home early," she said with a questioning scowl. "Tea?"

"Lovely."

"Here, have mine," she said, offering me her cup, "I'll make another."

I followed Alice into the kitchen.

"Where's your mum?" I asked, dreading the answer.

"She's not coming." *Get in.* "You'll be delighted to hear that she's decided to stay home. Apparently, she needed to plant her spring bulbs."

Under the circumstances, it felt like the tiniest victory, and I wanted to say that Eileen's lame explanation for wanting to stay home sounded more like an excuse to buy a shit load of nitrate fertiliser, but despite the good news, I wasn't in the mood to make jokes.

"Can you sit down for a second, there's something I have to tell you." Alice could read me like a book, immediately recognising the concern in my solemn eyes as my hands began shaking and my shoulders collapsed.

"Whatever's the matter? Oh God, just talk to me," she begged.

I had rehearsed what I was planning to say on the drive home, thinking I had the whole speech prepped and ready.

"Okay…" I paused, taking a deep breath. Then my lips started trembling. A sudden wave of emotion surged from my belly, it continued rising, swelling in my chest, then came gushing out of my mouth, as I inundated Alice with an incoherent blubbering of wracking sobs, dribble, and snot. I simply fell apart, dissolving like an inconsolable eleven-year-old girl trying to describe the devastating, world-ending, heart-rending tragedy of Take That's breakup.

It took about ten minutes for me to calm down completely. Alice rested on the edge of the kitchen table, utterly confused and anxious, hugging my head as she ripped another piece of kitchen towel from the roll. I blew my nose before wiping my face with more scratchy paper and taking a deep breath.

"Well, that was embarrassing," I said, placing Alice's hand in mine. Calmy, I looked up into her soft, cornflower eyes and began explaining what I'd done. Startlingly Alice looked somewhat relieved when I clearly recounted the near catastrophe and my complete lack of focus.

"Oh, thank God, I thought you were going to say something else."

"*Thank God? What? Did you hear what I just said?*"

"Of course, I did, but the way you crumbled just now and that look on your face, I was waiting for you to say you only had months to live."

In my confusion, I was struggling to understand why my wife appeared to be thankful that I'd tried to cause a major disaster.

"Do you blame *me* for what happened?" Alice squirmed.

"*What?* Why on earth would I blame you?"

"Well, you know," Alice said awkwardly, biting her bottom lip, "I did pick a *bunny girl* outfit," she admitted. *I knew it!*

"Don't be silly," I answered reassuringly, concealing the knowledge that I'd not been able to shake certain recurring visions, "there's no one else to blame except me. The always supportive and sympathetic Squadron Leader Koch made that quite clear."

Alice flinched at the mention of his name, grinding her teeth. I finished by telling her about the conversation in the office.

"That little bastard," Alice seethed.

"Yep, but let's not think about him. Besides, I'm absolutely wrung out and I just want to go and lie down," I pleaded.

"Okay. Go and grab a shower and then get some rest. What do you think will happen though?"

"I don't know, I've never screwed up like this before. One of the guys had an incident last year and he had to have a period of retraining."

"What's wrong with that?"

"Nothing, but he didn't nearly kill 400 people *and* it was under the old boss."

"*Oh.* Just get some shut-eye, I'll tell the boys to keep the noise down. I'll say that you're not feeling well and came home early. I still can't believe he made that dig about your career though."

"Can't you? Anyway, thank you for... you know... being you."

"Hey, we're a team you know. We'll get through this. It's not the end of the world."

"Isn't it?" I asked, instantly annoyed that I'd relapsed into despondency.

"*No, it's not!*" Alice raged, her chest and shoulders flaring into the dominant pose that she took whenever I needed a buck-up lecture. She quickly softened. "No, it's not. We'll be fine and you'll see things differently tomorrow." She paused. "I love you, Henry," Alice cooed, leaning over, and kissing me gently on my reddened nose.

"I love you too," I smiled.

"Are you okay though?"

"I'm not sure. I don't really know how I feel. It's weird because one minute it was all happening so fast and the next everything went into slow motion. It was pretty intense," I explained, lifting my arms, and showing Alice the huge tide rings.

"Oh God, you definitely need a shower, best you strip off and throw everything in the wash."

It suddenly struck me that the house seemed eerily quiet.

"Where are the boys?"

"They both got up and walked the dog with me this morning, which was lovely." *Thank you, boys.* "The biggun's popped to the shops for me, and our little angel's being horribly quiet up in his room." *Angel! More like a horny little devil.*


## CHAPTER 18

### The Bitterest Pill (I Ever Had to Swallow)

Stepping out of the bath I grabbed a large towel from the rail and started walking towards the bedroom. Feeling clean and refreshed, I relaxed, sinking into the softness of the comforting warm carpet underfoot. I had only taken a couple of steps towards the bedroom when a small shape darted between my legs, clawing me viciously on the inside of my right thigh, before dropping and darting along the landing. I glimpsed a ginger and white blur disappearing as it shot below the level of the top stair. I clearly heard the disturbing noise he made as he ran. I know that traditionally cats say, meow meow, but for a second I thought it sounded a heck of a lot like ha ha.

"*I'm going to cut your fucking pompoms off,*" I bellowed.

"Are you okay?" Alice hollered from the lounge.

"No. That little ginger ninja got me again."

The door to the boys' room cracked open behind me, and a single angry brown eye peered out. "*Can you keep the noise down please Dad?*" Jack demanded.

"Well, *excuuuse* me," I replied sarcastically.

"I'm trying to concentrate in here," the cheeky little sod said. I bet he was, and I knew what he was concentrating on too.

"*What?*" Alice shouted.

"Nothing, I was talking to Hugh Heffner."

"Really? Hugh Heffner? With the bunny girls. Not if he's any son of yours!" *Bitch.*

"Your bloody cat got me again," I complained, quickly changing the subject.

"Ah, Lucky's only playing," she called dismissively. "Just go to bed, darling."

That cat was lucky alright. Lucky that I'd never managed to catch the nasty little sod.

I lifted the towel, staring at the *playful* lines of blood oozing from the scratches on my inner thigh. A few inches higher and the furry assassin would have given me a vasectomy.

After dabbing my leg dry, I towelled off and then climbed into bed, naked, my head flopping onto a cold fresh pillow. The smell of crisp, clean cotton filled my head. Fresh bedding. Delicious. The stairs creaked and I lay listening to the soft thuds growing louder.

"Take these," Alice said, appearing from the landing with a glass of water. She handed me two small white pills.

"What are they?"

Pointing to each identical-looking pill in turn, Alice answered in the slow condescending tone of someone talking to a drooling, nose-picker.

"That… one's… crack cocaine… and… that… one's… heroin. Can you say that with me? Heh-rho-win."

"I just wondered," I glowered, ignoring her sarcasm, "if there was anything in them that might show up on a compulsory drug test. That's all! I don't want to get into trouble at work."

"I think I learned my lesson on that front a long time ago, don't you?" Alice said, raising her perfectly rounded, dark eyebrows. "Besides, as for getting in trouble at work, I think that ship has already sailed, hit a reef, and is currently taking on water." *Ouch.* "You definitely won't be getting tested this week, will you?"

"No, I suppose not. But what are they?"

"I call them 'Mummy's Little Helpers.' They'll knock you out for a few hours," Alice said, stepping onto the landing. Her parting words came echoing up to me as she trod downstairs, "Just take them like a good little boy and go sleepy bye-byes."

I'd never taken sleeping pills before and stared uncertainly at the innocent-looking tablets in my palm. *Ah, what the hell.* My tongue flexed in protest as the pills started fizzing and I grimaced as they dissolved, the acrid bitterness spreading. Grabbing the glass, I sloshed the contents into the back of my mouth and gulped. Yuck. I took another swig, washing away the last sour traces clinging to my taste buds. Resting on my back, my body began melting into the bed. The horrors of this morning were over, it had been a close call, but nobody had died. *Nobody died!* I looked at the ceiling, puffing my cheeks out, and blew. Lowering my gaze, I stared through the bedroom window, watching wisps of clouds scudding over the fern-green headland of Hayling Island, studying the waves foaming caps as they broke on an angry grey sea. The last thing I remember was thinking how quiet Jack was being, followed by the image of Sapphire's pert round bottom swaying against the backdrop of my heavy eyelids. In a matter of heartbeats, I drifted off and began *purring* so loudly it could have woken the dead.

## CHAPTER 19

### Smoke on the Water

Peeling one eye open I groaned, peering at my chest. I half-expected to find a young heifer sitting there, nonchalantly chewing the cud while pinning me to the mattress. Instead, I realised that the covers had been pulled to one side and the contents of my underpants had no underpants to contain them. I struggled to move my cold muscles; my body had turned to lead. Straining with the effort, I grunted and rolled over, pulling the quilt over me as I turned. *What time is it?* The feeble light through the slit between the curtains reminded me of a breaking dawn rather than dusk. *How can that be?* The confusing question made my thoughts as blurry as the numbers on the screen. Surely, I'd only slept for a few hours. But our bedroom was southeast facing, and that sunlight seemed to be… I shook my head, struggling to understand. Slowly, my eyes came into focus on the phone's display.

"07:07." *Holy shit!*

07:07 as in a.m. *Oh my God, it's Monday!*

I must have slept for, what, *eighteen hours!* I suppose I'd been so exhausted with the stresses and strains of…Yesterday happily kicked down the door to my memory, refilling my head with the horrors of the near miss, and the video loop restarted. Shuddering, I shook my head vigorously as if trying to clear an Etch A Sketch.

The familiar bubbling sound of a boiling kettle accompanied by the histrionic whimpers of Gypsy begging for food floated up from the kitchen. I imagined she'd been unrewarded as she came puffing and thumping up the stairs seconds later, with all the grace and nimbleness of a small elephant in hobnail boots.

The dog's head poked around the door.

"Hello, girl."

Her milky eye appeared to be having an argument with its clear neighbour, and was looking back towards the landing, her good one remained fixed on me. Tail wagging, she came bounding into the room. Bending down, I scooped my hand under her bottom, lifting her up, grunting with the effort.

"Blimey. I know a greedy little bitch that needs to go on a diet." She immediately turned her head towards the bedroom door, cocking it to one side as if her right ear had suddenly grown heavy.

"You'd better not be talking about me," Alice said, stepping into the room, laden with tea.

"Nooo," I replied, shaking my head, "I'd never call you little."

"Cheeky," she growled playfully, placing a cup on my bedside table.

"Thank you."

"So how are you feeling, Sleeping Beauty?" Alice asked, sitting down on the edge of the bed.

"Not great. The last thing I want to do is watch reruns of yesterday's nightmare, but I can't stop thinking about it. I know nobody died but that's not the point, they could have. Right now, there are over 400 people blissfully unaware of how close they came to never sniffing another tulip, eating Edam, or *schmoking* a pancake again. They could easily be splattered all over an Oxfordshire field amongst a load of wreckage, and it would all be my fault. 400 people, Alice. 400, all dead!" I felt like my heart had fallen into my stomach and put my head in my hands.

"But they're not, are they? Look at me. *Look at me!*" I flinched, raising my head slowly.

"But they could be," I answered feebly. Alice folded her arms, crossing her legs as she scowled at me. I gulped.

"We nearly won the National Lottery on Saturday," she said emphatically. I frowned. *What has this got to do with me trying to kill hundreds of people?* I also felt a slight buzz of excitement and couldn't wait to find out how much we'd won.

"Wh… what? How close?"

"We got number twenty-seven. We were only five numbers off winning 37.5 million."

"*What*? What *are* you talking about? Five numbers away, that's not even close." Alice uncrossed her arms, jabbing a finger towards my face.

"*No, it isn't, is it?* It's a long way off but that's life. Sometimes you're a million miles away from winning and sometimes you're horribly close to disaster, but when you have a lucky escape, you can either wallow in self-pity, pointlessly worrying about the *what if*, or you can be thankful and learn from it. Sometimes the only thing you have control of is yourself."

I hated to admit it but that made a lot of sense.

"I suppose so. Sorry, I don't mean to be such a pessimist," I bleated.

"Really? Because you're very good at it, I think it's in your genes. The other thing you're *really* good at is snoring. I hit your pillow, prodded you in the ribs, and then tried rolling you over. In the end, I just pulled the covers off you. That didn't work either, so I left you to it and went in the spare room."

"I was bloody freezing when I woke up."

"Good, you noisy sod. Had a nice long sleep though, didn't you?" I nodded, grinning widely. "You kept me up until gone midnight. Even the dog couldn't stand it and came in with me."

"Oh," I grimaced as a half-hearted apology.

"Well, you're awake now, Princess Aurora, so maybe you'd like to walk her?" Alice suggested, climbing in next to me. "I spent the night hunched up on a pathetic little single bed with a fat farty beagle. I think I'm entitled to a lie-in. *Don't you?*"

"Of course, my love."

"Don't let the door hit you in the *face* on the way out will you, my grunty little warthog," Alice instructed. She smiled as she put her hand out, leaning over to kiss me, inadvertently placing her entire weight on my belly. *Oh my God!* I almost swamped the bed.

"*Gotta go!*" I yelped, straining as I lunged out of the room.

A sudden, uncontrollable sensation of warmth had started flowing south like someone had pressed the supersize option on a drinks machine and the pipes had surged and filled ready to dispense but without a cup underneath. Scurrying towards the bathroom the expanding feeling inside swelled from uncomfortable to excruciating. Gravity was not my friend. Terrified I was about to water the landing, I grabbed my foreskin, pinching the end, and tried clenching my abdomen as I wobbled towards the toilet. It didn't help, flexing my stomach muscles only applied more pressure and intensified the unbearable, persistent tickling sensation. Looking down, I could see a small pink water balloon rapidly expanding and leaking slightly. I pinched harder. *Ouch*. Like King Canute, I couldn't hold back the tide and punched the door open, jumping into an unsightly squat over the porcelain and with the gay abandon of a free-range, nappy-less toddler, let go. The balloon erupted in an explosion of steaming, pale yellow liquid, surging up the wall, and over the raised lid and seat. It went

74

pretty much everywhere except into the bowl. Managing to direct the torrent downwards, I continued squatting like a small, bald naked sumo wrestler in a fighting stance. I closed my eyes, sighing and *aahing* for an eternity as my engorged rogue bladder blissfully emptied.

Letting out a long *phew*, I slowly opened my eyes. A sea of steam began rising from the cold porcelain and tiles, snaking upwards like twisting coils of smoke. Surveying the devastation, it looked as though someone had tried to kill a mosquito with a fire hose and somehow, I'd discovered a newfound level of self-loathing. I set about clearing up the mess. Inconveniently the wall-mounted toilet roll had taken the brunt of the tsunami and hung there, soggy, wrinkled, and looked as degraded as I felt.

"What the hell was that?" I asked myself aloud, on my hands and knees, mopping up the deluge with handfuls of squelchy paper. Yesterday had left me doubting my ability to control aircraft, and now I was having similar concerns about my body. I couldn't even bear to look at myself in the mirror. *For Christ's sake, I'm forty-four, not eighty-four! Could my crotch shot be an advert for the new Tena Man campaign? Well, I've definitely got the face for it!* I flushed, watching the mound of paper swirl as it was sucked down and then disappeared, along with my last remaining drop of dignity.

## CHAPTER 20

### Burning Down the House

I washed and dried my hands before grabbing my dressing gown from the back of the bedroom door, and carefully retrieved my phone and tea. The duvet-shrouded Alice had already started *purring*. Trudging down the stairs, I heard the familiar sound of the plodding beagle a few steps behind. Reaching the kitchen I put the tea to my lips, sipping then greedily gulping down the rich malty liquid. *This is the greatest cup of tea ever.* I realised why it tasted so good when the tea hit my stomach and my empty belly grumbled loudly, complaining that it hadn't been fed for over twenty-four hours.

"I don't know about you Gypsy but I'm starving," I said, walking towards the fridge.

As the door opened, so did the dog's mouth.

"Shhh, quiet!" I whispered testily. "She'll kill us. Well, me definitely."

The potential retribution for interrupting Alice's lie-in made me shudder. She often displayed what I described as an Israeli response in stressful situations, tending to result in a swift physical reprisal, although it never lasted six days. I tried desperately to shut the dog up but Gypsy kept innocently cocking her head sideways, panting and wagging her tail so hard that her whole body shook, continually whining, oblivious to the impending threat to my health from a would-be Mossad assassin.

I now faced the challenge of having to cook on a crap, standard, military-issue oven that had only two hob settings, Pathetically Lukewarm or Chernobyl Meltdown. Undaunted, I set about making myself a hearty English breakfast while repeatedly shushing the black, tan, and white, boss-eyed space hopper with a loud, squeaky valve. *Had they been eating breakfast on that KLM jet? I bet it had made a right mess.* I imagined the chaos on board, cabin crew stumbling, hot coffee and stroopwafels flying everywhere, passengers clutching their armrests and each other, screaming as they thought *this is it. They must have been petrified, those poor, poor people.* Gypsy started barking. I went to shush her when I spotted smoke wafting from the grill.

"*Bollocks!*" Yanking out the smoking tray, my mood suddenly felt darker than my overcooked sausages as I growled, frothing with anger. I tried crushing the handle in my shaking grip then threw the blackened, spitting grill pan into the sink. It clattered and clanged noisily. Irrationally, I couldn't care less if I woke up the whole damn street.

Breathing deeply, I shakily placed my foamy coffee next to my steaming plate, slamming my arse down into the chair. Gypsy sat quietly, staring at the food, willing it to fall on the floor, thin shoelaces of saliva hanging from her quivering jowls. My anger melted a little, my heart twinging with sadness as I stared at her milky blind eye. Rarely would I reward her begging, but *that face!*

"Right," I whispered, "don't tell your mum but you can have this if you can keep that ginger shithead off my back for five minutes. Just try being a proper dog for once," I suggested, sawing off a corner of my toast, "and this is just between us, okay?" Gypsy wagged her tail, which I took to mean that she understood my request and would try her best to worry the cat.

Pressing the small triangle into the dome of the egg yolk, it broke, oozing a stream of golden liquid. As the eggy crust sailed across the kitchen, Gypsy cowered, closing her eyes, shrinking away from the incoming projectile, and bracing for impact. It hit her in the face, bouncing off her eye socket. Flinching as if I'd just smacked her across the head with a leather belt, she pounced as the missile hit the floor, snaffling it up. Then, forcing her mouth as wide as possible, she began twisting, straining, and flicking her outstretched tongue, awkwardly attempting to reach the yellow goo on her face.

"Seriously? Are you sure you're a real dog?" I asked, shaking my head at the grotesquely contorted hairy creature in front of me, trying to lick its own eyeball.

With my belly satisfyingly full and my mood slowly lifting, I cleared away the breakfast things. Gypsy continued whining and dancing around my legs.

"Time for you to work off some of that lard. Come on girl," I said, grabbing her lead. "Walkies!"

Gypsy disappeared. Grumbling, I bent down and peered under the desk to discover a small furry shape trembling, cowering against the desk's backboard, presenting her blind eye. I rustled the bag of dog treats, shaking out a soft squidgy morsel, offering it a few feet from her muzzle.

"You really are crap at hide and seek you know," I said, clipping on the lead. The dog whistle hung next to the front door. I looped it over my head and then tried manoeuvring Gypsy into the porch.

"Move, fatty!" I snarled, jabbing my toe into her thigh, harder than usual and with more resentment than encouragement. Gypsy squeaked, then huffed, protesting through the doorway. I followed, my nose wrinkling with the stale blend of mouldy canvas and damp rubber filling the confined space. Slipping my arms into my rigidly creased waxed jacket, I shrugged it on and then peered nervously, before squeezing my feet into the uninviting dark, cold recesses of my wellies. Even as a fully grown adult I still had that fleeting moment where I expected some unseen tiny beast to sink its teeth into my toes. Opening the front door Gypsy flopped to the floor, impersonating a sack of potatoes.

"I'm not in the mood for your crap today," I rumbled.

The dog grunted in protest as I stepped over her and out of the front door, pulling on the lead.

"Come *on!*" I commanded through gritted teeth. The obstinate sack began sliding slowly across the tiled floor, making a low grouching whine. As her front paws collided with the door frame, stroppily, Gypsy got to her feet. Grumbling, she followed reluctantly, harrumphing into the cold October morning air as I shut the door behind her.

## CHAPTER 21

### Daydream

My carefree little companion merrily trotted off ahead of me, blowing plumes of steam into the crisp morning air, briefly looking back she appeared to smile. I had to admit it, this innocent podgy little hound had become such an integral part of my life that I couldn't stay angry with her for long or possibly imagine being without her. Even if I had paid over the odds for a half-blind duffer.

"Sorry about just now. I didn't mean to prod you *that* hard, I'm a bit stressed at the moment," I apologised to the dog's bottom as she stopped to sniff and lick something gooey lying in the gutter.

"Yesterday was awful Gypsy, I mean I've had bad days at work but nothing like that. Your mum didn't help with that whole bunny girl thing either. It was a bit of an extreme way to get her own back for our anniversary. Maybe I deserved it. Anyway, it doesn't really matter, as far as work goes, I really messed up. Maybe it's time to step away from controlling for good. What do you think?" Gypsy ignored me and continued assessing the goo's foulness and piquancy as I walked on. "At least I wouldn't have to work for that backstabber. I don't know, girl. I just feel a bit… lost. At least I've got you and hopefully you'll up your cat and dog game and that spiteful ginger tosser will end up on a missing poster."

The immovable, dead weight at the other end of the retractable lead reached its limit, wrenching my shoulder. Gypsy had upgraded from the gutter goo and anchored herself next to a badly tied, leaking black bin sack, deliberately licking the outside with the glazed, vacant expression of a flat earther sat next to their favourite flavoured window.

"Leave it!" I ordered, repeatedly pulling on the lead. Resisting with the force of an obstinate Shetland pony, she kept ignoring me and carried on slurping the gunk stuck to the black polythene. With a firm tug, the huffing mutt gave in, walking sideways, gazing forlornly over her shoulder at the retreating bin bag.

"You really are quite disgusting," I grimaced, shaking my head. Even so, I honestly had very few regrets about having this sometimes repellent yet adorable little dog.

Reaching the T-junction, I looked up. Two faint, thin, parallel lines of dusky pink emerged. Painted against the dark sky, they gently curved across the indigo backdrop of early morning, extending away from me towards the horizon. *Hmmm, what would a casual observer on the ground have seen if he'd been looking up yesterday as that C-135 and Jumbo crossed, seconds away from tragedy?*

The squeal of tyres and a car horn's deafening blare made me jump. Caught in the blinding glare of headlights, I instinctively yanked backwards on the dog's lead, as a white van screeched, swerved, and went speeding past.

*"Slowww dowwwn dickhead!"* I screamed, giving the English archer's salute to the back of the retreating van as it went wallowing down the hill. Panting loudly, I clutched my beating chest. *Jesus, that was close. That van could have flattened both of us. Idiot.* I then realised that I was standing in the middle of the road but couldn't even remember checking to see if it was safe to cross, never mind stepping off the pavement.

Unsteadily negotiating the wooden stile on the opposite side, I paused at the top, catching my breath before hopping down and setting off along the muddy, grass track, leading to the open parkland beyond. Relieved to be away from the road and in the safety of the field, I rested, letting out a long slow sheesh, unclipping the dog's lead.

"Off you go, girl!"

## CHAPTER 22

### I Don't Like Mondays

Through the half-light of the approaching day, I could just about make out the dog's podgy outline, walking off ahead of me sweeping the floor with her nose. Following steadily behind, I passed her as she stopped abruptly, excitedly sniffing a patch of grass. Bursting into a run, I watched as she ran off ahead, still nose to the ground. We exchanged places like this for a few hundred yards until she disappeared.

"Gypsy," I called. Nothing.

"*Gypsy?*" Still no sign of her.

Putting the whistle to my lips I blew, giving two sharp peeps. The distant whistle did its trick of firing a trigger in Gypsy's brain that went simultaneously to her stomach and legs and within seconds I heard the pattering and thud of paws as a familiar eager shape returned, bouncing into view, to sit at my feet, excitedly wagging her tail.

"Good girl," I said, as she stared at me, shaking expectantly.

Rummaging in my pocket, I found a star-shaped treat. Taking it gingerly between her front teeth, she snapped her mouth shut, gulping the whole titbit down with the elegance of a pelican swallowing a whole fish.

"Any idea what flavour that was? No, you greedy little bitch. You are allowed to chew, you know."

Head down, she set off again. Gypsy had only gone a few feet when her gait began slowing from its normal bouncing trot to a laboured wobble, her tail sticking straight up stiffly at a right angle, her legs rigid. Immediately recognising her signature shuffle, I started digging my hand into my trouser pocket.

I watched her waddling awkwardly, with her rigid tail acting like a defective rudder, as she carried out an imprecise bombing run. Her mission complete, Gypsy's tail went limp and with a small shudder she set off again with a noticeably lighter spring in her step.

*Yuk!* Preparing to collect my treasure trove, I spotted a sludgy layer of mire between Gypsy's steaming packages. I could feel my anger flaring at the thought that some careless owner hadn't bothered to clear it up. To be fair though, clearing that up would only have been possible if they'd gone for a dog walk armed with a bilge pump. Bending down, I looked up at the sound of Gypsy snuffling and watched as she happily plodded, licked, and sniffed tail wagging. I couldn't stop myself from replaying the heart-stopping moment of the white van appearing from nowhere and swerving to avoid us. I could still feel the fear and the sensation of the sudden rush of air as the van blew past, inches from my nose. *I nearly got that little dog killed just now.*

As I bent over, I definitely wasn't thinking about the dog whistle dangling from my neck. Breaking the tissue-thin skin of scum, it must have dipped silently into the dark, putrid slurry, glooping over the mouthpiece and filling the chamber. Collecting the last round from Gypsy's salvo, I tied the neck of the bag as I stood up, blissfully unaware of the ticking time bomb around my neck.

I scanned for a dog waste bin, getting a whiff of something unpleasant despite the cold. In the faint light of daybreak, I recognised a familiar rectangular silhouette waiting in the shadows at the base of a giant oak tree. Having disposed of the warm, lumpy bag, I walked on, scouring ahead of me for Gypsy. Long early morning shadows began creeping across the ground, the dawn light slowly intensifying with each passing minute. I could see a fair way ahead of me now but no sign of my dog.

"Gypsy. Here girl." Nothing.

"*Gypsyyy?*" Still nothing.

" *Gyyypsyyy!*" I shouted and waited, but she still didn't appear.

Instinctively running my hand down the smooth leather of the lanyard, I grabbed the cold whistle, put it to my lips, and blew hard.

The whistle failed to make a sound, but my hard puff generated enough force to fire a jet of slurry up my left nostril. Splatting forcefully against my sinuses and tonsils it began sliding down the back of my throat. The vile tang registered instantly in my brain as something repulsive, something I had smelled before, but never tasted and my brain began screaming as my stomach rolled over.

"*Oh God*," I belched, as my mind and body reached an instantaneous violent agreement. Wave upon wave of revulsion came sweeping through my body as I yawped more and more aggressively, honking like a klaxon with each forceful cramping spasm of my stomach.

"Hurgggh... Hurgggh..."

The grass, my Wellington boots, and most of my chin glistened, decorated with dollops of tomato, chewed burnt sausage, and soggy lumps of bread coated in light brown bile. I staggered, wobbling like a pissed weeble, struggling to remain upright, and thought I could hear what sounded like a small horse approaching at full gallop.

I imagine the sickly sweet scent had drifted through the cold morning air and eventually reached Gypsy's hypersensitive nose. Swelling with each thundering step, the smell must have made her fat little legs go like the clappers, bringing her barrelling towards the source. Jumping in surprise, tensing my back, I immediately relaxed when a very animated Gypsy came thudding into view.

"Hello girl," I mumbled.

My relief instantly turned to horror when, without stopping, Gypsy, quivering with excitement, barked fanatically and dove headfirst into my recently departed breakfast and started eating it.

"Gypsy, nooo!" I commanded weakly, but the determined little beagle couldn't stop. Ignoring my protestations, she started lapping feverishly at the steaming lumps of food. Lunging like a drunkard, I feebly threw my hand at her.

*"Stop it!"* I screamed. Jinking her rear end away from my slow, hooked fingers, I snatched nothing but a handful of fresh air. Gobbling and grunting noisily, her cheeks puffing like bellows, she slobbered with gusto. The sight of Gypsy eating my own vomit, on top of the horrible knowledge that I had just snorted and tasted dog shit, made my stomach cramp and squeeze and I started puking again.

Pronging like a fat, short-legged gazelle, Gypsy became even more animated, barking excitedly between mouthfuls as her platter refilled. With my last ounce of energy, I heaved again, and the ringing sound of Gypsy's animated barks started fading. Utterly spent, I groaned weakly, and my head started swimming, floating, tumbling, as Gypsy began melting into a blur of smudged black, white, and tan, her barks becoming softer and softer and...

## CHAPTER 23

### Barbie Girl

*Am I asleep?* I was faintly aware of an unpleasant wet sensation on my lips and face. Like being slapped with a hot, rasping, rancid flannel. Shivering, the cold clinging to my wet thighs and backside began slowly creeping up my back. *Maybe I'm in bed at home asleep and just having a really bad dream?* The recollection came crashing in through the saloon doors of my consciousness. My head kept pounding, a foul bitter taste was lingering at the back of my throat, and my neck and face strained as I tried swallowing. Sitting up, I opened my eyes as Gypsy leapt on me, her front paws on my chest as she tried licking my face.

"Geroff!" I grimaced, pushing her away, repulsed by the blended stench of gastric juices, coffee, and part-digested plum tomatoes on her fetid dog breath.

Weakly, I began looking around. *Nooo!* All evidence of my recent vomiting episode had disappeared, replaced by a large patch of flattened, wet steaming grass. Noticing that my wellies were gleaming with dog saliva too I retched. Gingerly getting to my feet, I stopped halfway up. Resting one hand on my knee, I groped in mid-air for an invisible support with the other to somehow steady myself as I caught my breath. Trying desperately to ignore the rancid taste burning the back of my throat, I sucked in several large mouthfuls of cold air to quell the nausea. Very slowly I stood up, wobbling slightly, then started retching again.

Gypsy crouched, barking excitedly in anticipation.

"No more, I'm empty," I muttered, "c'mon girl, let's go." Placing one foot deliberately in front of the other, I began heading home. I turned to see an extremely happy and content fat little beagle with a very waggly tail following.

The Sun continued its inexorable climb, peering over the top of the giant oak. Looking at my watch, I realised that I must have passed out for about fifteen minutes. *Why hadn't any other walkers found me and raised the alarm?* Nearing the road I spotted Barbie, a petite, young blonde woman, head to foot in bubble gum pink, crossing the stile. I often bumped into her on my morning treks with Gypsy, accompanied by her two annoyingly playful and mentally challenged red setters, Tinker and Belle. I knew her dogs' names like I knew Zamis the Dalmatian, Hogan the harlequin Great Dane, and Colin the annoying little Shih Tzu with the gammy leg, but I had absolutely no clue as to the names of their owners.

Even though we sometimes chatted, I'd never asked the attractive Barbie her real name. More than once, I'd found myself hypnotised, gazing into those dreamy, bright green eyes with inky black pools at the heart of a burst of gold, all set in a flawless ivory complexion with a cute, elfin nose and soft red lips. I became utterly lost, mooning like a lovesick puppy, adrift in a flight of fancy, picturing me and Barbie, hand in hand, skipping through a sunlit meadow. It was a perfect, innocent fantasy, right up to the point where she opened that sweet mouth of hers and noises came out.

Nature had clearly bestowed her with beauty to counter her irritatingly high-pitched, squeaky voice as if her lungs somehow converted air into helium. I recalled our first brief conversation that had convinced me that, not content with giving this flaxen-haired goddess vocal cords made of tightly wound piano wire, Mother Nature had been running short on human brains the day she was born and picked her out one from the box marked "BIRD."

One morning, when we'd found ourselves standing awkwardly as our dogs met, sniffing, and licking each other in their own unique way, she shattered the perfect illusion.

"You ain't workin' today?" she squeaked, splintering the beautiful silence.

"No, it's my day off. You?"

"Me neiver, I do lots of work for the charities now though," she explained, "but I woz a trainee assertishun."

"Sorry, you were a what?" I had no idea what she was saying.

"Assertishun."

"Bless you?"

"Wot?"

"Sorry, I still didn't hear what you said. An asser...?"

"Assertician, Bewty Ferapy silly," she giggled.

"Ohhh." An aesthetician. I suddenly feared for the charities she worked for, but by the same token felt consoled that at least one woman had narrowly escaped hospitalisation from a catastrophic Brazilian.

"So, where do you volunteer?" I asked politely.

"Everywhere really. I do all the big ones. You know, Oxfam, Barnando's, Mary Curry. I think it's really importunt to help those less unfortunate than yourself." *Oh, dear God!*

It was suddenly apparent that if Barbie and her dogs had been able to sit still long enough to take an intelligence test, she would have struggled to come third. Of course, I tried not to be rude, my parents had raised me under the strict mantra, 'If you can't say anything nice, Henry, then don't say anything at all,' which I always, consistently, and unswervingly stuck to. Sometimes.

## CHAPTER 24

### Who Let the Dogs Out

"Hiya," Barbie squealed loudly. If the pitch had been one hertz higher, I wouldn't have been able to hear her, and it would have set off all the dogs in the neighbourhood. I didn't feel like stopping, I just wanted to drag my sad, sorry arse home and clean my teeth. Gypsy spotted the other dogs and began baying loudly, really loudly, right behind me. The setters began booming in reply.

"Oh, please shut up!" I squinted, bracing against the cacophony of barking.

"Hiya," Barbie screeched again, waving enthusiastically as she unclipped her intellectual betters. The gundogs came bounding up the path, heading straight towards me, displaying all the grace, control, and coordination of a couple of half-cut giraffes on roller skates.

"Ow!" I yelled as the first dog flapped past, whipping me painfully across the knees with its hard, vigorous tail. The second beast continued juddering directly at me and I watched helplessly as its rear end started jack-knifing. It broadsided me at knee height, the slippery soles of my rubber wellies offering little resistance on the damp muddy grass. In a blur, my view of the world went from vertical to horizontal; I hovered for the briefest of moments before slapping face-first onto the ground. *Why me? Am I being punished for yesterday? I probably deserve it.*

"Oops a daisy, you okay, babes?" Barbie squeaked as she began walking towards my prone groaning body before clipping her dogs back on their leads. "Tinker vat was so norty. I'm so sorry, babes," she squealed with laughter.

"Oh yeah, you sound really sorry," I snapped, lifting my head off the floor, and spitting out mud and blades of grass.

"Norty Tink. I am really sorry," she twittered.

"I heard you the first fucking time," I growled, my rigid jaw flexing and clenching as I slowly got up.

Barbie flinched her nose, snorting in contempt. Her high-pitched apology mixed with squeaky laughter really, really pissed me off.

"Well, vat's just charmin'. Good mornin' to you too," she peeped indignantly walking past me.

No, not a good morning, it was a really bad morning. In fact, in the history of mornings, this could be rated as the worst morning I'd ever known. Okay, second worst. Barbie stopped, I imagined the cogs struggling to turn as she paused, trying to think of something else to say. She froze as I stood up facing her, her sweet lips parting in horror as she gawped at my dishevelled state. Quickly turning away, head down she trotted off, hurriedly dragging the confused Tinker and Belle behind her.

"Come on girl," I sighed, "let's go home."

## CHAPTER 25

### Homeward Bound

We crossed the road, *cautiously*, and five minutes later stepped through the front door with Gypsy straining on her leash. Home. I opened the inner door, plonking my backside down on the floor of the porch, and unclipped Gypsy. She bolted. The cool from the icy tiles radiated into my bum cheeks making them even colder as I sat huffing, puffing, and grunting. With two loud sucks, I finally managed to heave free my moist stockinged feet from the clammy walls of my boots then slowly got up, padding through to the kitchen.

90

"You have got to be kidding me," I tutted loudly, walking towards the sink. Gypsy sat next to her bowl, tail wagging, pleading for her breakfast.

"You horrible greedy little pig. I think you've had enough."

Filling a glass from the cold tap, I put it to my lips with a trembling hand. Swilling the cool water around my mouth, I threw my head back, gargling forcefully like my life depended on it, and spat. Hocking aggressively, I refilled the glass, drinking slowly as the cold and tiredness continued creeping right through to my bones. I felt like I'd swum a mile in a fur coat. *I really need to lie down.* I didn't plan on doing a great deal today but what I wanted to do, more than anything else in the world was wash my face and grab my toothbrush to get rid of that appalling taste.

"Fifteen… sixteen… seventeeeenuh!"

If Hercules had been faced with that stair climb as his twelfth labour, I think he would have asked Apollo if he could muck out the stables of another thousand cattle instead. Bending over the bathroom sink I rested, letting the swirling steam crawl across my face and wrap around my head. Plunging my flannel into the hot water, I began scrubbing the sopping wet cloth with a sweet, scented bar of golden coal tar soap and dragged it across my mouth, trying to erase every last foul trace. Feeling a little more human I grabbed my electric toothbrush, piping a healthy squeeze onto its bristles then scoured my gums, teeth, and tongue until the toothbrush alarm buzzed. Coughing and spitting, I repeated the process until my mouth felt as though I'd been chewing a whole packet of Trebor Extra Strong Mints at once. I had just finished purging my mouth and the back of my throat with the reassuring menthol sting of mouthwash when Alice appeared in the doorway.

"Did you have a nice, *oh my god you look terrible.*"

"I feel it too," I replied feebly. *What should I tell her? This has hardly been my finest hour.*

"What on earth's wrong with you?" she said, placing her cool fingers across my forehead. "You don't think it's that Parvovirus that's going around, do you?" I shook my head, smiling thinly.

Of course, Alice meant Norovirus and the pedant in me would normally have taken great delight in explaining the difference between the two, but not today. Besides, after what I'd had up my nose, Parvovirus would be a more likely candidate. *Do I lie or should I come clean?* I certainly didn't feel clean and Alice had an annoying knack for knowing when I was lying. She could have had a successful career breaking the most resilient terrorists and always managed to wheedle the truth out of me, although she hadn't tried waterboarding. Yet.

Sitting in the lounge, nursing a cup of sweet tea, I told Alice everything. Recounting the whole sorry tale, Gypsy kept occasionally popping her head around the door, almost on cue, apparently still hopeful for her breakfast. I still couldn't look her in the eye and my wife's reaction wasn't quite what I was expecting. I knew that her compassion tended to be fleeting, but not even she could make light of this so soon. Occasionally, she coughed, putting her hand to her mouth, but it sounded, well, forced. *Is she stifling a laugh? Surely not.*

"... and then, when I thought things couldn't get any worse, this dopey great Red Setter comes straight at me, takes out my legs, and knocks me flat on my face."

Alice burst out laughing and doubled over, crying, her whole body shaking so violently she was forced to cross her legs. Sitting there, wounded, I could only harumph, as Alice continued rocking, tears streaming down her face. Sulkily getting up from the table, I felt my neck flushing and tightening. Leaving my tea behind, I headed for the stairs, the sound of Alice's hooting still ringing in my ears.

Thumping up the staircase, she called after me.

"Wait … hang on … I'm … I'm sorry." She didn't sound bloody sorry, not in the slightest, as she continued impersonating a hyena. "Where… where are you… going?

"I'm taking myself to bed," I snapped irritably. Thump, thump, thump.

"Okay, you go… and get your head down." Still not a hint of remorse in her voice. "Just one thing, before… before you go to sleep."

"What?" I snapped, stopping to turn and glower at the red-faced Alice.

"I… I just… I wondered," she sniggered.

I crossed my arms and began tapping my foot, waiting for Alice to compose herself and finish asking her question.

"… have you fed the dog?"

# CHAPTER 26

## Wake Up Boo!

"Daaad? … Daaad? … *Daaad?*" Jack bawled the words, slapping awake my semi-conscious brain.

"Ugh?" Opening one eye I found him standing next to my bed, waiting, hands on hips.

"Hi Jack," I mumbled slowly.

"Mum said to ask you if you wanted a cup of tea if you were awake."

"What did she tell you to do if I was asleep?"

"Um, she didn't say, Dad, but you're awake now so do you want one *or not?*" Jack replied, throwing his hands in the air, with an exaggerated eye roll.

"But I was asleep," I pleaded.

"I know Dad, I could hear you in my room. It's very difficult to enjoy a lap dance when you can hear your old man snoring like a pig."

"*Jack!*"

"I'm joking, we've been downstairs with Mum while you were sleeping but you're not anymore, so what should I tell her about tea?"

"But Jack, *you* woke me up," I pined.

"*Duh!* I had to, so I could ask you if you wanted a cup of tea," he shrugged, "*sooo?*" Jack demanded tetchily.

"Yes please," I surrendered.

I watched, expressionless, as Jack stepped into the doorway, cupping his hands on either side of his mouth and bellowed, "*Yes Mum, Dad'll have one.*" Then, unbelievably, he walked down the stairs, went into the kitchen, and started chatting with Alice.

"Priceless."

Sitting up I peeled my dry mouth apart, running my tongue over my teeth. As the cold air hit my throat I gagged. *Ow, that's sore and why is my tummy so tender?* Then I remembered why. I knew that eventually, it would become a distant memory but for the time being that moment with the whistle would continually float about in my waking mind, bumping into the near mid-air disaster no doubt. *Can I still taste it?* I shuddered. *I'm imagining it, hopefully.*

A familiar, friendly canine face poked around the doorframe. I could tell from the small oscillations of her head that Gypsy was furiously wagging her tail and rear end but hesitating, uncertain whether she'd be welcome.

"Hello girl," I said encouragingly, patting the bed. I watched in awe as she took two strides and made an enthusiastic leap with all the poise and grace of a pizza-loving hippo in ballet shoes. Soaring very briefly, she yelped as she struck the side of the bed two-thirds of the way up, hitting the floor with a whimper.

"Come here, fatty?" I commanded lovingly. Placing my hand under her squidgy, hairy bottom, I hauled her up, her back legs scrabbling in mid-air until they gained purchase on the bedclothes. Immediately making for my face, she came at me with a flicking tongue.

"No Gypsy!" I shouted, holding her at arm's length until she lay down sulkily.

"Okay Gypsy," I said stroking her head, "I think we need to talk. Think of this like your midterm appraisal…"

I spent the next ten minutes explaining again to my lazy dog that she really needed to up her game as far as the cat went. The whole cat and dog thing clearly wasn't working, and she really needed to put a bit more effort in; sleeping and eating just wouldn't cut it anymore.

"So, like I said the other night, you need to start bothering that ginger tosser like a proper dog. Just keep him busy so he doesn't have the time to stalk me. Okay?" Gypsy lay on her front staring, twitching her eyebrows, cocking her head from side to side, looking utterly confused while I babbled on.

Her ears pricked up when she heard the tinkling of a stirring teaspoon coming from the kitchen and started watching the door at the sound of Alice's footfall on the first step.

"So," I whispered, "I just need you to try a bit harder okay. I mean, if you were to chase Lucky out of the cat flap and he just happened to run away and never came back, well that would be just awful, wouldn't it?" I winked. Ignoring me, she kept her attention on the doorframe, standing alert on all fours, her tail wagging briskly when Alice entered the room with a white china cup in hand.

"Who were you talking to?" she asked, placing the steaming drink on my bedside table.

"The dog, obviously." Alice looked at me like I'd grown a second head.

"Okayyy," she replied slowly, "and does she answer back?"

"No, it's wonderful. Maybe you could take a leaf out of her b…"

"Don't push your luck," Alice interrupted, gently guiding the inquisitive Gypsy away, making room to sit next to me. As she touched my forehead with the back of her hand, Gypsy forced her head and shoulders between us and slumped down.

"How are you feeling?"

"Much better for a decent sleep. I'm still feeling a bit *bleurgh* though and I'm trying not to think about the other thing. I nearly got run over this morning when I was out with the

96

dog."

"*What?*"

"Yeah, I was in a bit of a daydream and ended up in the middle of the road. The van driver saw us, but it was a bit hairy."

"Us! You nearly got my dog killed." I loved knowing exactly where I stood in my wife's affection hierarchy.

"And me, hello, I was on the other end of the lead," I protested.

"Yes, so you were in charge. Oh my God Henry, be more careful, she's irreplaceable." *Husbands on the other hand are obviously two a penny.*

"Sorry, I was miles away. I've got all sorts of weird crap going on in my head at the moment." *I've even had some up my nose.* "So, what did you tell the boys?"

"I just told them you still weren't feeling well."

"Okay, you didn't tell them why did you?" I feared that such a revelation would stock the boys' arsenal with a lifetime's supply of ridicule ammunition. Especially Jack's.

"Nooo," she said, looking at the ceiling. My heart sank.

"*Oh, come on!* I'll never live it down." *My life is over.*

"No, I didn't," she confirmed emphatically, "I'm joking, I didn't tell them." *Phew.*

"What time is it?"

"Four o'clock. You've missed lunch." My grumbling stomach agreed.

"Dinner's sorted. Get dressed and come down, the boys are watching an old horse opera. We'll eat at about six, then they need taking back to school. Are you okay to drive them?"

"Of course," I yawned, "you know how much I love those drive-time chats."

## CHAPTER 27

### We Are Family

I plodded down the stairs, Gypsy in tow. Reaching the bottom, I turned left into the front room, my faithful hound went right, hopefully going to annoy the cat, but more likely drawn by the smell and sounds of Alice pottering in the kitchen. Toby lay draped across a beanbag, lost in a packet of crisps, aimlessly depositing them into his mouth one by one. Jack was sitting on the floor, his back resting against the sofa, eyes glued to the screen, lost in the Monday afternoon movie. They could not have been more different.

Toby seemed to cruise through life, happily bimbling along in neutral, chilled, relaxed, and unriled, although his younger brother had a knack for knowing exactly which buttons to press when he felt like 'poking the bear.' Apart from his younger sibling, nothing seemed to faze or overly excite him. Jack, on the other hand, had inherited his mum's passionate personality and, like Alice, every emotion manifested in the extreme.

Alice's father had told me about the time he took his five-year-old daughter to the cinema to see Disney's The Incredible Journey. Alice hadn't just been watching the adventures of Luath the Labrador Retriever, Bodger the Bull Terrier, and Tao the Siamese cat, as they journeyed through the Canadian wilderness trying to get home, she was there, with them, living it. When the cat fell into the river, Alice jumped up on her seat and clenched her arms, straining her whole body, while repeatedly bawling at the screen, "*Get the cat out, get the cat out, somebody get the cat out!*" The usherette had politely asked Dougal to take his daughter outside because she'd made the rest of the children start wailing and calling out for their mums. I'd had a similar experience thirty years later when Jack had gone apoplectic, throwing his Kia Ora at the screen, screaming at the *very bad man* with the net, five minutes into Finding Nemo.

"Hi boys," I said, stepping into the lounge.

"Hi Dad" Toby replied, greeting me through a mouthful of soggy deep-fried potato.

Jack said nothing.

"Are you feeling better now? Toby asked.

"Shhh," Jack snapped.

"Yes, thanks. Just a bit of a dicky tummy, I think," I whispered.

"Maybe it was something you ate?" I eyed Toby suspiciously.

"What are you watching?" I murmured, flopping onto the sofa. Jack lifted his bum off the floor, and moved closer, leaning up against my leg.

"The Cowboys, shhh, it's really good," he hissed.

Grabbing a cushion, I placed it behind my head and leaned back, just as Bruce Dern shot John Wayne in the chest and he fell to the floor and died. I could feel Jack trembling. Putting his hand on the edge of the sofa, he pulled himself up, and then sat back next to me. I lifted my arm and he shuffled closer. Gypsy came plodding into the room behind Alice, who walked over and sat down, making a Jack sandwich. The dog took up her usual pose in front of the log burner with her head resting on the red brick surround and started baking her head, mesmerized by the dancing flames, no doubt wondering what they'd taste like.

"What's this?" Alice asked.

"Shhh, it's The Cowboys. It's really good," I replied, feeling a gentle prod in the ribs from Jack.

"Okay. Dinner's in half an hour," she whispered to the room, as she sat back. Looking around at my assembled tribe, a warm wave of contentment came washing over me. *You're a lucky man Henry Alder.*

## CHAPTER 28

### A Little Respect

The boys had brought home a huge pile of laundry, even though we paid for the school to do their washing. I'd just finished loading the boot when Toby and Jack opened the car doors and jumped in. Standing in the doorway, Alice lingered, waiting to see them off with Gypsy in her arms. I walked around to the driver's door and climbed in, thinking about the best route to take to Southsea when an idea struck me.

"I'll only be a sec."

"What did they *forget?*" Alice asked as I went flying through the porch.

Twenty seconds later I ran back out brandishing a driver and a 7-iron.

"Practice," I announced, bounding up the concrete steps two at a time. "See you later."

"Stick those behind my seat, Toby," I said, handing him my golf clubs.

"Are you off to the range then?" asked Jack.

"Yes, after I've dropped you off."

"Oh!"

"What?"

"I just thought you might want to get home to Mum, you know what she's like when we go back to school."

"She'll be fine," I said, uncertainly.

"Well, if we can give up strippers for five minutes to spend time with Mum, I think it's only fair that you should give up golf Dad. Don't you Toby?" Jack asked, crossing his arms triumphantly.

Toby nodded his agreement in the rearview mirror.

Alice remained in the porch smiling, blowing kisses, and waving the unimpressed Gypsy's paw. I could tell that behind her happy face, painted on for the sake of her two boys, she'd be crying inside. *Thanks, boys.*

The car grumbled as we pulled away. I couldn't have squeezed a wafer-thin mint into the boot and imagined it must have felt as stuffed as the boys did. They'd both had second helpings of shepherd's pie and somehow still had room for treacle sponge drowned in custard.

Taking the M275 towards Portsmouth, thankful for the light traffic as we approached Whale Island, I glanced out across the Solent, spotting the unmistakable outline of Cunard's latest ocean liner flagship.

"Look boys, there, that's the Queen Mary 2," I said, trying not to sound too excited, "I expect she's heading to Southampton Water."

"Where?" Toby asked looking out of his window with mild interest.

"*There*," I said pointing to the small single-funnelled shape on the horizon, "she replaced the QE2 a few years ago."

"What, that little splodge? Wow."

"I've met the Queen, you know," I said, trying to generate a conversation.

"Really?" asked Jack. "Is she as fat as she looks in the photos?"

"*What?* The Queen's not fat," I countered, defending Her Majesty's waistline.

"Well, she looked it in the photos I saw. They say the camera adds a few pounds."

"*What?* What photos are you talking about Jack?" I asked, confused.

"Those old black and white ones," Jack replied confidently.

"Sorry, you've seen black and white photos of Queen Elizabeth looking fat?"

"Ohhh, Elizabeth, the *Q, E, 2*, I get it now, Dad."

"What? Who did you think I meant?"

"Sorry, I thought you'd met Queen Victoria."

"Oh, ha ha. It was at Buckingham Palace actually, she awarded me my campaign medal."

"Really, you got one of your war medals from the Queen?" Jack asked, sounding genuinely impressed.

"Yes."

"Which war was that? Boer?"

"No, Gulf, cheeky git! How old do you think I am?"

"I dunno, seventy-two?"

"I'm forty-four, you little git."

"I know that's what you *told* us, but I think you're losing your marbles, Dad."

"Thanks a bunch."

"I know, I'll give you a test. Um, *did* you ever have a pet as a child?

"Yes."

"Was it a woolly mammoth?"

"*Nooo.*"

"*Did* you have a bike when you were a boy?"

"Yes."

"Was it a Penny Farthing?"

"*Nooo.*"

"Okay, when you were at school did you write in a book or chisel notes on a tablet?" Jack chuckled.

"Hilarious!" I sighed, shaking my head.

The Sun had set almost two hours ago, and I parked the car near the back entrance to St. John's College between two streetlamps, buzzing and glowing at the centre of large, misty orange halos. I helped the boys hump their bags to their boarding houses then the three of us walked back to the car. Time to say goodbye. They would only be gone for two weeks, but I could already feel my throat tightening. Reaching behind me, I tugged my wallet from my back pocket, producing two crisp, £20 notes.

"Toby. Jack," I said handing over the money, "and don't spend it all on lap dancers."

"Thanks, Dad," they laughed. Joining in, I revelled in the rare, precious moment of a shared joke with my teenage offspring. It felt wonderful to laugh, spontaneous, therapeutic, and normal.

"Since you're in a generous mood is there any chance you could top up my phone, pleeease?" Toby asked with a cartoon grin.

"Sure, just as long as you remember to use it to call your mum. Is £10 enough?"

"Yes, great."

"Jack?"

"Yes please."

"Anything else, that won't require me to sell a kidney?"

"Ugh, who'd buy that?" Jack asked, with a look of disgust. "Is there a big market for vintage organs?"

"Thanks very much," I replied, slightly wounded. I think Jack saw the hurt on my face and lingered behind as his big brother started walking off.

"*Dad, hang on*," Toby boomed, breaking into a run towards the back gate and disappearing through the wall into the darkness.

"What's that about?" I asked.

"Search me," Jack replied. He stood awkwardly, waiting, looking at the floor.

"I really liked that cowboy film today."

"Me too, son, me too."

As Jack loitered, rocking from side to side, I got the feeling that he wanted to say something and had waited until his big brother was out of earshot. Opening my mouth, I prepared to break the awkward silence when Jack spoke.

"Dad, I just wanted to…" he started but was cut off by the clanging of the gate and the appearance of an enormous sports equipment-shaped silhouette walking towards us.

"Oh yeah, we forgot," Jack said with the realisation of why Toby had run off, "our housemasters told us we had to bring our summer sports gear home at the end of last term because they needed the space."

"What the hell. It's October Jack!"

"Yeah, we're a little bit late." *Brilliant.*

I opened the boot and began loading the mountain of paraphernalia into the back of the car. By the time I'd finished, the briefly empty boot had been refilled with two enormous cricket bags, bats, pads, hockey sticks, a couple of tennis racquets, and two tubes of tennis balls.

"Is that everything? No cricket screens, hockey goals, or an umpire's chair?"

"Nope, that's it, almost," said Toby, pulling a folded brown envelope from his back pocket. I thought I saw Jack flinch, his gaze following the letter's path from Toby's hand to mine.

"I think it's from the bursar. Cheers Dad," said Toby and shot off again.

"Bye son, see you in a fortnight."

*Oh good, a letter from the bursar, what wonderful news will he have for me now? Maybe the board of directors has decided to reverse their decision about the six percent fee increase and he'll be sending me a big fat cheque.* There was more chance of Oscar Pistorius catching Athlete's foot.

"Are you okay Jack?" I asked, tucking the letter in my pocket, and closing the boot.

"Yeah, yeah, I'm fine," he replied, breaking his gaze.

Jack was still waiting as I got back in the car.

"Are you feeling better Dad?" Jack asked, his tone abnormally serious.

"Yes, I'm fine. Why?"

"Well, Mum said you came home from work because you were ill yesterday, you slept for ages, *and* you went to bed again after you walked Gypsy. I was a bit worried."

"Oh, that. No, really, I'm fine, don't worry son."

"Are you sure," he warbled, his face full of concern.

"Honestly Jack, your old man's fine."

Placing one hand on the door frame, he leant inside the car and kissed me. My heart glowed.

"I love you Dad, just remember that." Struggling to swallow the lump in my throat, I blinked away a tear.

"I love you too, son."

He stepped back from the car, his whole face smiling. Just for a second, under the weak glimmer of the streetlight's sodium lamp, Jack's expression reminded me of him as a toddler; small, innocent, and unworldly, then with an impish grin, he winked.

"*No, no, I don't want to,*" he shouted.

"What's wrong?" I asked, my forehead and brow scrunching in surprise.

"*No, I don't want to get in your car!*" he yelled.

"Jack, what are you doing?" I said, shaking my head, utterly flummoxed. *What's happening?*

"*I don't care if you've got some puppies!*"

"Jack, pack it in! That's not funny," I snarled through gritted teeth.

"*No, I don't want your Werther's Originals. Help! Stranger danger!*" he hollered.

White light flooded from the front door of a red brick bungalow opposite as it swung open and a bespectacled old woman wrapped in a shawl stepped out, craning her neck.

"*No, don't make me. Stop! Stop you pervert!*"

The nosey neighbour started down her garden path.

"Is everything alright, my love?" she shouted. I glared at Jack then looked back towards the bungalow, freezing when I spotted a burly tattooed skinhead in a blue

Portsmouth FC top walking past the garden gate.

"*Stay there you fackin' nonce!*" he raged, pointing towards my car, breaking into a run.

"Not funny," I growled at Jack, flooring the accelerator. I wasn't prepared to hang around and try explaining my younger son's sick sense of humour to a homicidal, rampaging Neanderthal in a Pompey shirt.

Shooting up Albany Road, my heart continued pounding. Shaking my head, a wry smile crept across my face as I caught sight of Jack in the rear-view mirror. Illuminated in the orange light of a streetlamp, doubled over, I watched him laughing hysterically, holding himself with one hand and waving goodbye to me with the other. *You little shit!*

## CHAPTER 29

### Pull Up to the Bumper

My pulse had almost normalised by the time I was cruising past the depressingly drab tower blocks of Fratton. The engine hummed, my mind drifting into autopilot as I continued home, passing by the dark waters of Mallard Lake along the broken hedge-lined Eastern Road. Rounding a long sweeping left-hand bend, I blinked, emerging from the darkness of the dimly lit coast road into the dazzling floodlights of Portsmouth Golf Centre. Slowing down, I leaned forward, glancing through the wire fence, watching the random tracer fire of range balls shooting up into the night sky, lit from all sides by the brilliant barrage of the monstrous bright lights. I turned left, crunching into a parking spot right outside the front entrance, and killed the engine.

*I'll only hit a few balls. Just a small bucket, then head home.* I needed the practice and was hoping to get at least one round in this week, possibly two, maybe three. *I could call Dougal; we could go for a drink too. Okay, maybe one large bucket of balls, but that was it.*

The vision of Alice holding Gypsy and waving goodbye appeared. What had Jack said? 'You know what she's like when we go back to school.' I did, she'd be home alone, trying to keep busy to avoid slipping into a state of melancholy. *Who am I kidding?* I knew I wouldn't be able to hit just one bucket, I'd be here until they threw me out at ten o'clock, and then, by the time I got home, Alice would be seething, or better still, asleep. She really didn't deserve to be abandoned for the evening, especially after she'd said goodbye to her *babies* for another fortnight. She'd been really supportive over the last two days too. *Maybe just one small bucket then.*

Five minutes later I found myself stuck on Eastern Road, after driving away and mournfully watching in the rear-view mirror as small bright dots went firing into the night sky. I couldn't leave Alice home alone; I could always rely on her in a crisis, and she'd be having a minor emotional one about now. *This traffic better start moving soon. I need to get back.*

I sat cursing, wondering why every man and his dog had chosen this moment to take my route home when the road ahead began opening up. *At last.* I accelerated, trying to catch the car ahead as it continued pulling away. Suddenly, its dazzling red brake lights flashed, and I lurched forward, the seatbelt strap cutting into my chest as I slammed my foot to the floor, feeling a crump behind me. Unfortunately, the boy racer who I'd seen tailgating me in a four-wheeled sub-woofer hadn't braked in time. Before realising I'd been rear-ended, the driver of the boom box reversed, turned around, and started wheel-spinning away up the road. Jumping out of the car, I could still hear the thumping speakers as I watched the car melting into the glowing sea of orange and white streetlamps and headlights. I walked to the next vehicle and began tapping on the windscreen. The driver jumped then squeakily wound down his window.

"Yes, mate."

"Hi, I don't suppose you noticed that guy's number plate, did you?"

"Wot guy?"

"The one in front of you that just went into the back of me and drove off."

"Did he? Sorry mate, I didn't see nuffin'. I was on me phone." *On your phone and 'you didn't see nothing.' Where do I start?*

Shaking my head and grating my teeth, I walked back to assess the damage. It looked expensive. The door of the boot had a two-foot-long crease starting faintly just below the rear wiper, that ran under the number plate, ending in a puckered V where it met the cracked bumper. Although *my* back end looked unsightly, I imagined that the fragile turbo-powered roller skate had come off a lot worse. *Thank the Lord the boys' sports gear isn't damaged. I mean, that would have been a disaster!* I thought about calling the police, quickly discounting the idea, knowing it would be pointless. Portsmouth and Fratton weren't exactly barren when it came to souped-up super hatch mobile discos, and I didn't think the Old Bill would get very far with my description of 'some little wanker in a small sporty red thing with blacked out windows and Carlos Fandango super wide wheels.' I shrugged, surrendering to the knowledge that I'd end up footing the bill for this hit and run, accepting it as another scoop of turd-flavoured ice cream being plopped onto my plate.

Standing by the car, I stared at the stagnant situation in front of me. Infuriatingly, the traffic on the bridge over Broome Channel looked to be solid as far as the roundabout junction 300 yards ahead. Beyond that, the T-junction had a solid line of traffic extending left and right all the way along the A27. The roundabout and bridge pulsed and flared with the flashing blue and red lights from a cluster of emergency vehicles surrounding a crumpled mess of twisted, steaming metal. It looked pretty bad. I'd be here for a while. Typical, I'd probably get home about the same time as if I'd stayed at the range. *I could have hit two large buckets of balls and just blamed the traffic.*

## CHAPTER 30

### Free Fallin'

The car crunched onto the gravel opposite number 12 around 9:30. Desperately tired, I stepped onto the road and stretched. Graunching the crumpled boot open we both groaned loudly as I started thinking about repair costs and the daunting sight of the mountain of sports equipment. *Why the hell can't you boys be more organised? If you'd done as you were asked at the end of term, I wouldn't be dealing with humping your pile of crap about single-handedly in the dark, in the middle of bloody October.*

Angrily assessing the cargo, I could feel my jaw tightening. *I should probably make two trips, or I could ask Alice to help me. Pah! What sort of man would I be if I asked my wife for help?* I dumped the contents onto the pavement, cringing at the noise of grinding metal as I forced the malformed boot shut.

The two navy blue canvas holdalls looked bulky, but I knew that the boys would have just shoved everything in. Undoing the zips, the small hairs in my nostrils recoiled, assaulted by the pungent smell of dirty socks, sweaty shoes, and fetid teenage musk. The contents looked more like the inside of a hurriedly loaded washing machine.

After repacking I was left to deal with two holdalls, two cricket bats, a couple of hockey sticks, and a single tennis racquet. *Piece of cake.* Laying the bats and sticks on top of one bag I bent down to pick it up. *Boy, this is heavy.* Next, I fed the racquet under my arm and tried picking up the second bag. The handles bit into my palms as I started shuffling towards the steps. *Cricket gear?* It felt like they'd each thrown in a set of dumbbells and a corpse.

On reaching the top, under the dull yellow streetlights, I could see the edges of the remaining steps almost all the way to the bottom. The last one lay shrouded in near darkness, as did the path all the way to the porch, shadowed by the sloping grass bank. If I'd known I'd be doing an impression of a Himalayan Sherpa, lugging a load of sports kit in the cold and dark when I got home, I'd have asked Alice to leave the porch light on. *Thanks, boys.* Although I'd only be traversing a set of eleven concrete steps on Portsdown Hill; not quite traversing the Khumbu Glacier on Everest.

Puffing, I clumped my way down, fearful of the bats and sticks falling off and disturbing the whole neighbourhood. Thankfully they behaved and stayed on top. On reaching the bottom step, everything below my knees slid into shadow.

"Nearly there," I told myself, bracing my shoulders for the final leg. Reaching the porch, my forearms felt like they were on fire. Bending my knees, I put the bags down and rested the racquet against the wall. My fingers had set into painful frozen claws. Flicking my hands, I felt the tingling of pins and needles as the blood flowed and my fingers came back to life, then nudging open the outer door I bent down, reassembling my load. *Blimey, these bags feel even heavier.* Stepping inside with one foot, I heaved the holdall on the same side as something smooth started misbehaving and began sliding down the canvas. I stopped, cocking my leg backwards, catching the bat's handle on my calf. Standing precariously, half in and half out, I wavered supporting the weight of two ridiculously heavy bags on one leg, the other hovering, bent backwards balancing a delinquent cricket bat.

The crunch of fatigued, breaking metal, combined with the yelp of a panicked cat in freefall made me look up. I shrieked as bits of corroded pipe and a writhing twisting set of claws hit me in the face, causing me to stumble backwards.

I imagine that Lucky had been crouched, unseen, waiting on the porch roof since I'd shut the car boot. He must have crept to the edge and sat on his haunches, resting his whole weight on the decrepit piece of half-pipe, watching. Of course, the cat had no idea that it had been rusting away for decades to the point that, unluckily for both of us, the thin layer of crumbling metal had become as brittle as a five-day-old pretzel.

Stumbling, I dropped the bags, catching my heel on the door frame as I went careering backwards, looking like I was trying to wind down the driver and passenger car windows at the same time. The night air was filled with the chaotic din of sticks, bats, and sections of guttering hitting the floor accompanied by the screams of a skydiving moggy. As I stumbled, one foot trod on something bony and squishy that screeched. Instinctively throwing my weight to one side to avoid squashing it, I stepped on the handle of a hockey stick, twisting my ankle, and fell, landing in the cold wet soil of the flowerbed at the side of the porch. Fortunately, the rose bush broke my fall.

Rolling away onto my knees, I delicately began peeling away the broken spiky branches. My throbbing arse felt like a perforated tea bag as I knelt puffing, looking for my assailant who'd almost been my victim. He'd made one hell of a racket.

The porch light began humming, flickering into life as the front door clunked open. Alice appeared, shaking her head, surveying the chaos.

"What *are* you doing? Are you trying to wake the whole damn street?"

"I fell over," I answered like a shamefaced small boy who'd taken a tumble on his new skateboard.

"You idiot. I thought the roof had come down." *Funny that.*

"No, no, I'm fine thanks," I huffed indignantly.

"And where did *that* come from?" she asked, pointing to the scraps of fallen guttering. With my index finger, I directed Alice's questioning gaze to a spot above just her head.

"The roof came down, or rather the gutter did when the cat fell off."

"*The cat!* Oh my God, is he alright?"

"I've no idea, I think he shot off somewhere. But yes, *I* really am fine apart from a punctured backside and a sore ankle." *Seriously?*

"Well get up, you'll catch your death on the floor, and you'd better not have damaged my rose bush," she remarked, oozing sympathy.

*It'll be damaged when I rip the bastard thing out of the ground and fucking batter you with it.*

"There's my boy," Alice chimed, "Lucky, are you alright, baby?"

I looked up the path, still on all fours, surrounded by my discarded cargo. Stepping daintily, Lucky picked his way around the fallen racquet, sticks, and bats. Stopping outside the porch next to me, he sat angelically looking up at Alice, purring.

"What are you waiting for, come in silly, it's cold out there."

Looking me in the eye he stepped inside, slapping me in the face with a flick of his tail. As the front door clicked shut, I heard a couple of strange cat noises that sounded smugly triumphant and nothing like meow meow.

After brushing off my knees, I'd made *two* short painful trips, limping up the stairs before unceremoniously dumping the boys' gear in the back bedroom. Alice could sort through it; if I'd had my way, I'd have dragged the bloody lot into the garden, doused it in petrol, and taken a match to it.

I trudged to the bathroom to freshen up. Looking in the mirror I felt unsettled by the dark bags, wrinkles, and lines on the face of the haggard old man staring back at me. *Wow, I think I've aged twenty years in three days.* I'd seen fewer creases on a bull elephant's scrotum. I thumped down the stairs and joined Alice in the lounge.

"Some idiot went into the back of me on the drive home," I reported, collapsing onto the sofa, instantly regretting not gently lowering my thorn-ravaged derriere.

"Is the car alright?"

"It's not great. The bumper's cracked and the boot's got a nasty dent, but you can still shut and lock it."

"Did you get the driver's details?"

"No, it was some boy racer, and he shot off before I got out of the car. It might be easier to just pay rather than go through the hassle of insurance and losing my no claims."

"That's annoying," Alice conceded, "you really are on a roll at the moment, aren't you?" *That's the understatement of the year.* "Do you think you can be trusted with a kettle?"

"Yes," I answered, feeling a bit insulted.

"Well go and make us some tea then and try not to electrocute yourself or burn the house down."

"Ha ha." I replied, easing myself up and trudging to the kitchen.

We sat, drank tea, and watched TV together. I say we; Alice watched the telly, I sat next to her, repeatedly bouncing my head off my chest while fighting to keep my eyes open, despite my recent mammoth nap. Just before ten, as my head rolled around for the umpteenth time Alice had clearly had enough.

"For God's sake Henry go to bed," she growled, with all the love and sympathy of a U.S. Marine Corps drill sergeant.

"*Ah'mawake, Ah'mawake!*" I mumbled loudly, forcing my eyes wide.

"Barely," Alice countered, "just give in my love."

"Okayyy," I conceded dreamily as I leant across and kissed her. I groaned to my feet, plodded out of the lounge, and shambled my way up the stairs, rubbing my sore bum. Feeling the crinkle of the envelope I thrust my hand into my back pocket. *Perfect, this should make for some pleasant bedtime reading.*

# TUESDAY

## CHAPTER 31

### Missing

Rolling onto my back, I peeled open my eyes, clenching my teeth as I tried sitting up. *Ouch, I hope the rose bush didn't make it.* I'd winced even more last night when I'd read that letter. For one, I'd cocked up and forgotten that because Jack had turned thirteen and gone up a year when he'd gone back in September, his fees came into the same top bracket as his older brother. I'd underpaid by £2,075, *two grand!* However, that was the least painful bit of news.

The more disturbing content regarded vandalism to one of the school chapel's priceless 17th-century stained-glass windows caused by some new Year 3 boarders. Reading the letter, I assumed there had been a mistake as Jack was in Year 9, so this clearly had nothing to do with him, but reading on, I began getting a sick, sinking feeling in the pit of my stomach. Apparently, when the stone-throwing culprits had been apprehended by the School Chaplain, they'd explained that their actions were the result of something one of the older boys had told them. According to Father Emmanuel, from the description he'd been given, it sounded like the older boy in question was his head chorister, Jack.

He might have had the voice and face of an angel but whenever I pictured my younger son walking to church for choir practice, I couldn't help imagining Jack's ringtone playing and the font starting to bubble as he got nearer. Thanks to his antics, I'd gone to bed with even more to worry about, not least the phone call I'd been asked to make.

Oddly, I'd woken before my alarm and reached across to check the time on my phone. Running my fingers over my nightstand's smooth wooden top I felt nothing. *Weird.* I turned slowly, looking directly at the spot where I'd left my mobile. Only a small white bedside lamp, the letter, and a silver framed photo of Alice and the boys sat on my bedside table. *Where on earth has that gone?*

"Have you seen my phone?" I shouted down the stairs, heading for the lounge.

"Are you *man looking* again?" Alice sneered from the kitchen.

"No, seriously, it's disappeared. I'm positive it was on my bedside table."

"Well, *I* haven't seen it. You know it'll turn up in the last place you look." *No shit!* I started lifting up the sofa cushions.

"Have you found it yet?" Alice shouted.

"Nope. Can you try calling me?" I cocked my head and listened.

As a faint muffled ringtone drifted down, I ran, scampering up the stairs.

"*Thanks, I think it's in our bedroom,*" I boomed, hurrying towards the music. I stormed into the bedroom to the sound of the ominous 'Imperial March' from The Empire Strikes Back. *If Alice twigs that I've given her Darth Vader's theme tune, I'll end up knowing the power of the Dark Side.*

"*Can you hear that?*" I shouted, fearful of Mrs. Vader's answer.

"Hear what?" *Phew.*

"Nothinggg!" I sang back.

The muffled blare of trumpets and trombones drifted from under the bed and crouching low I peered through the small gap between the floor and the base of the bedframe. Pinpointing the throb of light, I started wriggling up to my shoulder, groping, when my fingers hit something solid. *Got it.* I couldn't go any further but managed to hook my nail on the ridge of the case. Curling my finger, the phone started slowly nudging towards me, inch by inch. Teasing it under my palm, I gripped the sides between my thumb and little finger when the music cut out. *Gotcha.* Slowly withdrawing my hand, the phone stopped, like it was snagged on something. *Weird! What on earth?* The phone hadn't just stopped, I could feel the hard case slipping. It felt like it was being pulled in the opposite…

*"Aaargh!"*

Wedged under the bed I could feel the burning scratches as my hand was repeatedly slashed.

*"Ow, ow, ow. Stop you little fucker!"*

Frantically clawing at the carpet with my free hand, I dragged myself across the floor, wrenching my savaged hand out.

"For heaven's sake, what are you shouting about?" Alice bawled, climbing the stairs.

"He got me again," I said resting on my elbow, rubbing the back of my hand, "your precious little shithead."

"*He is not a little shithead*," she countered, stepping into the room, "he's like most cats, just a bit misunderstood." My jaw dropped. She had to be joking.

"*Misunderstood?*" I asked, looking up at her incredulously. Oh, I *understood* this cat alright, but prayed he'd just been playing with my phone and knocked it under the bed and hadn't actually set a trap.

"Yes, they're all lovely at heart, really. *Aren't you Lucky? Where are you boy?*" she clucked. "For such a clever man you really are quite ignorant when it comes to cats." If my phone hadn't been under the bed, I'd have thrown it at her.

"Go on then Mrs. Attenborough, dazzle me," I scoffed, inspecting my wounds.

"It doesn't matter, big cats, domestic cats, they're all the same, just furry, loving animals, but a bit misunderstood. *Poor Lucky? You're misunderstood aren't you baby?*"

"Are you flippin' mental? *Misunderstood!* There I was thinking that they were natural predators and born killers, hunting, and killing things by instinct and sometimes just for *fun*. Silly me," I tutted, with no attempt at hiding my sarcasm or contempt for her ridiculous claim. "Like that bloody great *misunderstood* tiger that attacked Siegfried and Roy on stage during their live magic show in Vegas. *Remember that?* I'm sure when Roy had his head stuck in that tiger's mouth, he would have found a great deal of comfort if Siegfried had said *calm down dear, it's not his fault, he's just misunderstood.*"

"Don't be dramatic, Henry."

"*Dramatic*, have you seen my bloody hand?" I whined.

"And mind your language potty mouth." Really? Bloody? What was her problem? She swore like a sailor and made Joan Rivers sound like a cloistered nun.

"No, my *bloody* hand. Look!" I meant it literally. "*Look*," I roared, thrusting my hand at her to reveal the crisscross of thickening red lines oozing blood.

"It's just a scratch," she snorted dismissively. Without warning, my blood boiled over, as a swell of raging lava erupted from deep inside me.

"*Shut up, for once just shut the fuck up!* It's *my* hand and it doesn't feel like just a scratch, it bloody well hurts. I've had enough of you defending that fucking cat all the time. He's a nasty little shit and yet you always take his side, every... single... bastard time... *I'm* your husband *and I've* had a gutful." Alice's bottom lip trembled. I'm not sure who was more shocked, Alice for being shouted at or me for telling her to shut up. I had never spoken to her like that, ever, I liked breathing too much.

"Sorry, I just thought you might have startled him," she replied meekly.

Gypsy appeared in the doorway, no doubt keen to see why the noisy people had rudely disturbed her slumber, hopeful that it might involve food. I heard Lucky behind me and turned my head to watch as he appeared from the end of the bed, stretching into a bristling, hissing arch. My brave protector took one look and turned around, fleeing back to her bed.

"Perfect, glad to know I can count on your support too," I seethed as Gypsy ran downstairs whimpering.

Lucky followed suit, running, jumping, and - "Ow"- using my buttocks as a springboard before bouncing off my head, shooting out of the bedroom, and disappearing.

"See, I think he's frightened, maybe you *did* startle him," Alice suggested passively.

"*I* startled *him*! He was under the bloody bed. How the hell could I have startled *him*. But don't worry, I will. Just as soon as I catch him and drag the little bastard into my shed," I raged.

"Please don't. I know you think he doesn't like you, but I still think he's lovely." The comment was punctuated by the sound of the lovely cat 'meowing' loudly to announce his departure, followed by the clacking of the cat flap as he left the house. I knew I couldn't win, and I couldn't bear to stay trapped inside those suffocating walls a minute longer. *I've got to get out of here.*

After a stinging application of TCP, a strong coffee, and a change of clothes, I banged out of the door, dragging the fat plodder behind me. Walking past the remains of the arse-wrecking bush of thorns, I felt the pressure inside my head melting away; it started the moment I set foot out of the house.

"Every time, Gypsy. She sides with that bloody cat every single time," I complained, mounting the cold concrete steps. "I sometimes wonder if a third child would have been easier, certainly a lot less painful… and you're no bloody help. Cats and dogs, you're supposed to be mortal enemies and *you're* meant to chase the cat, not run away you bloody coward." Gypsy looked at me uncertainly, deciding it would be less confusing to go back to sniffing the pavement.

"And where am I going to find £2,000 at the drop of a hat?" I asked the bemused dog. "Not to mention what the school might try and sting me for if they think Jack's behind that vandalism." Raising her head, Gypsy stared at me blankly, "… and don't give me that *talk to your wife* look, I can't tell her. Jack'll get away with a tongue-lashing, but she'll probably kill me. Mind you she can only do it once and the way I feel right now she'd be doing me a favour." Conceding that Gypsy obviously wasn't in a listening mood I shut up, deciding to try and clear my thoughts by simply enjoying the walk.

## CHAPTER 32

### Beautiful Day

What gorgeous weather, blue skies, a slight nip in the air, but hardly a breath of wind. It certainly outshone my dark mood. *This is perfect for golf.* I decided to call Dougal and tried three times, but the phone just kept ringing. *Oh well, I expect he got an early tee time. I reckon he'll already be on the second or third hole, or maybe he's still in bed recovering from a crib night and sleeping off one too many bottles of Monty Python's Holy Ail.*

Bathing in brilliant sunshine, I filled my lungs with the fresh, clean, cool air and within minutes we found ourselves bounding through a familiar open green space. Gypsy ran ahead then stopped and started circling, her tail wagging happily, barking enthusiastically. With my curiosity aroused, I hurried to see what had excited her. Nearing the flattened patch of grass, she began howling. I closed my eyes, shaking my head in disgust, recognising the haunting scene and the cause of my revolting dog's elation.

"You're quite horrible, you know that?" I reproached. "And you're unbelievably crap at chasing the cat, I'm ignoring you." Gypsy continued eagerly jumping off the ground. Avoiding eye contact, I hurried past yesterday's impromptu picnic site and carried on walking up the hill.

Despite being on the cusp of winter, I could feel the Sun's heat creeping through my clothes and the warmth crawling across the back of my neck and head. Deciding to sit for a while, I waited for Gypsy to grasp the fact that she wouldn't be getting a second helping from this two-legged mobile soup dispenser.

A simple wooden bench sat halfway up the sloping grass and according to its weather-worn, engraved brass plaque, it had been 'Sally's Favourite Place.' Looking out across the Solent on such a gorgeous day, I could see why. Sliding into a slouch, I yawned, watching a colourful flotilla of yachts with billowing spinnakers racing, cutting, and thrusting through the glinting blue-grey water. Gypsy appeared at my feet, then being ignored, walked away, and began burying her head and shoulders in a small bush. Sitting back, I spread my arms along the top of the bench, closing my eyes.

A bitter wind would usually howl up from the southwest and blow hard over this part of Portsdown Hill, but today only a light breeze breathed on the gently pulsing treetops. Savouring the Sun's warm rays I sighed, my cheeks and forehead relaxing as my body slumped. I allowed my eyes to sink and settle. A thousand thoughts had been whirling in my mind recently but now, away from the pressures of work and home, I felt a little lighter as if some of that burden was being lifted. With the added stresses of parenthood and life in general, I rarely had the chance to feel relaxed.

Melting into the bench, I noticed the sweet, pure song of a nearby Robin as a deep wave of inner calm began washing over me. A soft, soothing blanket began wrapping itself around my head, as my mind started drifting to another time and place where I had felt this way, tranquil, still, serene...

# CHAPTER 33

## Enola Gay

Beyond the glossy black railings of Royal Air Force College Cranwell, on a miserable grey, drizzle-soaked Thursday, I proudly marched off the parade square and up the steps of College Hall, immersed in the musty scent of mothballs from my sodden, steaming, Air Force blue, No. 1 uniform. Moments later, a flock of officers' hats rose in the air, carried upwards by the cheers of the graduates below. I'd done it, I'd completed eighteen weeks of Initial Officer Training. Pilot Officer Henry Richard Alder. I was somebody.

Four months later, my inflated opinion had swollen even more as I stood grinning, posing with my award during my graduation ceremony from the Central Air Traffic Control School, RAF Shawbury in Shropshire. I had won the Bunting Trophy, having attained the highest practical scores on my controllers' course. Before the camera's flash had faded, I'd been told to hand the trophy back, ready to be held by the next course's winner, who'd also get to keep it for a whole fifteen seconds. Having passed my professional training, I was no longer just a nineteen-year-old pilot officer, I was a Royal Air Force air traffic controller. I thought I was the dog's knob. I was half right.

My bubble burst on arrival at my first unit, RAF Valley, a fast jet training base across the Menai Strait on the North Wales island of Anglesey, famed for its Easy Care sheep, welcoming locals, and 70 MPH fog. I wish I'd recorded my arrival interview with my first boss, Squadron Leader Derek De Vos, a brusque, red-cheeked, and impressively moustached misogynistic dinosaur. I could have used it years later for lessons on 'How to Make Your Staff Feel Valued.'

"Well, we're up to our eyes in it, Alder, no time for slackers. We've got a shed load of Hawks and it's a full-on flying programme every day." By every day he meant Monday to Friday, I'd joined the RAF; we didn't tend to do weekends.

"If you can't hack it, you'll be chopped and sent to some sleepy hollow, like Manston. Ever been to Kent?"

"No, sir."

"Well, don't bother, it's full of strawberry farmers and loose women."

"Okay, sir." *Note, must visit Kent. I bloody love strawberries.*

"Sir, do you know when I'm likely to start training?" I asked, eager to display my enthusiasm and desire to get going.

"Hmmm, I suppose you can't have been completely crap if they sent you to Valley." I didn't realise it at the time, but that would be the nearest I'd ever get to a compliment in my three-year tour of duty.

"We've got a huge training backlog. I don't know why they sent you really, the last thing I need is to be a damn wet nurse to a baby pilot officer. Anyway, I can't see you starting training for about six months, four at a push." This was not the news I'd hoped for.

"In the meantime, why don't you try and get yourself on some adventurous training courses. There's all sorts of stuff, mountain climbing, hang gliding, skiing."

"I'd like to try skiing, sir." I immediately pictured myself in Cortina d'Ampezzo, wearing a once-piece belted yellow Campri ski suit, gliding, like Roger Moore, down the sun-kissed slopes of the Dolomites and spending the evenings on a fur rug by a roaring fire with a raven-haired Italian beauty wearing nothing but a beckoning smile.

"Well, they run courses up in Aviemore?"

Aviemore, *Aviemore*, what a beautiful name.

"That sounds lovely, sir. Where is Aviemore? France? Switzerland?"

"Scotland, in the Cairngorms, bloody miserable place, you'll freeze your balls off."

Wow, he was really selling it.

"And you really don't mind, sir?"

"Mind! Why would I mind? I don't want you hanging around here doing nothing. You're about as much use to me as…"

He then proceeded to explain just how useless I was. In the three years that followed, despite becoming a fully validated controller, Squadron Leader De Vos would introduce me to several colourful idioms to explain my uselessness. My favourites included a bra on a snake, an inflatable dartboard, and nipples on a breastplate.

However, less than one year later, I'd not only started training, but I'd also gained three controlling endorsements. Squadron Leader De Vos rewarded me with an enticing 'character development' opportunity to broaden my service knowledge by nominating me for an exchange with the Royal Navy. I was lucky enough to be selected from a volunteer list of one, for a six-month tour of duty with the senior service on board one of Her Majesty's aircraft carriers.

Joining the ship in Portsmouth at the beginning of March, I walked up the gangway to board HMS Ark Royal with a sense of foreboding. *An RAF officer at sea for six months with no long weekends? Outrageous!*

The detachment to the Royal Navy's flagship included a twelve-week tour of the Pacific, which had been some consolation, as life on board proved to be worse than I'd imagined. Even as a very junior officer, the Officers' Mess at RAF Valley provided me with my own room with enough space for a sink, two chests of drawers, and wardrobes. It even had things called windows through which I could see the 8th hole of the station's golf course while sprawled out on my huge double bed. Now I shared a long, narrow cubicle with five other men. I couldn't sit up in my tiny bedspace without hitting my head on the bunk above and I had to cram all my worldly possessions into a shoe box. Rolling to my right gave me a view of a dark grey wall, or three feet to my left my snoring neighbour's hairy back and arse crack. I really struggled with the cramped living conditions, the lack of personal space, and the constant, rigorous routine; not that I would have been able to play golf or go to the pub if I'd been given a day off anyway.

In a little over a year and a half, I'd been indoctrinated into life in the British military, well, the Royal Air Force at least. Naively, I thought I'd become hardened to base humour, but in the Wardroom and officers' cabins nothing could have prepared me for some of the language and the depths of depravity of my so-called 'shipmates.' These shining examples of morality, decorum, and respect should have either been in prison, on some sort of sexual deviants' register, or at the very least getting psychiatric help. They did unspeakable things to each other's toothbrushes if left unattended and my jaw literally dropped when a fellow officer gleefully began explaining the practice of teabagging. I prayed I was being made the subject of another 'wind up' created especially to unsettle the token RAF 'Crab' officer.

That night, sleeping nervously, I was awoken by a horrible coughing fit in the early hours. Fearing the worst, I took drastic measures and from that moment on always went to sleep wearing my issued full-face anti-flash hood.

As the days turned into weeks the Navy began grinding a routine into me, through assimilation to the matelot way of life. Surprisingly, I actually started enjoying myself, and made some friends, although not in the unsavoury, intimate way of the Royal Navy's reputation. Being part of the small ATC team providing 24-hour cover for Ark Royal's Sea Harriers and Sea King helicopters left me longing for my bunk most days, but the long hours and hard work finally paid off with the captain's promise of four days' shore leave when Ark Royal reached the coast of Japan.

Those allowed aboard the Liberty Boat to Yokosuka had mostly headed for the obvious diversions of the bars, clubs, and other establishments for adult entertainment in Tokyo. Tagging along with three other officers, we bucked the trend, deciding on something completely different. We planned to visit the site of the first use of a nuclear weapon in anger, Hiroshima. I felt that I *should* visit the city, after all, I would probably never get the chance again and, I don't know, it could have been some sense of wanting to show respect. Hoping that the other lads felt the same way, I secretly suspected that their intentions might be less cultural and humanitarian and somewhat more ghoulish.

We hired a compact Toyota for our road trip without realising that the journey involved a ten-hour drive. If we'd known we'd definitely have considered a slightly roomier and better-ventilated vehicle for four men who'd spent the last month living off the ship's tinned rations.

Arriving in the late evening, we found Hiroshima to be a bright, clean, modern, and vibrant city, humming with the sound of cars, buses, and trams. I hadn't really been sure what to expect but had been pleasantly surprised. Being tired after such a long drive, we quickly found a hotel for the night then grabbed a couple of welcome beers at a nearby bar before sloping off to bed.

Our party of four started the next day with an early breakfast and, after an uncomfortable chat with the receptionist, we discovered that we'd chosen a hotel situated just a five-minute walk from the Hiroshima Peace Memorial Museum. I feared it was going to be tricky trying to explain where we wanted to go, but Craig 'Soapy' Watson, a hairy old salt and the most forthright, but least tactful member of the group, saved the day by drawing a picture of a four-columned building to denote a museum. Then I nearly died of embarrassment when the insensitive Soapy started impersonating a B-29 Superfortress executing a high-level bombing run, followed by a toe-curlingly graphic and unmistakable mime of an atomic bomb exploding and people running away screaming.

Initially wandering around as a group, we were eventually drawn by different distractions, agreeing to go our separate ways. My mind hoovered up the information while drifting through the exhibits on a rollercoaster ride from shock to anger to revulsion. The thing that stuck in my mind the most were the artefacts on display, revealing the effects of when Little Boy detonated on the 6th of August 1945, killing 80,000 people. Display cases held tattered clothes, charred sandals, stopped watches, and coins that had fused together and been melted into barely recognisable lumps by the extreme heat.

The gentle movement of a flock of hanging paper cranes drew me to the story of Sadako Sasaki. The two-year-old girl had been at home when the explosion occurred, about one mile from ground zero. She'd been blown out of the window and her mother, who had fled the house suspecting her to be dead, found her daughter alive with no apparent injuries. However, while they were fleeing, Sadako and her mother were caught in the 'black rain.' Ten years later she developed lumps on her neck and behind her ears and became hospitalised after being diagnosed with leukaemia and given only one year to live. Despite her rapidly weakening condition, Sadako set herself the goal of using her remaining time by folding 1,000 paper cranes. Before she died, she had folded almost 1,300. The small origami figures became adopted by the people of Hiroshima as a symbol of peace and determination. But it was the contents of a large glass case that upset me the most.

At the heart of the clear box sat a tiny, scorched child's tricycle. Everything organic had been incinerated in the fireball leaving behind a pitiful burnt and blistered brown metal frame with charred, disfigured wheels.

Shinichi Tetsutani had been only three years and eleven months old and riding his tricycle in front of his house in Motomachi when the unstoppable ball of fire engulfed him. He died that night. His father, who had been inside the family home, survived, and not wanting to separate his son from his favourite toy, had buried Shin with his trike in the backyard. Forty years later, the father dug up his son's tiny corpse and transferred it to the family grave, donating the remains of the tricycle to the Peace Memorial Museum. Standing there, reading the notes, I breathed heavily, swiping away the stream of tears running down my face.

Drifting listlessly around the museum, my thoughts and emotions became completely overwhelmed. I needed some air. Walking outside, I followed the signs to the Peace Memorial Park. Stepping through a leafy archway, I found myself in a small courtyard, surrounded by an outer wall of perfectly trimmed green bushes and russet shrubs containing a ring of ornamental cherry trees bursting with pink blossom. They stood sentinel to a pair of ornate carved wooden benches at their centre.

Detecting a hint of Jasmine I sniffed deeply, inhaling the flower's sweet heavenly scent. After feeling so wrung out, I simply sat there, alone, with the Sun warming my face, and closed my eyes, listening, cocooned in the trill of birdsong. I had never felt so calm before and imagined this was what meditation felt like. I drifted off, drinking in the sunshine, my senses floating in a hypnotic cloud of perfume.

Opening my eyes, I gazed at the vibrant cherry blossom, giving my arms and back a long and leisurely stretch before checking my watch. I'd only dozed off for about fifteen minutes, but it felt more like an hour, and deciding to return to the museum, I set off to find the others.

I spotted them huddling around a lectern at the end of a long walkway, the sides of which were covered in giant, colourful, lurid murals depicting the pain, suffering, and anguish from the catastrophic effects of the atomic bomb. As I approached, they looked up sheepishly, acting a little startled. Recognising me they visibly relaxed, acknowledging my presence with nods before returning to whatever it was that was holding their interest. Seeing that they were writing comments in a visitors' book, I felt that after such a poignant day I had to express my own heartfelt thoughts. A glass cabinet stood nearby with translated excerpts of previous entries, written over the years by famous visitors from all over the world. Richard Nixon, Jean-Paul Sartre, and Pope John Paul II had all left a personal mark. The head of the Catholic Church had written, 'God's hope is one of peace, not one of pain.'

Feeling my heart swell as I read the tenderness and depth of feeling of some of the other comments, I began soul searching, desperately struggling to find something meaningful and fitting to write. Shuffling off towards the cafeteria, the others said they were going to 'grab a wet', leaving me alone with my thoughts. I might have been mistaken, but as they sidled off, huddled conspiratorially, they appeared to be enjoying a shared joke.

Standing before the open pages, I took up the pen, sighing heavily, still trying to evoke some sage and profound prose. It was then that I spotted the last entry, a comment that one of my party had written. I couldn't believe my eyes.

I had been completely overawed by my visit to Hiroshima, upset by the horrors and the tragedy that were catalogued from the fateful day that had brought a nation to its knees, and I could not comprehend the note before me. Blinking slowly, I hoped that the text would be erased but stubbornly the writing remained in plain sight. I stood aghast, shaking my head in disbelief, staring at the inappropriate words, written by my matelot colleague from Her Majesty's Royal Navy written in the Hiroshima Peace Memorial Museum visitors' book.

*'Lieutenant Craig "Soapy" Watson R.N. Air Warfare Officer, HMS Ark Royal.*

*THIS PLACE LOOKS LIKE A BOMB'S HIT IT!'*

A cold wet nose started prodding my hand and, yawning, I opened my eyes to find Gypsy wanting to play. My moment of blissful escape dissolved as I stretched, getting up from the bench in search of a stick. Gypsy had a habit of eagerly chasing after whatever was thrown, picking it up, then immediately dropping it and running back empty-mouthed. After a fruitless ten-minute game of non-return fetch, I turned for home with the puffing stick dropper in tow. I kept thinking back to that trip to Hiroshima. It seemed like a lifetime ago.

Funny that I should think about that now. One devastating impact and all those people had been snuffed out in a huge ball of fire. More than sixty years later, I'd come close to creating a similar moment, admittedly on a much smaller scale, but the result would have been the same. Bodies engulfed in flames, screaming, panic, sheer terror, and the heartbreaking aftermath of relatives trying to identify the charred remains of loved ones, and all my fault. Nobody else, just me.

## CHAPTER 34

### Poison

"We're baaack," I shouted into the porch, opening the door.

"I'm in the kitchen. Do you want a cup of tea?" Alice chimed.

"Please," I replied, as my boots sucked then released my feet. Stepping into the hallway I welcomed the embrace of the house's inner warmth. Gypsy came trotting in behind me, heading straight for her dog bowl. When she was ignored by Alice, she sulked off towards the lounge.

"How's your hand?" Alice asked solemnly.

"A bit sore. Sorry, I snapped, I don't know what came over me," I said contritely.

"It's okay. Just go and put your feet up darling," Alice suggested. I about turned. "I'll bring your tea through in a minute."

"Thank you," I shouted, stepping into the front room.

"Then maybe you could cut the grass," Alice added.

"Yeah, later," I grumbled, my hackles flaring. Gypsy lifted her head off the fireplace, her gaze following me as I sat down. For some reason, her good eye appeared to be giving me a look of contempt. I turned on the television and began scrolling through the irritatingly endless channels of the TV guide, struggling to find something to watch that wasn't soul-crushingly dull when Alice appeared.

"There you go, my love," she said, placing a steaming, white cup down on the coffee table.

"Thank you. I am really sorry about earlier. I'm a bit tightly wound at the moment."

"I noticed, I know you must be stressed," she replied sympathetically, producing a box of dark chocolate-coated ginger biscuits and placing it next to my cup.

"Ooh, lovely. I thought I'd eaten the last ones." I felt sure I had because I'd checked the biscuit barrel and scoured the cupboards last night when I'd been making tea.

"You did but I popped out and got these for you while you were walking the dog. At least there's one bitter ginger thing that you quite like," she smiled apologetically. I felt my mood's tightly coiled wire relax.

"You know what, you can be an insensitive moo at times, but it's little gestures like this that remind me why I love you. That and your amazing knockers."

Alice tutted, shaking her head. Turning to walk out, she stopped.

"What *do* you think will happen at work?" The question made the wire tighten back up a notch. *How the hell should I know? I'm not a bloody fortune teller.*

"Honestly, my love, I haven't got a clue. Who knows what my sneaky boss is planning?" I rolled my head back, testily hunching my shoulders and stretching my neck.

"But we'll be okay, won't we? The boys are settled in school, and we'd be in real trouble if you lost your job. And I really like it here."

Losing my job hadn't even entered my mind but Alice's question suddenly triggered a worrying thought. When I joined the RAF, it had numbered about 90,000 personnel. Over the years, through several Strategic Defence Reviews that number had dwindled to almost half and I'd discounted the imminent tranche of voluntary redundancies. Disturbingly, I knew that if the MoD didn't get sufficient personnel to take the severance package voluntarily, then some people were going to get a nasty surprise. I'd just realised that my cock-up could make me a nasty surprise candidate.

"I *said,* I don't know," I answered sharply. *I don't need you telling me the bleeding obvious. Of course, we wouldn't be able to afford for the boys to continue boarding. What a stupid thing to say and we'd not only have the stress of all being back together again, living under the same roof, we'd have to find them places in a state school, and have to find somewhere to rent and the money to pay for it.*

"Sorry, but do you think we'll be alright?" *Go on, tell her, tell her why you're worried.*

"*I said I don't know!*" I shouted in exasperation. *Coward.* Alice recoiled. *Well done, way to go, shouting at the one person who genuinely cares.*

"Look, I'm sorry," I sighed, instantly softening after seeing her blanch, "honestly, I just don't know." Alice mutely walked out, reappearing briefly with an armful of laundry.

"Right, I'm just going to make a start on the ironing. Maybe you could watch last week's episode of Top Gear that you thought you'd missed but *I* recorded just for *you*," she suggested, making me feel even more crap, "… and enjoy your biscuits," she added, piling the guilt on as she left.

Hitting the remote's green button, I tried ignoring the wave of self-reproach. The planner revealed a recorded and unwatched, episode of my favourite show. Pressing play I leaned forward, putting the remote down and gently pulling apart the packet's cellophane wrapping before silently sliding the tray of biscuits out. Gypsy moved, rolling her shoulders as she groaned, her nose twitching. Her eyes remained firmly closed and she settled back again as my fingers hovered, deliberating over which of the identical biscuits to take when… the doorbell rang.

*For Christ's sake, what know?*

"Sorry, can *you* get it?" Alice shouted from the other room.

"Okayyy," I grumbled, getting up and stomping towards the front door. I turned, glancing at the tray of biscuits, then at Gypsy, who gave a loud snore. Ignoring the voice in my head that said '*hey, whatever you do, don't leave those there,*' I left them there, stepping into the hallway.

Two overly enthusiastic-looking figures, each well-groomed and wearing a crisp, long-sleeved white shirt and hideous matching beige and navy chequered tank tops, were standing on the doorstep both bearing a pamphlet. *Perfect, this is all I need.* They waited, sporting grins so irritating I had to resist slapping them off their faces as soon as I opened the door.

*No, I had never considered secular society to be morally corrupt, and neither did I think it was controlled by Satan. No, I did not think that the establishment of a kingdom of God on earth would save mankind and I absolutely did not believe that Armageddon was imminent.*

Despite being raised Catholic, I'd fallen from the religious wagon in my late teens, giving Eileen another reason to hate me. I really didn't have the patience to get embroiled in a protracted, religious debate with unyielding door-to-door evangelists, not today.

"No, thank you... Sorry, yes, I'm sure my soul *has* been corrupted... Yes... uh huh... probably but I'm a little bit busy."

As hard as I tried to be, what I considered abrupt, it wasn't working. These unwavering Jehovah's Witnesses evidently had skins thicker than a rhino's calloused hide. I'd had no problem venting at Alice just now, but for some reason, I couldn't bring myself to be curt enough for these two grinning zealots to take the hint and leave. My wife however could be formidable in these situations and came to my rescue over my shoulder.

"Excuse me, I don't mean to be rude but right now I need my husband to take me upstairs, throw me on the bed and do wicked, ungodly things to me until I call the Lord's name. Good luck with the Apocalypse. *Bye-bye*," she chirped, waving, before slamming the porch door in their shocked faces, and pulling me inside.

"Ummm. You're a very bad girl, Alice Alder. Your soul is going to burn in hell for all eternity for that. I know because those smiley men in the horrible tank tops just said so." Alice tutted while looking through me with her deadest eyes.

"I would have got rid of them in the end you know," I protested feebly, feeling slightly emasculated.

"Not before Judgement Day, my love," she replied, breaking into the thinnest knowing smile.

"Well, they still would have gone, *eventually*," I contested lamely.

"Yes dear, I'm sure they would, *eventually*. Although I imagine they'd have faced quite a dilemma having to choose between spending all day trying to convert you and dying from malnutrition," said Alice, without any attempt at hiding her condescension.

"Hilarious," I groaned. "Just out of interest, did you say that thing about me taking you upstairs just so that they'd bugger off or…?" *Well, it's a long shot, but there's no harm in asking.*

"*Really?*" Alice sighed, shaking her head, "I mean it's hard to say no, it's such a turn-on when you're a grumpy bastard. Besides, I've got housework to do, beds to be made, clothes that need ironing and bathrooms to be cleaned. I can't just drop everything for a quickie."

"Who said anything about dropping *everything*?" I winked.

"Seriously?" Alice exhaled, looking at me sideways.

"Thanks for getting rid of them though."

"Well, I just couldn't bear listening to you rabbiting on."

"Aw, you cow."

"*Oh, come on then Casanova,*" she conceded, taking me by the hand, "I've just plugged the iron in, it should be nearly up to temperature by the time *you've* finished." She just couldn't help herself.

Nearing the bottom of the stairs, I heard Gypsy panting excitedly, accompanied by the unusual sound of her galloping paws, thudding on the carpet as she went whizzing around the front room. Then I saw the mess scattered across the floor.

The dog continued doing thundering laps of the furniture at such high speed she could have performed the Wall-of-Death trick without the aid of a motorcycle. Alice frantically phoned the vets.

"They're asking how much she's eaten," she said, her eyes wide with panic. I could feel my pulse quickening, chocolate wouldn't just make Gypsy poorly, it could be fatal.

"Hang on," I said, scrabbling through the debris on the floor.

Frenziedly sifting through the mess of chewed cardboard and plastic, I searched anxiously, desperately trying to find the ingredients' label. Gypsy continued her high-speed lapping of the lounge stopping occasionally to jump at my face and bark then reverse her circuit. I found half of a chewed white sticker stuck to the carpet, covered in a mixture of dog slobber and brown ooze.

"She's eaten all eight biscuits, that's 175 grammes, and it's fifty percent, no hang on…" I could barely read the small print on the mashed paper coated in chocolatey opaque dog saliva "…no, seventy percent cocoa, dark chocolate."

Alice relayed the information, nodding, her glistening eyes wide with fear, listening intently to the vet's instructions.

"Okay… yes… right away, thank you." Tears began rolling down Alice's cheeks as she looked up from the phone.

"The vet said she's eaten enough to kill her. We have to get her to the clinic, *now!*"

Driving at breakneck speed into Portsmouth, I ran two red lights en route to the North End Animal Hospital, normally fifteen minutes away. It had felt like forever. Five minutes into the journey, the writhing Gypsy, who Alice had been struggling to restrain in the front seat, had suddenly gone from wriggling piglet to rigidly stiff as her muscles locked and spasmed. Then she started fitting, letting out a fading yelp, her eyes becoming fixed and lifeless, as her flaccid jowls bubbled with a thick white, foaming froth.

"You stupid, greedy little bitch," I raged. *If she dies, it's my fault. Idiot.* How could I have been so stupid to leave the biscuits out? I knew I had to make sure I put my socks *in* the laundry basket because she couldn't be trusted to not try and eat them, never mind chocolate bloody biscuits. I'd left a whole packet within easy reach of a greedy dog whose nose could sniff out a single Malteser in Wembley Stadium. *If those grinning idiots in the tank tops hadn't come to the door my dog would be home right now, asleep. Fucking Jehovah's Witnesses!*

A screech of tyres announced our arrival. Abandoning the car near the entrance, I left the engine running, grabbed the rigid trembling beagle from Alice, and ran into reception.

"We called in, um, chocolate poisoning, Alder, errr Gypsy," I explained, panting wildly.

I had given CPR to an old man in Fareham after he'd suffered a heart attack, I'd been first on the scene at a horrific M5 seven-car pile-up on the way home from an exercise in Cornwall, and in Kosovo, I had seen a colleague's leg reduced to, what I could best describe as, kit form after stepping on a land mine. In those incidents, my military training had instinctively kicked in and I'd remained relatively calm and focused. Right now, I couldn't stop shaking. I loved this little dog like a daughter, and I had been the stupid fucking idiot who'd left out, what was essentially dog poison. *What is wrong with me?*

The receptionist directed us to the waiting area where a vet stood half smiling, calmly waving us through. Immediately, a young woman in pale green scrubs appeared, and took the drooling spasmodic dog from my quaking arms, hurrying off with the vet through the same door she'd just come through. An eternity after the nurse had taken Gypsy away, the vet came back out.

"Okay, we've got her. There's really nothing more you can do. I suggest you go home," he instructed plainly.

"Can't we stay?" I begged.

"Really, it's best that you go."

"*I want to stay. She's my bloody dog!*" I thundered.

"*Henry!*" Alice chastised. "Calm down."

"*And don't tell me to calm down!*" I seethed.

The vet, Alice, and I stood awkwardly, immersed in uncomfortable silence.

"Sorry," I muttered, "it's just..."

"It's okay Mr. Alder, I do understand," the vet said calmly, placing a comforting hand on my forearm. I gulped down a sob. "Honestly, she's in good hands. My team and I will do all we can. It's really a matter of time and a waiting game now. We'll do our best to save her."

## CHAPTER 35

### So Emotional

I found out later that Alice took the call from the duty vet around seven o'clock. He reported that Gypsy was still a little groggy, but she would be okay. I had no idea; I'd been feeling all at sea after leaving my dog's fate in a stranger's hands. Alice and I had struggled to eat lunch and spent the afternoon drifting between rooms, turning the TV on and off, neither of us could remember what we'd been watching, leaving cups of half-drunk tea to go cold. With each passing hour, I started feeling increasingly suffocated, the weight of worry and guilt piling up. By late afternoon I couldn't bear to stay indoors a minute longer and went out for a drive to get some fresh air, leaving Alice to man the home phone.

I drove to Porchester Castle, where I sometimes walked Gypsy, spending an hour sitting on the pebbled beach, gazing out to sea, watching the sunset as the tide lapped at my feet. I kept replaying the moment I'd got up to answer the door but this time imagined picking up the biscuits before the horrible vision of Gypsy fitting and frothing reappeared. *Oh God!* I'd started making blunders with horrendous consequences. I prided myself on being competent in nearly all aspects of my life and I struggled to understand why other people made such huge cockups when the inevitable outcome of their actions always seemed so blatantly obvious to me. I was Henry Alder, the go-to person, the problem-solving guy who rarely made mistakes, but lately… Maybe, at forty-four, I should be thinking about hanging up my headset for good. At the very least it would remove the risk of me killing anyone. *How can I expect the RAF to trust me again when I don't even trust myself?* Worst of all, I wanted to unload my worries and unburden my soul by sharing my thoughts and feelings with my furry little confidante. Instead, I kept imagining my vulnerable little dog hooked up to tubes and monitors, scared, alone, and fighting for her life or, worse still, lying dead on a cold metal table, limp, and lifeless, and all because of me. *Fuuuck!* Looking along the shoreline I pictured Gypsy running by the water's edge, happily jumping and barking at the waves breaking at her feet. My heavy head drooped as my breath came in short, ragged gasps. Looking down I watched my tears falling, colouring the pebbles with dark splashes of unbearable shame.

Strangely, I got back in the car and automatically drove to the local convenience store, for no apparent reason, picking up bread and milk that we didn't really need and a newspaper. Reaching the front of the queue, I was handing my basket and a fiver to the cashier when my pocket started buzzing. Frantic for any news I immediately pulled my phone out, seeing that I'd received an SMS from Alice. My heart began racing and my quivering finger became a blur. I took a deep breath, preparing to touch the screen.

The young female cashier handed me my shopping and tried offering me my change, repeatedly extending, and gesturing with her outstretched palm. Standing, transfixed by the text, my wrist began slowly collapsing and I let go of the bag. The heavy plastic bottle slammed into the floor, popping the lid, and the contents came bursting out, just like my tears, right in front of the open-mouthed checkout girl in the Farlington Tesco Express. My knees melted and, collapsing to the floor, I tried covering up my blubbering mouth with the Daily Telegraph.

My wracking sobs weren't caused by relief from knowing that my little canine friend had survived, unburdening me from my guilt. It wasn't the knowledge that an hour ago Alice had received a call saying that Gypsy was fine and could be collected. Neither was it the fact that Alice couldn't bear to wait for me to get back and had picked up our sickly pup by taxi and brought her home. No, it was the fact that in her excitement and haste to relay the good news to me, Alice had meant to type 'Gypsy's home.' She had been in so much of an eager hurry she had pressed send without checking her text. Instead of getting good news, as I stood at the front of the queue with a broadsheet, four pints of semi-skimmed, and a loaf of Hovis granary, I received a message saying, 'Gypsy's gone.'

Trembling, I picked myself up off the floor, lunged out of the shop, and with an icy claw crushing my heart, shakily tried calling home.

"Hello."

"Oh God, what happened?" I sobbed.

"What do you mean?"

"With Gypsy, why couldn't they save her?"

"… What are you talking about? She's here." My heart leapt but in the fog of emotions, I had to be certain I'd heard Alice correctly.

"What? She's there? How come she's there? You said she was dead."

"*Dead?* Don't be silly, she's right here, she's a bit poorly but I told you, she's home."

"She's home?"

"Yes."

"Gypsy's home?"

"Yes!"

"*Check your bloody phone,*" I snarled, hanging up.

Overwhelmed by the good news I dissolved into a snivelling mess of tears again and, after managing to compose myself, walked back into the shop and apologised as I collected my change, offering to help clear up the spilled milk.

## CHAPTER 36

### You're My Best Friend

You could have cut the tension with a flip flop and Alice kept apologising, saying that she'd make it up to me. All I wanted to do was grab Gypsy and squeeze her. Alice said that the dog had been very woozy and judging by the pained look in my wife's bloodshot eyes, I realised that we'd all had a pretty rough time. I couldn't stay angry with her. *Anyone can make a mistake. Can't they?*

"Are *you* okay my love?" I asked.

"I am now, but I never want to go through that again. It was horrible."

"Me either, I'm sorry I snapped at you on the phone. I was so upset."

"I'm sorry too, I should have checked but look," she said, pointing to our sleeping pup, "we're all still here and we're fine."

Looking at my sickly dog, overcome with remorse, my heartstrings twanged. "Sorry but I just need to hold her for a while," I whispered.

"Okay," Alice smiled.

"I think she'd be more comfortable on *our* bed," I said, bending down and tenderly lifting the poorly beagle from her basket. Weakly, she raised her head, looking at me with her droopy, sad, red-ringed good eye. Cradling my sickly little companion like a newborn, I gingerly carried her upstairs, gently placing her next to my pillow and laying down. Gypsy sniffed, wriggling her shiny black nose into my armpit, making a couple of contented grunts. With a huge sigh, she closed her eyes and went back to sleep. Laying completely still, I began stroking her velvet-soft ears, reminded by the shaved pink patch and bloody scab on her foreleg of how close we'd been to losing her. *More like how close I came to killing her.*

"I'm sorry, I am so sorry, girl," I muttered, gazing at her sleeping face. I'd just started drifting off too when I heard the voice of Carly Simon coming from downstairs. Answering the call, Alison started chatting and I could clearly hear her animated babbling and occasional laughter. She chatted for a few minutes before coming up the stairs, her face lit with a huge beaming smile.

"It's for you, it's Danny," she said, handing me my mobile.

I already knew, and my spirits had started lifting the moment I heard my phone playing 'You're So Vain.'

## CHAPTER 37

### Lean on Me

Being posted to a new RAF station every three years made it difficult to maintain any long-term friendships. However, I considered Danny Ansell to be my best mate. Annoyingly, Danny had a natural rapport with almost everyone and he had dated a string of stunning women that should have been way out of his league, and quite a few of them overlapped, sometimes simultaneously, in the same bed. He didn't have the chiselled handsome features of a typical ladykiller though and with his pockmarked skin, short stature, and mousy brown hair, he could have passed for Bryan Adams and Rob Brydon's love child. Danny simply won people over, men and women, with his charisma, zest for life, and relentless pursuit of having fun. Irritatingly, his success with women went hand in hand with his aptitude for sport. Danny took naturally to whatever he tried, be it sailing, golf, or skiing. It didn't matter if you put him in charge of a yacht, put a golf club in his hand or strapped a pair of skis to his feet, he would instinctively trim a sail, blithely drive a ball miles past yours, or glide effortlessly through powdered snow, as if he'd done all three from birth. If he hadn't been my best friend, I would have hated him, except that he would have just been his usual likeable, charming self and won me over. Alice handed me the phone.

"Hi, Danny."

"Hello fella, have you tried to commit genocide lately?" Bad news clearly travelled as fast as the good type did.

"So, you've heard then."

Danny had left the RAF three years ago but remained connected through a spider's web of social media friends, most of whom were still serving in the Armed Forces. I just hoped that someone hadn't been insensitive enough to plaster something about the near-mid-air disaster all over Facebook or worse still, leak it to the Press.

"Yeah, why didn't you call me you muppet?" That was a very good question.

"I dunno." *Why didn't I call Danny?* If there'd been anyone who would have immediately understood and been the ideal person to turn to in a crisis it would have been him. *So, what stopped me from picking up the phone and calling him?* I genuinely had no idea.

"Mate, my head's like jelly at the moment, sorry, you should have been the first person on my list."

"Don't apologise, I'm just a bit shocked. I would have called you."

"Great, are you trying to make me feel worse?" If he was it was working.

"No, I just mean you're a genuinely good person and I know you'd be there for me if I was in trouble. Anyway, Vlad called me and told me what happened, you numpty. He said that you'd been called in to see the pint pot Mussolini, who we both know is a real *people person*. I thought you could probably do with hearing a friendly voice." If I'd been given a choice of friendly voices to hear, I'd have chosen Danny's every day of the week and twice on Sundays. I was still really struggling to understand why I hadn't thought to call him.

"So, how's that lovely little dog?"

"She's fine now," I answered guiltily, watching Gypsy's chest gently rise and fall.

"Good. More importantly, how are you, *honestly?*"

"Well, I've had better weeks," I answered evasively. Danny waited.

"Wow, you don't hold back do you fella? Maybe we need to do this over a beer. I can drop everything and meet you somewhere or come over to you if you want to talk."

"No, it's fine."

"It's no trouble, I can be at yours in no time."

"Honestly, it's fine."

"Alright, as long as you're okay. Anyway, Wheezy Boy said you'd taken some leave."

"Yes, mate, I'm off until Monday then I have to go and see Squadron Leader Arsestabber and face the music."

"Arsestabber?"

"Yes, he's not tall enough to be a backstabber."

"Ha. Look, don't worry about it, we both know he's a little knob." Danny had a history with my boss too and didn't include Isaac on his Christmas card list.

"I know, but I did screw up, it *was* my fault, and I really don't know what's going to happen."

"Look, you're not the first and you won't be the last. You're in the RAF, and it's not like you're a civvy and they can sack you, is it? *Shit happens!*"

"Funny you should say that, but things are a bit different now mate."

"What d'you mean?"

"Well, there's a massive round of redundancies coming up. I could be right in the poo if they don't get enough people willing to jump ship."

"No way, you're Mr. Golden Bollocks, you'll be fine. *Won't you?*"

"If you'd asked me before Sunday, I'd have said I had nothing to worry about but now…" I let the words hang in the air, "I might be in the crap because the decision for who gets *voluntold* will be based on age, the likelihood of promotion, and performance."

"Oh, in that case, I'd say that's three strikes and you're fucked."

"Thanks a bunch, *mate.*" Danny was right though, I was no spring chicken, and this incident alone would certainly impact my slim chances of promotion and put a nasty, indelible stain on my conduct sheet. On the whole, my future was looking about as safe as a greenhouse on the San Andreas Fault.

"Sorry fella but I think it makes sense to have something up your sleeve, just in case."

"I know." *But what the hell am I qualified to do?* After recent events, there was one job that sprang to mind but I had no idea if we could survive on my salary modelling incontinence pants.

146

"What does Ali think?"

"Erm, I haven't exactly mentioned it," I cringed, knowing that I really should tell my wife. "I don't want to worry her unnecessarily."

"*Seriously?* You haven't told your wife? But hey, it's your funeral."

"It could well be. Promise you'll say something nice and won't try to shag one of Alice's friends at the wake."

"Well, you know me, I can guarantee I'll say something nice."

"Typical."

"Oh, for God's sake cheer up fella. You make Marvin the Paranoid Android sound like a lifestyle guru. Nobody died you know."

"I know," I sighed.

"*Oy!* Pack it in."

"Sorry."

"Right, what are your plans for the next few days?"

"Oh, I don't know, nothing set in stone really," I replied despondently. "I thought I might try and get a round of golf in. Actually, do *you* fancy a game?"

"Sure, how about a couple of rounds, in Scotland?" Danny asked enticingly.

Immediately I felt myself being lifted from my melancholic state.

"Scotland? What are you talking about?"

"We're going away mate, Thursday and Friday. Just you and me for a boys' weekend. Fancy it?"

"How can it be a boys' *weekend*, if we're going Thursday and Friday?"

"Don't be a dick, have a day off."

"Sorry, no, sorry, I mean that sounds great." *But what about Alice?* The thought of getting away from it all for a couple of days could be a lifeline, but how could I just disappear and abandon my wife. *Should I go?* Especially after what we'd been through lately. Danny beat me to it.

"… and don't worry about Ali. I cleared it with her just now. I just have to promise to bring you back in one piece or at least return the most important ones," he joked. "So, what do you reckon, are you up for it?"

"Does a pig's arse taste of pork?" I replied, barely able to contain my excitement, "So, what's the plan?"

"I'm just sorting out a few bits. There's a bit of a snag with accommodation, but I'm sure it'll be fine. Just leave it all to me, I'll sort it."

"Awesome. I can't wait," I beamed.

"We'll probably fly from Southampton early Thursday morning, but I'll message you once it's all squared away. Now bloody well cheer up, you're off work and you get to spend some time with me."

"Thanks, Danny."

"Catch you later."

*Fantastic, two days' golf, in Scotland, with Danny, just, just, yes! Could this be my salvation?* I wanted to grab this opportunity with both hands, but I'd had a couple of nasty surprises from the school bursar, and I needed to get the car fixed too, not forgetting that Christmas wasn't far away. *Can I afford to go, but then again can I afford not to?* Although I felt that I'd be abandoning Alice, I also had an incredibly strong urge to put as much

148

distance as possible between her and my bad mood and more importantly my current streak of bad luck. That whole thing at work, what a mess, and I'd almost killed the dog, twice. *Is Alice next? Or am I being ridiculous and overthinking things? Maybe I should sleep on it or at least express my thoughts, fears, and worries to a dependable, loyal individual who understands me, like my dog. Maybe even my wife. Or I could just bottle it all up, say nothing, and hope that everything works out.*

## CHAPTER 38

### She Drives Me Crazy

Alice hadn't said a word after we'd gone to bed last night. She never got the chance. I'd quickly decided that the matter didn't need to be discussed, with her or Gypsy, concluding rather selflessly, that flying to Scotland for a two-day golfing trip with Danny would be best for everyone. I feared that if I stayed, I'd be a danger to those around me, but Alice didn't need to hear that or about the bursar's letter either. I didn't want to stress her out about money or, more honestly, give her a reason to stop me from going.

Content with my excellent and selfless decision, I'd launched into an animated monologue about the boys' weekend and started jabbering about shopping for some new gear, golf courses in Scotland, and how I really needed some practice. I had just started explaining the science of how the grooves on a golf club impart spin and its effect on ball flight in different wind conditions when I looked across to see that Alice had already fallen fast asleep. She must have been tired.

Luckily for her, when I woke up the following morning, I remembered roughly where she'd dropped off during my animated golf lecture and carried on over breakfast, even though she seemed a bit distracted. I put it down to the close call with Gypsy. I was still feeling giddy with the same twitch of excitement in my belly that had started when Danny phoned. I had a million and one things to do before tomorrow, including a quick shopping trip, but I couldn't possibly leave before I'd finished explaining to Alice how a Stimpmeter measured green speed and telling her about the main differences between a parkland and a links course.

Getting up from the table I gave her a quick peck on the cheek, but she remained motionless and glassy-eyed, staring out of the window, occasionally stabbing herself in the back of her hand with a fork.

"Hello? Alice? What are you doing to your hand? Alice? Hello? I'm heading off now. Hello?" No response.

"Are you okay? Can you walk Gypsy if I take her out later? *Alice?*" Not even a flicker. I waved my hand in front of her face.

"Huh?" she muttered, looking up as the fork clattered on the table.

"Sorry," she began, shaking her head while blinking slowly, "I was just trying to imagine what would give me greater relief, shoving my hand in the food processor, or smashing you in the face with a Le Creuset frying pan, but it's okay, you're leaving now."

"Oh, ha, ha, ha."

"No, it's great, thank you so much. You know how I have trouble sleeping, so I'm just going to replay your little golf presentation in my head, and I'll be out like a light every time."

"Rude! There are women out there who'd appreciate me taking the time to talk to them."

"About golf?" Alice scoffed.

"Yes, even about golf."

"I'm sure there are, dear, but I expect they're extremely lonely, are surrounded by cats, and have dentures."

"There *are* benefits to dating a lady who hasn't got any teeth!"

"Oh God, are you still here?" Alice grinned, reaching for the cupboard door. "Where's that frying pan?" Stopping halfway she turned, her expression thoughtful. "Look, I know that you're off work because of what happened, and you need to relax. And I'm really glad that you've got the chance to get away, but do you think you could cut the grass today?"

I instantly bristled. I couldn't put my finger on why I resented Alice's perfectly reasonable request to do one of my allocated chores, but irrationally, I did. I'd put it off once and done very little to help over the last two days, yet for some reason I felt her question had been spiteful, probing, and said to highlight my complete lack of effort around the house. Basically, I felt she was calling me lazy. Worse, I knew that mowing the lawn could completely scupper my carefully timetabled plans for the day. *Why the hell can't you cut it for a change?*

"Fine," I groused.

"Don't worry if it's too much trouble," she said, smiling apologetically, "you know I get nervous about using your Flymo but I can give it a go," she added, offering me a way out of doing the only job she'd asked of me all week.

"*I said yes,*" I snapped, "I'll do it when I get back. I'll only be gone a couple of hours. See you later," I grumbled as I skulked out of the kitchen. Before Alice had time to say goodbye, I grabbed my golf clubs, wallet, and car keys, went stomping up the concrete steps and drove off.

## CHAPTER 39

### Money, Money, Money

Pulling into the deserted underground car park, I couldn't believe my luck. Gunwharf Quays resembled a post-apocalypse shopping centre this morning. No jostling throng of angry shoppers, no screaming brat-laden buggies, not even a shell suit-wearing, gang of lumbering members of the hard of thinking. *Perfect.* Despite my bank balance looking about as healthy as a one-lunged chain-smoker with emphysema, I happily set about trying to put it on the critical list, treating myself to everything for a boys' golfing trip I considered to be essential, plus a couple of things that would sit comfortably in the category of extravagant and completely unnecessary. My reckless purchasing complete, I checked my watch, thinking about going straight to the range for a quick bucket, then heading home for lunch and spending the rest of the afternoon relaxing with Alice. *Oops*. I'd been out for nearly three hours already, but surely Alice wouldn't mind, she said it herself, I needed to relax. *Grab lunch here, go to the range, and then head home? I'll still be back at about two o'clock and have time to cut the grass. She'll be fine with that, won't she?*

The customer count in Caffè Nero had doubled when I walked in and lounging in a soft leather armchair, I continued flicking through my new golf magazine while indulging in a deliciously gooey cheese and ham panino. After my second two-handled bucket of frothy coffee, I fell for the seductive charms of a huge slice of outrageously sugary and tangy lemon meringue tart, so sharp and sweet it almost turned my face inside out and left me feeling like a foie gras goose.

Sinking further into the armchair's soft cushions I began surveying my expensive collection of bags, surrendering to the realisation that now might be a good time to tackle the nightmare subjects in the bursar's unsettling letter that I'd been deliberately avoiding. Battling guilt and a soporific food coma, I called the personnel clerk at work first.

"Admin, Corporal Bromley."

"Hi Claire, it's Flight Lieutenant Alder."

"Oh, hi sir, what can I do for you?"

"Boarding school fees. My younger son moved up into Year 9 in September and I just wanted to check that the RAF will cover the fee increase, it's just over two grand," I asked hopefully, crossing my fingers.

"Of course, they will, sir," *Great, one down,* "you'll get the full subsidy when you apply next term." *What?*

"Next term? What do you mean next term?" *No, not next term, now, I can't just make £2,000 appear out of thin air, I need it now.*

"Yes sir, your latest application has already been processed and the window for all claims closed last Friday." *Nuts.*

*"Seriously?"*

"Sorry sir, I wish I could help you, but I really can't. Once we're past the cut-off date I can only view the claims, I can't amend them. I'm really sorry."

"No, no, it's fine." *It's anything but fine.* "It's my cock-up." *Again.*

"Is there anything else I can help you with?"

"No, thanks." *Not unless you can get me a bucket to throw up into and know where I can find a money tree and a body shop that does free repairs.*

"Oh sir, before you go, are you okay to pop into the office and sign something in your personal file please?" Immediately my mind started racing. I'd signed for my annual report two months ago and I couldn't think of anything else that needed my attention.

"Sure, what is it?"

"Um, it's just the formal acknowledgment of the warning you got from Squadron Leader Koch." *Warning, what warning?* I began fast-forwarding through the conversation in Isaac's office.

"I'm a bit confused Claire, what warning are you referring to?"

"Oh, sorry, this is a bit awkward then. The squadron leader's put a note in your file to say that he issued you with a formal warning on Sunday." Still whizzing through the conversation, I remembered the moment he'd said, 'take this as a warning.' I thought he just meant to be careful. I hadn't realised he'd make it official, the snake.

"No, it's okay, he did say. I'll come and see you on Monday."

"Thanks, sir."

"Any more good news for me? I've not been specially selected to retrain as a mine clearance diver or anything?"

"No sir," she chuckled sympathetically. *Pity. So, I've got an official warning and I'm two grand out of pocket. Well, I'm clearly on a roll, I may as well call the bursar now, then drive to Southsea Esplanade and throw myself off the pier. Knowing my luck, the tide will be out.* I ended the call and taking a deep breath, started dialling the boys' school.


## CHAPTER 40

### Sweet Child o' Mine

Trudging down the steps to lower-ground parking I kept shaking my head. *For Christ's Jack, £15-20,000 worth of damage. What the hell were you thinking son?*

The chat with the bursar had been more than a little tense, causing me to repeatedly raise my hand in apology to the shocked barista when I'd caught myself shouting. The school was still investigating the incident, but they sounded fairly certain of Jack's involvement. According to Father Emmanuel, he'd caught a small group of tearful eight and nine-year-olds red-handed, trying to throw stones at one particular stained-glass window of the school chapel depicting St. Nicholas of Myra. The distraught group had reported that they all wanted to go home and were only throwing stones because of what one of the older boarders had told them.

Jack had allegedly been spreading the supposedly well-known 'fact' that if you could knock out one of the thirteen stars around the figure of the saint, who over time had evolved into Santa Claus, he'd grant you an early Christmas wish. However, there was a forfeit, if you hit him, then Christmas would be cancelled. I imagined that most of the new boarders had simply dismissed it as an urban myth or had either been too sceptical or too frightened of missing out on presents. However, a group of three highly strung and emotionally overwrought youngsters had been so desperately unhappy and homesick, they'd been caught after dinner, hurling stones at the saintly image. The trio included one inconsolable little girl who the priest had found slumped on the grass, screaming about not getting a My Little Pony after putting a stone straight through St. Nick's forehead.

I felt certain that neither of my boys would have fallen for something like that at eight. Toby would have found it far too energetic, whereas Jack would have simply been too sharp, but I could easily imagine him spinning a yarn to a few impressionable, dewy-eyed new kids and chuckling to himself as they set off towards the chapel. Of course, I defended my younger son.

"Even if it was Jack, and you said yourself you don't know that it was *for sure*, he never put the stones in their hands, did he?"

"Actually, Mr. Alder he did. So, to speak."

"Pardon."

"The older boy in question sold these young boarders *magical runes*."

"*Magical runes?*"

"Yeees Mr. Alder runes, which just happen to look exactly like the ornamental pebbles from the chapel garden with some crude symbols drawn on them." *For God's sake Jack.* That definitely sounded like something he'd do and by crude I don't think the bursar meant rudimentary either. Unsettlingly this wouldn't be Jack's first offence or the first time the little wheeler-dealer had got up the nose of the school's head of finance. I'd been called in for a meeting with the headmaster only last year after Jack's housemaster had uncovered him running a highly lucrative Black Market tuck shop from his bedroom. He'd been buying and splitting multipacks of chocolate bars and fizzy drinks from the local Co-op and making a pretty penny by significantly undercutting the school's cafeteria. I couldn't help but admire his entrepreneurial spirit on that occasion but this…

"Well, I'm sorry but if they're that gullible it's hardly Jack's fault. If it *was* him that is."

"That's not the point Mr. Alder, and we are seriously looking at him as the instigator. If we can prove it was him, we *will* be seeking recompense for the damages. And it's an act of sacrilege." *Oh, piss off. I've had a gutful of 'believers' lately.*

"Well, I don't see how you can pin it on my boy, it all sounds a bit circumstantial to me and nobody was coerced were they?"

"No, Mr. Alder, it's worse than coercion. When young children start boarding, they tend to be extremely vulnerable and highly susceptible to older influence, and I'm sure you'll agree that Jack can be rather…" *Manipulative?* "…persuasive." *I can't argue with that.* "It appears he was playing on their emotional vulnerability for his own amusement and personal gain." *Yes, well he gets that from his mother!*

"I'm sorry but as far as I'm concerned you don't have proof and it's just a silly schoolboy prank that I won't be paying out for."

"But Mr. Alder…"

"We'll just have to agree to disagree I'm afraid. Good day." I hung up shaking, crapping myself at the prospect of being asked to make amends to the tune of almost half my annual salary. This scam had Jack written all over it and, rummaging in my pocket for notes and loose change as I wandered over to the ticket machine, I continued worrying that I hadn't heard the last of it.

I jumped as the machine ripped the piece of thin white card from my hand and then stood waiting. It whirred momentarily before ejecting the ticket so hard it flew past my head. I watched dumbfounded as it went fluttering to the floor. Huffing as I bent down, I picked up the rejected ticket, blew off the fine specks of dirt, and tried once more. Greedily gobbling again, the machine decided it still didn't like the taste, violently spitting the ticket out. *Seriously?* Wiping the card clean and double-checking the orientation on the diagram below the slot, I tried for a third time. Again, the machine snatched the printed card from my hand, and began whirring, then nothing. Looking at the screen I kept waiting for the ransom demand to release my car to appear. Nothing. Just my reflection and silence, apart from the sound of cracking enamel. *You've got to be kidding me.*

On any normal day, I'd have pressed the HELP button, asking for assistance as I calmly explained that the machine had malfunctioned. Instead, driven by despair, an angry sugar rush, and four shots of espresso, I decided to give the bastard thing a damn good kicking. Raging, banging, and slamming my open palm on the hollow metal box, the car park echoed with the sound of my meltdown.

"*AARGH!*" Placing one hand on either side I started shaking it, "*YOU SHITTING PIECE OF A MOTHERFU…*"

"Can you stop doing that mate?" The machine rocked to a squeaky stop, as I let go panting, scanning frantically for the source of the voice coming from inside. Looking across the expanse of the almost empty car park, I spotted a dark figure waving at me through the tinted office window near the exit barrier. Guiltily craning my neck, I put my mouth up to the microphone, leaning my forearm against the machine. Screeching loudly, it shook as it wobbled backwards a few inches then stopped. *Shit! Maybe it was already loose.*

"Um, I've lost my ticket inside your machine, I think it's broken."

"Well, if it weren't before it is now innit," the dark figure sneered, "can you come to the ticket office mate?" *Mate, don't fucking call me mate!*

Throwing my extravagant guilt-laden purchases in the back of the car I growled, clenching my teeth and grinding the misshapen boot shut before storming across the car park.

Twenty minutes later, gripping the steering wheel so tightly it squeaked, I set off for the driving range with my wallet lighter by £60, while fantasising about me repeatedly smashing the smug, overfamiliar cark park supervisor in the face with a credit card reader.

I'd protested at first, stubbornly refusing to pay the standard fee for a lost ticket but immediately softened when he started using phrases like 'criminal damage' and 'police matter.' I buckled completely, staring in disbelief when he started playing me the CCTV footage of my 'Falling Down' moment.

*Bollocks, sixty quid on top of the school fees.* I couldn't bear thinking about making a crippling donation to the stained-glass uplift for Father Christmas. How on earth was I going to generate an additional £2,000, get the car fixed and pay for a golfing mini-break? At my age, I didn't think hanging around Portsmouth Dockyard after dark was a viable option. *I really don't have the energy for it or the legs for that matter.*

## CHAPTER 41

### I'm Going Slightly Mad

At the driving range, my day continued deteriorating. It started badly when I inattentively placed the mesh plastic bucket under the ball dispenser. I'd been replaying the CCTV footage of me beating the shit out of a ticket machine when I heard the racket of balls clattering onto the concrete. Scrambling to catch the deluge, I righted the bucket, that had been knocked on its side as the first balls came spewing out, managing to catch the last dozen or so. I then spent several humiliating minutes picking up over sixty escapees, that had bounced, rolled, and trickled all over the place.

After whacking over a hundred range balls the dark clouds continued gathering. Wrongly assuming that hitting a couple of buckets would be the textbook preparation for the upcoming trip, I'd also been hoping it might lighten my mood a little. It didn't.

The spray of scattered dots clearly indicated my inability to hit a small yellow sphere in something resembling a straight line. A couple of really wayward shots had managed to not only clear the top of the high protective netting along the sides of the driving range but the road beyond too. No matter what I tried adjusting, stance, posture, or grip, nothing seemed to be working. I even started hitting *shanks*. Striking the ball with the club's hosel, I then angrily began slamming my club repeatedly into my golf bag, seething, after watching yet another ball squirt away to the right at a bizarre angle before clattering into the fence. Worse still, I nearly added 'injury to insult', coming close to hospitalising myself when I tried hitting my brand-new driver.

Lovingly peeling the cellophane from its huge, glossy red head, I thought that even if my iron shots were rubbish, I couldn't miss with this beauty. Throwing the clear wrapping in the bin, along with the shameful receipt, I peeled off the extortionate, incriminating price label too. It would be beneficial to my health and well-being if Alice didn't discover that I'd gone a bit mad in the range's shop. In her terms, this club alone equated to about four and a half handbags or the repair bill for my battered estate car's dented bottom.

Bending down, I placed a ball on the practice mat's long rubber tee. Waggling the club, I took one look down the range before starting my swing, drawing back the expensive metal wood.

Thud! Clunk! Clang!

Thumping into the bottom of the tee, the clubhead almost went completely under the ball and sent it rocketing vertically off the domed top of the driver. Smacking into the corner of one of the thick metal rafters, it rebounded into the corrugated steel roof, then came whistling past my head before thudding into the thick green Astroturf mat.

Uncurling my arm, I stood up, looking around. A sea of disapproving looks stared back, shaking their heads and murmuring. The errant shot had left an ugly scuff mark on the crown of my formerly pristine driver and staring at the dull graze on the shiny red lacquered surface, I felt a bit sick, wishing I'd never bought it. I also had the feeling that coming to the range might have been a bad idea too. I'd come to practice because I didn't want to travel to Scotland and look like a complete idiot on the golf course. Instead, I managed to humiliate myself before leaving England. *And I haven't even packed!*

Annoyed, frustrated but mostly embarrassed, I doggedly tried carrying on.

"Come on Henry," I muttered irritably, "you can do this."

Taking a deep breath and gently rocking my weight, I sank into my shoes. Staring at the ball, then down the range at the '250' board, I turned back to the ball. Breathing out I relaxed, feeling calm and in control as I started smoothly drawing the clubhead back low and slow to start my swing.

The ball came cracking off the clubface with a satisfying crunch and standing, perfectly balanced, holding my follow-through, I gazed as a yellow dot went rifling into the sky, ripping through the air, gently arcing to the left, climbing over the 50-yard marker, 100, 150... Approaching the 200-yard board, still climbing, I spotted another ball, closing from the left, rising to meet it. Watching intently, my mouth fell open as they hit, smacking off one another before hearing the delayed click of impact. *What are the chances? Two airborne bodies meet at the exact same point in time and space.*

As they dropped, I didn't see two yellow range balls falling from the sky. Instead, I stood picturing two distant objects, trailing dark ribbons of smoke, tumbling towards the ground. The vision of dead bodies strapped in their seats, burnt and lifeless, others blistered but barely conscious. Then the unlucky few, fully aware of the horror, choking and screaming, helpless, trapped inside a giant screeching metal coffin, drowning in the rolling boil of black and orange, as their blazing, aluminium alloy casket spiralled uncontrollably, rushing, unstoppable, plummeting towards oblivion.

I really didn't feel like practising anymore. I felt like screaming and crying and curling up into a tight ball and gently rocking myself to sleep.


## CHAPTER 42

### Little Lies

Parking the car just after three o'clock, I stretched, yawning widely. That stressful range session on top of a heavy lunch seemed to be taking its toll. Unloading the car I scanned the windows, spotting the top of Alice's head in the lounge. She appeared to be sitting on the sofa watching the TV. *Perfect.*

Easing the porch door handle down, I slipped inside, then slid the key in, silently opened the front door, and tiptoed into the house.

"Hello, my love," I shouted into the lounge, leaving my golf bag in the hall and dashing upstairs with an armful of carrier bags before Alice had a chance to get up. I stashed the new purchases in the spare room.

"Is that new?" she asked, standing in the hallway, pointing accusingly at my driver's immaculate head cover as I walked back down. *How the hell does she do that?* Thankfully she hadn't spotted my new putter.

"This old thing," I said, taking the club out and slipping off the head cover, "Nooo, I've had this ages. You can see how old it is, it's even got a scuff mark. Look!" Beads of sweat started forming on my forehead and I felt myself getting warmer, while inside my heart gently wept as I pointed to the sickening graze.

"Hmmm, really," Alice said, doubtfully, "so, are you going to make a start on the grass then?"

The remaining good parts of my mood dissolved instantly, and I stiffened at the question. I'd only been in the door a few minutes and she'd already started nagging me. *Jesus woman, give me a break.*

"Ow." I felt a pricking in the front of my leg and looked down to see Lucky sitting at my feet, brazenly pawing at my shin with his talons bared.

"Are you seeing this?" I asked Alice, as the audacious cat continued openly raking at my trouser leg.

"Ah, he just wants your attention and thinks you're avoiding him. I know how he feels," Alice jibed.

"Ow, I'll give him my attention alright. *Pack that in!*" I shouted, flicking my leg to make him stop.

Lucky darted out of the way and simply walked around then started again, this time dabbing my calf with his claws.

"*Stop it,*" I barked and tried donkey-kicking the bare-faced bully but missed. *The little shit can't even be bothered to hide his malice now.* I'd had enough.

"*Right, I'll cut the bloody grass,*" I surrendered stroppily, thumping upstairs, leaving Alice in the hall suspiciously eyeing the contents of my golf bag.

I undressed, ripping my clothes off and yanking the drawer open. Piling my dog walking gear on the floor I sighed, sitting back on the bed, trying to muster the enthusiasm to tackle the lawn. *Oh boy, this mattress feels so comfortable. It'll only take about an hour to cut the grass, plenty of time.* My throbbing head sank into the pillow, and I closed my eyes, listening to the pulsing rush of blood as it surged past my eardrums. Puffing my cheeks and pursing my lips I blew out, long and slow then yawned. *Five minutes, I'll just have five minutes, then I'll get the mower out.*

## CHAPTER 43

### Get Lucky

I didn't know how long I'd been asleep but I knew I had to sort the garden out or Alice would be furious. Jumping out of bed, I winced. Looking down I saw the reddish marks on my shin and calf and the three-day-old scabs on my thigh. The back of my left hand was a mess of scars, and I still had that scratch on my heel too. Enough was enough, I had to do something about Lucky once and for all. *Carpe cattus!*

I had one sore, bloodied leg in my scruffy jeans when Gypsy appeared, giving me an idea. Pulling my jeans up, I sat on the floor, beckoning her towards me.

"Right girl, here's what you're going to do..."

Sitting on the bedroom floor, I carefully laid out the plan for Lucky's 'accident', explaining it three times to Gypsy. She kept zoning out and I couldn't be sure that she completely understood, even though at one point, worryingly I could have sworn she said 'okay.' My plan was to knock on the glass-panelled lounge door that led into the garden and show her a dog biscuit. This would be her signal to find the cat, scare him out of the house through the back door that I'd leave open, then chase him across the lawn to where I'd be waiting with my lethally sharpened Flymo. I even promised her a cooked beef bone once the job was complete.

"Any questions? No? Good. *Operation Kitty Mince is a go!*" I confirmed high-fiving Gypsy's raised paw.

The cold October weather had stunted the lawn's growth, but the blades of grass had still managed to stretch themselves upwards, creating a messy garden well overdue for a haircut. It felt rather unsettling because bizarrely, I believed I could see the grass regrowing as soon as I'd cut it. Banging on the collection box, I emptied my third load onto the mountainous compost heap, then carried the machine up the small flight of steps and started trimming the final top strip.

The cold and damp combined with the dangerously sloped bank made it a treacherous task. I fell twice as I lowered and swung the hover mower from side to side while trying to trim the sharply angled bank, my front foot slipping and clipping the edge of the mower. If it had gone under, I'd have lost a toe. *Can I really do the same to the cat? It'll be quick, but then again, what if it's not? I might just horribly mangle it and there's no way I could afford the vet bills.* If I'd been half my normal sane self, I would have been horrified by the thought alone but flicking through the painful catalogue of war wounds inflicted by my spiteful enemy, I somehow justified my horrific plan, deciding to press on.

Pushing the thrumming mower in front of the lounge's rear door, I released its power lever, the high-speed whine instantly dropping as the blades juddered and the hovering orange box dropped to the floor. Gypsy lay sleeping in her bed and twitched when I began tapping on the window. Rolling her head towards the sound, she eyed me lazily then tried unsuccessfully to jump up at the sight of the treat in my hand. I pointed at her, then at the biscuit, giving her a thumbs up, then stood watching as she flipped, wobbled, and floundered like a beached seal before scrambling out of her bed and went bolting out of the lounge. *Game on!*

With shaking hands, I lifted the metal-framed handle and began panting heavily as I squeezed the lever. The hover mower started rocking as it whirred into life.

An almighty bang announced that something had hit the cat flap at high speed. Keeping my eyes fixed on the corner of the house, I waited, nervously anticipating the appearance of the ginger menace before I turned him into cat tartare, the bars of the whirling, scything blades of death gripped firmly in my hands, poised, ready…

I gasped, flinching violently as a creature came flying round the corner, tearing across the grass, and heading straight towards me.

I didn't see any sign of the cat though; I don't think Gypsy had either. Instead, I was staring at the sight of a bounding, tail-wagging, greedy beagle desperate for a biscuit, wearing a cat flap like a square plastic ruff.

"You are absolutely *rubbish*," I said, chastising my incompetent accomplice.

We both turned as something moved into view in the bottom pane of the lounge door. Lucky sat, staring back, licking his paw.

"You had one job," I said, turning to Gypsy who continued wagging her tail as she looked up at me expectantly, sporting her boxy white necklace.

Alice appeared, marching across the lawn with a frown of concern so big it wrinkled her whole face.

"*What the hell is going on?*" she thundered.

"Nothing," I sang innocently, avoiding Alice's gaze by checking to see if the guttering at the back of the house looked secure. "I think Gypsy got a bit carried away and tried to fit through the cat flap," I answered as, content with the integrity of the pipework, I redirected my attention into trying to pull the plastic frame over the dog's wriggling head.

"I know," said Alice, "there's a bloody big hole in the door."

Relieving Gypsy of her new jewellery, I gave her the unearned biscuit. With a couple of thumps, I managed to wedge the frame of the cat flap back into place, refitting the clear swinging door that had pinged off when Gypsy the Wonderdog had headbutted it, going hell for leather. Waiting until Alice went back into the lounge, I then crept back upstairs.

Heaving that mower around for an hour, tackling the grassy slopes plus the adrenalin rush of my botched assassination had taken its toll. I needed a proper lie-down. I slipped out of my clothes and climbed back onto the bed. *Oh yes, have a quick nap then get the dog out.* It would be the perfect opportunity to evade Alice's interrogation about what I'd been up to all day.

## CHAPTER 44

### Escape (The Piña Colada Song)

I woke to find my clothes piled on the floor and not a green stain or a single blade of grass anywhere. *Strange.* I could only assume that Alice must have taken them outside, beaten the cuttings off then put them back on the floor, ready for the evening dog walk. Peering through the window I stared in shock as I surveyed my lamentable handiwork. I could see that I'd missed several patches and left quite a few ugly brown scars and clumps of twisted, chewed-up grass. A casual passer-by might have thought I'd been drunk or hired a blind gardener. Dressing quickly and having checked that the coast was clear, I crept back down, stealthily grabbing the bag of dog treats. Gypsy appeared at the sound of the gently rustling packet, and putting my finger to my lips, I slipped her a treat while silently clipping her lead on.

"See you later, I'm just taking the dog out," I shouted, dragging Gypsy and scarpering out of the front door to avoid any chance of Alice getting the thumbscrews out. If cornered I knew I'd crumble like an oatmeal ancient ruin and, after my recent aggressive behaviour, feared how I'd react if put under pressure.

An impromptu walk with my beloved pooch had been the perfect getaway and I'd pulled it off. I couldn't be too long though; I'd been out all day and imagined that Alice would already be surveying the freshly cut grass and picking the perfect site for a husband-sized hole.

## CHAPTER 45

### How You Remind Me

"Well, that was a complete balls-up earlier, wasn't it?" I griped at my hapless partner in crime, who completely ignored me by sniffing the ground instead.

"If I'm honest, I'm not sure I've really got it in me, Gypsy. It seemed like a good plan, but on reflection I'm ashamed. I can't believe you didn't talk me out of trying something so horrid either. Well, you can forget the bone."

Gypsy stopped and lifted her head, looking at me attentively at the sound of the word 'bone.'

"Oh yeah, now I've got your attention, any mention of something you can eat, and suddenly you're all ears. You'd have gone through with it too, wouldn't you, and all for a bone?" Gypsy started barking and wagging her tail. "Why couldn't you have been the voice of reason and given me some moral guidance? Oh, and if your mum asks you about any of it, stay strong and deny everything!"

I clambered over the stile and was bending down to unclip Gypsy's lead when I heard the unmistakable boom of two daft red setters. They came bounding towards us and Gypsy plodded off to meet them for another unsavoury sniff and 'lickfest.' Bubble Gum Barbie came trotting behind. I raised my hand, but she obviously didn't see me and carried on walking.

"Evening," I called, preparing to stop, and daydream. Barbie didn't reply and continued thumping down the path.

"I said good evening." *She wasn't still upset that I'd shouted at her yesterday, was she? Surely, she'd be over it.*

"Prick!"

*Maybe not.*

As Barbie continued flouncing past, I walked on, stepping into the shadow of the giant oak, when my phone began buzzing, and Bruno Mars started singing in my pocket.

*"Today I don't feel like doing anything…,"* this was a pleasant and unexpected surprise, *"…I just wanna lay in my bed…"*

"Hi, Toby."

"You're a git." Not his normal friendly greeting.

"Pardon."

"You, you're a rotten git Dad."

"Why, what have I done *now*? And is that really any way to address your father?" I grumbled, feeling my hackles starting to flare. *Strange.* I'd been wound up countless times by Jack, yet I couldn't remember a single occasion when my elder son had come close to riling me. "You've got about one second to explain yourself young man and tell me what you think I've done."

"It's not what you've done *now*. Oh no, not *now* Dad. It's what you did *then*?"

"Then when? You've lost me."

"When we lived in our old house near Stubbington."

"What? For Christ's sake, just spit it out, boy!" I barked testily.

"Two words, Dad, *Junction Bingo*."

"*Oh*." Instantly, I knew exactly what Toby meant. If he'd settled on git, I was getting off pretty lightly. "Yes, about that…" I said, walking across the field, recalling the ploy I'd devised to trick the young Toby and Jack into behaving. I began wondering if nowadays it might be considered mental cruelty. *Oh Jesus, on top of everything else, am I a bad parent too?*

## CHAPTER 46

### Wicked Game

I'd invented Junction Bingo about ten years ago, during my first posting to Swanwick. We were living as a young family in Stubbington, a seaside village in the district Borough of Gosport, six miles west of Portsmouth. At the time, Toby had been seven and Jack only three when we were told by friends about Paulton's Park. Located just over twenty miles away, near Romsey, the family-oriented amusement park promised a host of rides, and attractions, including exotic birds and kids' shows. It sounded like the perfect recipe for a full and exhausting day out.

However, looking at the road atlas, I reckoned the drive, mostly along the busy and often slow M27 between Portsmouth and Southampton would take about half an hour. That could be a problem. Thirty minutes for the parents of two squabbling boys, strapped in the back of a car would feel like a week in Dante's Fifth Circle of Hell.

One Saturday morning, as I checked the route, bracing myself for a painful journey, I noticed something odd. Slowly running my finger along the bold blue line, I double-checked to be sure. *No way.* In a moment of pure inspiration, an ingenious way of keeping them quiet suggested itself. As the engine hummed into life, I turned to face Toby and Jack, preparing to deliver my masterstroke.

"Ahem. Right boys, we're going to play a game today."

Blank stares.

"… and the prize for the winner is a £50 note." Two bored little faces suddenly lit up.

"*Fifty pounds?*" they shouted in unison.

"Really?" asked Toby doubtfully, having been duped by me on a technicality more than once.

"Yes, I promise, I'll give *this* to the winner," I nodded, producing a large red and brown banknote from my wallet, and holding it up for them to see. They lost their tiny minds.

"Hooray! Hooray! How much is fifty pounds, Daddy?" asked Jack.

Toby turned to his younger brother; he couldn't get the words out fast enough.

"Fifty pounds Jack, *fifty pounds*. We could buy our own sweet shop with that."

"Cowabunga," exclaimed Jack, slapping his thighs excitedly.

Alice scowled at me, but I gave her a confident trust-me-darling-I-know-what-I'm-doing wink and nod.

"Can I touch it?" asked Toby.

"Of course, if you win you get to keep it," I said, handing it over. Toby and Jack sat open-mouthed, staring, mesmerised.

"What's the game, Daddy? What's the game, Daddy? Tell me, tell me," Jack asked, as he bunched his tiny fists excitedly against his cheeks.

"Okay boys, it's really easy, it's like I Spy. The first one to spot Junction 6 on the M27 gets the £50 note." Stunned silence.

"What's a junction?" asked Jack innocently.

"It's the big blue sign on the motorway, darling," Alice explained. "When you see a big blue sign with a number six on it you shout out."

"Shout what?" Toby asked.

"Erm, Bingo," Alice added glaring at me. *Fair enough.*

"Okay, *Bingooo*," they screamed.

The scene was set, the rules were simple, and the air crackled as we drove off.

When, several minutes later, we joined the motorway at Junction 9, the car filled with squeals of excitement.

"Right, keep your eyes peeled boys, here we go…"

You could have heard a pin drop and I could almost hear the strain of their little eyeballs as they tried searching for the prizeworthy Junction 6. A blue sign appeared in the distance.

"Bingo!" shouted Jack.

We approached and passed Junction 8.

"Nooo, that's number eight Jack, keep looking."

"Bingo!" shouted Jack again as we approached Junction 7.

"Nooo, that's number seven, very close."

The normally relaxed Toby, unlike his brother, knew that 9 was followed by 8 then 7 and then the hallowed 6, sat, waiting like a coiled Slinky.

Another blue sign appeared in the distance; Toby nearly burst.

"Bingo, Bingo, there it is, Junction 6. I win! I win!"

"That's poo!" Jack huffed, crossing his arms angrily.

Toby sat grinning on the back seat with a huge prize-winning smile on his face, but it faded as we approached and then passed the huge blue road sign with a large number 5 on it.

"Oh dear, that was Junction 5, you must have blinked and missed it. Oh well, you can try again on the way home."

"Loser!" Jack chuckled, delighted that his brother hadn't won. Toby remained perplexed, his face twisting in confusion and anger, as he frowned, sulking until we pulled into the car park. Distracted by the novel attractions of Paulton's Park, they soon forgot about the game.

Nearing the end of a full day of rides, ice cream, and fresh air, Toby was the unfortunate victim of a bombing run from a Herring Gull. Jack took great delight in calling him names and, as I unlocked the car, he continued chuckling as he nimble-footedly evaded his brother's lumbering attempts to grab him.

"Right boys, stop that. Who wants to play Junction Bingo again?"

"I bet Poohead does?" Jack said, climbing onto his booster seat.

*"That's enough Jack,"* Alice snapped, "now say sorry."

"Okay, Mummy. Sorry, Poohead."

"Right boys," I interjected, trying not to laugh, "let's see who can win Daddy's £50 note, okay?"

They both nodded and I could see from Toby's determined expression that he planned to win this time.

Five minutes after pulling out of the car park, we re-joined the M27 at Junction 2.

"Here we go again…"

"Bingo, Daddy," Jack cried loudly, on sighting Junctions 3, 4, and 5. A crushing silence fell each time, seconds after I declared, "Ahhh, no, not quite Jack, keep trying."

Toby's gaze remained firmly fixed, glued to the horizon. Watching his mouth in the rearview mirror, I noticed him silently counting off the exits 3, 4, 5… I was just thinking that he hadn't blinked for the last eleven miles when suddenly his eyes went wide.

"*Bingo! Bingooo!* There's Junction 6, yeeessss," Toby bellowed victoriously, erupting with joy, and punching the air.

"Agh, double poo," Jack harrumphed.

"*Yeeesss! Fifty quid,* I'm going to buy a Super Soaker, a giant bag of Quavers, and all of the Pick 'n' Mix in Woolworths and… Huh? *What the...*"

"What's wrong?" I asked, feigning surprise.

"That was number *seven* on that sign," said Toby, his voice warbling as his brow furrowed.

"*Was it?* Oh well, never mind son, you must have missed it again."

"But… I…"

"Well, I never. Where could that naughty Junction 6 have gone?"

Alice gave me a cold, hard, murderous stare. Toby looked daggers at me in the mirror, red-faced.

"Stop that," Alice ordered as Toby began kicking the back of her seat.

"That's your fault," she mouthed.

Jack affably suggested one answer to the conundrum of the missing junction.

"I expect some thieving pikey nicked it, don't you, Daddy?"

"Well…erm… I really couldn't say, Jack. I don't know where they pick these things up!" I scoffed, looking out of the driver's window. "When we get home, remind me to have a word with the staff at Jack's nursery."

We played Junction Bingo about eight or nine times after that, during every trip to Paulton's Park and all the other journeys down the M27. Of course, no matter how determined they were, how hard they tried, or how much they concentrated, the cash remained unclaimed in my wallet. The boys couldn't possibly win, of course, Junction 6 simply didn't exist.

Thankfully, before the boys were old enough to realise they'd been hoodwinked, I received orders for an overseas posting to RAF Akrotiri. Our family upped sticks and moved to the Mediterranean island of Cyprus, and the mysterious Junction Bingo simply faded from memory, lost forever in the mists of time. Until now!

# CHAPTER 47

## Hanging on the Telephone

"Junction 6, eh, Dad?"

"Yes, about that," I didn't know what to say, "so how did you find out?"

"We had a rugby match today against a school near Ringwood."

"Really, how did you get on?" I asked, trying to divert the conversation.

"Nice try. We were on the M27, you know the motorway that we used to drive down when we went to Paulton's Park when we were little."

"Um, I vaguely remember." Clearly, my inability to lie convincingly to my wife extended to my children too.

"Well, we were going along in the minibus, and I remembered that game you made us play as kids."

"I didn't really *make* you. You were both really keen."

"Yes, but we couldn't win, could we?"

"Er."

"Could we, Dad?" Toby insisted.

"Um."

"*Daaad?*"

"No," I ashamedly admitted.

"You made me cry. *I must have only been about six.*"

"Seven actually," I corrected, not that being one year older excused my ruse.

"Oh well, that's alright then. Making a six-year-old cry is unforgivable but seven and over is fine! I told Jack and even he remembered."

"Yes, well *he* would," I replied, rolling my eyes. "Talking of Jack, do you know anything about the damage to the school chapel?"

"The smashed window?"

"Yes."

"Look, Dad, it's just one of those stupid things like the story about the theatre being haunted and it wasn't just Jack telling the new kids, a few of his mates were winding up those little ones too." *I bet he was the ringleader though.* "The school's as much to blame."

"How come?"

"Because one minute there's a Science lesson teaching Darwinism and the next you've got an R.E. teacher talking about God creating the world in six days. No wonder the younger ones have a hard time separating fact from fantasy." Toby had evidently reached the same conclusions regarding theology that I had at his age.

"I see your point, son, but you do go to a Catholic school, so I wouldn't let your teachers hear you saying that. And if the subject ever comes up with Grandma Eileen, for God's sake don't repeat what you just said and my name in the same breath or I'll get the blame. I don't fancy getting an I.E.D. for Christmas."

"Ha, I think you're fine, Dad. She gets me and Jack muddled up these days and she's a bit shaky, so I don't think she can be trusted with separating red and green wires or handling tilt switches." *I am so proud right now.* "Anyway, it's stupid if they try to blame Jack."

"That's what I thought." *I still have a horrible feeling the school won't see it that way though and there's the small matter of fraudulently selling magic stones too.*

"So…" Toby continued, getting back to the main reason he'd called, "I explained the whole Junction 6 thing, and I said you were a git. Jack said you were something much worse that I won't repeat. He reckons that when the time comes, we should put you in a really shitty nursing home."

"I'm sorry. You were such little horrors we tried everything to keep you from fighting."

"*We?* What do you mean, *we?* Mum said it was all your idea."

"Oh. You've spoken to your mum then?"

"Yeah, I just called her, she seems to be in one of her *moods.*" *I can't imagine why.*

"Anyway, Mum said she asked you not to play it and thought Jack and I might end up talking about how we'd been mentally abused to a therapist one day. Well, you've seen how Jack turned out, that's all on you Dad." *Of course, it is.*

"Anyway, we've decided that Mum's going to go into a luxury Five-Star home when the time comes and we're going to pay the staff extra at your retirement hovel to abuse you."

*Charming. When Alice bailed, she really bailed.*

Of course, Toby had been joking and wasn't genuinely upset. He said he thought it had been quite a clever scam, funny even, a bit of a sick game to play on young children, but still funny. *Hmmm, maybe Jack does get it from me.* Chatting for a few more minutes, I avoided any mention of what had happened at work. My elder son might have exuded a generally laid-back approach to life, but despite this, I knew he'd have been worried sick about the potential fallout from my unsuccessful attempt at Shooting the Gap.

"So, I'll pick you up a week Friday."

"Okay Dad, speak to you soon."

"Okay."

"Oh Dad, one quick question."

"Yes?"

"What's six feet two, thirteen stone, and hangs up?"

"No idea. What's…" Click "…Hello? Toby? What's? Hello..." *Damn it.*

## CHAPTER 48

### Suspicious Minds

We walked through the front door and as soon as I unclipped her, true to form, Gypsy went straight to the kitchen, checking to see if her bowl had magically refilled. Washing my hands, I heard heavy footsteps growing louder, as Alice came stomping down the hall.

"*What the hell are you playing at?*" she roared.

"What? I've been walking the dog."

"Not just now, you were out *all* day, *shopping* apparently. I thought you were only going for a few hours." I shrugged. "Then you came in for two minutes acting all secretive, said you'd cut the grass, then disappeared upstairs for a sleep before you buggered off out with the dog. I've hardly seen you and I tried calling you."

"Alright, I've just been busy. Don't get on my case, I just needed some space."

"Is that all it is? You just wanted time alone?" Alice warbled.

"Yes. Why? What on earth did you think I was doing?"

"Nothing." Translation, *something* and not good.

"Come on, what is it?"

"It doesn't matter. It's silly," she replied softly, her voice cracking.

"Come on. What?" Alice paused, looking at the carpet before lifting her head to face me.

"I thought there might be someone else," she murmured, her blue eyes glistening with tears.

"Oh, my God. Alice no! *Nooo!*" I protested, my heart suddenly aching for making her feel that way.

I couldn't believe that she'd think that, but I suppose my recent behaviour had been a bit odd. I definitely didn't feel myself at the moment. I'd hardly been thinking straight, and my normally long fuse seemed to have grown shorter by the hour. I felt like I'd become a ticking time bomb and was anxiously hoping this trip to Scotland would be the perfect way to defuse me before I went off and did some real damage.

"Don't be ridiculous. Honestly, on the eyes of our children, there's no one else. *You're* my girl."

"Really?"

"Always."

Alice grabbed me, squeezing so hard I thought she might pop a lung. Hugging her back, I began smoothing her shoulder as she sobbed. Talking her down, I tried explaining why I needed some time alone after the stress I'd been under, and she seemed somewhat placated, saying she understood. Telling her about the conversation with Toby she threw her head back, hooting, wiping away her tears as she continued laughing.

"Well, I told you I'd dob you in it if they ever found out," she admitted, dabbing her eyes with a tissue.

"I know and I'm so glad that you're a woman of your word."

"See, you don't know how *lucky* you are," she chuckled. "Anyway, I told Toby that I was an unwilling accomplice to your emotional torture and psychological abuse."

Although I knew Alice was joking, hearing the term psychological abuse reignited a genuine question I'd asked myself earlier regarding my suitability as a parent. I'd been prepared to repeatedly upset and frustrate my own children, rather than try and entertain or distract them and it was easy to see where Jack got his inspiration from. *Does that make me a bad father and a poor role model?* There seemed to be a mounting orgy of clear evidence that pointed to me being a bad person and Alice obviously hadn't felt like putting me in a favourable light after neglecting and abandoning her for most of the day. *I've brought this all upon myself.*

Admittedly, I'd been more than a little self-indulgent with my time today and my plan to have a bit more practice before tomorrow's trip could easily result in divorce or at least a visit to casualty. Instead, I offered to take Alice out for dinner to make up for my *away day,* figuring that an intimate meal for two would make everything better or at least limit the bruising.

"We should be able to accommodate you, sir..." The restaurant manager said, pausing, "I do have a semi-private function booked from six but just let me check for you... yes, we have one spare table for two available aaat *seven.*"

"Perfect."

"What's the name?"

"Alder."

"Okay Mr. Alder, we'll see you at seven."

*Excellent, dinner at 7:00. We should be back by 9:00, I'll still have time to hit some practice balls in the garden.*

# CHAPTER 49

## When You Say Nothing at All

I had been waiting in the lounge, alone with my troubled thoughts, since 6:15, spending the last half an hour listening to Alice spluttering and cursing as she got ready. When she came jiggling down the stairs, a buxom vision in tight blue jeans and an eye-popping, low-cut, frilly pink top, twenty minutes later than I'd planned, I could still hear her teeth grinding.

"There she is," *at last*, "my very own Botticelli," I said as Alice stepped into the lounge.

"Hmph," she sneered, "more like a jelly botty." *Oh great, here we go again.*

"Everything alright?"

"No! I just had a complete nightmare." I'd avoided going anywhere near the bedroom while she got dressed. The coughing, thumping, and swearing had clearly indicated that it should be treated as a 'Demaritalised Zone' and I'd never witnessed more accurate, effective, or devastating friendly fire than my wife's. I started having the horrible thought that somehow, this would end up being my fault.

"I was just putting my mascara on when I had a sneezing fit. When I looked in the mirror, I saw Alice Cooper staring back. Honestly, I looked like something from a Tim Burton movie. I'd have given you nightmares." *You mean more nightmares.*

The manager had squeezed us in at 7:00 and by my watch, it was 6:45, so we really needed to get going. If I hadn't been in such a rush, I might have chosen my words more carefully.

"Well, I don't think you look *that* bad my love," I offered with a great deal of sincerity and support, "anyway, it's dark now and when we get to the restaurant I'll see if they can put us in a corner."

"……" Alice replied furiously.

She gave me a look that could have split stone. Sometimes, Alice asked for my opinion because, like any woman, she needed the reassurance that she looked good, and just wanted some form of acknowledgement from me for the effort she'd made. However, when she didn't directly ask for my opinion, I could avoid any chance of hostilities by saying nothing at all.

"*What's wrong?*" I gulped.

"What's wrong? *What's wrong you shit?*" she snapped. "I said I *had* a sneezing fit, and I *looked* a fright. Past tense. *Past tense!* I wiped my mascara off and started again. That's why I'm a *tiny* bit late." *Tiny!* I bit my tongue.

"This…" Alice continued, circling a bright and rather frightening red fingernail around her face "…is how it's *supposed* to look."

"Oh," I replied sheepishly, checking to see what colour shoes I had on, "I er, I, um… you look *lovely*."

"Just get in the car and don't speak to me again until you've got a wine list in your hand."

"Mmhum," I nodded pathetically as she stormed out of the room.

## CHAPTER 50

### Cold As Ice

To describe the atmosphere as icy would be an understatement. Polar bears in winceyette pyjamas, woolly hats, and sheepskin slippers would have found it chilly. I thought that the evening couldn't get any worse and took Alice's instruction literally, avoiding eye contact and all forms of physical and verbal communication, concentrating on the road ahead.

Arriving at Bellamy's Brasserie, fifteen minutes late, Alice's mood had thawed a little to one degree above Arctic sunrise. Within seconds, the thermometer plummeted. The semi-private function turned out to be for a local rugby club whose members appeared to be several pints into a very convivial evening. Walking to our table, the jeers and comments were not subtle, turning the already self-conscious and frosty Alice into a volatile glacier.

"Would you like a glass of wine?" I asked meekly, chipping away at the frigid 'wifeberg' with a toffee hammer.

"No," she growled coldly, "I'd like a *whole bottle!*" *Well, if it's not chilled enough, you could just look at it.*

I ordered a bottle of Pinot Grigio, Alice necked the first glass and was draining her third when the starters arrived. She glowered, swinging her wine glass as she drummed her fingers, enjoying my discomfort, deliberately remaining silent, waiting for me to start the conversation. I clearly needed prompting.

"*So*, talk to me then," she demanded, crossing her legs as she sat back deliberately, taking another swig. My brain froze. For some bizarre reason, uncharacteristically, I had nothing to say. I just clammed up. She might as well have said 'be spontaneous.' As the pages of a thousand flickering thoughts blurred, the sudden noise of crockery hitting the floor threw a vivid image to the front of my mind. Two huge jet aircraft screamed across my vision, seconds from impact, then smashed into each other. *No. Get out!* I sat shaking my head, the echoing din from the kitchen generating drunken cheers and cries of 'sack the juggler.' Alice remained unmoved and sat staring, waiting, as the jeering died down.

"*Well?*" she said, cocking her head dramatically to one side, expressionless, as I struggled to provide an icebreaker. She looked about as stable as out-of-date gelignite and one wrong word could easily set her off. Leaning forward, Alice picked up a large prawn, placing it deliberately between her teeth. Looking me in the eye threateningly she chomped the tail clean off. *Help! What to say? Just say anything. Talk about, the um, the weather? No, shopping? No, idiot, definitely not shopping. Bad dog. Family? Yes, family, family was always a safe bet. Good boy. Phew.*

"Sophie's lost a lot of weight," I said, pulling the pin and rolling a conversational hand grenade across the table. Alice slammed her hand down, her eyes widening as her top lip began curling.

*Oh my God, she's going to kill me. Mayday! Mayday! Mayday!*

In my defence, Alice's younger sister, Sophie, *had* recently lost a lot of weight. I also knew that my wife claimed to be having her own body issues. 'Nothing fitted anymore,' and she 'looked hideous,' and she had 'an arse like a dray horse.' Sophie had always been her cute, chubby little sister, but recently had transformed into a curvaceous green-eyed stunner. Alice always suspected that I had a soft spot for her sweet, innocent, and much younger sibling. I didn't, not in that way. But I had to admit that if I'd had a spot for Sophie, it definitely wouldn't have been soft.

Alice stopped chewing and glared. Slowly raising her eyebrows at my opening gambit, she swallowed. Then she started choking.

"Are you okay?" I asked stupidly as she began gagging, her eyes suddenly bulging and watering as she pointed to her throat.

"Alice? Are you…" I stopped, seeing her face turning an aggressive shade of puce. *Shit!*

Rushing around the table, I sent a chair skidding across the wooden floor and began smacking Alice on the back. The food didn't budge, and she continued gasping. Grabbing her from behind, I clasped my hands in a double fist under her ribcage and began thrusting.

The first two attempts did nothing, and I could feel Alice beginning to wilt as she started to make horrible, strangled rasping noises. Squeezing my arms tighter, I pulled her limp body towards me.

"Come on, come on," I pleaded, pumping violently.

Alice felt like a giant ragdoll as she flopped in my arms. *No, please God no!*
In desperation, I set my jaw and summoning all my strength, pulled hard with an almighty, adrenaline-fuelled thrust.

As the ejected prawn went sailing across the restaurant, Alice did an impression of a turbo-powered leaf blower set to reverse, as she tried sucking in the entire room's supply of air. I thought the windows were about to implode. Awkwardly, as the partially chewed crustacean popped out, so did Alice's left breast. Her strapless bra and the low-cut top had been gallantly trying to contain her large boobs, but when Alice went floppy, one side must have been defeated by a combination of my vigorous thrusts, critically stressed elastic, and gravity.

Standing up, gorging herself on air, the crimson-faced Alice found herself immersed in an eruption of hoots, catcalls, and clapping. Unaware and bathing in the attention, I smiled, holding up my hand, waving and nodding appreciatively to the cheering diners, wrongly assuming that they were applauding me after my successful Heimlich Manoeuvre. Turning to look at Alice, I saw the real reason behind their enthusiastic cheering. We didn't stay for dessert.

Overwhelmed with embarrassment, Alice clutched her chest and grabbed her coat, fleeing from the restaurant, closely followed by me. Apologising to the waitress as I left, I slammed two £20 notes down on the table before running after my mortified wife.

Reaching the car, I found Alice panting and frothing with rage, she appeared to be battling with conflicting emotions.

"*Oh my God Henry!*"

"Are you okay my love?"

"No, I am far from okay. Not quite the date night I was hoping for."

"I know. I'm really sorry."

"First you disappear for the entire day, you ignore my phone calls, make a thoughtless comment about my make-up as we're about to walk out of the door and your idea of a conversation starter is to tell me that I'm fatter than my little sister." *What phone calls? And that is not what I said.*

"Not exactly a romantic evening is it, getting my boobs out in a restaurant full of pissed-up footballers?"

"Boob actually and I think they were rugby pl…" Alice's widening eyes cut me off, her terrifying glare intensifying, "…nothing, you were saying."

"I nearly choked."

"I know, I know," I muttered sheepishly, continuing to study the dust cap on the driver's side front tyre.

"*Aargh*," she growled, stamping the floor, "I don't know what to feel. You practically saved my life, but… Oh my God, that was so humiliating. I don't know whether to kiss you or punch you in the bollocks."

"I like the first one."

Unfortunately, she chose the latter.

# CHAPTER 51

## Should I Stay or Should I Go

Alice stormed off to bed as soon as we got home. From the faint clicking sounds coming from below the bedroom window, she probably thought I was just dicking about in the dark. I really didn't want to be spending our last night together with me standing in the garden, freezing my nuts off at nine o'clock in the evening, trying to chip plastic golf balls into a flowerpot by moonlight. I would rather have been tucked up in bed with my warm-bodied wife, but I thought it would be safer to stay away. Not just because she probably wanted to finish her boxercise class, but because I had a genuine fear that I might kill her. I didn't plan to wait until she fell asleep then sneak into the bedroom and smash her over the head with a 1-iron. What a ridiculous notion. I could never do that, I'd choose a 5-wood, I couldn't hit a thing with a 1-iron.

In truth, I felt that death had been stalking me for days, nipping at my heels, edging nearer with each passing hour. Shooting the Gap had been close, the two attempts on Gypsy had been progressively closer, but tonight Alice nearly choked to death. The thought of losing her terrified me. I felt indescribably mad at myself. I'd said something stupid and nearly killed my wife. And not forgetting of course that I'd actually planned to kill the cat. *What is wrong with me?* I genuinely preferred the company of animals to most people. Admittedly, Lucky might have been an exception, but the thought of chopping him up with my Flymo… I'd expect to see that kind of sick stuff in a really nasty horror movie. It certainly didn't belong inside my normally sane head. I suddenly felt horribly sick at the thought that, despite being distraught after nearly killing hundreds of people, the next minute I'd been planning to take a life. A cat's life, but a life, nonetheless. Had that really happened, or had my poor stressed mind been playing tricks on me? I couldn't be certain I hadn't imagined the whole thing. *At this rate, I'll be spending time in a secure room weaving baskets or rubbing shoulders with the inmates of Strangeways.*

I studied the newly cropped lawn; it had definitely been cut but I couldn't believe the mess I'd made and the number of patches I'd missed. I must have been distracted, thinking about dispatching Lucky. Thank God I'd concentrated when I'd driven the boys back to St. John's and delivered them into the safety of their school in one piece, distancing them from my potentially fatal reach. *Maybe I should ring Danny and call off the trip. Even his good luck must have its limits. Perhaps it would be safer for everyone if I just disappeared altogether.*

Click... click... click...

I swung the club listlessly, staring at the same patch of chewed grass. Hitting the hollow white balls absentmindedly, my mind clouded in a sinister dark swirling fog as I continued tussling with my anxiety. *Am I really a Jonah or could this all be nothing more than a run of bad luck? Maybe getting away will break the spell. I really don't know.* I began wondering if a couple of days of playing golf might stop me from having despicable murderous thoughts and help me get back to being the old me. I desperately hoped so. The one thing I knew for sure, my eyelids felt heavy, and my body ached with cold. I needed my bed.

## CHAPTER 52

### Smells Like Teen Spirit

Around ten o'clock I climbed under the covers and surprisingly, the disgruntled Alice hadn't succumbed to sleep. Instead, she lay awake on her side rubbing the insubordinate dog's belly. I probably deserved worse than a punch in the bollocks. Any fair, balanced, and unbiased jury of twelve divorced feminists would have found Alice 'not guilty by means of neglect' if she'd decided to wait up, with malice aforethought, and set about me with a meat cleaver.

I picked up the October edition of Golf Monthly I'd purchased earlier and began flicking through the pages, stopping at the article I'd been searching for, 'The Majesty of Scotland.' Alice watched me, then huffing, stopped smoothing Gypsy, and turned her back. Snatching her Kindle from her nightstand she thumped into her pillow.

I had been so engrossed in the article about golf in the Highlands I didn't notice the gentle rocking motion next to me, but I couldn't ignore the progressively louder, disgusting noises.

Slurp, slurp, slurp.

Gypsy sat bent double, engrossed.

"*Stop that!*" I commanded, prodding her shoulder.

"Oh God, that's *enough*!" I ranted, jabbing her again. She eagerly carried on.

"Oh, leave her alone she's just keeping it fresh," Alice growled, spinning around to defend her dog.

"I don't care, it's disgusting. Does she really have to muck out now? And she shouldn't even be on our bed?"

"Just be grateful that she keeps herself clean," Alice grumbled, turning to the industrious pooch. "You're just keeping yourself clean, aren't you girl?" she cooed. "Such a *good* girl, *ye-es*, keeping yourself clean like that. Just ignore the horrid grumpy man." Gypsy ignored both of us and continued slurping.

"Well thank God we don't have to do that."

"*Really!* You always have to take it too far, don't you? I didn't want to go to sleep with that disgusting image in my head but thank you *husband*," Alice snarled, turning her back again.

"Sorry," I began, "besides, you'd probably have to give her a biscuit first before she'd let you."

Honestly, I think she cracked a rib.

Deciding that, in the interests of self-preservation, sleep might be my best option and, nursing my side, I got out of bed. Picking up the magazine, I headed for the spare room, planning to pack it with the rest of my golf gear before calling it a night. Walking along the landing I caught Lucky sneaking out. We froze, eyes locked. Staring at one another with the intense glare of duelling gunslingers, I rolled my shoulders back, preparing to draw.

"What are you up to?" was what I planned to say but I only got as far as 'Wh' before he bolted past me and went scampering down the stairs. I was certain that I heard 'ha ha' as he shot through the cat flap. I unzipped the inner compartment of my rucksack, slid the magazine inside, and began sniffing. *What was that smell?* We didn't use this room very often, perhaps it just smelled a bit, stale, and funky. *Mould again?* I looked up to see a faint bloom of green and black speckles starting to emerge through the recently repainted ceiling. *No, it doesn't smell like mould.* More likely the festering contents of the boys' cricket bags, a long-forgotten pork pie, a dirty set of whites, or maybe a sticky unwashed cricket box. The little buggers could be practically feral at times.

## CHAPTER 53

### Land of Confusion

I walked back into the bedroom and climbed into bed. Content that her undercarriage was sufficiently sanitised, Gypsy rolled onto her back, flopping her rock-hard head into my lap, and slapping me between the legs. I winced, suddenly aware of the weak dull ache in my testicles, a faint reminder that they had been used as a punch bag. 'Rocky' meanwhile had stopped reading and bolstered her pillow. Propping herself against the headboard, she sat up waiting, arms crossed, with an I-want-to-talk-to-you-even-though-you've-been-a-selfish-insensitive-shit face.

"All packed?" Alice asked.

"Ooof, yeah, just about," I replied, lifting the dog's head off my sore plums, "I need to throw my washbag and a few other bits in my suitcase, but I'm pretty much there. I am going to *miss you*, you know," I confessed, battling with feelings of guilt for leaving versus a desire to protect her with my absence. Alice leaned over, playfully prodding me in the side.

"Ow!"

"Sorry. I'll miss you too. Not that I'll notice, it'll be like replaying today twice over," she said with a half-hearted smile. "Look, I don't want to be a nag, but when you get back do you think you could try and help out with a few more jobs around the house?"

"Okay. What sort of things, besides cutting the grass?"

"Well, that would be a start."

"Okay. I can cut it again when it needs doing, what else?" I asked. Alice's face wrinkled with confusion.

"What do you mean *again*?"

"I'll do it *again* when it needs cutting," I replied flatly and somewhat irritated.

"*Really?*"

"*Yes, really!*"

"Are you trying to be funny?"

"No. Why?"

"*I* cut the bloody grass!" she blurted, looking as confused as I suddenly felt.

"When?"

"Today." *Today? What? I thought I'd done it.*

"Are you joking?"

"No. When you eventually came home, *five hours* after you left for a *two-hour* shopping spree, you said you'd cut the grass then stomped off upstairs in a huff. I was in the lounge expecting to see you appear any minute chucking the mower around, but you never did. I came upstairs and heard you snoring before I got to the landing. You were in such a shitty mood I left you to sleep."

"But what about Gypsy going through the cat flap?" I asked, worrying that I might be on the verge of a psychotic break.

"What *are* you talking about? She was snoozing all afternoon. Well, until you rustled her treat bag and slinked off to do your Greta Garbo, *I want to be alone* thing," she sniped. My mind gave a huge sigh.

"So that's why it's such a mess," I muttered.

*"What?"* Alice snarled.

"Er… I… I said thank you for letting me rest." *Phew, well done.*

"Hmm, really? Well, it's all yours from now on Alan Titchmarsh."

*Oh, thank God, halleflippinlujah. The pile of clean folded clothes, the badly cut lawn, the talking dog, it all made sense now.* I could have cried. *I can stop beating myself up about my plan and failed attempt to Magimix the cat too. Obviously, I don't have it in me to kill Lucky after all. No, obviously I only try to kill people.*

193

"Are you okay?" she asked.

"Yes, sorry… I'm fine. I was just having a moment."

"You will be careful, won't you?" Alice asked earnestly, returning to the matter of my imminent trip, her tone noticeably softer and pleading.

"It's golf in Scotland, my love, I'm not going to Pamplona for the running of the bulls!" I joked as waves of reassurance continued to wash over my relieved mind.

"Oh, I know, it's worse, you're going away with Danny. You know what happens when you two get together."

"I have no idea what you mean?" I lied sarcastically, drawing a halo above my head, and pressing my hands together in prayer.

"Hmph," Alice replied, rolling her eyes. "Just be careful, *please*," she implored.

"With my luck what could *possibly* go wrong?" I answered affably, leaning over and kissing her goodnight while ignoring the little voice in my head that kept excitedly putting its hand up shouting *Ooh, ooh, I know, I know, ask me, ask me.*


## CHAPTER 54

### Don't Stop Believing

As much as Alice liked Danny, who was the only person I knew who ever got away with addressing her as Ali, she'd always considered him to be a bad influence. Well, not really a *bad* influence, not even a bad lad, naughty would have been a better description, or mildly delinquent. Although she encouraged our friendship, Alice said she lived in constant fear that whenever Danny and I got together, I'd end up completely penniless in a casino or drunk and broke in a strip club and would ultimately wind up in a police cell or possibly on a mortuary slab. She said it wouldn't have been a surprise to turn on the television and hear our names in a Sky Newsflash report of a hostage situation or watch shaky footage of our two figures being winched into a Search and Rescue helicopter from a stricken stolen speedboat.

Although I'd shared most of the stories about the scrapes Danny had gotten me into, I had never told Alice the whole truth about what *really* happened the night I bumped into him. I had the feeling that she always suspected there was more to the version I'd given her, about how the two of us made the Northeast of Scotland think that RAF Lossiemouth was under attack from the Provisional IRA. Besides, she'd read the story headlined, "RAF Stupidity Hits New Heights," in the local morning paper.

Within months of meeting, I realised that Danny had Lady Luck firmly on his side. By comparison, I always felt that she was taking a permanent sabbatical or had gone into a witness protection programme the second I'd been born. The charmer constantly got away with murder, everyone liked him, and he had the uncanny knack, that no matter how deep the trouble he appeared to be sinking into, he would always rise smelling of roses. I, on the other hand, tended to come up covered in something hot, brown and steaming. It had always been this way from the moment we first met.

## CHAPTER 55

### Rocket Man

On the same day that children across the country were ripping open the first window on their 1993 advent calendars, I arrived at the gates of Royal Air Force Lossiemouth, an RAF airfield near Elgin in the north of Scotland. Situated about forty miles northeast of Inverness, 'Lossie' was home to the few remaining specimens of the maritime strike Blackburn Buccaneer and its shiny new replacement, the Panavia Tornado GR1B.

Almost six months later, on a Thursday night at the end of May, a series of events and circumstances collided to bring about an incident that would be reported on BBC Scotland news, make headlines in The Inverness Courier and Forres Gazette, and even attracted a small column on the front page of The Scotsman. Most importantly, it marked the beginning of a firm friendship.

The recently arrived 617 Tornado Squadron, the famous Dambusters, was hosting a dining-in night and although not a squadron member, I had been invited as the Squadron Liaison Officer from Air Traffic Control. The newly arrived Danny had spent a few winters allegedly teaching the squadron boss's daughter 'how to ski' and had been invited as a last-minute hanger-on. The event had been like any other dining-in night with amazing food, free-flowing drink, and a venerable, World War II guest speaker. The elderly Dambusters' pilot had enthralled the attentive diners, regaling them with tales of derring-do, from the view of one who'd actually flown wartime missions in the Avro Lancaster four-engine strategic bomber.

After sinking several beers, a few glasses of wine, and half a bottle of port I kept falling forward with my eyes closed, bouncing my head off the table before climbing back skywards where I soared briefly before stalling and dropping again, to make another pass.

Staggering my way to the bar, long after the loyal toast, I stumbled sideways into a small huddle of pilots and navigators positioned near the hatch. I nudged one man's elbow, spilling his beer.

"Oopsy, excuuuse me," I slurred apologetically to an unfamiliar face.

"No worries fella. You okay?" asked the stranger, moving his pint glass into his left hand and flicking the spilled beer from his right.

"I'm bloody marrrvelous and poss'bly a bit pissed. Sorry 'bout that," I said, pointing to his dripping fingers, "can I getchew another?"

"I don't take drinks from strangers, so best we get acquainted. I'm Danny," he smiled, extending his wet right hand.

"Henry, Henry Alder. Pleas'd t'meet you, Danny. Just arrived?" I enquired still gripping and shaking vigorously, well past the length of a normal handshake.

"Yes fella, I got here yesterday but I don't officially start until Monday," Danny said, reclaiming his hand.

"Where, 617?" I asked, assuming that Danny had been posted to the Dambuster squadron.

"No mate, Air Traffic."

"Me tooo," I squeaked, "well bugger me!"

"Only if you buy me that drink first."

Taking a little longer than usual for the joke to filter through to my pickled brain, eventually, I laughed. Even in my alcohol-induced state, I warmed to him, knowing instinctively that Danny and I would become friends.

Introducing myself to the others, Danny and I re-joined the group and we happily carried on chatting and drinking. The night seemed to be rolling along quite merrily and, up to this point, had been unusually humdrum. It would have remained that way too if Jamie Mason, one of the pilots in our group, hadn't announced that, as far as dining in nights went, this one was rather boring.

"It's nearly midnight, what did you have in mind fella?" asked Danny.

"I don't know. It's pretty lame, just something to make the evening go with a bang," sighed Jamie. I noticed Danny's eyes light up with a puckish expression that I would soon learn to love and fear.

"Funnily enough, I might have just the thing," he grinned. "Can you get onto the mess roof?" *Why on earth would he want to go clambering around on the mess roof in the dark?*

"Yeah ye'can, but whyyy?" I slurred, looking at him quizzically.

"Jamie, do you know how to get to it?" Danny asked. Jamie nodded.

"Right, we'll meet you up there. Henry, are you feeling strong?" Danny asked.

"Like 'n ox," I slurred.

"Okay fella, you come with me. It's time to have some fun boys," he winked.

Minutes later, shuffling across the car park with our booty, we headed towards the side door, listening to the dull thuds, boisterous yelling, and occasional crack of breaking furniture, signalling that a bloody game of gladiatorial mess rugby had started in the Ante Room.

Lugging a rough wooden crate backwards, up two twisting flights of back stairs was not my idea of fun, and I realised that ox might have been a bit of an exaggeration.

"Stostostop, putddit down again," I panted, clunking my end onto the stairs for the third time.

"Come on fella, you can do this, we're nearly there and I've got all the weight," Danny said encouragingly, resting the box on his bent knee. The git hadn't even broken a sweat.

"I know but I've got a hurty hand, look it'sa mahoosive splinter," I whined, thrusting my hand towards Danny.

"Fella I can only just see your fingers from here, come on."

"Oh. Well, take my word f'rit, it's mahoosive." Holding my hand under my nose I began pawing at the large shard of wood sticking out of my palm.

"*Goddit*," I sang triumphantly, dropping onto my haunches to grab the box again.

Banging our way through the double doors into the corridor, I trundled backwards and then hoisted my end of the massive rectangular box onto the windowsill.

"Here, grab this," Danny grunted, lifting, and shoving the box through the open window. Jamie and one of the other guys rushed over, guiding it through as I leant against the wall puffing. Carefully they lowered the huge container onto the roof. Danny followed gently dropping onto his feet. Then me, who for some reason thought headfirst would be a good idea. Bracing my thighs against the thick wooden frame, I tried easing myself down until my legs gave out. Falling face down, I tucked my head under, managing to perform some sort of forward roll, ending up sitting, looking at the other five who looked back shaking their heads. Danny walked over, helping me to my unsteady feet before turning his attention back to the large wooden crate. Gathering around the box, on the flat roof space about thirty feet below the level of the impressive red brick building's twin-pitched roof, we all started shuffling closer.

"Welcome to the House of Fun," Danny said with a flourish, unclipping two catches and opening the lid. We all gasped and stood gawping at the treasures within.

"Where the *hell* did you get those?" asked the wide-eyed Jamie.

"I met a bloke in a pub near Thetford who does professional displays. He'd imported a load from China for a 4th of July party he's doing for the Yanks at Lakenheath."

"What, and he just gave them to you?"

"No, I just bought him a drink and talked him into letting me buy some off him, at cost," Danny winked.

Walking across the car park towards Danny's car, he'd told me that he had a 'couple of little fireworks in the boot' but now, when I actually saw the size of them, despite being three sheets to the wind, my eyes almost popped out of my head.

"Jeez Danny, don'chew need a licence for thuz things?" I asked with concern.

"Well, um, yeah, kind of. Don't worry, it'll be fine, what's the worst that could happen?" he shrugged.

"How many have you got?" Jamie asked.

"Two dozen," Danny beamed proudly.

"Havenchewgotta stick 'em in the ground?" Strangely, I was having a moment of clarity, thinking I'd stumbled on a major obstacle that would prevent them from being launched.

"Normally you do," Danny replied, "I've got the launch tubes in the boot but this way's much more fun."

"What way's that?" asked Jamie.

"Just watch," said Danny, kneeling down and starting preparations for blast-off.

Untwisting the wire that locked the two halves of each firework's individual metal cage, he pulled the framework apart, revealing the head that resembled a large, pointed beer can. Sitting at the base I could see a bright red plastic cap covering a fuse; he pulled it off and then, with two hands, lifted out the giant firework. The thick, hinged launch stick was last and when unfolded looked to be about five feet in length.

"Here goes," Danny said, removing a long packet from inside the box. Tearing it open, he removed a book of matches and a long rod resembling a giant incense stick. He struck a match, holding the flame to the top of the taper until it started burning, then touched the glowing tip to the exposed fuse and waited. I wavered, pondering whether this might be illegal, or at the very least a bit naughty. Acting like a bunch of impish schoolboys, we must have all felt too giddy to stop and consider the consequences, and at that moment, the RAF's well-honed principles of officers acting responsibly and with sound judgement went up in smoke.

Only a few seconds passed before we heard crackling and hissing, as small bursts of spitting white sparks started lighting up our eager faces. Extending both arms, Danny held the huge rocket by the bottom of the launch stick. Silently we all stood, watching, waiting, spellbound. The fuse seemed to be taking forever to burn and then… *WHOOSH!*

With a loud fizz, the rocket's fuel ignited, illuminating Danny with bright spraying sparks, as it went shooting from his hand, screaming vertically into the clear, starry sky. It screeched, hurtling away from the launch site, leaving a streaming white trail and a moment of complete silence before, KABOOM! Cheering erupted as the rocket exploded, lighting the night sky, and shattering into a thousand shards of glittering blue light.

"*Awesome*," Jamie shouted, hopping excitedly from one foot to the other before turning to Danny.

"Let's have a go," he pleaded over the sound of the hooting and hollering. Grabbing another titan from the box, Danny handed it over, grinning. Leaning forward, he lit the fuse that caught immediately and started hissing.

Attempting to go one better, Jamie stood snorting manfully, determined to launch his rocket one-handed. He started trembling. Even I could see from his contorting face that he was struggling to keep a firm grip as the long fuse continued burning. As the hand of the unstoppable countdown approached zero, the rocket began drooping, and realising that he was losing control, Jamie tried bringing his other hand up, but too late. The rocket went shooting off at forty-five degrees. Just clearing the mess roof, it went sailing on a perfect arc over the main gate before detonating above the Guardroom.

Another round of cheering rose, echoing around the rooftops of the Officers' Mess.

"Right, 'smy turn," I said, presenting myself in front of Danny. "Fewzleer Alder reportin' for rocket jewty *sah!*" I saluted, snapping my heels together and wobbling slightly.

"Go on then you silly bugger," said Danny unwisely, handing me the largest of the colossal fireworks. Proudly holding the monster in both hands at arms' length, I inadvertently pointed it directly at Danny's face.

"Keep a tight hold of it fella," he instructed, before picking up the taper and moving it towards the base of the rocket. Touching the glowing tip against the exposed fuse until it caught, he then grabbed my wrists, angling them up so that the rocket stood vertically. I assumed he felt reasonably confident that I had control of it and grasping my shoulders, he locked me in place before standing back. "Now, just hold it there," he ordered with a wink.

A strange rising and falling warbling sound began filling the still night air. Everyone stopped jabbering, holding their breath, and straining to listen.

"That's weird," said Jamie, "isn't that… yeah… it sounds like the air raid warning siren." After about five seconds the wailing faded as a frantic voice erupted from the station Tannoy system.

*"Standby for broadcast, standby for broadcast from the main guardroom. The station is under attack. All personnel are to take cover. I say again, the station is under attack. All personnel are to take cover."*

As the echoing message died, we stood still on the rooftop, immersed in an interminable surreal silence, apart from the fizzing of a monster unlicensed pyrotechnic. Exchanging puzzled glances, the rest of the party looked like they were trying to comprehend what we'd just heard when suddenly, a collective light bulb came on.

"Oh fuck!" said Jamie and immediately they all appeared to understand *exactly* what was happening and started scrambling towards the open window.

*"Henry, leg it!"* Danny shouted, turning to join the growing, panicked fumble of grappling bodies.

"So pretty," I purred, ignoring him, looking up like a grinning idiot, hypnotised by the dazzling shower of yellow sparks above my head.

In the ensuing melee, I was knocked sideways, cracked my skull, and being too dazed to get back up, lay on the roof semi-conscious. While bravely running away, the other five would have heard the unmistakable whoosh of a professional firework display rocket going off, that a moment before they'd left in the care of an untrained pissed amateur.

The rocket fired near my head, burning my scalp, its screams drowning out mine as it began shooting around the rooftops like a scalded cat. Whizzing and deflecting off the brickwork at sharp angles, the screeching, sparking projectile glanced off a chimney stack and fishtailed along the flat roof, bouncing, skidding, and narrowly missing my face, before whipping away and taking off again, ricocheting off a piece of guttering and smashing through a senior officer's en suite bathroom window. Hitting the toilet door, it detonated in a huge ear-splitting explosion, blowing out the remaining windows and setting fire to a small pyramid of toilet rolls and a blue quilted smoking jacket.

Weeks later, I discovered that in the subsequent panic-filled minutes, several things happened. Jamie heard the bang and then saw smoke coming from under the bedroom door. He had the presence of mind to hit the fire alarm and called the Station Fire Service but in the confusion, no one in the Officers' Mess knew what protocol to follow during a terrorist attack when the building they were taking shelter in was on fire. A whole building full of RAF officers, yet not a single one could decide if they were supposed to risk burning to death to avoid the threat from IRA mortars or leave the burning building and take their chances with flying shrapnel. Meanwhile, Danny had grabbed a fire extinguisher, smashed the bedroom door in, and single-handedly managed to put out the blaze started by the burning loo rolls. Ironically, he received a Station Commander's commendation for his presence of mind and bravery.

In no time, anyone within five miles of RAF Lossiemouth could hear the wailing of sirens, as blue flashing lights washed over the station's roads, hedgerows, and buildings. Absolute bedlam reigned for several hours before a continuous high-pitched wail began signalling the ALL CLEAR, allowing people back into the mess. Members of Scotland's Counter Terrorism Unit and the RAF Police had questioned several officers, including Jamie and Danny, who at that point had no idea what had happened to the rest of the group, including me. I hadn't moved, I was still lying on the roof with a large bump on my head and a singed bald patch, oblivious to the commotion, snoring loudly in a state of severe inebriation with a mild concussion. Danny was still explaining his story to the Station Provost Officer and within earshot when a witness interrupted, beckoning the senior policeman to one side to report what he'd seen.

"Excuse me, sir, but it wasn't mortars, it was fireworks and I know who set them off."

"What do you mean *fireworks* lad?" asked the Provost Officer.

"Rockets sir, they're in a box up on the flat roof of the mess and so's the guilty party sir. I think he's very drunk sir and asleep."

"Who is?"

"Henry Alder sir, he's an air trafficker, I work with him."

"You'd better show me then, um, what's your name."

"My name sir, oh yes, sorry sir, it's Koch sir, Pilot Officer Timothy Koch."

Even though Danny, Jamie, and I had been the main culprits, I took full responsibility. The others wanted to come forward, but I insisted that as I'd been stupid enough to get caught red-handed, I couldn't see any point in everyone else getting into trouble. Initially, the Station Commander grounded the entire Tornado squadron but after I'd taken the fall, they had been back screaming low level across the white-capped waters of the Moray Firth that same afternoon. I never bought another drink if there was a 617 Squadron member in the bar after that. Danny said he felt terrible, but I refused to let him own up. I said he'd just have to owe me a favour, a very big favour.

The incident could have resulted in a court martial. At any other time, an impromptu firework display might have been put down to high jinks or at worst resulted in a smack on the wrists, but the whole country had seen the news reports of the IRA attacks, and all military bases been placed on a heightened alert state. I might have only been a flying officer but I should have known better and hoped that it wouldn't seriously impact my career prospects.

Reporting to Strike Command Headquarters, I had my future read to me, during a delightful one-way chat, also known as 'an interview without coffee', with an angrily moustached, ex-Buccaneer Air Commodore. While giving me a world-class bollocking, his whole head changed colour to an impressive hint of maroon.

"Are you trying to have the shortest career in the history of the Royal Air Force, Alder?" the Deputy AOC roared, loud enough that he could have drowned out the noise from the Rolls-Royce Spey engines of the old jet he'd piloted.

"No, sir," I muttered with trembling lips.

"No sir, no sir, three bags bloody full, sir, you senseless brain-dead cretinous oaf. I wouldn't expect this sort of idiotic behaviour and buffoonery from a lobotomised airman, no matter a commissioned officer. If I had my way, I'd have you strung up, shot at dawn, or at least publicly flogged, but I'm not allowed. I asked the Chief of the Air Staff but sadly he said no. Lunacy, this is utter bloody lunacy."

I wasn't sure if the 'lunacy' referred to the denial of his request for corporal punishment, his eccentric rant, or my unauthorised firework display. I thought it best not to ask, or at least wait until he'd finished raging and turned back to a normal colour.

"… and if you ever darken my door again, young man, I'm going to see to it that you spend the rest of your career stuck in the bleakest, wettest, nastiest, most inhospitable, and miserable place on God's green earth."

I thought that was a bit harsh, I quite liked Anglesey.

## CHAPTER 56
### Wind of Change

Alice jabbed me awake.

"Ow, huh, what?"

"Your phone," she said, pointing to my nightstand.

Blearily scrunching up my eyes, I waited until they focused, allowing me to see that Danny had sent a text message detailing the plan for our trip.

'0730 pick up. Flying SOU to EDN, Perth 2 nights. Bring golf gear, best drinking trousers, and smile (if you can't find I have spares). Always said I'd owe you one, well this is it, the whole trip is on me, no arguments!' He ended the message with emojis of an exploding firework and a wink. Placing my phone back down I felt a warm glow flooding through my body. *Fantastic, maybe my luck's changing after all.*

## CHAPTER 57

### I'm So Excited

The alarm's rhythmical strumming started at six and I woke groggily to discover that I'd

had a nosebleed during the night. I remembered deliberately lying face down before I fell

asleep, but must have woken Alice with my snoring, *again*. She said sharing a bed with me

was like sleeping next to a corpse fitted with a six-litre diesel tractor engine being

repeatedly cold-started on a frosty morning. I imagine, at some point, I must have rolled

onto my back and, as my soft palate had started to rumble, she'd instinctively tried

whacking my pillow to make me stop. In her stupor, she obviously hadn't realised that she'd

fallen asleep with her e-reader in her hand and must have flung her arm across the bed,

smashing me squarely in the face with her Kindle. As I tried lifting my head, the pillow

came with it. With a soft ripping sound, I gently unpeeled my face from the bloodstained

cotton cover, then peeled the pillowcase from the pillow, throwing it in the laundry basket.

Lumbering into the bathroom I looked in the mirror to discover a nose encrusted with

reddish-brown flakes. *God, I look tired.* I felt it too, I'd hardly slept. I'd been so excited by

the message from Danny I had lain awake, mentally checking off what I'd packed then

started playing out the coming days. Then I'd started feeling guilty, revisiting the week's

events, work, the money situation, and last night's frightening date with disaster. When I

eventually dropped off, my disturbed mind had insisted on treating me to a reel of crazy

dreams that had centred around golf, homicidal prawns, and Alice using my dangling

scrotum like a boxer's speed bag.

My bladder gave me a polite nudge that I acknowledged with indifference; that

deceitful troublemaker had an extremely long way to go before I'd be allowing him back into my circle of trust. Relieved, I washed my hands, rubbing away the cracked, rusty red stain on my weary cheeks. Noticing my bulging washbag, a smile crept across my face. *Two days' golf with Danny. I can't wait.* I bounced back into the bedroom, eagerly jumping into my dog-walking clothes. I wouldn't be seeing Gypsy for a few days and felt like treating her to a good long walk before I left. It also meant I could give Alice the luxury of a lie-in.

## CHAPTER 58

### Don't You (Forget About Me)

After a lengthy, slightly chilly, but thankfully event-free stroll, we returned. I fed Gypsy before showering and changing. Sitting waiting in the kitchen, I kept anxiously checking my watch, sharing some toast and a cup of coffee with Alice.

"How do you feel this morning?" I asked, last night's choking incident still painfully fresh in my mind.

"Well, my ribs are a bit sore but it's a small price to pay when you consider the alternative."

"Don't say that. You really frightened me last night. I honestly thought you were going to…" the final word stuck in my throat, the sudden ache in my heart stopping me from saying it out loud, "…I'm just glad you're okay."

"Well, it was certainly memorable. I can't remember the last time you took me out for dinner, grabbed me from behind, and got my tits out."

"That's not funny. Besides, I think you'll find it was only one."

"Sorry, *tit!*" Alice tutted.

"How can you joke about it? It really upset me. Are you sure you're, okay?"

"Apart from my ribs, I'm fine. It frightened me too but look. *Ta-dah!*" Alice exclaimed leaping up from the table. Jumping into a star-shaped pose in the middle of the kitchen she began twirling on the lino floor in her pyjamas and furry leopard print slippers, bursting into a short rendition of Elton John's, 'I'm Still Standing.'

"...*yeah, yeah, yeah.*"

"You're a nutter." I smiled through the pain, watching her jump around singing. She made my heart leap, reminding me how much I loved her while at the same time feeling that I'd come horribly close to waking up a widower.

"I know but I'm *your* nutter," she beamed, rejoining me at the breakfast table, "Mwah" and kissing the top of my head. "I am sorry though. I do feel bad about smacking you in the goolies. I hope I didn't break anything."

"Well, you might want to check your Kindle. I think you tried to kill me with it last night."

"What?"

"I'm pretty sure I snored, and you smacked me in the face with it. I think you tried hitting my pillow but luckily my nose got in the way!"

"Oops."

"Anyway, it's not broken, and thankfully neither are my balls. If you're a good girl, I'll let you give them a test drive when I get home. Just to be sure."

"Ah, thank you. That's *so* romantic. At least it'll give me a chance to calibrate my egg timer."

"Ha ha. You're on form this morning. You're very quick aren't you."

"No, my love. You're the expert in that department!" I tried changing the subject.

"Well, Danny should be here in about twenty minutes," I said, checking my watch again.

"Well, I hope you've brushed your teeth and have matching underwear on."

"What? Why?"

"Because you're fidgeting like you're about to go on a first date."

"I'm just excited about going away. I can't wait."

"Thanks very much."

"You know what I mean."

"Of course I do. I'm just glad that you can go and do something that you love for a couple of days. And not have to think about work. Even if it is with the least responsible person I know," she smiled. The corners of Alice's mouth dropped, her tone suddenly sounding earnest. "Go and enjoy yourself but *please* be careful and try to have some fun."

"Okay, okay. I promise."

"Which bit, the being careful or having fun?"

"Having fun of course. I can't make any promises about the other one. I'm going away with Oliver Reed's more delinquent twin!"

"Exactly. That's what worries me. Right…" she said, leaning across the table to kiss me, "I'm going back to bed, say hi to the Prince of Mischief for me, and *be careful*," Alice commanded, heading out of the kitchen, taking Gypsy with her.

"Love you," I said as she walked away.

"I love you too," she chimed. "Come on Gypsy, two days without the loud noisy, snoring man in our bed. *Yay!*"

# CHAPTER 59

## Shut Up and Drive

The lounge TV burst into life, not that loud but certainly loud enough to disturb Alice. I pushed the door shut with my foot while lunging at the coffee table. Desperately grabbing the remote, I violently prodded the minus button. Sitting for five minutes, I listened to the latest news, scanning the scrolling ticker tape. Still no reports about a near miss caused by an air traffic controller. Maybe the incident hadn't been newsworthy or hadn't filtered through, yet. Hopefully not the latter.

Sneaking upstairs, I went to collect my golf gear. Bending over, I noticed that smell again and looked accusingly at the boys' sports holdalls. *Hopefully, Alice will sort through that stinky lot while I'm away.* Picking up my luggage, I eased my way out of the funky spare room and began creeping back down with my golf bag carrier, small backpack, and suitcase. The loud creaking of the stairs faded, swallowed up by the familiar growl of Danny's BMW M3 pulling up outside. Tiptoeing back up the stairs, I snuck into the bedroom to say goodbye to my two special ladies.

"I love you girl," I whispered.

"Lub you too," mumbled Alice. I tried sneaking out of the room as quietly as possible in the hope that Alice didn't realise, I'd been talking to the dog.

Grabbing my bags, I slowly pulled the front door until it gently clicked behind me and stepped out of the porch. Lugging my gear along the path, I shuffled up the steps to the waiting car and the beaming Danny.

"Morning fella, are you ready for some fun?" Danny asked, dazzling me with his playful Colgate smile, taking the bags and loading them into the boot.

"Hell yes."

Slipping my jacket off I strapped in. Danny spotted my new golfing top.

"Wow, nice shirt, Liberace. Pink suits you."

"Poke off, it's salmon."

"No, it's pink Sweetie."

"Salmon!"

"Pink!"

"It's salmonnn," I insisted.

"And exactly what colour is a pink salmon?" He beamed triumphantly.

"God, I've missed you. Just shut up and drive smart arse," I grinned. Danny leaned forward, pressing a button on the sports car's dashboard. Above my head, a widening crack of daylight appeared, the roof lifting, arcing backwards, before lowering. After a few whirrs and clunks the car juddered as the roof clicked, locking into place.

"Please keep your arms and legs inside the ride at all times," Danny instructed lowering his mirrored Ray Bans, grinning at me as he repeatedly gunned the sports car's load, throaty engine.

"You're such a dick," I said, rolling my eyes. As the tyres squealed, my head jerked back, thumping my skull into the thick leather padding. Turning for a farewell glance at home, I noticed a familiar figure sitting on the porch roof. Lucky's head followed me as we went roaring up the road. I watched him lifting his front leg to lick his paw. I'm pretty sure he was simply cleaning it, but for a split second, it looked like he was poking his tongue out while giving me the finger.

# CHAPTER 60

## My Ding A Ling

Danny's handling of the back roads and narrow, high-banked country lanes reminded me of watching the boys on their PlayStation, skilfully evading the police with a car full of drugs and a loosely moralled, scantily clad stripper in the passenger seat. Maybe he thought this route would be more fun or he just wanted to show off. He looked irritatingly cool in his Top Gun shades, expertly manoeuvring the car around tight bends and the occasional hairpin as we flew through the sleepy villages of Boarhunt and Funtley. He hit long sweeping curves at such speeds that the car screamed onto the motorway, just outside Whiteley, in fewer than ten minutes. At legal speeds that journey would have taken me about twenty, my knuckles wouldn't have turned white, and I wouldn't have said three Hail Marys.

Once on the three-lane highway Danny began opening up the throttle and quickly had us cruising at a terrifying 135 MPH. I had never travelled this fast in a car and the roar of rushing cold air made it feel like we were in a wind tunnel. Feeling equally exhilarated and sick I kept checking my wing mirror for blue flashing lights. None appeared, of course, because *I* wasn't driving. Four minutes later we arrived, windswept and speeding fine free. Gliding onto Southampton Airport's service road we started following the signs for the long-stay car park.

The terror of the journey over, I felt tears pricking my eyes as my heart started swelling with nervous excitement. *This is really happening. I'm going to Scotland for two days of golf with my best mate.*

"Danny, I don't think you realise how much this trip means to me."

"Well, it's the least I can do after the amount of shit you've had to deal with this week," *I haven't just dealt with it, I've been doing lines of the stuff,* "and I promised you I'd pay you back for taking the blame for impersonating the IRA. I'm just sorry that it took so long."

"Don't be daft. You'd have done the same for me."

"I would, in a heartbeat, and Isaac would have happily stabbed me in the back too."

"Yeah, if he could reach."

"Ha."

"Well, it means a lot. You're a real lifesaver."

"You're welcome fella, and when you feel like talking, I'm all ears."

Danny put the roof up while I got the bags out. We jumped on the shuttle bus to the terminal, checking our bags in before heading towards Airport Security.

Danny, of course, walked straight through the metal detector without a hitch and stood waiting for me on the other side. After removing every possible metallic item, I could think of, I stepped into the rectangular steel frame. After my third try the red lights above my head started flashing again, accompanied by the irritating blare of the alarm.

"Raise your arms please, sir," ordered the unnervingly effeminate security guard, approaching me with a handheld device. Sweeping it across my shoulders, the back of my arms, lower back, backside, and legs the scanner remained silent. Moving to the front he swept it across my chest and abdomen before kneeling down. Passing the detector over my crotch it bleeped and started buzzing.

"Maybe it's your piercing, Henry. I told you to whip it out," Danny suggested unhelpfully.

"Ooh," said the guard in an overtly camp show of surprise.

"Not funny, Danny," I growled, shaking my head, suddenly feeling a flood of tingling warmth as my neck and face flushed and prickled.

"I didn't realise those things were so sensitive," Danny said to the theatrically wide-eyed and open-mouthed security guard. "I'm amazed that it picked up something that small."

I heard giggling coming from the growing line of passengers behind me and could feel myself getting hotter. Clenching my jaw, I shook my head, glaring at my 'best friend' who sadly, was about to be killed in a freak departure lounge accident.

"If it's not a personal question sir, do you have a..."

"*If it's not a personal question!*" I hissed through gritted teeth. "It's very... I mean... how much more personal could it be?" I stood blinking, open-mouthed.

"Piercings are quite common now you know. I come across about two Prince Alberts a day," the guard replied, winking conspiratorially at Danny. Rocking from side to side, I squirmed, tugging nervously at my collar as the laughter behind me kept growing. I would have felt more comfortable if I'd been getting a prostate exam from Captain Hook.

"Well, *I* don't have one!" I growled, my jaw locking even tighter as my eyes glared murderously at Danny. I was in the frame of mind to thump someone.

"Thank you, sir, probably just your zip and not a cock ring, have a nice trip."

"*For the last time, I haven't got a bloody...*" Walking away I continued shaking my head, relieved but still red-faced. Snatching my belongings from the X-ray tray I set off after my travel companion who waited, snorting, and clutching his ribs as he wiped his eyes with the back of his hand.

"That... wasn't... funny," I snarled, punctuating each word with a punch to Danny's upper arm.

"It was a bit," Danny sniggered, half cowering.

"I had visions of him giving me a full body cavity search," I added with a sense of relief, starting to see the funny side.

"You wish!"

# CHAPTER 61

## Up, Up and Away

The Flybe De Havilland Dash-8 lurched to a stop. I imagined the pilot pressing the balls of his feet firmly against the pedals, holding it in position, lined up ready for take-off. Easing the throttle levers forward, the twin turboprop engines strained against the brakes. The loud whining rose to a deafening thrum as he eased towards full power, causing the whole fuselage, me, and everyone inside it to start vibrating.

As the disc brakes released their grip, the plane leapt forward and began swaying rhythmically, accelerating down the runway's glistening tarmac. I rocked back gently, craning my neck to peer out of the cabin's small oval window as a blur of green and black went rushing past, then, with a gentle leap, the tyres lifted, and the ground fell away. We were heading for Scotland.

It felt like I was watching a stuttering movie reel of sinister light and dark grey images that kept swirling and twisting as the plane ploughed upwards, bumping, and shaking, as it continued climbing through seemingly endless layers of thick clouds. Then, suddenly, the film flicked off the reel, the screen filling with a bright brilliant blue, as we popped into an infinite expanse of sunlit sky. The oppressive cloak that had been weighing so heavily on me seemed to shift, lightening slightly as if it was starting to lose its powerful grip. I thought of Alice, the boys, and Gypsy, feeling a twinge of sadness that we'd be apart, but a greater sense of relief that with every passing second my loved ones were retreating further and further from my fateful touch and, as a bonus, I'd be beyond the reach of Isaac, and that bastard cat.

The seatbelt sign and chime faded and pressing the circular silver button below my thumb, I tried pushing my head and neck back. The backrest faltered, reclining about a foot, before stopping. I pressed the button harder, shoving my weight against the back of the seat;

it refused to budge. *Wow, this is amazing, it's almost as if I'm lying down.* While my body might have relaxed a touch, my mind began racing. As the twin engines hummed loudly, pulling us ever skywards, I closed my eyes, gripping the armrests tightly, my fingers straining as I braced for an onslaught of horrible, distressing images.

During our drive, when I'd been praying to the Virgin Mary as Danny treated me to the terrors of being his seat-grabbing speechless co-driver on the Drayton to Whiteley stage of the Lombard RAC Rally, I'd wondered if this morning's flight might trigger a series of flashbacks. I tensed, waiting for a bombardment of video clips of the near miss in HD. Instead, looking at only the blackness of the inside of my eyes, I collapsed, sighing with indescribable relief as my mind remained blank.

"So, where are we going?" I asked, turning to Danny, who I hadn't realised already had the undivided attention of one of the air stewardesses.

"One second," he said, holding up a finger to the female flight attendant and turning to face me, "Scotland, it's the big lumpy bit above England." She continued laughing as he re-engaged. I tapped him on the shoulder.

"Where's exactly in the big lumpy bit above England smart arse?" Danny turned, pointing to the printed white card in my seat pocket.

"Edinburgh. It says it on your boarding pass."

"Oh, you're flipping hilarious," I huffed. Danny had remained tight-lipped from the moment the tyres of his BMW had squealed away from home earlier that morning, but in a moment of weakness, he must have decided to tease me with a solitary breadcrumb.

"Okay, I've chosen Perth because it's central to the two courses we'll be playing. Happy now?" *No, that doesn't really help.* I knew that Scotland had hundreds of magnificent golf courses dotted all over its rolling, rugged green countryside, especially around Perthshire and Fife.

Submitting to the fact that he clearly had no intention of letting slip where we'd be playing, I relaxed my grip, sinking back into my seat, revelling in the almost prone soporific angle afforded by reclining my headrest five degrees and a whopping twelve inches. *How am I supposed to sleep when I'm practically vertical?* It took three whole minutes for me to start purring like a cold-started tractor.

## CHAPTER 62

### Beautiful Liar

A little over an hour later, after a slightly turbulent, but otherwise uneventful flight, we landed at Edinburgh Airport. I found myself skimming through Thursday's edition of The Daily Record, sitting on a hard plastic chair inside the car hire office while Danny stood at the counter, collecting the keys. He leaned in, chatting, and joking with the chubby female rep, who I could hear giggling while talking him through the paperwork. I found it odd because she could only just fit behind the desk and definitely wasn't Danny's usual type. She looked like the sort of girl who'd be on first-name terms with the staff at Dunkin' Donuts and he usually went for tall, striking, leggy women, like the gorgeous, bubbly blonde Flybe stewardess on our flight from Southampton who I assumed he'd chatted up for most of the journey.

"Right let's go," Danny ordered, heading for the exit. Weirdly, the car rental girl seemed overly friendly, smiling, blowing kisses, and waving at us animatedly as we made off to find the hire car.

"Will this do?" he asked, dropping his bags, and jutting his chin skywards as he stood proudly, hands on hips in a superhero pose.

"Are you serious?" I asked, eyeing the shiny black Range Rover Sport. Typical

Danny, the dedicated bachelor with no commitments and cash to burn. Obviously, I should have expected him to hire a brand-new Range Rover. *What have I got? I'm saddled with school fees for the next five years and pootling about in a crappy old estate with a crinkly bottom.*

"Yes, fella, Holly gave me a free upgrade," Danny winked.

"*Holly* gave you an upgrade, did she! And what does *Holly* get from you in return?"

"Nothing," Danny replied, "well not from me, anyway," Danny mumbled, deliberately avoiding eye contact.

"What was that? What do you mean 'not from me'?"

Danny ignored me, pressing the key fob, the Range Rover winking and chirping, as the boot lifted automatically.

"Oy!"

"Oh, that, it's nothing. I just promised that you'd take her out for dinner tomorrow."

"*What?* You... what? That is not happening. You go back and tell her and get a bloody Golf or a Ford Focus or something."

"Alright, alright, calm down, dear. I didn't actually promise, I just said you'd try," Danny replied calmly, trying to smooth my ruffled feathers.

"Why would you do that? You know I'm married. Alice would kill me... and you for that matter. And even if I wasn't married it would be impossible. We're in Edinburgh now and staying in Perth for two nights, there's no way I could get back."

"Look fella, *I* know that, and *you* know that," Danny replied coldly, "but *Holly* doesn't have to know that does she? I'm not trying to stitch you up, I never would. It's not like I said you'd marry the girl. I'm doing all of this for you, remember. So, take a chill pill, let your hair down, and *try* to enjoy yourself."

I decided to try, but even though I really fancied lording it up in a Range Rover, I still felt guilty about Holly at the car hire desk, who, through no fault of my own, I was going to stand up tomorrow night. I gave a wry grin as I stood admiring the beautiful glossy 4x4, reminding myself that even though he could be a total and utter heartless git sometimes, Danny's charms certainly had their uses.

## CHAPTER 63

### Do You Know Where You're Going To

Approaching lunchtime, we continued motoring north. The radio traffic reports had said that the M9 roadworks were causing significant tailbacks, so Danny had chosen to completely avoid Stirling. He reckoned the new route past Loch Leven might take a little bit longer than he'd planned but it would be much prettier.

"It should be just over an hour to get there." He still wouldn't say where *there* was and had avoided using the satnav, no doubt wanting it to be a surprise. *I wish Alice was here, she'd crack him in under a minute.* Then again, I needed someone to play golf with and he'd have struggled without any fingernails.

"I think we're going to be tight on time though, fella. We need to go straight to the course, and then find the hotel later, okay?"

"Sure, fine by me, which course did you say that was again?"

"Hah, I didn't." *Worth a try.*

Crossing the murky turbulent waters of the Firth of Forth, I tried thinking of potential candidates for our imminent round. Obviously, I knew of one particular and very special 'old' course that lay in this general direction, but we couldn't be going there. *Could we?*

I felt dwarfed by the enormity of the eponymous bridge and a little nervous about the huge drop as the car swayed, side-swiped by the strong winds rushing up the brooding channel. Trying not to think about getting blown over the edge, I continued looking straight ahead when my nose wrinkled.

"Can you smell that?" I hoped I was wrong because it smelled a bit like the spare room.

"Smell what?" Danny asked, turning his head to sniff.

"It's probably you then. Have you farted?"

"No cheeky, you'd know if I had. Are you sure it's not your arse twitching, it's a long way down you know?" Danny observed, wide-eyed as he whistled and mimed a dive with his finger.

"Shut up, I was trying to think happy thoughts until you dropped one."

"Not me fella, check your undercrackers when we get to…"

"Get to *where?*" I asked.

"G'wherever we're going?" Danny replied. *Damn, nearly.*

The Range Rover started rocking violently halfway across, threatening the integrity of my unblemished boxer shorts, forcing Danny to slow down. Thankfully, on reaching North Queensferry on the far side, the wind abated and the black 4x4 sped up again, roaring through the lush greenery of the Fife countryside. Six miles later I held my breath, waiting for Danny to indicate and turn off towards St. Andrews.

"Oh," I sighed.

"What's up, fella?"

"Nothing, I thought we were going somewhere else," I shrugged as we continued barrelling along.

"Trust me, you won't be disappointed," he grinned. "So, you still haven't told me the *full* story about work," he said, leaving the way open for me to give a complete account of events surrounding the Shooting the Gap incident.

"Okay," I sighed, taking a deep breath, preparing to give Danny a candid and *almost* full version of the last few days.

Leaving out some of the more personal and embarrassing aspects, I went into great detail about the air miss and Isaac's lack of compassion. I also mentioned the dig about fireworks; even Danny bristled. Looking across the car he shook his head and snorted

"I'm not surprised, that twat has zero empathy. It's probably because he didn't get any love and attention in the enclosure after his mother abandoned him as a runt at birth, or possibly just because he's a complete wanker."

"I'll say b, final answer. Although complete is a bit of a stretch, he's not exactly fully grown."

"Okay, little wanker then. Anyway, I reckon you've had a pretty good run if this was your first incident though," Danny suggested sagely.

"What do you mean?"

"Well, how many close calls have you had since you've been controlling?"

"*Close calls*. Well, none, really."

"Exactly, that's not normal fella. All controllers can expect to have at least one really scary 'nasty', even you Mr. Perfect." I'd studied countless post-accident and airprox reports and tried taking on board the lessons identified. However, they were like works of fiction to me, and I felt dissociated from those events because they'd happened to someone else. Other controllers would be reading about me and learning from my mistakes soon enough, though what lessons they'd learn I had no idea. *Animal-based sexual role-playing and the threat of a visit from your terrorist mother-in-law may cause a monumental fuck up?*

"You should be thankful you had a near *miss*."

"*Thankful?*" I said, spinning around.

"Yes fella, *thankful*. If they hadn't *missed*, we'd be having a very different conversation right now. Well, *we* wouldn't, you'd probably be talking to a murder detective."

"True," I nodded, grimacing, "so, what about you then?" I asked, knowing that I'd never heard Danny talk about screwing up at work.

"Yes, mate, I was on Tower at Lossie and nearly welded two Tornados together in the fog, but the pilots cocked up too. You never heard about it because we sorted it over a beer in the mess and never reported it. It was pretty hairy."

"You never reported it?" *I would have, probably, even if I'd known I was at fault.*

"No and we agreed to never talk about it again but I'm breaking radio silence and telling you now. You see, we're all human and we're all fallible, even you."

"I guess I am." The evidence clearly couldn't be refuted.

"It sounds like a classic scenario too, only one aircraft. You were probably under-stimulated. Your brain wouldn't have gotten out of first gear. You know that most ATC incidents happen when there's very little going on upstairs or way too much."

"Yeah, apparently." I had no intention of telling Danny that despite only having one aircraft under my control I had plenty of stuff *going on upstairs,* and it was the stuff that had gone on upstairs that had been partly to blame, just not ATC stuff. Not to mention the traumatic memory of being attacked by rabbits and the worry of coming home to a depressed, septuagenarian bomb-maker.

Twenty-five minutes later, we continued cruising along the motorway. *Wherever we're going we must be making good time.*

"Wow!" Looking to my right, the rippling sunlit waters and lush banks of Loch Leven, framed by the distant slumbering giants of the Lomond Hills, filled my passenger window. "Scotland is gorgeous when the Sun's out isn't it," I said dreamily.

"Yes, fella. When!" Danny chuckled and I joined in. It felt so freeing to laugh but the sensation quickly faded when the traffic began slowing, and a sea of flashing hazard lights filled the road ahead.

"Oh, come on!" Danny growled.

Approaching the police car parked sideways, blocking both lanes, we could see a dayglo-clad figure waving the traffic off the motorway and onto the Junction 6 slip road. I grinned to myself. *The M90's got a junction 6, maybe I should take a picture for the boys.*

"Kinross and Milnathort," Danny read disdainfully passing the road sign, "I was more than happy on the motorway, but I haven't got a clue where to go now?" he confessed. Leaning forward, he began tapping the large display screen. I watched and felt my heart leap as he typed in the destination.

"Sorry to spoil the surprise fella. I just hope we can make it."

"Gleneagles!" I screamed, with all the poise and decorum of a small girl who'd just been given a pony.

# CHAPTER 64

## Ain't That a Kick in the Head

*"Set in 850 acres of breath-taking countryside, Gleneagles sits proudly among lush rolling hills and beautiful Scottish glens, boasting three championship golf courses. The PGA, King's, and Queen's are considered to be amongst the finest courses on the planet and the envy of golfers the world over.* I can't believe it, I was reading this article last night in bed," I said, tapping the cover as I closed the magazine, while my warm insides continued dancing their happy jig.

"I bet Ali loved that. Not exactly the most stimulating bedroom material, is it?"

"Eh?"

"Well, I think you'd have had more luck with something a bit racier fella," Danny joked. "Mind you, you've got a choice of fifty-four championship holes at Gleneagles, how many holes were you hoping to…"

"Stop right there, unless you want to try eating sweetcorn without any teeth."

"Whaaat?"

"You know what, there are such things as boundaries Danny," I said, wagging a finger.

"Boundaries? Never heard of 'em!"

"Well, there's a surprise."

"Anyway, we're on the King's Course at 11:20 and if we can get out of this traffic, we should still make it."

The King's Course at Gleneagles had always been number three on my golfing bucket list, just behind Pebble Beach in California, with the St. Andrews Old Course taking the top spot. I checked my watch. In less than an hour I'd be stood on the first tee, surveying the majestic Scottish Highlands.

Despite Danny using all his overtaking skills and with a flagrant disregard for the sanctity of my underpants, the detour had still eaten into our time. When we'd finally got going, we'd flown past the trees, hedgerows, and farmhouses lining the leafy lanes and B roads before joining the fast-moving flow of vehicles on the A9. Unbelievably, we'd just passed somewhere called Broom of Dalreach when the traffic on the dual carriageway started slowing before coming to a grinding halt.

"Can you believe this?" Danny asked pointing ahead.

"I can, yes. *I'm* in the car. Do you think we'll make it?"

"Hmm, I don't know, fella. If this traffic doesn't start moving soon, we might not. Come on, come on," he muttered impatiently, drumming his fingers on top of the steering wheel.

I felt a buzz in my pocket followed almost immediately by, "*Tumble out of bed and stumble to the kitchen. Pour myself a cup of ambition…*" I froze. The display said 'Work.' *Who could this be and what on earth did they want with me?*

"Hello, Henry Alder."

"Ah, hello Henry," I stiffened at the sound of the familiar voice. "It's Squadron Leader Koch. I normally like to do this sort of thing face to face and I'm really sorry to break this to you over the phone," he didn't sound it, "but there's been a last-minute request for someone for an Out-of-Area detachment and your name's come up." The sunlight, that had shone briefly on me began fading, smothered by gathering clouds of despair.

After several minutes of prattling, he ended insincerely with, "Sorry, but there's nothing I can do about it," and, "I'll make sure the family is looked after," and, "I really don't want to lose one of my best operators." He finished his disingenuous monologue with, "but we all have to do our bit." Unbelievable! Admittedly, I'd been in the RAF a few years longer than my boss, but I'd completed operational tours in Pristina, Basra, and Kandahar and only last year had spent four months at Mount Pleasant airfield in The Falklands. Even more galling, I knew that Isaac had reached the rank of squadron leader, and the most threatening places the Air Force had dispatched him to had been Luxembourg and Norwich.

"I really am sorry but it's out of my hands. Come and see me on Monday for a chat and I'll be able to give you more details." I could almost hear the little bastard smirking.

"Well, that's just pissed on my chips?" I grumbled, hanging up.

"What has?" asked Danny, knowing that it couldn't be good news.

"Looks like I'm off to Afghanistan *again*," I surrendered.

Danny turned to say something, but I held up an open palm. The mood in the car changed instantly and sitting with my arms crossed, I looked out of the window, sulking. Danny simply sat in silence, concentrating on the traffic jam ahead.

## CHAPTER 65

### A View to a Kill

Five minutes later we still hadn't spoken, the traffic hadn't moved, and Danny kept checking the time.

"I think we're gonna be late fella," he said anxiously, tapping the steering wheel again.

Clutching my phone, I sat thinking about how to break the news to Alice, just as the display lit up and Dolly started another rendition of '9 to 5.' *Seriously, the work switchboard number again. I bet it's Isaac, he's probably found another handful of salt to rub in.*

What I wanted to say was, 'What the hell do you want now you draft-dodging little

227

tosser?' but settled for an irritated and aggressive, *"Yes!"*

"And a good day to you too, Mr. Grumpy?" wheezed Vlad.

"Oh, sorry Vlad, I thought it was someone else from work calling."

"It sounds like he's already rung you about your unplanned Central Asian holiday then?"

"The boss, yes. I just put the phone down. *How the hell did you know about it before me?"* The jungle drums must have been very fast this morning.

"Mate, listen, you can't say where you got this information from, but you're not going to believe this."

Five minutes later, as Vlad finished explaining just what my sympathetic, caring, line manager had done, my mind was still racing, struggling to comprehend how Isaac could have stooped so low. Vlad was about to hang up then remembered the other reason why he'd called.

"Look, why don't you come for a kickabout tomorrow? A bunch of us are going to play 5-a-side after work." I enjoyed a game of football, but my boots hadn't seen the light of day in almost two years. I'd probably have jumped at the chance if I'd been at home but wasn't exactly feeling sociable. I couldn't focus my thoughts on anything other than ways to dispose of a mutilated stumpy squadron leader's remains.

"Thanks mate but I'm up in Scotland."

"Scotland?"

"Yes, you called Danny and he called me. Mini golf tour, boys' weekend. We flew up this morning."

"Niiice. Well, enjoy." He was about to hang up, but added, "And like I said, please don't mention that you heard it from me. God knows what he'd do if he found out I told you."

"Your secret's safe with me and I do appreciate the heads up."

"No worries. See ya."

I had never felt so angry and by the time Vlad and I finished talking, I could feel my entire body shaking with rage.

"That bastard, that complete and utter lying little bastard," I seethed.

"What's he done now?" Danny asked, genuinely intrigued.

"I knew he'd be up to something, but he's outdone himself this time, just wait until you hear this," I snarled and began relaying the conversation I'd just had with Vlad.

Apparently, the 'last-minute' request had actually been made nearly two weeks ago when, according to the rumour mill, an RAF air trafficker working with the Army in Lashkar Gah had suffered a mental breakdown, or as it was more widely reported, had 'gone wibble.' He'd not reported for duty and had been found sitting on the end of his camp cot, sharpening his bayonet and gently rocking while repeatedly singing the first three lines of 'I Feel Pretty' from West Side Story. He'd been medically evacuated, and one of Vlad's friends from Brize Norton had been earmarked to fill the post and had already started his pre-deployment training. According to Vlad, his mate had been told yesterday there was a chance he was no longer required as I'd *volunteered* to go in his place. By the time I'd finished speaking, Danny looked furious too.

"Nooo, that's pretty despicable, even for him."

"Just give me a minute, okay?" I said, digging my fingers into the leather seat and fuming.

Danny gave me about three seconds.

"Right," he began, "you know you can't change this. However, it's come about." I immediately knew from his tone that Danny planned on delivering one of his inspirational pin-your-ears-back-sunshine speeches. "Isaac is a nasty piece of work. You can't do anything about that. If the signal has been sent and your name's on it, you can't change that either. If you're going, you're going." I shrugged mutely. "Personally," he continued, "I'm really looking forward to two days' golf with my best mate. So, you can either sit and whine like a little bitch, or you can man up, say screw it, and really kick the arse out of this trip. Now, am I right or am I right?" I felt like I'd just been told off. Similar to the feeling I got after one of Alice's robust buck-up chats but without the threat of physical violence. Danny's words lightened my dark mood a little and I knew he was right. *I can't change the inevitable, so why not make the most of the next two days.*

"I hate to admit it but, yes, as always, annoyingly, you're making sense. Okay let's make it a trip to remember but there's still one small problem," I said trying to muster some enthusiasm and pointing to the two lines of traffic ahead that had moved about ten feet in the last five minutes.

"Don't you worry my friend," said Danny confidently, "I have a cunning plan."

Although not signposted, a couple of taps on the satnav had revealed an alternative route and the turning we needed for the A824 to Auchterarder waited for us only a few hundred yards ahead.

"If that back road is clear I reckon we can still make Gleneagles in time if I really floor it." *Floor it! Oh Christ, sorry Calvin Klein.*

The two lanes of traffic slowly began nudging forward. *If only we could just move a few more feet, we'd be able to turn across the opposite carriageway and get going.* The car ahead rolled and stopped leaving a gap that I judged to be too small even for a Fiat Cinquecento, no matter a hulking great Range Rover. Danny confidently edged forward, somehow managing to squeeze the large SUV between the other car's bumper and the central reservation, and now faced the challenge of crossing the opposite side of the dual carriageway. Unlike our side of the road, the eastbound A9 hummed with fast-moving, morning traffic, and I couldn't see any sign of a suitable space between the cars as they continued rushing past.

"Come on, come on," said Danny impatiently, scanning for an opportunity to get us on our way. Suddenly, the Range Rover's tyres screamed as the black brute leapt, lurching across the path of the fast oncoming vehicles. I heard a heart-stopping screech as the shape of a red transit van filled my passenger window. Closing my eyes, I braced for impact, waiting for the crunch and slam of being t-boned, but only heard the blare of irate car horns. I felt myself being flung across the car and looked up as we went sailing past the blurring signpost for the A824, leaving the cacophony fading in our wake.

"Bloody hell, Danny, I didn't think we were going to make that."

"Well, luckily for you, one of us *is* capable of avoiding traffic and shooting the gap."

"Ha bloody ha." *Smart arse. I'd have been proud of that one.*

"Right," Danny said, "I reckon we've got about ten minutes," he added, checking the satnav display. The Range Rover growled, hungrily eating up the road, speeding us towards Gleneagles and the small, sleepy town of Auchterarder.

Incredibly, it looked like we might just make it, after all. Annoyingly, we'd been slowed down by the morning traffic in the centre of town, but fortune had been on our side and the traffic lights had stayed green. Once we'd passed the row of small shops, the road had been completely clear and now, rushing past a blur of small grey houses, the satnav display indicated we were tantalisingly close. *Five more minutes and we'll be there.*

Thundering through the sleepy village towards Gleneagles, I began thinking about the Kings' Course, hoping that the first tee wouldn't be too crowded. Butterflies started flitting but I didn't feel too worried, I just didn't fancy teeing off in front of a large audience after yesterday's awful practice session.

"Now we're talking," Danny beamed, looking down to locate the + symbol by his left thumb. The rising dulcet tones of Irene Cara came pouring out of the speakers but I wasn't going to complain, it was drowning out his singing.

Darting from the grass verge, a small shape went shooting across the road into the speeding car's oncoming path. I gasped as Danny twitched, catching the briefest glimpse of the thing to his right, moving low and fast, but even his lightning-quick reflexes didn't fire in time. He instinctively tried braking, but before his foot reached the pedal, we felt and heard an appalling dull thud and a small bump as the front wheels ran over whatever had just failed to cross the road. The sound of squealing rubber on the tarmac filled my ears as Danny slammed his foot to the floor, bringing the Range Rover to a juddering halt.

"See anything?" I asked, watching Danny search in the rearview mirror.

"Nope." I tried checking my wing mirror, but I couldn't see anything either. We both turned, frantically looking through the rear windscreen. Oddly, the road appeared to be completely clear.

"I'll go," I said reluctantly. Danny pulled over to the left side of the road and stopped the car, putting the hazard lights on. As gregarious, confident, and charismatic as Danny was, I knew that the tiniest drop of blood could make him pass out. Walking back the fifty or so yards towards where I estimated the bump had occurred, I could see nothing in the road except for a clump of orangey brown hair. It lay several feet before where the black

232

tyre marks began. Then, scouring the side of the road, I heard a loud mewing.

A sloping, grass-topped dry stone wall blocked the view to my right, but taking a few more steps, I saw that it sloped down to meet the road and my eyes met with the sight of an animal lying almost motionless amongst the grass. Through the thin blades, I could see light brown fur. The creature started twisting and, noticing that the brown mingled with black and white stripes, my panic dissipated quickly, realising that thankfully, it was just a cat. Moving closer, assessing its condition as it lay on the grass verge, I watched its front paws weakly twitching, its back end not moving at all. I tried blocking out the cries as a swell of nausea rose in the pit of my stomach. There was no sign of any blood but the moggy's back legs appeared locked and stiff, nothing moving from the rib cage down. Assuming that the poor thing had a broken back and knowing exactly what I had to do, I started walking back towards our car, my forehead gleaming with sweat.

"Where's the wheel brace?" I demanded, manually forcing open the automatic boot.

"Why? Have we got a flat?" Danny asked. I think he was fairly sure why I needed it but was obviously trying not to entertain that thought.

"No *Stig*. You know we haven't got a bloody flat. You ran over a cat. It's in a right state and I need to put it out of its misery."

"Can't we just leave it? We're going to be late." The corners of Danny's mouth twitched nervously. I could tell that he desperately wanted to drive off and get the hell out of there.

"No! I'm not just leaving the poor thing. I don't care if we're late. Maybe you want to do it," I suggested angrily.

Danny kept looking forward, breathing slowly while shaking his head, his face changing colour to match the seat's pale cream leather. Even though we'd parked about fifty yards from where the cat lay, with the boot open, we could clearly hear the animal's loud cries over the sound of Irene's singing, so Danny turned her up.

"*I can't leave it like that,*" I shouted over the music, pointing in the direction of the screeching moggy.

Dragging the golf clubs hurriedly out of the boot, I dumped them on the ground, frisbeeing the boot cover out in my frenzy to access the tool kit.

"Right, you load this lot back up. I'll be as quick as I can," I instructed, walking back down the road, my pulse racing. My white knuckles locked, clutching the quivering wheel brace. Steadying myself with a deep breath, I stepped up on top of the wall, heading towards the calls of distress. The creature hadn't moved, its back legs remaining motionless, its front legs flicking feebly in the air. Raising the metal bar, I paused, my trembling arms held above my head, ready to deliver the merciful fatal blow. The cat must have sensed my presence as the crying stopped for a split second before its mouth fell open, and the sickening racket struck up again. Slamming the bar down, I heard and felt a nauseating crunch. The cat screamed. Bizarrely, the pain and shock on its face made it look like it was grinning from ear to ear, and for a brief moment, the strained expression reminded me of someone. I breathed loudly, my nostrils flaring, and my temples throbbing. Driven by a desire to give this poor animal a swift release, while having a really strong craving to smash my boss's smug face in, I took another deep breath, slamming the wheel brace down repeatedly.

"I'm sorry," *thwack.*

"You bastard!" *thwack.*

"I'm really sorry," *squelch.*

234

# CHAPTER 66

## Don't Fear the Reaper

Last night, I'd stood in my garden, aimlessly swiping at small white plastic golf balls, wrestling with the thought that death had been stalking me. I'd felt that he had been shadowing my movements for days, repeatedly swinging his scythe at those around me but thankfully missing. I'd been wrong, oh so wrong, and too close to those near-fatal events to see the truth. Death hadn't been tracking my every step, he hadn't been hovering at my shoulder ready to pluck a soul at will, *I was Death*. I hadn't slipped the cloak of despair that had been weighing me down at all, instead, it was me who bore the hooded robes of the Bringer of Death, *I* had become the Grim Reaper. Okay, so maybe not the actual Reaper, he clearly had the whole soul collector thing down pat. I was more like his YTS apprentice who'd missed all of his training targets and just needed a bit more practice.

# CHAPTER 67

## Run to the Hills

Isaac had stopped grinning and some of his brains was *al fresco*. Cocking my wrist, I wiped away the tears from my cheeks and the sweat from my dripping brow, smearing blood and clumps of kitty matter as I dragged the back of my hand across my face. I couldn't leave the body here, but where could I dispose of the corpse of a bludgeoned cat? The answer was sitting on the opposite side of the road in the form of a large black wheelie bin, placed at the end of a gravel path leading away from a tiny grey bungalow. I gently picked the cat up by the non-gooey end and crossed over, holding the leaking, feline cadaver at arm's length to avoid getting any more of the dribbling gore on my shoes and clothes. I looked like I'd pulled an all-nighter in an abattoir and my new 'salmon' shirt had probably been ruined before it had been anywhere near a golf course. Opening the bin, I unceremoniously dropped the deceased moggy inside with a juicy thud. Lowering the lid, I looked up and found myself staring into the shocked eyes of a white-haired old lady gazing out of the bungalow's kitchen window. I didn't have a clue how long she'd been standing there, watching, or how much she'd witnessed. I smiled weakly, slowly raising my bloodied hand holding the dripping wheel brace, and began waving to her. With a look of sheer dread, she very slowly raised a trembling hand and tried feebly waving back.

I probably should have knocked on the door to explain, simply telling her that my friend had just run over her neighbour's cat, and I had then beaten it to death out of mercy, but at that moment I was feeling rather emotional and had a thousand scenarios running through my head. Unblinking, she continued staring out of her window, her open mouth and pale features appearing frozen in terror. Given what she'd possibly just seen me do, I couldn't think of any outcome where this would end with a pleasant chat over a nice cup of tea and a Tunnocks wafer. Thinking it would be best to say nothing and simply walk away, I slowly turned around, then started running.

"*Go, go, go!*" I bellowed, jumping into the passenger seat still holding the bloodied murder weapon. "Oh God, I can't turn up to the Clubhouse looking like this," I exclaimed, staring down at my crimson hands. Speeding away, Danny leaned forward, tapping the satnav a couple of times, searching for Local Services. He must have known that I had blood on me, he could probably smell it and I knew he would not be able to look at my spattered clothing without passing out.

"There's a garage two miles away. You'd better get cleaned up there," he suggested, his eyes locked forward as he stopped and started putting the car into reverse.

"Okay," I mumbled, then looked at the screen. "Stop, where are you going? Isn't there another one? That's in town, back the way we came. I don't want to revisit the crime scene."

Danny started tapping the screen.

"There," he replied, not allowing his gaze to go any further left than the satnav display, "Blackford, we'll be there in... six minutes."

"Thanks, and Danny ..." I started dejectedly.

"Yes."

"I'm really sorry but I feel a bit sick, and I don't think I can play golf today." Danny concurred with a sympathetic nod, and I noticed a familiar smirk starting to form at the corner of his mouth.

"Well, at least you got to swing a club," he chuckled.

"*Too soon!*" I scalded, shaking my head in disbelief.

"Sorry," he offered with the look of a berated schoolboy as he drove away, concentrating on the road ahead.

## CHAPTER 68

### Red Right Hand

The Range Rover crunched onto the gravel as we pulled into the small rural garage, parking opposite the forecourt.

"Are you going to fill up while we're here?" I asked, nodding towards the solitary antiquated petrol pump.

"Er, not at these prices, no," Danny answered, his face twisted in shock, stunned by the garage's exorbitant cost for a litre of petrol. "I'll wait until we get to civilisation and a proper services. You go and sort yourself out, I'll ring Gleneagles and cancel. Maybe I can get a refund."

"I'm really sorry," I said, turning to face Danny.

"Don't worry about it," he replied, still avoiding eye contact, "we'll have a nice lunch and a few beers, and we've still got tomorrow."

Halfway to the entrance of the garage's small shop, I came face to face with the shuffling, flat cap-wearing, elderly forecourt attendant in tatty green overalls and scuffed brown corduroy slippers. The old man stooped, as he lumbered towards me.

"Can I help ye, laddie?" There was a clear hint of intolerance in his tone.

"I'd just like to use your toilet please?"

As the old man looked up, I saw his mouth slowly drop open. He gawked, staring at my face and the dark red splatters of clotted blood on my salmon shirt, the sticky wheel brace still firmly clamped in my glistening, gooey fist.

The old man said nothing but slowly moved his trembling finger, pointing past the pump towards the door of the shop.

"Thank you," I breathed, heading for the small white building. I heard the old boy dragging his feet, shuffling behind me, and shadowing me to the door.

Inside, I saw the WC sign in the corner to my left and stepped into the toilet, shutting the door behind me. The cubicle echoed as the bolt slid shut. Looking in the mirror I jerked back as a bald, middle-aged Carrie stared back. Opening the taps fully, the sound of rushing water mingled with the echoing clang as I dropped the bloody wheel brace into the sink, turning the water the same colour as my salmon golf shirt.

From the faint noises I could hear in the shop, I suspected that as soon as he heard the bolt go across, the old man had shimmied around the desk, grabbed the old telephone from behind the counter, and with a trembling hand started dialling. I turned off the tap for a moment, holding my breath as I put my ear to the door.

"Emergency, which service do you require?" I imagined hearing.

"Police," I think the old man whispered. Then nothing for what seemed like an eternity to be connected.

Given where we were, I imagined a voice saying, "Perth and Kinross Police, how can I help you?"

"Hallo, come quickly, I think there's bin a murder."

*Did I imagine that too? Or was that exactly what he said?* I grabbed the bar of soap, plunging my murderous, tacky hands into the warm pink water, and began scrubbing.

Having cleaned up, I unbolted the door and saw the old man sitting, reading a newspaper, seemingly disinterested in my presence. Sloping off quickly through the door, I strode across the forecourt to the waiting car. Glancing back, I caught him staring, his head instantly dropping behind his newspaper as I met his gaze.

"Alright?" Danny asked as I jumped in.

"Um, yeah, I think so," I replied uncertainly, looking quizzically towards the shop.

We'd barely set off when the flashing blue lights greeted us.

## CHAPTER 69

### Stray Cat Strut

As late morning rolled into early afternoon, Danny and I continued silently contemplating the depressing sludge-green walls of Auchterarder Police Station's holding cell. We'd been detained by the wiry, fox-faced Sergeant Fraser and had been over our story at least three times. The Duty Sergeant said he couldn't make his mind up. He supposed he could charge us with animal cruelty, but our case was strong. He reckoned we had to be guilty of something, even if, in my case, it was only possession of an English accent and an offensive blood-spattered bright pink shirt.

He said he had received two calls that morning and although he knew Danny and I hadn't murdered anyone, he still needed to get to the bottom of what the other distressed caller had accused us of, and the old lady that owned the dead cat had given him an unerringly accurate description that fitted me perfectly. The grating of a turning key caused us to look up.

"Gentlemen you're free to go but I need to show you something first," the grinning sergeant reported proudly, looking as if he'd single-handedly cracked the cases of Jack the Ripper, the Zodiac Killings, and the disappearance of Lord Lucan.

Despite feeling relieved at the news of our release, we both shrugged, exchanging a puzzled look as the self-satisfied policeman led us out of the detention room. Escorting us out of the station's back door, we followed, thankful yet confused as he began walking towards our waiting vehicle. The car sat exactly where Danny had parked it, after our police escort almost three hours ago. Handing Danny the key fob, Sergeant Fraser started walking confidently towards the front of the Range Rover, beckoning us to follow, pointing at the left front wheel. Danny spotted the tip of a white and ginger furry tail poking out a split second before me.

"*Nooo!*" I gasped, putting my hand to my mouth. Sickeningly it dawned on both of us what we'd done, or to be more precise, exactly what I had.

Sergeant Fraser spent ten minutes eagerly revealing his detective prowess and grinning proudly, whereas I spent the whole time trying to apologise while feeling utterly wretched.

"I thought yous and the auld lady were both tellin' the truth but couldnae fathom how that cud be. Then I realised I had tae take another look at yer car and here's the answer," he beamed, leaning down. Grabbing the cat's tail, he began peeling away the body wedged inside the wheel arch. He interrupted me mid-sentence as I prepared to say how bad I felt and how sorry I was for the eleventh time.

"Dinnae fess yerself, sir, it was a genuine mistake an' done with the best o' intentions."

"I know but…"

"Jest an unfortunate mistake. No harm done," the policeman said with just the faintest hint of irritation in his voice. "An' dinnae worry about this wee fella," he said, holding the dead cat up by its tail. "I'll try an' find his owner or at least give him a decent send-off. A'm sure there's a nice wheelie bin here aboots."

I definitely didn't feel ready to make jokes about wheelie bins just yet. I also felt that, as far as inappropriate phrases went, 'no harm done' had to top the list considering that I'd caved in the skull of an old cat happily playing in the grass, in full view of its distressed owner. Strangely, the cat we'd run over, looked almost unharmed, apart from the extremely startled expression frozen on its face and the weird angle of its head. The deceased moggy bore an uncanny resemblance to my least favourite ginger feline and, for some strange reason, the weight of guilt in the pit of my stomach started to feel even heavier.

## CHAPTER 70

### Suicide is Painless

Danny got in the car. Solemnly, I climbed into the passenger seat beside him and leaning forward let my head thud onto the leather dashboard. Neither of us moved. Instead, we simply sat there in silence for a few minutes. Leaning back, I began watching the raindrops collect and run down the windscreen, quietly mulling over the morning's events.

"You know, maybe you did that other cat a favour," Danny suggested. My head spun around so fast I almost gave myself whiplash.

"*How the hell did you work that out?*"

"I was just thinking, you know, in the long run."

"A favour? *Are you serious?* I beat a perfectly healthy animal to death. I smashed its head in with an iron bar, Danny, and got bits of it all over me. Have you seen my shirt?"

"No. You know I can't look at it," he said, staring straight ahead, then turning his head away to emphasise the point. "I know you killed it, but, well, that's my point, it wasn't perfectly healthy. I'm just saying, the copper said it was quite old and completely deaf. You know, maybe it was better than, well, getting *really* old."

I turned the idea over in my head, thinking I sort of knew what Danny meant before concluding that actually, I had absolutely no bloody idea what the hell he was jabbering about. I had no problem with euthanasia in principle, Alice and I had discussed it, although neither of us felt in any great rush to see if those Sunday School teachings about heaven were true. We both agreed that if one of us became terminally ill and in so much pain that it removed any real quality of life, or we ended up in a vegetative state with no chance of recovery, then death would be preferable to a long, drawn-out miserable existence. I had similar feelings every time Alice's mum came to stay.

Exploring Danny's idea a little further, I could see why someone might make a conscious decision to take a one-way trip to Switzerland, choose to lay in a comfortable bed and peacefully slip away in a calm, dignified manner. However, falling asleep and never waking up was one thing, having some madman burst into your private room and beat you into oblivion by caving your skull in with a large metal rod could hardly be classed as

242

dignified.

"Well, Danny, I don't know about you, but whenever I turn on the news and there's a report that someone's been murdered, I'm horrified, you know, like a normal person would be. I don't then think, *oh, actually those thugs did that old dear a real favour because she was eighty-five. Bloody good job they smashed her head in and saved her from making ninety. What is wrong with you?*"

"That's not what I meant," Danny protested.

"Whatever you meant, it's irrelevant now. I'm not going to argue, and I don't want to talk about it."

"But…"

"Just leave it," I growled.

"But…" he protested.

"*Leave it, Danny!* I'm pretty sure I'm going to have even more bloody nightmares as it is and I never want to talk about this again, it never happened. You don't mention it to Alice, to Vlad, to anyone. Understand? Never."

"Never?" Danny asked.

"Never!" I replied, sliding my finger across my throat in a cutting motion.

"Alright, cross my heart and hope to die… but not until I'm at least eighty-five."

Looking past the small rivers of water trickling down the screen, I stared blankly, picturing the terrified look on the old cat's face.

"Danny…," I sighed.

"Yes, mate."

"I think we could both do with a drink."

"Okay, just let me suss out where we're going," Danny said, typing the destination into the satnav.

"Seriously?" I asked in horror, staring at the name on the screen.

"Yeah, sounds charming, doesn't it?" he said, chuckling nervously.

## CHAPTER 71

### Highway to Hell

It should have been a twenty-two-minute journey, but it had taken us closer to forty for the satnav to guide us from Auchterarder Police station. Judging by the bizarre route we'd taken, the device must have been a unique Scottish version with a special setting for English visitors; *Most indirect with as many road works, potholes, cattle grids, and unnecessary diversions down B roads as possible*. Eventually, the Range Rover's in-built navigation system directed us through the centre of town and onto Glover Street, passing behind Perth railway station before telling us to turn left down a narrow, filthy alleyway. Crawling along the unnamed road, we kept peering ahead for something resembling a hostelry. I began having the sinking feeling that either Satnav Ally had got us completely lost, or was leading us into an ambush, when his cocky robotic voice rang out, just as we were scraping past a thick mess of brambles.

"You have arrived," he announced.

Looking at the name of the foreboding building in front of us, and the way I was feeling, I think I would have preferred it if it had said Dignitas.

The hospitality of the alarmingly named, Axe Hotel, awaited us at the end of a cul-de-sac or, more appropriately, a dead end. Pulling into the small car park, we scanned the area nervously before Danny reversed the incongruous, luxury SUV into a parking space that appeared to be the only remaining one without broken glass, bags of rubbish, or an abandoned shopping trolley. He stopped the car, turned off the engine, and we both sat, staring at the ominous, sooty grey building. Silently, exchanging wide-eyed glances, we looked again, checking that our minds weren't playing tricks on us. It was definitely our hotel, Satnav Ally had said so, the black and white chequered flag on the display said so, and tilting my head to the right, reading the faded hotel sign hanging off the side of the building confirmed it. I don't know what disturbed me more, the burnt-out Ford Capri at the bottom of the car park, mounted on four piles of bricks and with a scaffolding pole through its windscreen, or the chap leaning against the back door of the hotel relieving himself against the wall. I assumed the shuffling, stumbling, shabbily dressed figure to be a tramp although, for all I knew, he could have been a regular.

"Wow, I mean… wow. This looks truly horrible, Danny. Who needs London and The Ritz when you've got Perth and The Axe?"

Danny made a funny, nervous nasal noise, sounding a bit like a laugh, before lamely suggesting, "You never know, it might be quite nice inside."

Having unloaded our gear, we gazed worriedly at our upgraded hire car, so completely out of place in these unsavoury surroundings.

"We'll just have to hope the local oiks will think it belongs to a local gangster or drug dealer and leave it well alone," Danny offered uncertainly. Crossing the car park, we trod carefully, negotiating the dog turds, empty beer cans, and a discarded swollen condom before walking around to the front of the hotel. En route, we gave a wide berth to the hobo who had either finished peeing and appeared to be repeatedly shaking himself dry or had decided he'd like some 'happy time.'

Pushing our way through the double doors, we entered a dimly lit hallway and heard muffled voices, the clinking of glasses, and the sound of Deacon Blue's Ricky Ross belting out 'Dignity,' coming from behind the door immediately to our left. Placing my bags down, I pushed open the door and took one step into the bar.

"...*isn't she pretty, that ship called...*" All conversation ceased too, and the small groups of early afternoon drinkers turned to look at me, the audacious English invader who had just dared to enter their lair. *Gulp.* Towering behind the bar, stood a short-cropped, daffodil blonde hulk, who in his youth could have doubled for a member of the Hitler Youth on steroids. He gestured for me to enter with a commanding backward nod. Danny followed, the paused music and chatter starting up again as if someone had just pressed 'play.'

"Can I help, ye?" asked the former Aryan poster boy, placing his massive hands on the bar top, his eyebrows rising sharply as he began studying my speckled shirt. I couldn't help noticing the downward pointing star tattooed on the side of his thick neck and the four dots on the knuckles of each hand. *Oh good, we appear to be staying in a hotel run by a police-hating Satanist.*

"I think we've been lucky enough to book two penthouse suites in your fine establishment," Danny chipped in over my shoulder.

"Wha's the name?" the barman growled, ignoring, or more likely not understanding, the sarcasm.

"Ansell," Danny responded. From the look on his face, I think he'd realised that for the first time in his life, even his charm had its limits.

"Wait here," the barman ordered. I half expected him to slam his heels together and goose-step out of the bar. We waited, obviously both thinking it best to do as our genial host commanded, and watched as he pulverised the carpet. On second thoughts, I decided he wasn't so much Nazi but looked more like Raoul Moat's less stable older sibling.

A minute later, the enormous bartender reappeared, holding up two sets of keys, and began jangling them at us. Like Pavlovian test subjects, we immediately responded to the stimulus, grabbed our bags, and obediently followed Raoul's big brother towards the back of the hotel.

"A'm Stevie," the illustrated giant, and suspected Devil worshipper said, introducing himself as we clambered up the backstairs, "I run the hotel on ma ain as barman, hotel manager, and porter." He had clearly forgotten that this last role normally involved more than carrying keys, leaving us battling with our bags up three flights of narrow stairs before fighting our way through the final constricted stairwell at the top of the building. Danny stopped a couple of steps down; we couldn't fit three people on the small landing leading to the two single rooms on either side, not unless we'd done the conga.

"Take yer pick, then," Stevie said temptingly, holding open the palm of his large hand, presenting me with the choice of two identical-looking sets of keys, numbered 13 and 14.

"Unlucky for some, Danny," I shouted, picking up the number 14 key. Turning around I unlocked the door with a triumphant grin. Grabbing my bags, I backed into the door, flicked the light switch then began shuffling sideways into my room, feeling that I'd had a minor victory. *So long sucker!*

The creaking of room 14's door, like the sound effect from a 1970s' horror movie when Peter Cushing lifted the lid to Christopher Lee's coffin, preparing to drive a stake through his heart, should have been a portent for what lay beyond. The cracked tiled floor had been partially covered with a long piece of poorly cut but properly stained beige carpet and the air had a distinct odour. I sniffed, identifying the sickening, synthetic scent of cheap flowers blended with the stench of bleach, damp mop, and dead rodent. Similar to the smell of an embalmer's apron. The room itself couldn't have measured more than twelve feet by eight; there literally wouldn't have been enough room to swing a cat and immediately I thought of one that I'd have been happy to grab by the tail to check. Despite its cramped dimensions I still managed to squeeze myself and my bags inside, leaving just enough room to shut the creaking door.

The single bed, crammed into a recess on the left-hand side, looked reasonably clean and thankfully had space underneath for my luggage. Danny had said that when he'd booked the rooms, he'd managed to get each of us a single, both with a private bathroom and tea and coffee-making facilities. Looking around, I considered calling Trading Standards. They'd have had a field day.

When I initially entered the third-floor catacomb, I'd shuffled in sideways and not noticed a frosted glass door recessed into the wall behind me. Pushing the door in the centre, it folded in on itself, sliding open to reveal a compact and delightfully bijoux shower cubicle. The acrylic tray had been white at some point in its long life, but with age had greyed around the seals. Worryingly, it looked to be cold and slimy underfoot and I hoped that the gelatinous gunk glooped across the drain hole was nothing more sinister than a spurt of old hair conditioner.

"Hmmm," I mused aloud, "I can't wait to get in there."

Opposite the end of the bed stood a small, scratched sink decorated with a dust-covered bowl of ancient, desiccated potpourri, and next to it a small corner shelf had been hastily fixed to the wall. It held the world's smallest grey plastic travel kettle, a chipped St Johnstone FC mug, a used plastic teaspoon, a couple of tea bags that could easily have been exhibited by the Imperial War Museum, and two half-filled jars. One contained Mellow

Birds and the other a crusty ridgeline of Coffee-mate that at some point in the last century had been powder. Between the jars, I discovered a small clump of tiny, dark brown pellets but couldn't tell how fresh they were. *Hmm, looks like I could be sharing. Hopefully, it's only mice.*

Looking around, I then realised that my room had no windows. Room 14 might well have been furnished as an upstairs bedroom at some point, but it had the appearance of a storeroom and held all the allure of an en suite crypt. Lifting my suitcase onto the bed, ready to unpack, I noticed the absence of a wardrobe. There wasn't even a set of drawers, just a flimsy, white metal clothes rail wedged at the foot of the bed. It might be a free trip, but this room, well, it would probably have been luxury for a Royal Navy officer, but if I'd been livestock, it would have violated the Animal Welfare Act.

## CHAPTER 72

### Rat Trap

At first, I thought I'd locked the door, although I couldn't remember going anywhere near the button on the Yale lock. I tried pulling again, but the door still wouldn't budge.

*Oh great, I'm trapped.* I started banging repeatedly.

*"Danny! Danny! Can you let me out?"*

No response, except, I could just about make out the theme tune to the film Flashdance that had been playing earlier when Danny ran over the cat. It was coming from the room opposite. As the walls of Room 13 resonated to the voice of Irene Cara, singing 'What a Feeling,' I could also hear the unmistakable backing vocals of the tuneless and lyrically challenged Danny Ansell.

"Firrrst when there's nothing but a slow, moving train…"

*"Danny! Danny! Let me out, I'm locked in."*

Still nothing except Danny screaming, *"...being's believing. I can have a ball..."* He might not have known the right words, but I couldn't knock his enthusiasm.

*"Danny? Danny? Hello? Please stop you're upsetting the rats. Hellooo? I hope your room is as shitty as mine... I think I might die in here... please tell Alice that I love her and make sure that she sprinkles my ashes upwind so that you can choke on them... Danny?"*

After several fruitless minutes, I gave up and tried calling him on my mobile.

The fifth member of Il Divo, still in full flow, answered after two rings.

*"...take your pants down and make it happen...* Hello mate, why are you calling me you lazy sod? You could just knock."

"Yes, I could, couldn't I. If I wasn't locked in!" I replied, my jaw set.

"Whaaat?" Danny chuckled.

"Don't laugh, I'm locked in," I replied tersely.

"Ha, you're on form. We've only been here two minutes. Are you really locked in?"

"Yes, really," I replied with well-rehearsed exasperation.

I took my key off its keyring, sliding it under the door for Danny to try. The lock wouldn't budge, the door remaining firmly shut.

"Hang on, mate, I'll try to find Stevie. I'm sure he'll be *delighted* to come upstairs and help," Danny suggested, plodding down the staircase.

Sitting on the bed I waited, looking around, enjoying the majestic sweeping view of the drab, nicotine-yellow walls of my private tomb. A few minutes later Stevie from Axe Customer Care, Guest Relations, and Facilities Management arrived, and pointlessly knocked on the door.

"Hello, are ye in there?" he asked. I resisted the temptation to tell Stevie that it was a stupid bloody question.

"Yeees. I'm *still* in here," I replied derisively.

"I'll have ye oot in a jiffy, wee man," Stevie shouted. I could clearly hear Danny laughing to himself on the other side of the stubbornly locked door. There followed a lot of rattling, scraping, and thudding.

"Come on ye wee fucker" Stevie growled. He could clearly add amateur locksmith or possibly burglar to his resume as, in under a minute, with a resounding clunk, the lock came free, and the door creaked open.

"Sorry aboot that, this storeroo…, sorry, uh, bedroom door can play up now an' again."

Stevie then proceeded to spray the mechanism with a can of lubricant until it ran out of the front of the lock, through the keyhole, and down the pale yellow door. He waggled the lock, turning the key in it a couple of times until it moved freely.

"Good as new," he said with a smirk. "Room okay?"

"Lovely," I lied and immediately started cursing my Englishness.

"Um, about the door…" I started as Stevie turned to walk away, "…what if it's not as good as new and there's a fire?"

"Och, it'll work fine now wee man, but if it disnae, I'm sure yer pal here will let ye oot," Stevie said, turning to Danny. "You will let him oot, won't ye? Ye'd be a basta'd not tae."

So, my life, in the event of a fire, rested on the malfunctioning lock behaving itself, or

I had to expect Danny, who would hopefully *not be* a bastard, to be within earshot if the hotel set ablaze. I wanted to express my dissatisfaction, but Stevie stood wielding a six-inch screwdriver and a nasty-looking piece of bent coat hanger wire while sporting the expression of an unhinged panel beater. I also couldn't help noticing the large green vein pulsing under the pentagram in the handyman's neck. Nodding, I agreed that the door probably would open, or Danny probably would let me out, *if* the fire alarm worked, and I'd be fine, probably. Danny agreed, he had no intention of letting me burn to death. Knowing him he'd probably get an award for it.

"I don't know about you, but I'm Hank Marvin," I commented, my stomach loudly announcing its presence. Danny concurred. It had been a long time since we'd grabbed a coffee and Danish at Southampton Airport.

"Right, fella, shower and change, and then we'll see what culinary delights Perth has to offer."

"Twenty minutes?" I suggested loudly, competing with the long, agonising creak of my crypt door.

"Make it twenty-five," shouted Danny, retreating into his room, "some of us still have to do our hair."

## CHAPTER 73

### Hot N Cold

I had planned to run the shower to rinse away the 'hair conditioner' and let the water warm up, or at least check the temperature before I climbed into the cramped space, but this proved to be impossible. The bi-fold door opened inwards and almost touched the opposite wall, trapping the shower unit behind it. Unable to reach around the door and turn the shower on, I had to get in it first.

Having undressed, I pushed on the opaque glass, gingerly stepping inside, just managing to shut the folding screen door without taking my kneecaps off while manoeuvring myself into the cramped space. The shower head had been cemented into the wall at a fixed angle, the only adjustable thing appearing to be the temperature dial. Turning it to halfway between the red and blue arrows, I began praying that whatever was about to come out of that rusty, encrusted spout would be at least tepid. Backing away a few inches into the corner, I could feel the cold coming off the ceramic tiles behind me as goosebumps started sprouting on my lily-white backside. Raising my left leg, so that my thigh covered my genitals, I clenched my left arm against my chest like a folded wing, squeezing one eye tightly shut. Looking like a cross between a weirdly contorted human being and a hideously disfigured, one-eyed, white-arsed flamingo, I gulped, nervously moving the index finger of my free hand slowly towards the ON/OFF button. Trembling, I held my breath as I pressed it. I could hear and feel a faint bubbling under my feet travelling towards the far side of the cubicle and up the tiled wall. My eyes started climbing the grubby grouting between the off-white squares, following the sound of the rising gurgle. The shower head appeared to be clearing its throat, gargling for a few seconds before it abruptly stopped. An eerie silence fell, the only sound was my rapid breathing. I thought something must be blocking the pipe and cautiously edged towards the inert menacing silver head. A couple of droplets swelled on the face of the shower rose, bulging and kissing to form a single droplet before falling into the tray. Squinting, I leaned forward for a closer look, craning my neck to investigate, peering into the lifeless spiral of holes. Without warning, the shower struck.

Danny told me later that he thought I had my television on max volume while watching the slashing scene from Psycho. The surprisingly high-powered shower's aim had all the accuracy of an Imperial Stormtrooper, firing random streams of ice-cold needles at various parts of my naked body. I jumped back, pressing myself against the freezing tiles. I even shocked myself with the volume and pitch of what came out of my lungs.

Twiddling and blindly fumbling, I let out a panicked moan as I struggled to turn the dial towards the red arrow before violently wrenching the stubborn knob around as far as it would go. The pressure dropped and the sound of more gurgling came bubbling up from beneath my feet. Warmer water started spurting and flowing. *Aah.* I stopped screaming as the warmth of the gentle spray began rising, my racing heart slowing.

The shower paused briefly at pleasantly warm before ejecting rockets of hot liquid in which you could comfortably boil potatoes. Fearing that my own spuds were about to get cooked, I let out another blood-curdling girlie scream while red-hot pokers continued pummelling my delicate flesh. Poached and half-blinded, I frantically scrabbled about trying to locate the controls. I began punching anything that felt like an ON/OFF button before wrenching the folding door back and leaping out.

There was a knock on my door.

"Yes?" I answered breathlessly, dripping all over the floor, attempting to regain my composure.

"Did you have a nice shower?"

"*Piss off!*" I snapped.

"Seriously, fella, are you okay?" Danny asked, his tone suggesting something approaching mild sympathy.

"Yeah, but I think I'm a bit beyond al dente," I answered, softening slightly at Danny's seemingly genuine concern. "I'm pretty sure that my shower's possessed."

"We can share my bathroom if you want. Why don't you have a shower in mine, it's fine?"

"Thanks, mate," I sighed, grabbing my towel. *Of course, yours is fine. Why wouldn't it be?*

I creaked open the bedroom door. The lock thankfully appeared to be behaving itself. Danny covered his mouth at the sight of my blotchy pink skin with the distinctly rosy hue of a freshly slapped arse.

"Oh mate, you look like you've been parboiled."

"I have," I replied testily.

"Seriously, are you okay?"

"Just peachy. Now can I use your bloody shower?"

Looking over my shoulder, Danny's jaw dropped seeing the size of my pathetic room.

"Bloody hell, fella, I've seen bigger rabbit hutches," he laughed, noticing me flinch.

"Are you alright?"

"Yes, just suffering from mild PTSD." Danny shook his head. "Post Traumatic Shower Disorder," I deflected.

"Look, it's too late to sort anything for tonight but do you want me to try and find somewhere else for tomorrow?"

"Could you?" I asked, even though I knew it would be a ball ache to move for one night.

"I'll try but I doubt we'll have much luck. It was a nightmare getting two rooms in this place. There's some Scottish arts festival thing called the Mòd going on. Would you believe every single registered hotel and B&B around here is booked solid? The only places that still had vacancies, like this place, were classed as *not recommended* by The Scottish Tourist Board."

"Really, this place isn't in The Scottish Tourist Board's Top Ten places to stay. I hope Stevie appeals."

"Sorry, I did try."

"No, I'm sorry. I know you've gone to a lot of trouble sorting this trip. It's only two nights, it'll be fine, as long as we can share your bathroom."

"I already said it's not a problem, *mi casa es tu casa*. When you're ready to join up all those patches just give me a knock," Danny offered, pointing to my belly resembling a map of the world in pink and white.

I gazed in disbelief when the door swung open silently, and I stepped onto the soft, warm carpet of Room 13. Admittedly it would never be described as palatial or plush, but his room had to be at least three times the size of mine and the en suite bathroom had a bath with a separate shower and toilet. *A toilet! I haven't got a toilet.* If I wanted to relieve myself, I had the unsavoury choice of a demonic shower needing the attention of a plumber, or possibly a young priest and an old priest, or my crappy little sink. Danny's room even had a queen-sized bed and a double wardrobe. Stepping into the capacious shower cubicle I tutted loudly. I emerged from the bathroom ten minutes later relaxed, warm, clean, and grinning, having made aggressive use of his lavatory.

"You might want to give it five minutes, maybe ten," I said, wafting my hand across my nose. "I'll see you down in the bar," I added, shutting the door behind me, smugly satisfied with a slight spring in my step.

I dressed quickly and because, as Danny had so kindly pointed out, I had no hair to do, arrived first in the bar. Danny walked in to find me sitting on a barstool, the one next to me unoccupied, with two pints of foam-topped, golden liquid waiting. Stevie lurked nearby and nodded to Danny.

"Cheers," we chimed, chinking our glasses.

"Sorry about today, Danny, I can't believe we missed out on a round on the King's Course. I'm gutted."

"Me too but don't worry about it. I managed to get my money back."

"Really, how?"

"I just said we'd had a sudden bereavement." *Unbelievable.* "Anyway, we've still got tomorrow to look forward to."

"Absolutely. Come on, let's finish these and go and get something to eat," I replied.

"Yous'll be very welcome if ye want to pop into the bar for a wee nightcap when ye get back," Stevie offered.

"Thanks," I replied, slightly confused. *Of course, we'll be welcome, you great lummock. We're guests. We've paid for two rooms or rather one room and a refurbished cleaning cupboard.* As we headed out of the bar, the lummock growled, "I'll be seeing yous both later fer a bevvy then." It sounded less like an invitation and more like a threat.

## CHAPTER 74

### I Just Called to Say I Love You

The earlier rain had turned to a light drizzle, and despite a slight chill in the air we decided to walk. Heading into the centre of town, we scoured the streets fruitlessly, searching for a pub en route. After asking a group of lads for direction, we found ourselves plodding through the shopping precinct, before turning right and slapping along the grey wet pavement of Methven Street to find Sportsters, an unimaginatively titled sports bar.

"They must have spent weeks thinking that one up," I said to Danny, looking up and pointing at the dilapidated awning. Through the doors I could hear and feel the booming and thudding coming from within and fearing that I wouldn't be able to hear her once inside, I decided it would be a good idea to try calling Alice. *The way I feel at the moment, I definitely won't be in a fit state to chat later.* Reaching my hand in to get my phone, my pocket started playing Darth Vader's walk-on music. *Uncanny, she does that a lot.*

*Idiot!* I still hadn't told Alice about Afghanistan. I'd be leaving her, the boys, and of course Gypsy, for another six months. It had completely slipped my mind to call her. So much had happened since that unpleasant call from Isaac almost seven hours ago, although it felt more like seven days.

"It's Alice," I mouthed pointing to the phone.

"Yes, he's here… Uh-huh… I'll tell him… Windscreen… Yes, I've got it," I said, putting my hand over the phone.

"Alice says hi and to tell you that if you ever sit outside our house again and wake her up revving your engine, she's going to *put a dustbin through your fucking windscreen.*"

Danny laughed.

"Trust me, she's not joking." Danny stopped laughing.

"I'll go get us a table then," he suggested.

Leaving me in the cold and rain to continue my call in private, Danny stepped through the door, disappearing into the wall of noise. I suddenly felt guilty for leaving it so late but not guilty enough that I would tell her everything about today.

"Are you okay my love," I asked, trying to delay the inevitable.

"Yeah, I was just in the garden clearing up dog shit and it made me think of you." *The cheek.* She sounded bright and bubbly, but my news would soon change that.

"So, how's my favourite girl doing?"

"She's fine and I'm okay too. Thanks for asking."

"I meant you, my love," I protested half-heartedly.

"Of *course,* you did," Alice said sarcastically, both knowing that I'd meant Gypsy.

"I don't know what you mean, you've always been my favourite bitch."

"You're very brave when you're hundreds of miles away on the phone, aren't you? You do realise you'll be back within striking distance of a cast iron saucepan on Saturday?"

"So, how was your day?" I asked, diverting the conversation.

"Fine," she replied flatly, "not as much fun as yours, I expect. How was golf?"

I lied, saying that I felt fine and that the weather had been too bad to play and, obviously, I never mentioned the cat or to be more precise, cats. According to my version of events, we'd just had a relaxing morning, found a coffee shop, and read the papers and now Danny and I were heading out for a very late lunch, adding that we might get a drink later. She seemed to be satisfied with my report, even if she sounded disappointed that I'd missed out on a round of golf.

"I'm just glad you're enjoying yourself. You sound like you're relaxing."

"I am," I fibbed, steadying my nerves, preparing to spoil her day. "Alice," I began sombrely, "there's something else I have to tell you and you're not going to like it."

By the time we'd finished talking, Alice had been through a whole raft of emotions and, at one point, had cried down the phone. She'd sounded shocked, upset, then angry, really angry, but as usual, had rallied quickly and gone into her instinctive, stoic manner she adopted whenever she knew I had to go Out-of-Area. Her resilience and inner strength had been two of the many traits that had attracted me to her and each time I got deployed at the RAF's behest, I took comfort in knowing that she would switch into her practical, survival mode and just get on with everyday life; unlike some of the wives. There were several that, as soon as their husbands went away for more than forty-eight hours, would dissolve into blubbering wrecks, and couldn't even face the thought of changing a light bulb without a bottle of Pinot Grigio and a dose of Prozac large enough to cheer up a suicidal donkey.

"We'll be fine. Of course, we'll miss you, but we'll be fine. We always are." She tried sounding stolid, but I detected a slight warble in her voice. "I love you, Henry, see you in a couple of days. Be safe and don't talk to any strange women."

"I won't," I laughed, "I love you too." I sighed, putting my phone in my pocket as I pushed open the heavy wooden door, bracing myself against the dreadful racket within.

## CHAPTER 75

### Maneater

It would have been generous to classify Sportsters as a dive and it sounded as noisy inside as I had hoped it wouldn't be. Squinting against the harsh din, I jostled through the throng of bodies but couldn't find Danny. I expected to see a penitent man, alone with his thoughts. One who'd been upset that he had been complicit in the death of two cats and guilty of robbing an old lady of her beloved companion. A sorry man who'd spent the morning in police custody and would be in desperate need of an afternoon of introspection and meaningful conversation with a close friend over a beer.

Sitting in a corner booth at the farthest end of the bar, with a very attractive young woman next to him, I immediately recognised Danny and his dazzling grin. He clearly hadn't lost his touch; he'd just mislaid his conscience and moral compass. I'd been in the bar for less than a minute and could already feel my temper starting to simmer. I just wanted to have a few quiet drinks with my best friend and to keep having quiet drinks until they became noisy ones, and I could no longer remember anything, not even my own name. I certainly didn't feel in the mood for entertaining. Walking towards the booth, Danny started waving enthusiastically and introduced me to our guests. Thankfully, he had found a table far enough from the huge, wall-mounted speakers which made normal conversation just about possible.

"Henry, this is Sandra," he said, indicating the pretty young brunette under his arm and then pointed to Sandra's friend who, by judging by her size, could have been Sandra's bodyguard. "And this is…"

"Rebecca, but Becca for thort," she added.

"For what?" I asked, frowning. Danny went wide-eyed, shaking his head at me. I wasn't trying to be rude, I genuinely hadn't heard what she'd said.

"Hi Henry, it's Becca for *short*," Sandra interjected, standing up and extending her hand towards me.

"That'th what I jutht thaid!" Becca snorted at her friend. The penny dropped.

"Nice to meet you," I replied, raising my hand at Becca as I sat down.

"Nithe to meet you too." *Oh dear, you poor girl. What a terrible lisp.*

Becca must have seen the expression of pity on my face.

"Ah, it'th okay. You don't have to look at me like that. Thith ith why I talk funny," Becca explained, opening her cavernous mouth, and tilting her head forward. Staring into the dark recess, I could see a steel ball attached to a thin silver bar pierced through the middle of her thick tongue.

"Ouch. Isn't that painful?" I winced.

"Nah and bloketh *love it!*" she winked, a little too eagerly for my liking.

"Could I have a word?" I asked, standing up and walking a small distance away, beckoning Danny to follow until we were out of earshot.

"What are you playing at?" I whispered through clenched teeth.

"What do you mean, fella?" Danny shrugged innocently.

"I've had a really shit day. Okay, we both have, and I said I wanted to have a nice quiet drink. Just you and me, remember?"

"No. As I recall you said you wanted a drink in a nice warm pub. You never said anything about quiet or a romantic date for two."

"Well, it was implied. I can't do *this*," I said, nodding my head towards where the girls were sitting, "let's go somewhere else."

"It's just a drink with a couple of young ladies. Nothing more."

"*Young ladies!* Are you taking the piss? Have you taken a good look at Sandra's mate?"

Even Danny had to admit that Becca wasn't the daintiest or prettiest thing he'd ever clapped eyes on. She had the biggest set of shoulders that either of us had ever seen on a woman and had been cursed with a chin to rival Desperate Dan's.

"Now, now, be nice Henry," Danny said calmingly, "it's just a couple of drinks."

"I am being nice. I know that lisp is self-inflicted, but nature's not exactly been kind to her, the poor thing."

"I know fella, she makes Geoff Capes look like an Oompa Loompa," Danny snickered.

"Don't. It's hardly her fault."

"Alright. So, are we staying?"

"Okay, as long as it's only for a couple," I conceded, feeling that I didn't have the strength to argue.

"Good lad," Danny grinned, patting me on the shoulder, and giving me that devilish look that I knew only too well, "I might even treat you to a packet of pork scratchings."

"Are you sure? Is that within budget?" I joked and then tried being serious again. "Just a *few* drinks, though. I'm not playing gooseberry all night," I added, begrudgingly resigning myself to being Danny's 'wingman.' I hadn't agreed through any sense of loyalty or bonhomie, the truth was, I had no fight left in me. What mental respite I'd been enjoying on the flight and during the drive from the airport had been crushed the moment I'd killed that cat, although my true descent back into a melancholic slump had probably started before that with the phone calls from work. As the world around me kept bubbling, laughing, and chattering, I felt nothing, empty and uncomfortably numb.

As the afternoon dragged on into the early evening, I reneged on my 'few drinks' limit, graduating from beer to pouring glasses of Jack Daniels down my neck as if my throat had an unquenchable fire. I'd said to Danny that I'd stay; I didn't say anything about sober. Meanwhile, Becca completely outpaced me, 'yamming' pint after pint, that in her hand looked like a sherry glass. I reckon she'd have seen off any professional darts player.

Looking across drunkenly at my beer-guzzling 'date', I had to lean back to focus and fit her all in. Whatever romantic antics Danny had planned this evening, he needed to understand that *I* wouldn't be entertaining anything more than polite chit-chat. Re-joining the party, I interrupted the indiscreet Danny before he got to the end of a story about a skiing expedition in Germany, involving me mistaking a hotel lobby plant pot for a urinal. I changed tack, deliberately mentioning that I was happily married with two children but didn't notice so much as a flicker to break Becca's unnerving leering stare. I was trying to make it quite clear that I would not be appearing on tonight's menu although, looking at Becca, I'd probably have been an hors d'oeuvre.

"So wha's the story with you girls then?" I asked, feigning interest.

"We're students at Perth College. I'm from Cheltenham and doing Applied Sciences then I want to study Medicine at St. Andrews," the bubbly, petite, Chardonnay supping Sandra announced. Not wanting to be outdone and trying to impress, Becca rudely cut in.

"I'm from Canterbury but grew up in Bathildon. I'm doing Beauty Therapy and I'm going to open my own thalon one day." I knew what she'd meant by 'thalon' but couldn't be sure if she'd tried to say Basildon and, worrying that she'd be offended if I asked her, decided not to, thanking my stars it hadn't been St Swithun's. *And did she really say Beauty Therapy?* To be blunt, Becca cast an impressive shadow and hadn't exactly been blessed when it came to looks either. I couldn't help worrying that she was going to have a tough time ahead of her. Not that I could imagine anyone being stupid enough to criticise the aesthetic handiwork of a 6'4" beer-swilling giantess wielding a pair of scissors.

I contemplated doing a runner and sneaking back to The Axe, but having volunteered to be Danny's unwilling fourth wheel I knew I had to stay, I'd never let him down before. Predictably, he appeared to be getting along famously with the attractive Sandra. Meanwhile, my attempts at a pleasant exchange with Becca stuttered painfully, but at least the drink continued flowing freely. Almost as freely as her saliva. Even though I'd started slurring, had trouble focusing long enough to pick up my drink, and at times was being blunt bordering on downright rude, Becca's unremitting ardour remained completely unaffected. She continued shuffling closer, stroking the back of my arm. Disturbingly, we'd now reached the stage where she'd reverted to ogling me while panting and gently grunting. *Any moment now she's going to leap up on this table and start beating her chest.*

Sandra must have noticed the uncomfortable lull in the conversation and tried rescuing the drowning dialogue.

"So, what star sign are you, Henry?" asked Sandra. "Becca's really into astrology. Aren't you?" she added timidly, trying to grab her friend's attention. Becca said nothing, instead continuing to study me while downing another pint, her face so close to mine I could feel her snorted breath warming my neck. "I'm a Capricorn. I've got horns." Sandra yelped, as Danny squeezed her thigh under the table.

I had always had unflattering preconceptions about the mental capacity of beauticians. Blondie had done nothing to dispel those, but the phrase that came out of Becca's mouth only reinforced my prejudiced view. Breaking her gaze she banged the empty glass down, wiping her mouth dry with her sleeve.

"Yeth, I'm into shtar thignth. I'm…" she began. *Not Sagittarius, not Sagittarius, please not Sagittarius.* I waited, fearful, anticipating a tidal wave of more dribble.

"…Canther. I've got crabth. Get it?" she grinned, slamming me on the back and revealing a set of crooked teeth like an abandoned graveyard.

"Pffft," I spat my JD and Coke across the table and started coughing.

"Drink anyone?" Danny interposed, leaping to his feet and walking around the end of the table towards me, trying not to wet himself laughing as he patted me on the back. Catching my breath, I stood up, pulling Danny to one side.

"Please, Danny, come onnn. Let's go, she's doin' my head in. Seriously? '*I've got crabs.*' Tha's not *funny*. Mind you, she cud stuff a'coupla Maine lobsters in that bloody great frizzy hairdo of 'ers and no one'd notice. Wha's wors'is she won't take the hint an' she's gettin' a bit *handsy*. I can't take much more. I jus' wanna g'home, pleeease."

"Ah mate, come on, stay. For me? Look, we'll have some food and one more little drinky. Just one?" Danny begged, pressing his palms together in prayer. "Come on fella, have a burger or something and I'll get you another JD and Coke, then we'll go. I promise."

"Really? Jus' one more an' some'ing to eat?" I implored, with a sneaking suspicion that I'd end up being conned.

"One more," Danny confirmed and made a crossing gesture over his heart.

"Okay, but if she tudges me ubbagain," I said sternly, "*I am outta here*," I added emphatically, throwing my hand away and pointing dramatically towards the entrance.

We fought our way to the bar, returning with four more drinks and bar menus.

"Ladies," I started in an attempt at pleasantness, "it's bin a pleasure but we're gonna have *one* more drink an' then we mus' get goin', but firs' food," I slurred, passing around the menus. Danny seemed to be faring quite well on a liquid diet, but I needed something more than the single packet of scratchings he'd treated me to.

"I've got thomething you can eat," Becca snarled, her eyes lighting up. I sucked in aggressively, desperately trying not to eject pieces of deep-fried pork rind soaked in bourbon and cola all over the table.

"Right, who's hungry?" Danny cut in, picking up his menu.

"I am," growled Becca, winking at me again as I tried to calm my churning stomach while my temples started throbbing.

"Okay. We should have time to eat, but we'll have to be quick. We're supposed to get back by seven," Sandra announced. I had to stop myself from standing on the table, punching the air, and cheering. The reason that Becca gave for their early departure nearly caused me to have a seizure.

"Alright Miss Bothy," Becca sniped before turning to me, "sorry but we've got to attend the Thtudent Union Annual AGM Henry, there'th a dithco afterwardth, they have one every year."

"What, a disco?" I asked.

"No thilly, the AGM."

"The Studen' Union Annual AGM, really? They have one ev'ry year, eh?" I couldn't help myself.

"Yeth, they have one every year," Becca confirmed adamantly, creasing a frown on her massive forehead.

"An *annual* AGM ev'ry year. Well, wha' are the chances a that?" Danny tried kicking me but missed. I didn't care anymore if I upset her, my well of sympathy had run dry about three leg squeezes ago. I'd become increasingly cranky and could see absolutely no reason for remaining pleasant, even if I might ruin Danny's chances with Sandra. *Screw him*. I was fed up with watching my best friend trying to charm his way into an attractive young woman's knickers while getting molested by a relentless, half-witted female Wookiee.

"I think you're really funny, Henry," said Chewbacca, nudging me playfully with her massive elbow, knocking me off balance.

"… and I thing you nea'ly broke my ribs," I whined, muttering, and rubbing my side as I climbed up off the floor.

"We've got over an hour Becca, but we don't *really* have to be there," Sandra countered, trying to appease her friend. Panicking, my brain started sweating.

"*Butchew must,*" I insisted in a rather desperate high pitch.

"Henry's right, my tutor pathifically thaid I had to be there, and I don't want to dithappoint her."

"Pacifically?" I asked.

"Yeth."

"Your tutor *pacifically* said you had t'be there?"

"*Yeth!*"

"Well, you'd bedder nobby late then, y'know, if she said you had t'be there, *pacifically* f'the *annual AGM* they have *ev'ry year.*"

"*Okay then,*" agreed Sandra sharply, tactfully intervening while glaring at me, "we'll go, but we can still eat here if we're quick."

I caught myself staring, as Becca's open mouth started moving slowly while she pored over the menu, captivated by her cakehole's sheer enormity. *I don't think eating quickly is going to be a problem.*

The bar menu listed fairly standard pub fare and Danny and I quickly made up our minds while our dinner dates continued mulling over their choices.

"I don't really eat much," said Becca. Danny's aim had improved, kicking me squarely on the shin as soon as he saw my mouth opening.

"Ow! Whaaat?" I cried, protesting loudly. *I wasn't going to say anything.*

"I'll jutht have the healthy option, macaroni cheethe with bacon bitth pleathe."

I rubbed my leg, struggling to believe my ears, and had to check the menu to be sure. Amazingly Becca was right, printed next to Macaroni Cheese I could see an (h) symbol, denoting it as healthy.

"How's pasta 'n' cheese healthy?" I asked, shaking my head. Sandra held the answer to my rhetorical question.

"This is Scotland, Henry. Compared to some of the stuff that the others in the halls eat that's practically a green salad. I've got a Glaswegian girl on my course who's convinced that pizza is health food."

"Tellme tha'sa joke?"

"No," she replied matter of factly.

"An' does she'plan on becomin' a doct'r too?" I joked, unprepared for the reply.

"No, a dietician. I've read her dissertation on healthy eating. She actually suggested that grilling a pizza was a positive contribution towards tackling heart disease in Scotland because it wasn't deep-fried."

I put my hands over my ears, trying to block out the nonsense. It hurt my brain.

# CHAPTER 76

## She's a Lady

We finished our meals a little after 6:15 and I watched in horror as Becca finished her last mouthful, then picked up her bowl and began licking it clean. Danny and I exchanged looks of disbelief. Clunking the glistening bowl down on the table, I was half-expecting her to rip off a chair leg and start using it to pick at the clearly visible bacon bits stuck between her tombstone teeth. Instead, taking a deep lungful of air Becca produced a belch that must have been drawn from her boots, loud enough to drown out AC/DC's 'Thunderstruck' momentarily. The noise alone was horrific but the smell… I found myself enveloped in a noxious, eye-watering cloud of gastric fumes that singed my nasal hairs and smelled like a combination of lager, pasta, and the part-digested troll she'd evidently eaten for lunch. I almost barfed.

"Oooh, that'th better," Becca said, tapping her sternum with the flat of her palm. *A salon, why not go the whole hog and make it a beauty and finishing school!*

This soiree from hell couldn't end fast enough for me. As the time sailed past 6:30, a beautiful light started appearing at the end of the evening's tunnel when Sandra announced that they'd have to leave soon. Blithely, I insisted on settling the bill and eagerly paid, delirious that momentarily I'd be free. I kept checking my watch. Content in the knowledge that our guests would soon be gone, I relaxed, briefly.

"Tho, can I thee you later?" Becca asked with what looked like a flirtatious smile but could have been trapped wind.

"Later?" I squeaked drunkenly, completely shocked by the unexpected question. "Well, no, no' really. It was lov'ly t'meet you Becca, an' it would've been nice t'spen' more time witchoo, but I jus' carn't. G'luck with yer course though."

"But *I* want to see you *later*," she grumbled. *Jesus!*

269

"Sorry," I said, trying to let her down gently, "we're playin' golf t'morrow, an' we have t'be up early," I explained. "Don't we Danny?" I added, desperately seeking support. "An' I'm old enough t'be yer father." I started floundering but thankfully my best friend had my back, which he amicably stabbed.

"He's right, Becca, we can't kick the arse out of it tonight. Besides, how old did you say you were, twenty-two?" Becca slowly nodded her planetoid noggin. "Well, there you go. He's a lovely fella but I mean, look at him. He's nearly fifty, a bit podgy and he's practically bald."

"Sod off. I'm nowhere near fifty y'cheeky bast'rd."

"Doethn't bother me. I like older men."

"And he's only got a small cock," Danny eagerly added.

"Er, hello, thang you. I'm right here! I c'n hear yooou." I retorted, glaring in disbelief, and waving angrily at Danny.

"That'th fine by me," said Becca resolutely as she leant over, sliding a gigantic hand under the table, and grabbing me by the crotch as she lisped in my ear, "you can thtick it up my arth."

"*TIME T'GO!!!*" I bellowed, erupting from the table, knocking the remainder of the drinks over in the process. Grabbing my jacket, I drunkenly bolted and started pushing past people, wrestling my way to the door before Danny reacted.

"Hold on, fella," he shouted at my escaping figure wriggling through the crowd.

I stopped, red-faced and exasperated, turning in time to see Danny hurriedly tapping on Sandra's phone. Bending down he whispered something to the girls, who both giggled, before grabbing his jacket and walking towards me.

# CHAPTER 77

## Show Me the Way to Go Home

The journey back to The Axe had been a quiet and sombre event. The combination of travelling, 'Moggygate' and a belly full of booze and pub food had me feeling so tired that I suggested we should head straight back to the hotel and go to bed.

Danny and I pottered along, hardly exchanging a word. He was first to break the long, cold silence as we continued plodding cautiously along the unlit alleyway beside the hotel's car park.

"Come on let's get another drink," he suggested encouragingly.

"No thang you. I'd rather slam my *little cock* in a car door than 'ave a dring in tha' bar."

"Really? You don't fancy a few swallies and some witty and urbane conversation with our genial host then?"

"Wha' with Stevie the Devil worsh'per? Nooo flippin' wayyy. I've 'ad a skinful."

"No worries fella," Danny nodded agreeably.

Emerging from the alley I noticed that the hotel's tramp had taken up residence inside one of the Biffa bins in the car park and lay sleeping on top of a pile of black rubbish bags. I felt quite envious, at least he had a view. Entering the hotel, we were hit with the hubbub from the bustling, noisy bar, and found the door leading to it wedged open. Taking one sneaky look inside we silently agreed that we didn't fancy listening to Runrig and knew we'd never get away with having 'a' nightcap, both understanding that we would have been press-ganged into a heavy drinking session, resulting in a lock-in with the intimidating Stevie. Neither of us needed that, especially as we had to be up tomorrow morning to play golf.

Danny kept watch, waiting until Stevie wasn't looking. As he turned to pour a drink from one of the optics behind him, Danny gave me a thumbs up and we crept past the open door, unseen, before giggling nervously and sprinting up the back stairs to our rooms. Breathing hard, I fumbled for my key before ramming it in the lock, the door complaining loudly as I flung it open.

"G'night, Danny. Le's try not t'kill an'thing tomorrow."

"Deal. Night fella, see you in the morning."

Slamming the door shut I panicked. Quickly turning the knob, I slid the button on the Yale lock, pulling the door to make sure the catch was working. It opened. Phew.

"Hello again. You alright?" Danny asked, turning back as he opened his door.

"Yep, jus' checkin' the lock. See you in th'mornin'."

Safe in the knowledge that Danny could come to my rescue, I pushed the door to and half-heartedly tried getting undressed, giving up halfway, "*Ah fuggit,*" I said, as I tottered sideways, flopping into a heap on the bed.

## CHAPTER 78

### Getting Jiggy With It

A fat old tabby cat sat on the roof of a shiny black Range Rover, wearing a hearing aid and a bright salmon golf shirt. I lay on my back, stretched out on the bonnet, my head resting on the windscreen as I slept. Disturbingly, the cat only had one eye, and half of its head was missing. It started speaking, trying to wake me up as it tapped me on the forehead with the wheel brace it held in one of its paws.

"Hellooo?" tap tap tap.

"Hellooo?" tap tap tap.

"Henry, wake up," tap, tap, tap.

The cat kept hitting me.

"Henryyy?" tap tap tap.

"Are you in there?" tap tap tap.

It just wouldn't stop.

"I've got a thurprithe for you."

Lying face down with my arms flopped at my side, my arse still stuck up in the air, I stopped breathing and listened. Silence. Peeling one eye open, I peered around the dark room, my breathing suddenly loud, shallow, and rapid. *Was that? No, it can't be. I'm just having a bad ...*

"Are you athleep?" an unmistakable voice asked from the corridor.

I froze. She'd found me. *Oh, God. How? How the hell could she be outside my door? Tracked my scent probably... Seriously though, how on earth?... Danny!* That git must have given Sandra his phone number before we left that dreadful sports bar.

"Henry," tap tap tap, "it'th Becca."

I didn't move, my perturbed mind spinning wildly. *Go away, please go away, please go away.*

"Hellooo?" Knock, knock, knock.

I gulped and could feel my heart pounding, hearing the blood rushing in my ears as a prickle of sweat bloomed on my forehead. Keeping deathly quiet and perfectly still, like a small furry rodent being stalked by an apex predator, I held my breath, listening. My blood was pumping so fast and loud that I began worrying that she'd be able to hear it. *She can probably smell my fear seeping under the door.*

"Henryyy? Wakey wakey."

Why couldn't she just take the hint, give up and leave? *Dear God, please God, make her leave. Please, God, I'll even go back to church if it helps. Just make her go away and leave me alone.*

"Hellooo?"

Whatever she used to knock on the door, her fist, head, or an uprooted tree, did its job and I shuddered, listening to the most terrifying noise of my life. Worse than the scream of a dentist's drill, worse than a child's first recorder recital, it was even worse than the dreadful sound of Katie Price's nails-down-a-blackboard rendition of 'A Whole New World.' The sound that turned me to stone, bringing me close to tears was two loud thumps on the door of room 14 of The Axe Hotel, Perth followed by a long, low, creaking sound. Like the noise made by Van Helsing forcing the hinges on a vampire's coffin.

"There you are," Becca said with relief, "wake up thleepy head?" she added, trying to coax a response from me as I lay quivering on the bed, dimly lit by the eclipsed landing light.

I slowly sat up, shaking. Becca stood in the doorway, pretty much filling it. She ducked and came drunkenly lumbering into the room and filled that too. I didn't know what to do. I still felt utterly sozzled, but even more terrified. My mind was shouting and slapping itself, trying to sober me up but failing, badly. Distressingly, I resigned myself to the knowledge that she was blocking my only escape route, not having the highly appealing option of throwing myself out of a third-storey window.

Striding into the room with very little clearance on either side of her massive shoulders, she flicked the light switch on and then shoved the door closed with her enormous bottom. Groaning loudly, the swinging door thumped into its frame, thudding closed like the sealing of a tomb. Thankfully the catch held.

The light bulb in my room seemed to be housing a small, brilliant sun, and straining my eyes, I tried focusing on my intruder.

"I've brought you thomething," she said proudly, proffering a large yellow box in one hand, the smell from which was already making me feel queasy, and in the other, an ice bucket.

"Thurprithe!" *Yes, it is, and not a nice one.*

"Please get out. I need t'sleep," I begged.

"But I came here thpethially and I've brought you thome prethents, look," she said, opening the polystyrene box and showing me the contents of the ice bucket.

Semi-blinded, I tried focusing again. A doner kebab smothered in some thick red sauce with chips and plastic cutlery, plus a bottle of Thunderbird in a Babycham ice bucket. *You had me at thurprithe.*

"Shdn't you be atchor annual AGM?" I slurred.

"No, thilly, that finithed ageth ago."

"Oh."

I really wanted her to go. I desperately needed to sleep, I felt horribly drunk, a little scared, and, in my half-dressed state, extremely vulnerable.

My sinuses recoiled, being assaulted by an array of strong odours. I couldn't pinpoint exactly what was making me feel worse, the alcohol with which I'd poisoned myself, the greasy smell of the kebab, or the stench of Becca's cheap scent. I thought she'd fallen into a bath of it, a bloody big bath that is. Not only had she been wallowing in a vat of Panache but she was also plastered in make-up. Squinting at her through one eye, I assumed she'd applied it in a blackout during an earthquake. I also noticed that she'd changed her outfit.

Despite feeling blotto, tired, and increasingly irritable, once again I found myself feeling guilty. Admittedly she'd stalked me and barged uninvited into my room, but I couldn't help wondering if this was somehow my fault. *Had I not been clear enough? Had I done something to encourage her?* I could have sworn that I'd rebuffed her advances all evening to the point of being downright rude. *Hadn't I?* Regardless, I absolutely didn't want to be hosting an uncouth female colossus, who had seemingly enjoyed one too many in the Student Union Bar, in my room at God only knows what time of night.

"Look, Chewbecca…" I began drunkenly.

"*What did you thay?*" she asked, her forehead creasing into deep furrows.

"Sorry, sorry, Rebecca, sorry. I don't feel well an' I'm not hungry. I'm really tired, an' I'm jus' a liddle bit drunk. Please, jus' leave me t'sleep. Pretty please." I beseeched.

"But I got all dressed up," she pined, turning around to display her billowing floral wigwam.

"Very nice but I need t'be up early in the mornin'. Jus' go would you."

"No, I came pathifically to thee you thexy," she griped.

*Sexy!* My head felt like a faltering gyroscope, I reeked of booze, and I was wearing a crumpled white t-shirt and a pair of saggy boxer shorts, and I only had one sock on. Oh yeah, one look at me and George Clooney would have been put on suicide watch.

"Please Becca, jus' go. I'm so tired," I grizzled.

"Well, that'th tough. *I am not leaving*," she insisted grumpily.

At first, she sounded upset at being spurned. Now, worryingly, she started sounding a bit pissed off, bordering on aggressive. She harrumphed, opening the polystyrene box as she sat down on my bed. The bed protested. Grabbing the kebab in one hand she started ruminating noisily.

"Oh no, come onnn. Don't eat that in heeere. Jus' look at the mess you're makin'," I groaned, as pieces of chopped cabbage fell from her lips, and went tumbling onto the bed and carpet. Ignoring my pleas, she continued shovelling large handfuls of pitta bread and kebab meat noisily into her mouth. Thick red liquid began oozing down her large fingers and over the back of her hand and she bent down, grabbed the bottle, and started guzzling noisily.

Belching seductively, through a glistening mouthful of semi-masticated doner kebab swimming in fortified wine, while rubbing her chest with her free hand she asked, "Don't you want me?" I nearly threw up.

"How m'ny times? For God's sake Becca, I'm married. I'm goin' home on Sat'rday and *pleeease stop touchin' yourself like that!" This is getting out of hand.* I couldn't look. Seeing her attack that greasy kebab, while massaging one of her mammoth boobs made my stomach gurgle. I most definitely didn't feel *in the mood*, nothing could have been further from my mind. Besides, I never strayed and if I had, I definitely wouldn't have tried 'getting fruity' with King Kong's half-cut sister.

"Jus' take your k'bab and your booze an' go. *Please!*"

"No! And I don't care if you're married," she snarled.

"Well, I bloody well do."

"Well... ithn't... that... a pity," she replied in a frighteningly determined and deliberate tone as she dropped her kebab and lunged. I squealed like a frightened vole. Becca's enormous physique reminded me of a giant silverback gorilla, and I discovered that she had the power to match. Scooping me up with one hand, she lifted me off the bed before placing me gently on the floor. Looking up at her huge frame, backlit by the dazzling ceiling light, I half expected machine gun-toting biplanes to appear from the bright glare and start circling her.

"Please, lea'me alone. I've got kids too," I pleaded in an equally plastered and petrified squeak. I couldn't guess exactly what form it would take, but I sensed that Becca was preparing to attack. Sinking to her knees she began manhandling me, forcing my nose into her huge cleavage, my head becoming shrouded in the black nylon fabric that had been obscuring Becca's gigantic breasts. In the darkness I started struggling to breathe as I felt her reaching down, grabbing at the front of my boxer shorts. They stretched momentarily, giving me a brief wedgie. A loud ripping sound followed by a cooling sensation around my tackle, announced the unceremonious passing of my underwear as it fell away in tatters. Unsurprisingly, I was feeling far from aroused, kneeling naked from my waist to the top of my sock on a bed of half-chewed cabbage. Feeling sleepy and light-headed but conscious enough to realise that my family jewels were swinging freely, I had the terrifying realisation that I was slowly suffocating.

Becca began rumbling, obviously disappointed with the uncooperative former contents of my recently deceased pants. Her voice took on a worrisome tone as she reached around me.

"I bet your wife dothn't do thith to you," she rasped, spitting erotically into my ear.

Leaning over me, Becca's hands started groping down the small of my back towards my buttocks then began probing.

My eyes suddenly flew open, nearly popping out of my head, and started watering. I let out a muffled scream into the chasm of her heaving nylon-swathed cleavage as an uninvited giant chubby finger began driving in the wrong direction up a one-way street. Not only was I being brutally violated by an unwelcome invader but there was also a definite warm, no, hot feeling, growing inside me. *Holy Mary Mother of God, that red stuff's chilli sauce.* Managing to wrench my head free I panted, desperately struggling for air.

"*Oh, my God!*" I screamed "*.... that's so hot.*"

"Oh yeah, you love it don't you?" Becca purred, mistakenly thinking that I was enjoying having my prostate gland prodded with a chilli-glazed digit. *Like it! Like it! If I had the strength right now, I'd knock your fucking teeth out. Where's my slayer's touch when I need it? Typical.* I didn't necessarily want the girl dead, but the ability to cause mild incapacitation would be very welcome right now.

The room began swimming, and I sucked in hard, fighting the feeling that I was fainting. Mustering every ounce of strength possible I reached back, grabbed Becca's wrist, and pulled, throwing my weight backwards.

"Jesus, I'm on fire," I cried breathily.

"*Yeth you are you horny little bathtard!*" Becca whooped excitedly, slamming my face back into her chest. My head continued reeling, the searing pain between my arse cheeks feeling so bad I feared I was definitely about to pass out. Taking two aggressive breaths, trying to fight the wooziness, I managed to remain conscious, just, and slapping my palms onto Becca's huge shoulders I pushed with every last fibre. *Timberrr!* As Becca fell, I tried getting to my feet but with jelly legs like Bambi, I collapsed, flopping back onto my knees, swaying gently, weak, and helpless. Tears began streaming down my face as Becca began rising, unstoppable, climbing towards the ceiling, enveloping me in her dark, ominous, monolithic shadow.

"I want you," she growled, unbuttoning her waistband.

"*Help,*" I sobbed, my body frozen, staring in horror as her skirt parachuted to the floor. Followed by her enormous knickers. I started screaming. If I could have reached the plastic fork, I would have happily tried gouging my own eyes out. I didn't have the words to describe the sight in front of me, but I'd seen something similar in a horror movie and that thing had ripped out the throats of three members of a polar research team and eaten their dog. It started just above her knees, but I couldn't tell precisely where it finished, as, thankfully, my view was interrupted by the hem of her blouse. I gazed blearily, assuming it carried on as far as her massive chest and across her back.

Earlier, I had drunkenly mused that Chewbacca was a more suitable name, without realising how accurate that thought had been. I'd never seen anything this hairy, man, ape, Elton John's toupee. More worryingly she was currently presenting herself so forcefully that she could have passed for a sex-crazed female sasquatch that had sat on a lipstick.

"You know what I need, don't you," Becca asked in a chillingly deep, forceful rumble.

"A shave?" I squeaked. I had absolutely no intention of going anywhere near that *thing* not even with a local guide, machete, and an armed escort.

"Yeth, a thlave." *That's not what I said. Then again, a slave would probably involve a lot less work.*

"You're my thex thlave now and I want you to…" the next two words she uttered made me shudder, and I started gagging, tasting the bitterness of bile and sour mash whisky swelling in the back of my throat. I heaved, as another wave of fear and panic started washing over me while the melting nuclear reactor in my arse continued burning. Praying that I'd misheard her, my worst fears were soon realised. Through the blurry fog of my tears, I could see enough to make me grasp what the maniacal Becca wanted, as she came stomping towards me, legs akimbo.

Kneeling on the floor, rocking, I frantically tried thinking of ways to escape and more urgently where I could get hold of something really cold. *The ice bucket!*

"Yes!" I exclaimed, unfortunately out loud, vocalising my eureka moment.

Becca eagerly grabbed me by the ears. Turning my head away at the last moment, the side of my face went bouncing off a rippling mattress of bristling, moist warm flesh, as my left hand continued fumbling around on the floor. My flailing palm hit the side of the ice bucket, knocking it over and spilling its contents. My fingers started scrabbling over the carpeted surface, desperately grabbing at the slippery blocks that kept sliding and popping out of reach. Becca meanwhile continued grunting and grinding against my cheek. Clawing at the wet carpet I trapped an ice cube, immediately thrusting my hand between my legs. The instant relief felt heavenly.

"Oh yes. Tha's so good. Ohhh yeeesss. Swee'baby Jeeesus yes."

Becca, encouraged by my apparent enthusiasm, started grinding even harder.

Fatefully, at that precise moment, I heard the groaning door to the mating pit open. Blissfully unaware of anyone coming into the room, I continued resting my head against Rebecca's writhing belly while enjoying the sublime, cooling effects of the small cube of frozen water on my inflamed starfish.

"Becca stop, let go, it's time to leave," I heard Sandra saying, trying to coax Rebecca into releasing her death grip. The blood began painfully throbbing back into my mangled ears the instant she relented.

Hastily grabbing her things, Becca started stomping seismically towards the open door. Sandra repeatedly told Becca to ignore me as, semi-naked, I knelt on the floor, shouting a foul tirade and barrage of verbal abuse at her, breathing raggedly, nursing my poor throbbing sphincter.

I felt Danny trying to lift me up. Helping me to my unsteady feet, he guided me to his room where I spent twenty minutes leaning against the cubicle wall with the showerhead pumping cold water between my arse cheeks. After guiding me back to the lovers' nest and putting me to bed, he kept watch, waiting for me to fall asleep, which he later said took about five minutes after I'd stopped crying.

"Hey, mate, are you okay?" he whispered, pulling the covers over my shoulders.

"Oh yeah, peachy. Jus' fuckin' peachy."

# FRIDAY

## CHAPTER 79

### What's Going On

It looked like I'd hosted a mini rave. A plastic ice bucket lay on its side in a huge wet patch and half of my bedding lay abandoned on the floor, along with my crumpled clothing and a scattering of chopped white cabbage. I leaned out of the bed, pulling the crushed remains of a polystyrene box towards me. *Why on earth did I buy a kebab? I must have been really hammered.* Worse than the thought that I'd actually eaten some of it, the horrible sight and smell of the cold doner meat, covered in red sauce and congealed, white, waxy fat kept making me heave. I didn't have a clue how my room had ended up in this state and scowled, trying to remember anything about last night. A sudden horrific image of a hairy, fleshy midriff popped up. *What the hell was that?*

Had I been beaten up by a flange of ruffian baboons? My whole body ached, but actually, being beaten up didn't seem quite fitting. On reflection, it felt more like I'd spent the whole night wrestling. Wobbling to my feet I staggered to the sink to look in the mirror. Splashing cold water on my face I shook my head, my reflection becoming a little clearer, instantly wishing it would go back to being blurry. The dark wrinkled bags, sagging jowls, and deathly pall didn't just make me look like the walking dead, they made me look like the walking dead who'd had a skinful and partied all night with Keith Richards.

The trickling water woke the slumbering liquid-filled giant within. *Not again! Damn it.* I remembered that I'd picked the tomb. Danny had the proper guest room with a bathroom and a toilet.

"Danny, I need your loo. Danny?" I shouted, banging on his door. I tried pushing it open, but the door remained shut. *Bugger.* I could feel the water backing up, half expecting my eyeballs to start floating any second.

I'd never make it down three flights of stairs, and realising I didn't have any pants on, leapt back inside my room, slamming the door shut. That left me with two disgusting prospects. It would either have to be the satanic shower or my waist-high hot and cold flushing urinal.

As the contents of my bladder swirled in the sink, spiralling down the plughole, I looked down, gasping at the foaming stream's shocking colour. Overseas tours in hot and hostile environments had taught me about the dangers of dehydration and I knew that dark yellow pee put you in danger of heat stroke. I stared in horror, wondering how life-threatening brown was.

I ran both taps, flushing away my foul-smelling shame while gazing at the creeping red vines snaking across the whites of my gunk-encrusted eyes. My tongue had a thick mottled coating of white fur that turned pale green around the edges and looked like it belonged to someone lying on a mortuary slab. Filling the chipped mug I took a mouthful, swirled the cold water around, and spat. Long strings of drool hung from my open mouth as I fell forward, leaning against the sink, my forehead thumping into the glass as I wilted, enjoying the coldness of the porcelain against my thighs. A wisp of cold air swirled around my backside, reminding me again that I didn't have any underwear on. Scanning the room, I saw what looked like a dead fruit bat draped across the foot of the clothes rail. *Who on God's sweet earth do these belong to?*

I could make an educated guess as to why my bedding, clothes, and a half-eaten kebab were on the floor of my room, but I had absolutely no idea why I was standing holding the most enormous pair of scarlet silk knickers. *How the hell did these end up on my floor?* I dropped the massive bloomers, resuming the search for my own drawers, spotting them lying under the head of the bed. They'd been shredded and... *Is that blood? For the love of*

*God what the hell happened in here and… ow, why do I feel like I've got a glowing lump of coal between my arse cheeks?* Bending down to examine my boxer shorts I regretted it immediately as blood began rushing to my head and the contents of my delicate stomach tried making a bid for freedom. I stood up, hooking the boxer shorts out with my foot, and picked them up between my toes. Sniffing my tattered pants, I knew instantly that it wasn't blood, it smelled like… *Is that, yes, it's chilli sauce. Of course, the kebab, but why are they ripped in half. And what the hell is going on with my backside?* Flexing my cheeks, I squirmed uncomfortably, making it worse. I couldn't even remember going to the toilet, but I must have gone into Danny's room during the night and that kebab had obviously gone right through me.

Another wave of queasiness started washing over me. Standing over the sink, shaking, I concentrated on breathing through my mouth, suppressing the feelings of nausea. *I really need to lie down.* Having grabbed the first pair of underpants I could find from the top of my bag, I very slowly put them on, not caring if they were clean. Climbing slowly back into bed, belching, and groaning loudly, I flopped onto my pillow. *I hope Alice opts for a church service and I think I'd like oak.*

## CHAPTER 80

### Girls on Film

Danny knocked on the door.

"Hello? Are you up?"

"Whaaat?" I grumbled, "Come back later." I desperately wanted to be left alone.

"It is later you old lush. I left you to sleep for as long as possible. I've been up nearly two hours."

My nose started twitching, hoovering up the scent of sweet, warm milky coffee coming from the hallway. Dragging my tired and sore body out of bed I shuffled towards the door, feeling like I'd been hit by a bus and wishing it had reversed back over me and finished the job. I pulled the door handle, the graunching hinges reminding me of my aches and pains.

"Wow!"

"What?" I asked grouchily.

"You genuinely look like a dead man walking," Danny observed with unbridled glee.

"Thanks a bunch," I muttered.

"You'd better have this," he said, swaying a large, red paper cup in front of my cadaverous face. "Massimo vanilla latte with an extra shot for…" Danny said, reading the name written on the cup, "Han Solo!" Screwing up my red eyes, I stared, confused, frowning at Danny. The drink had cooled a little, but the cup felt reassuringly warm. An injection of caffeine was exactly what I needed.

"Han Solo?" I asked, peering at the writing.

"Yes, *Han Solo*," Danny replied sardonically, wondering why his joke had fallen flat. I shrugged, shaking my head, and looking at him blankly.

"You don't remember last night, do you?"

"Well, it's very fuzzy," I answered vaguely.

"Yes, she was, wasn't she?" Danny grinned.

"*What?*"

"Fuzzy," Danny smirked, taking a sip from his cup.

"What? Fuzzy? I… I don't get it. Who was?"

"Never mind." Danny obviously didn't feel in a rush to fill in the blanks.

"Last night," I continued, "it's really… well… blurry. If you can call a total blackout blurry. I remember going to that awful sports bar and meeting those two girls. I know we had a few drinks and I think we had food but that's about… oh yes, I do remember you, you git. *He's only got a small cock.* Thanks, I'm going to make you pay for that. Just as soon as I've drunk this. Cheers," I said, clipping our paper cups together.

"What time are we teeing off?"

Danny looked at his watch. "We've got about two hours, sorry fella but I couldn't let you sleep any longer."

"Thanks, mate. Sooo…" I started, still desperately trying to dredge the seabed of my mind for any snippet of the previous evening's events, "I remember you saying I had a tiny knob and that's when we left, right?"

"Yeah. Seriously, that's all you remember, nothing else?" Danny asked, surprised at how much of the evening I'd had apparently blanked out.

"No, no, hang on, we walked back and… *did we end up in the bar?*" I asked hazily.

"No," Danny laughed, "you were pretty hammered, so we called it a night. We walked back, well, I walked, you staggered."

"What time was that?"

"I'm not sure but it was pretty early, we'd been on it all afternoon and I reckon you smashed your way through a whole bottle of Jack."

I closed my eyes, shaking my head. Even that hurt.

"I am never drinking again," I lied. "Wait, I still don't get the Han Solo reference?"

Danny's whole face lit up, even his eyes were smiling, "Oh, I haven't got to the best bit."

He admitted that he'd exchanged numbers with Sandra before we left Sportsters and had sent her a text, inviting her back to the hotel, but said that he honestly didn't think that Becca would tag along. Danny and Sandra had been in his room when they heard the screaming.

"She screamed. You're definitely making that up! Oh God, what the hell did I do? Tell me," I insisted, suddenly worried that I'd be up on an assault charge for molesting a young woman.

"Not her, you muppet, you!" Danny flatly replied.

"Okay, now you're definitely making it up."

"Oh no. She let herself into your room and tried to jump you. I think we arrived in the nick of time." I blanched, slowly pacing backwards into the room, putting my coffee cup down by the sink. I'd suddenly gone off it.

"Don't expect me to thank you if you hadn't…" I began accusingly.

"Whaaat? It's not my fault, I was, you know…"

"…just being you, you complete and utter shagbag. You're unbelievable."

"That's what she said."

I shook my head again, it still hurt. *I really must stop doing that.*

"Is the lucky lady still here?" I said, gesturing with my head towards Danny's room.

"No, I walked her home, then grabbed us some coffee on the way back."

"Okay, but you *still* haven't explained about Han Solo," I asked tetchily, resigned to the fact that Danny seemed intent on telling me everything.

"Well, you were swearing like a docker, you kept calling her Chewbacca and telling her to, colourfully, *go away*" he added.

"I called her Chewbacca and told her to fuck off?" I closed my eyes, stretching my neck, feeling awkwardly ungallant.

"Yep, I'd say about twenty times. Screamed it if I'm being honest, along with a variety of creative insults. Let me see…," he paused, tapping his chin, trying to recall just how offensive I had been, "…there was *Chewbacca*, obviously, that was your go-to phrase, um, *you ball-grabbing sasquatch*, what else …. oh yes, *Cousin It,* I thought that was quite funny. Oh, and then my personal favourite *you sex-mad orangutan.*"

I shook my head shamefully. Nothing could excuse that sort of hurtful verbal abuse.

"And…" Danny continued.

"*Oh God*, I thought you'd finished."

"Do you want me to stop?" he chuckled.

"Stop, oh no Danny, why would I want you to stop? This is as much fun as the time I went for a bladder check and had a camera shoved up my penis. Like I said to the urologist, is there much more?"

"We're almost there." *That's what he said.* "Sandra told her it was time to go, and you said she should call Han Solo, hitch a ride in the Millennium Falcon and see if they could make the Kessel Run in less than twelve parsecs again."

"Ohhh," I groaned, staring at the ceiling.

"Sandra told you to shut up and said she'd call Becca a cab. You told her she should call a big game hunter and tell him to bring a bloody big gun, tranquiliser darts, and a flatbed truck."

I felt mortified, remembering how I'd thought she resembled Han Solo's Wookiee co-pilot from Star Wars but couldn't believe that I'd been so insensitive and rude enough to say it out loud, plus all of those other horrendous insults. I must have deeply offended her and really hurt the girl's feelings.

"That's awful. That poor girl. Don't get me wrong, Danny, I wasn't her biggest fan but those are dreadful things to call a young woman."

When I woke earlier, I wouldn't have believed it possible to feel any lower than I had at that moment. I did now, by a mile. I don't think I could have felt any more of a despicable arsehole if I tried.

"I think I should call her and apologise," I said, putting my head in my hands. "Do *you* think I should apologise for last night?" I asked, looking up at Danny of all people for moral guidance.

"Oh... no... I wouldn't worry about it. Sandra said she was pretty hammered last night too and *apparently* can't remember a thing."

"Well, she might want these back," I suggested, bending down to pick up the dead fruit bat.

"*Holy moly,*" exclaimed Danny, his eyes widening like saucers, "stick those in your hand luggage. They might come in handy on the flight home tomorrow if we lose an engine and have to bail out!"

"I can see why women can't say no to you, you silver-tongued devil," I jibed. "I still think I should call her though. I feel terrible."

"Um, maybe you should see these first," Danny replied slowly, pulling his phone from his pocket.

On seeing the first image, the remorse that I'd felt and my strong desire to apologise to Becca started dissolving. By the time I'd seen the fifth incriminating horror shot any remorse had vanished completely. I felt certain that the last few close-up shots would have got me a lifetime ban from all social media platforms and attracted an investigation by the RSPCA. The graphic photos, combined with the tattered and stained boxer shorts convinced me that my initial fears had been way off. I was the one who'd been assaulted. My stomach heaved again as my head continued spinning.

"What on earth possessed you to take those?" I asked angrily, realising that Danny must have stood idly by, snapping away while I was being molested.

"Well, you didn't look like you were in any *real* danger, and I felt it was important to capture such a special moment."

"*Really?*" I snarled.

"Whaaat? Okay, honestly, what would you have done in my shoes?" Danny asked. *I'd probably have taken a load of photos to rub your nose in it, but I'm not going to admit that.*

"That's not the point. You're a bastard and you can bloody well delete those," I demanded, looking up from the phone until my incensed bloodshot eyes met Danny's. He could see that I appeared to be simultaneously shocked, upset, and deadly serious.

"Come to think of it," I continued, "just to be on the safe side, erase everything on your phone, then smash it, then burn the broken bits and throw the scorched remains in the Tay. I'll buy you a new one." The intense look I was giving Danny should have left him with no doubt there would be serious consequences if he didn't destroy all of the evidence.

"I don't care how long we've been friends Danny, if any of those, and I mean *any*, see the light of day I will hunt you down, I will find you and I *will* kill you."

"Okay, okay, relax," Danny said and began tapping and swiping the screen before shoving it in my face. The picture thumbnails had vanished into the ether and with that, all proof of last night's drunken shenanigans had disappeared, forever… except for the mess on the floor and the uncomfortable sensation in my swollen ringpiece.

"See, look, they're gone, do I still have to throw it in the river?"

"I guess not," I said, fixing Danny with an even more intense and deadly stare, "now listen very carefully, Daniel Ansell. I know that I've told you things in confidence before and that you've basically been crap at keeping it a secret. You've even blabbed about stuff to Alice and broadcast certain details to our mates, but not this time. Not one single word. Danny FM needs to go off the air, permanently. Understand?"

"Absolutely, fella. Not a word," he promised, gulping down a grin. For once, I believed he might actually mean it.

"My door's unlocked, help yourself to a shower."

"Thank you."

"Do you want me to order you some breakfast?" Danny asked heading downstairs. *I don't feel like it, but I suppose I should eat something.*

"Yes please," I shouted, as he disappeared below the landing, "*...and a nice coffee.*"

A thumb popped up above the top step. "See you in a minute."

## CHAPTER 81

### Grease

I showered quickly in the relative luxury of Danny's room, before changing into my golf gear, including my second brand-new shirt. Walking down the backstairs my nose started wrinkling, assaulted by the unpleasant smell of burnt toast, Nescafé instant, and dirty hot grease. As I'd been getting dressed, I'd realised that I didn't know the location of the dining room, if indeed there was one.

I popped my head around the door of the bar, spotting Danny amongst the tables of other unfortunate guests, sitting alone in the corner, and walked over. He couldn't resist commenting on my new golfing attire.

"Wow, nice shirt, Tiger, it suits you."

"Thanks," I preened.

"Red's a good colour for you, it matches your eyes."

"Ha, ha. So, this is the dining room," I said, sitting down. "Well, I must say, it's lovely and so much nicer than that scruffy bar."

"I believe it's also the conference room and children's play area. I don't know what they use the rest of the building for."

"I do," I offered, lowering my voice, "satanic rituals and storage for the bodies of all the slaughtered virgins."

"Virgins, in Perth?" Danny asked with surprise. "And when you say *they*, you mean Stevie right?" he added uncomfortably loudly.

"Shhh, yes. I am Steven for we are many."

"Hmmm, I think you need to get out more," he said, frowning with apparent concern.

"Well, it's the nicest Satan Worship House I've ever stayed in. You certainly know how to spoil a girl, Danny Ansell."

"Only the best for you, sweet cheeks. Five Pointed Star hotels and top-quality restaurants run by Michelin chefs. It took me at least, ooh, minutes to plan this trip you know, you ungrateful shit!"

I opened my mouth to say that all joking aside, I genuinely appreciated the effort he'd made when the door to the kitchen opened. Our own pentangle-starred chef walked in, placing two huge plates of fried food and a rack of toast in front of us. Stevie clearly had an impressive CV and great time management. Apparently, he could add chef and waiter to his ever-growing list of qualifications and somehow still made time to sacrifice maidens and pray to Beelzebub.

"Two full Scottish, eat up lads."

"Thanks," I said, looking down at my plate as he backed away into the kitchen. *I don't care how scary or threatening Stevie sounds or how 'in league with Lucifer' he is, I am not putting this greasy food anywhere near my mouth.* The platter of Scottish fried breakfast glistened, swimming in cloudy, black-flecked oil. I looked from Danny to my plate to Danny again, giving him a cold, filthy stare.

"Everything I just said about spoiling me, I take it all back. You're a git. Cereal and toast, I asked for cereal and toast."

"Fella, you never asked for anything except coffee."

"Are you sure?"

"Yes, I asked you if you wanted me to order breakfast and you said yes and a nice coffee. Sorry Princess, if you were feeling that ropey, I'd have got you an Alka Seltzer instead."

"I wanted cereal and toast."

"Well, you could have, if you'd asked. I'm not a bloody mind reader."

Surveying the plate of food, I wondered if I could stomach any of it. *"Oh, my God! What the hell is that?"* I asked covering my mouth in horror, pointing at my Scottish 'lardfest.'

"Um, that's white pudding. It's like black pudding only they use fat instead of blood. It's like a heart attack in sausage form."

"No not that. *That!*" I spat, pointing aggressively at the fried egg on my plate.

Danny leaned forward and we both sat gawping at a tightly curled black hair, lacquered in grease, partially buried in the white of the egg.

"Ohhh, yeah, that," said Danny, "um, I think that's a pube." Quickly identifying the disturbing thing poking out of my food, unperturbed, he then started shoving forkfuls of bacon and beans into his mouth. My stomach rolled over.

"Do you want me to call the chef so that you can make a complaint or possibly reunite them?"

"What and get filleted at the table or wake up inside a giant wicker man. No thanks," I said, pushing the plate to one side. The smell of fried food had made me queasy, but that pubic hair poking out of the egg made my stomach cramp. Danny's hysteria clearly only surfaced at the sight of blood, and he happily carried on with his own fried breakfast, transferring the sausage and bacon from my plate to his own. He didn't bother with the hairy egg though. He paused, pointing his fork at the rack of semi-charcoaled slices between our plates.

"Sorry mate, I'll get you cereal next time but there's some toast there. You'll feel better if you get something down you. Come on we're leaving in twenty minutes," he ordered.

I tried nibbling one slice of burnt toast with a veneer of margarine and cheap marmalade, taking a few unenthusiastic slurps of bitter instant coffee. *What a perfect start to my day.*


## CHAPTER 82

### Green, Green Grass of Home

Danny sat waiting in the car with his shades on, annoyingly perky and without the slightest hint of a hangover. After loading my golf bag and small holdall into the boot, which took me two attempts, I climbed into the passenger seat, fastened my seatbelt, and sat back, letting out a long, hung-over sigh. I spent the first ten minutes of the journey looking like a Labrador, with my nose poking out of the window, sucking in the fresh cold Scottish air, my sweating, shiny head reflecting the early morning sunshine. By the time the Range Rover hit the eastbound A90 towards Dundee, my forehead had gone numb, but I'd started feeling like myself again, well almost.

Half an hour later, as we were nearing the far bank of the River Tay, I watched a lone herring gull effortlessly glide across my view before dipping below the level of the bridge. I turned to Danny.

"So where are we off to then?" I asked, trying once again to wheedle a name out of him, as the water beneath us gave way to sand and rocks, then grass and trees.

"You'll see fella, not far now."

Gliding off the bridge, Danny eased off the gas as we approached and slipped onto the roundabout, taking the second exit straight ahead. The name at bottom of the road sign caught my eye, making me catch my breath. I glanced across at my grinning friend, realising we were travelling towards a particular famous venue.

"Are we going where I think we're going?" I asked, my insides giving a little jolt of excitement.

"Yep," Danny smiled.

"You are kidding me, Danny?" I asked, my pulse quickening.

"Nope" Danny replied, seeming genuinely pleased to see me looking so happy, "I'm taking you to the home of golf."

I quickly looked back over my shoulder at the retreating road sign that read 'A92 St. Andrews,' then across at my best friend.

"I bloody love you." I could have kissed him.


## CHAPTER 83

### Shake, Rattle and Roll

Slowing down, we turned left into Golf Place, past Auchterlonies and then the imposing red brickwork of the magnificent Hamilton Grand hove into view to my right, followed by the grey, solid stone structure of the world-famous Royal and Ancient Clubhouse. At that moment, a strange feeling in my belly started growing.

"Are we going to make our tee time?" I asked, anxiously looking at my watch.

"Yeah, relax fella. We've got fifteen minutes, loadsa time."

Annoyingly, we couldn't find a space in the small car park at the front of the clubhouse, so Danny turned the car around, taking a right into The Links, parking next to a low, white, wooden fence running along the edge of the 18th fairway.

"We won't be warming up then," I stated. The prospect of going straight onto the tee without the chance to loosen my muscles or hit a few practice shots was going to be more nerve-wracking than opening a heavy, lopsided ticking parcel from Eileen.

"You'll be fine, relax. It's meant to be fun you know."

"It's fine for you, you spend half your life in the gym. I spend all day sitting in front of a radar screen or in the Crew Room, or at home in front of the telly. The only exercise I get is walking the dog. Unless you count the few panicked days when I try running and do some sit-ups and press-ups three days before my annual fitness test."

"Alright Stressy Susan, *calm down*. You'll be fine. Aren't you excited? *Look!"* he enthused, sweeping his hand across to highlight the stunning vista of the bay and The Old Course, "It's St. flippin' Andrews."

"Sorry, I am. Yes of course I am."

"Well, tell your face then, you miserable git!"

Having driven in our golf gear, we just had to change our footwear, slip on our jackets and hats, and we'd be off. Danny opened the boot, pulling out both sets of clubs as I went to grab my golf shoes. Hooking my fingers into the back of my golf shoes I felt my middle finger breaking through a fine crust, squelching into something cold, thick, and squidgy inside the left shoe.

*"You're fucking kidding me?"*

"What's up, fella?"

"Look!" I said, thrusting the shoe at Danny.

"What the hell is *that*?"

Curled in the bottom of my left shoe was what could best be described as a feline Walnut Whip but without the walnut.

"I'm telling you I am going to murder that bloody cat."

"Maybe the poor little bugger got a bit desperate," he laughed.

"*Don't you start!*" The last thing I needed was my best mate to join Alice on Lucky's team of defence lawyers.

"Jeez, what's your problem?"

"You wouldn't believe me if I told you." He wouldn't, so I didn't. I realised that if I ever tried to explain the unique love/hate triangle between me, my wife, and our disturbingly calculating ginger tomcat and the special attention I got as Lucky's plaything, anyone would think I'd been at the sherry.

Thankfully, I kept a packet of tissues and wet wipes in my travel bag. Using two wipes and a golf tee I scrubbed and gouged my defiled digit and fingernail then turned my attention to Lucky's size nine leather portaloo. After banging, scraping, and scouring the inside of the shoe, I gave the insole one final vigorous rub with a wet wipe. Lifting it to my nose I sniffed. I was getting a delicate bouquet of citrus with strong floral notes, a whoosh of antibacterial disinfectant, and just the merest hint of a litter tray. *As soon as I get home, I must remember to sharpen those secateurs.*

The first tee on The Old Course was controlled by a splendidly attired old Scotsman. He sat waiting on a shooting stick, sporting tweed breeks, a flat cap, and as it turned out, to my misfortune, a biting sense of humour.

"Good afternoon, gentlemen." He greeted us, checking our tickets and handicap certificates before ushering us towards the first tee. "We'll just wait fer a wee while 'til yer playing partners get here," he instructed dourly.

I knew that due to the popularity of St. Andrews, visitors were expected to play in groups of four, but as the time to tee off arrived, the other two still hadn't shown up. I couldn't believe our luck. It would just be me and Danny; at least that took some of the pressure off, although with the next group of four arriving, and a line of visitors lingering nearby we'd still have a small audience. The starter spoke to us briefly, explaining a few local rules before inviting us to tee off. Danny tossed a tee in the air. The white peg landed pointing directly at me.

"Right, fella, you're up. Play well," Danny said, standing back as I prepared to tee off.

Reaching into the bag for my new driver, which could really only be described as 'nearly-new,' I could feel my hands trembling. Initially, the nervous flitting in my belly had been mild, but now, walking onto the tee, golf club in hand, the feeling started swelling. I felt my stomach lurch as it thought about evicting its contents and I must have looked shakier than OJ Simpson's alibi.

I gave my driver a couple of ritual waggles. My last practice session hadn't instilled much confidence, and that ugly mark on top of my driver was still upsetting me. I tried not to think about how it got there. My mind, however, had other ideas and decided to clearly replay a clip of me back on the range, hitting shanks and ducking as a golf ball tried to kill me. Danny could see me shaking.

"Just relax fella and have a good game," he said encouragingly. I looked up and gave Danny a wan smile as my guts continued writhing and the blood drained from my face. Taking aim, I started thinking that the feeling of a few butterflies was growing into a maelstrom of whirling fruit bats. *Fruit bats!* Suddenly, noticing the head of the shiny red driver glinting in the sunshine, a pair of massive shiny knickers began flapping before my eyes.

"Come on, fella, we're playing golf, not statues," Danny said, breaking my trance.

"Sorry. Just keep your eyes on this beauty," I said in a pathetic attempt at quelling my nervousness while trying to erase the sight of Becca's titanic flying bloomers.

I drew the club back slowly, cocked my wrists, and turned my shoulders, winding my body into a tight coil. I paused for a split second and as I started turning my hips back my buttocks gently peeled apart, reigniting the fire in my ring, causing me to clamp my cheeks shut and stand up, as I vigorously swiped at the ball.

The large, metal clubhead whooshed low and fast. Following through, I looked up, hoping to see a small white ball disappearing into the blue yonder and go bounding down the fairway towards the Swilken Burn. Instead, I saw nothing but a lot of blue sky, a golf course and the seaside. I had felt a strange knock and heard the faintest click as I swung but had no idea where my shot had gone. Searching the heavens in vain, out of the corner of my eye I became aware of something scuttling off to my left. *Oh God!* Turning my head shamefully, I saw my ball skipping towards the 18th green. Incredibly, I'd brought the club down on such an extreme outside path that I'd somehow managed to hit the ball off the heel of the club and it had shot off, between my legs, at roughly ninety degrees. I watched it skidding through the grass, bouncing over a couple of mounds, before running up and rolling onto the putting surface. Coming to rest just seven feet from the flag of the famous final hole in front of the clubhouse, it earned a ripple of applause from the four Japanese golfers standing there lining up their putts. I felt my cheeks flushing as Danny clutched his knees, bent double laughing, the waiting four-ball joining in.

Setting off to retrieve my ball and apologise, I took a few embarrassed steps towards the green when the chuckling Starter cut me dead.

"I'd take yer putter, laddie. If ye sink that ye'll be seventy under par!"

After such a shameful tee shot, unsurprisingly, my already unstable golf game completely fell apart. By the 9th hole, my confidence felt like my arse, in tatters, and I'd amassed a score of fifty-one, fifteen over par. My dreadful tally included two shanks, *aargh, bollocks*, four brand new golf balls that had been swallowed up by the impenetrable thick gorse, *shit, shit, bugger, shit,* and one ridiculously wild sliced tee shot that ended up on the beach, *oh for fuck's sake, FORE!* While encouraging me to calm down, play well, and not stress, Danny couldn't resist mentioning my opening tee shot every few holes. To be fair I'd have probably done the same if the tables had been turned.

Miraculously I hit a reasonable 3-wood into the narrowing throat of the tricky par 4 13th, avoiding the cavernous Coffin Bunkers, leaving me a short iron to the immense double green. The satisfying compressed, crunch of my approach shot gave me my first glimmer of hope, making me think I'd hit a perfectly controlled low spinning draw into the wind. Annoyingly, the ball sailed right over the flag, *damn it,* hooked left, *no way,* and kept going, *WTF,* landing where the two holes merged and about eighty feet from the hole, *oh come on, you've got to be kidding me.*

"Seriously! I thought I'd nailed that," I grumbled, ramming my pitching wedge into my bag before angrily ripping the cover of my putter as I wrenched it out.

"Does somebody need a hug," Danny sang.

"Shut up," I growled, stomping off to assess the monstrous snaking eighty-footer I'd left myself.

After hitting a dreadful lag putt that came up fifteen feet short, I almost topped my second effort, leaving myself a simple two-foot tap in for an annoying bogey. *For Christ's sake, come on Henry, just knock this in for a five and move on.* The ball clicked off the putter's face, rolling straight towards the hole. I started walking to pick the ball out of the cup, just as it broke left, caught the rim of the hole, and horseshoed around, stopping right on the edge. I waited and waited but irritatingly it sat there, mocking me, refusing to drop.

"*Bollocking bastardy shitbags!*"

"Okay, fella, pick it up, I don't think I could handle watching you miss that!" Danny chuckled.

"Fuck off!" I snapped while flexing the shaft of my new Scotty Cameron putter against my knee.

"Now now. Calm down, dear," Danny suggested, "it'll be a fortune to replace." It would and if Alice knew how much I'd spent on it she'd probably have bent *me* over *her* knee.

"Fggnshtnbllcks," I muttered, relaxing the pressure on the club, and shoving it back in my bag.

*A four-putt for a double bogey, aaargh!* I'd become more than a little fed up, feeling dragged down by my poor play and Danny's occasional ribbing wasn't helping. Standing on the 14th tee, preparing to tee off, he started again.

"Come on, mate, you're much better than this. Let's see one of your big booming drives, straight down the middle... I mean the middle of this hole; you do know where that is don't you?"

"Seriously Danny. *Enough!*"

"Whaaat? I'm just kiddin', fella."

"Well, it's getting a bit much."

"So's your score. I'm going to need an abacus at this rate."

"Just *stop it*."

"Alright, alright, mind your blood pressure. You've had more than enough strokes today. You don't want another one."

*"Enough!"* Raising my nearly-new driver above my head, I lunged, preparing to crack Danny's skull when the absurdity of my behaviour suddenly dawned on me. Okay, so I'd made a complete fool of myself on the first tee and currently, I felt like I couldn't hit a cow's arse with a banjo. However, I was standing on the hallowed turf of St. Andrews, fulfilling a lifelong dream of playing a *free* round on the historic Old Course. If I had wanted to get wound up and stressed, I might as well have stayed at work, if I'd been allowed to. I began reminding myself that I'd flown to Scotland on a boys' holiday with my best mate who was paying for everything. I wasn't at work trying to kill people or poisoning my dog, upsetting my wife, or getting molested by a crazy hairy beast; simian *or* feline. I was on a golf course, the most famous golf course in the world, so why not try relaxing a little and enjoy it?

As Danny cowered and the ridiculousness of my behaviour washed over me, I began laughing. A chuckle at first, but it soon started growing, building to full-blown belly-shaking laughter. My shoulders rocked as tears ran down my face and I felt the angst and frustration I'd been suppressing come pouring out of me. Laughing so hard that it hurt my ribs and made my legs go weak, I ended up sitting down on the cold grass. Danny joined me, relieved that I'd called off my attack and drawn in by the infectious happiness. The two of us sat on the 14th tee box of the Old Course, St. Andrews, guffawing and reeling. It must have looked like two villages had given their idiots the day off.

# CHAPTER 84

## Feeling Good

As my ball went sailing upwards, climbing into the panorama of blue and white, I felt my whole body sigh. I watched dreamily as my ball kept flying, carrying the Beardies sand traps, before bouncing, bounding, and rolling down the wide fairway known as the Elysian Fields, stopping 290 yards from the tee. I sent my second shot screaming miles over Hell Bunker and beamed as it ran through the fringe, trickling onto the green of the Par 5 in two shots. I made a birdie. Punching the air in celebration, I could feel my confidence restored. The magic kept going, having a dream finish to the round. One under par for the last five holes, including a satisfying par save out of the bunker on the notorious 17th Road Hole. I felt happy, free, released, and overcome with a sense of joy I hadn't felt in years.

"Thanks," I said, smiling inanely at my best friend. "I mean it, really, thanks, mate." I couldn't remember the last time I'd been this happy and meant every word as we stood shaking hands on the 18th green.

"Come here," I said, grabbing him in a manly embrace, overcome by a warm wave of emotion, "this was amazing. Thank you so much. I still can't believe I'm stood on the 18th green of the Old Course."

"Well, you are," he grinned, "for the second time today!" *Twat!*

The clubhouse clock's red face showed it was approaching five p.m. when we walked off the final green. Heading back to the car, the light began gently fading as the Sun continued dropping behind Aytounhill. According to the satnav, our drive back to Perth would take us just under an hour. Hopefully, it would be reliable enough to take us directly back to The Axe. I felt so hungry I could have eaten one of my golf shoes, though maybe not the left one. Having changed our footwear, we loaded the clubs into the back of the car and drove off, heading northwest, towards the soft, pink glow of sunset and the promise of another night of the delights of Perth.

"So, what do you fancy for dinner?" Danny asked pulling left off the roundabout onto the A91 exit, following the signs for the Tay Bridge.

"I really don't care but if it's alright with you I'm going to close my eyes and keep playing the last five holes in one under, over and over."

"Henry my old friend, knock yourself out. Whatever makes you happy." *Spending time with you buddy, spending time with you.*

## CHAPTER 85

### Size of a Cow

I kept dozing on and off on the journey back. Satnav Ally was clearly in a good mood, directing us straight back, and with only one minor tailback on the ring road around Dundee we crunched back into the same parking space just after six o'clock. After clomping our way upstairs, Danny let me shower first.

Clean, shaved, and refreshed, I was sitting at the bar chatting to Stevie when I felt a hand on my shoulder.

"Is that mine?" Danny asked, pointing to the foaming pint glass next to me.

"Yes, mate, cheers, and thanks again for today. I loved it."

"You're welcome and thanks for taking a massive dump in my bathroom."

"Sorry, it was meant to be a revenge poo, but I did feel slightly bad and opened the window," I grimaced.

"Revenge? What did I do?"

"Well, you beat me at golf today."

"Fella, my granddad could have beaten you on the front nine and he's been dead ten years! Next time, do you think you could flush?"

"Oh, my God. I did, *didn't I*? I know I did. I always do."

"Well, it didn't work because I walked in after you, lifted the lid and was greeted by Tarka the Otter. Seriously, it was massive. I had to cut the stubborn bugger in two with the bog brush to get rid of him."

"Oh, God. I'm so sorry." I cringed apologetically.

"Are you hungry? Judging by the present you left me I reckon you're practically hollow," Danny chuckled.

"I'm famished," I confirmed before turning to face our barman. "So, Stevie, where's a good place to eat," I enquired, "apart from Sportsters!"

## CHAPTER 86

### Spice Up Your Life

Our genial hotel manager, barman, and porter-excused-heavy-lifting had given us directions and recommended a few eateries. However, I wasn't totally convinced that Danny and I shared the same culinary tastes as our menacing host, although he did mention a curry house as one option. Tandoori Nights sounded reasonably inviting and hopefully free from human sacrifice.

Crossing the bridge over the railway line, we continued walking purposefully towards the centre of town.

"Hang on I think we need to go right here." Remembering that Stevie had said not to go past the purple and green-fronted Cheryl's Hair Salon, I replayed his instructions in my head. "Yes, it's definitely this way," I confirmed, before crossing to the pavement on the far side of Charterhouse Lane, as we continued heading into town.

Stevie's directions had been unerringly accurate, and as the St. John's Kirk bell tower chimed nine o'clock, we turned right at the Costa on Scott Street and entered the pedestrianised zone of Perth's main thoroughfare.

"Still up for a Ruby Murray?" Danny asked.

"Yep, it should be down here," I nodded.

Stevie had said that the curry house could be found about halfway down the main row of shops on the right-hand side. Driven by our grumbling stomachs and the thought of beer and a balti, we walked quickly, scouring the shopfronts.

"There it is," Danny announced, pointing to a building two doors down, "right there, next to the pet shop."

The name was actually Tandoori Knights and it looked nothing like any curry house either of us had ever seen. Coats of arms adorned either end of the restaurant's awning, the space filled with the silhouette of armoured men on horseback jousting with forks. From the outside, it could definitely be classed as the world's most un-Indian Indian.

"That is just weird," I said, shaking my head.

We looked at one another and in a 'what the heck' way, shrugged our shoulders and started walking towards the entrance. It didn't get any less strange on the inside.

Admittedly, the interior of the restaurant looked like any typical curry house, with an orange-patterned carpet, fresh, crisp white tablecloths with saffron yellow napkins, and the obligatory red flock wallpaper. However, the usual background tunes of 'Now That's What I Call Bhangra' had been replaced by a recording of 'Greensleeves' played on sitar. It appeared devoid of diners, apart from us.

A freckled ginger late adolescent, evidently not from the Indian sub-continent, welcomed us unenthusiastically, wearing a badly tailored gold doublet and embarrassingly tight green hosiery, so close-fitting you could tell his religion. The emerald-clad youth could almost have pulled off the whole mediaeval look too if it hadn't been for the pair of silver Reebok trainers on his feet. Greeting us in a bored drawl, he couldn't, or rather didn't, try that hard to hide his strong Scottish accent or complete indifference, sounding like a monotone 7th-century android from Dumfries.

"Good evening, squires, I am Lancelot. How can I serve thee this fine evening?" he droned apathetically. The three of us stood awkwardly, Danny and I taking a moment to check for signs of a hidden TV crew. *Dear God, this is going to be painful.*

"Um, table for two please?" Danny asked, breaking the silence.

"Verily," Lancelot replied robotically.

I tried stifling a snigger and from the look that Lancelot gave me, I thought I might be challenged to a duel or at least a game of 'stone, parchment, shears.'

As my appointed second, Danny intervened. "Look, *Lancelot*, this is all a bit odd mate and as much as we appreciate the effort you're going to with this whole *knights' thing*, me and my mate are the only people in here. We just want a curry and a few beers, so you can drop the forsooth, hey nonny nonny sire bollocks if you want."

Lancelot looked at us warily, his eyes darting suspiciously from Danny to me and back again, wondering if he was being tested, then his shoulders dropped.

"Thank God fer that. A'm fed up wi' all this pish."

Lancelot a.k.a. Robbie had been waiting on tables for six months, trying to make a dent in his growing student debt and pay his way through university as an Engineering undergraduate.

"I'm not surprised that you're fed up. I would be too if I had to talk like that and wear that ridiculous clobber every night," I offered sympathetically.

"Och, I don't. I'd never ah taken the job if ye'd told me I'd be talkin' like a saft in the heed Englishman an' wearin' a poncey jaykit an' tights," he confessed.

Robbie explained that the Indian-born owner was obsessed with the Arthurian legend and the restaurant name had been his idea. He'd also thought that during Perth's hosting of the Mòd, it would be fun for his staff to dress in period costumes and role-play to match his themed menu, for the whole nine days of the event! I found it a bit peculiar, considering that King Arthur and a prawn bhuna had to be the strangest of bedfellows.

We ordered two pints of Kingfisher and Robbie handed us each a 'Bill of Fayre' that had been printed to look like an olde worlde tariff made from a sheaf of velum and handwritten with a quill. He left us for several minutes to mull over the bizarre menu.

"What do you fancy then?" asked Danny.

"Well, I like my curry how I like my women," I replied smarmily with a wink.

"Really? I don't see a Bigfoot Balti on the menu!" Danny chuckled.

"*Oy Ansell, I warned you!* Kneecaps are for life not just for Christmas," I growled, wagging my finger slowly. He held up his hands in surrender, mouthing sorry. "I meant saucy," I continued, "with a hint of fire."

"Ooh, get you, Omar Shariff," Danny mocked. "So, what are you having then?"

"Korma probably," I shrugged. "Actually, I've no idea, I was waffling because I'm only halfway through the starters. I'm loving this menu, it's like something from Monty

Python."

Having eventually settled on our choices, we placed our order including two more beers.

"…and just bring everything out together please fella, we're starving," Danny added, as Robbie slouched off to the kitchen.

Twenty minutes and two more pints of Kingfisher later, our green-legged serf appeared pushing a wooden trolley.

"Right A've got a Gawain the Green Goat Goan Curry with Pellinore's Pilau an' the Bedivere Beef Bhuna with Mordred's Mushroom Pilau an' there's Arthur's Aloo Gobi and a plain naan."

"No fancy Arthurian-based name for the naan then?" I asked with an enquiring smile.

"No," replied Robbie with a condescending grin, "it's plain."

"Okayyy," Danny interceded, "I ordered the Goan curry and my friend there," he said pointing to my Camelot placemat, "ordered the bhuna and, please, forget all the fancy names."

"Ye'll no be wantin' Merlin's Magical Mango Chutney then or Lady O' the Lake Lime Pickle?" asked Robbie.

"*Oh, dear God*," Danny tutted, "pickles, chutney, and that mint yogurt stuff would be great thanks, to go with the poppadoms. Plain old poppadoms, not Sir Kay's Courageous Crispy Shields or whatever you call them."

"Right ye are," Robbie grunted, plonking down two plates of curry, "yers is tha green un, an' yer mate's is orange. Enjoy."

Surprisingly my orange curry tasted unbelievably good, rich, meaty, and very cheekily spiced, and even better when accompanied by several more pints of lager.

By the time we'd finished, I'd started crumbling from the impact of seven beers. Danny obviously saw the effect that last night's trauma, a round of seaside golf and several pints were having on my plastered face.

"Had enough?" Danny asked. I imagine he decided that it would be a good time to go before I did or said something stupid. Too late.

"Verily, forsooth 'twas a mighty fine repast, Squire Ansell," I replied before turning to bellow my orders at Robbie. "Lancelot you fine fellow, tally the bill, my good man, saddle our charges, and fetch them to the front of the inn," I ordered, wafting my hand at our serf. Luckily for me, the themed decorations didn't extend to Robbie having access to a mace, lance, or crossbow. Danny rolled his eyes.

"Sorry about that fella," he said apologetically to the snarling Robbie. "Could I just get the bill please?"

## CHAPTER 87

### Cigarettes and Alcohol

While navigating a safe path to the hotel, I could clearly hear Sharleen Spiteri coming from the bar halfway down the alley. Stumbling inside we saw that the night appeared to be in full swing, with animated conversation floating from the sea of heads bobbing above a swirling, broken layer of thick smoke. I couldn't tell if the dense cloud had been made deliberately with dry ice or was a byproduct of having a room full of natural-born smokers, probably a mixture of the two. The patchy fog pulsed and flashed, lit by the spinning coloured lights on the DJ booth. The bar-cum-dining room had been turned into a Friday night disco and, even though it was before eight, the floor seemed to have been electrified as we walked in. Stevie the DJ spotted us. He had obviously spent a good part of the evening keeping himself as well-oiled as his inebriated clientele and continued to multi-task with his usual aplomb. From the open doorway, we watched in admiration as he bopped away while serving drinks behind the bar, a stubby cigarette wedged in the corner of his mouth, before nipping behind the mixing deck in the corner for a quick spot of DJing. While cueing the next song he spotted us, waving wildly, and came bounding over.

"Awright lads, what'll ye have," he shouted over the thumping music. Dropping his glowing cigarette on the carpet, he squashed it with the toe of his shoe before putting Danny and me in a vice-like, convivial headlock and dragging us into the bar.

"I wondered where ye'd got to ye wee basta'ds. It's yer las' night so these ones are on tha' hoose."

I had to admit that I had been scared of our hotel manager cum chef cum DJ cum suspected Satanist, but in my drunken haze I decided that Stevie didn't scare me at all, he just had the misfortune of being one of those overly aggressive friendly types. The sort of bloke who genuinely wanted to be your pal and buy you a drink, but who you mistakenly thought would kill you if you refused. Stevie released us from his bone-crunching embrace and walked around behind the bar to serve us.

"So, what'll ye have? Whisky?" he asked in his inimitable hospitable but threatening manner.

"Lovely jubbly," I agreed, rubbing my sore neck, even though I much preferred bourbon, "and keep 'em coming."

# CHAPTER 88

## Rag Doll

Danny had been pacing himself all night while trying repeatedly to slow me down and stop me from embarrassing myself. He failed miserably. I was clearly 'on a mission' which I successfully completed, entertaining the whole bar in the process, and probably deserved a medal. By midnight I became two things: a local celebrity and absolutely plastered.

"Fella, I think it's time for bed," Danny suggested, peeling the microphone from my grasp. *How dare you?* Blinking slowly, I nodded with an imbecilic grin then tried to punch him and missed. *Okay, we'll call it a draw.* Closing my left eye, I raised a wavering finger, taking a bearing on the open doorway. Lunging and careering in the general direction of the opening, I stumbled three steps sideways before standing up, almost vertically. Screwing my face up into an exaggerated squint, I raised my finger for a second time, checking my bearing again, then set off once more, lurching across the room. Staggering wildly, I tripped and fell over. Danny stood, watching in awe. It was proving to be a tricky crossing, mainly caused by trying to traverse the confusingly patterned carpet through the thick mist. Eventually, I made it, resorting to crawling the last ten feet on all fours, the whole bar stopping, acknowledging my exit with rousing cheers and rippling applause.

"C'mon fella, up we go," Danny offered encouragingly, stepping over me as he mounted the stairs.

"Oh yeah, look atchoo, Mister Fancy Pants. Always *showin' off*, walkin' about on two legs an' everythin'. You flash git."

"C'mon, you silly sod," Danny replied, laughing, as he bent down, helping me off my knees, "let's get you to bed."

Putting his head under my arm, lifting me up, he half-carried, half-dragged me up to my room. In my current condition, if you'd pitched me against Wayne Sleep in a cage fight, Danny would have thrown in the towel before the bell for fear of me getting my arse kicked.

"Open ses'mee," I said, producing the key from my pocket, and waving it in Danny's face. He unlocked my door, sliding me along the wall before lowering me onto the bed and slipping my shoes off. I insisted that I wanted to take my own shirt and trousers off but couldn't, although I felt like I'd conquered Everest when I managed to unbuckle my belt unaided. Grabbing the hem of my trousers, Danny squatted and pulled. The trousers didn't budge, I stayed slumped on the bed, but the mattress happily came sliding off the metal frame, slapping onto the bedroom floor. We both started giggling.

"You're not helping," he said, "lift your arse."

Arching my back, he tugged again. This time the trousers slipped off my legs, taking my boxer shorts with them.

"*Oy, what's your game?*" I shouted, grabbing and pulling my underwear back up.

"Don't worry, fella, you're not my type."

"Pah," I scoffed "you cudn't afford me."

"Come on, mate, we need to put the mattress back on."

Staggering to my feet, Danny and I grabbed an edge and flipped the mattress back over.

"Oh bugger," I said, looking at the upside-down made bed.

Danny wrenched the covers out, scattering them on top. Standing back, he watched as I wrestled with my shirt, managing to undo most of the buttons before ripping it off, sending the last two pinging across the room. Taking two unsteady steps towards the edge of the bed, I pirouetted and collapsed back onto it. Danny then attempted to put me in the recovery

314

position. It had obviously been quite a few years since his last RAF annual first aid course, but he tried giving it a go and by the time he'd finished manhandling my uncooperative limbs and adjusting my body, it looked like a crash test dummy had been dropped headfirst from the roof of a multi-storey car park. Laying on my front, my head rested at a funny angle with my arse sticking straight up in the air, but I wasn't complaining.

"That'll do," he said, standing back to admire me impersonating a half-dressed contorted mannequin.

"G'night," I mumbled, "an' thangs for a really great day."

"Yer welcome, fella, sleep well. I'll see you in the morning."

I heard Danny creeping out, pulling the groaning door that clunked as it wedged shut against the thickly painted frame. *Goodnight.*

## CHAPTER 89

### Wake Me Up When September Ends

Yesterday, I woke up feeling pretty shabby. It didn't come anywhere close to the sensation in my stomach this morning. I felt like I'd chewed my way to the final of The World Pickled Toad Eating Championships and wanted to throw up. Then I wanted to crawl away into a dark corner and be left alone to die. Irritatingly, Danny appeared to have escaped *another* hangover, sounding his usual perky self when he knocked, then pushed the door open that complained with its familiar groan. Announcing his entrance, he stepped into my penthouse suite.

"*Goood morninggg Vietnaaam,*" he shouted, annoyingly loudly. It hurt my head. Everything hurt my head, even breathing. *I've changed my mind, I want to kill Danny, then I want to die.* I rolled over, pulling the covers over my head.

"Sod off."

"How are you feeling?"

"Terrible."

"Don't you want some breakfast?"

"Nooo," I moaned.

"Really?"

"Positive."

"Can't I tempt you with a hairy egg on toast?"

"*Hurgh,*" I wretched from under the bedding. "Please go away and just leave me to die in peace."

"Go back to sleep then, Princess," Danny replied sympathetically. "I'll leave you alone and give you a knock later."

"Thank you," I moaned, feeling like the creaking door, as it grouched, groaned, and thudded shut.

## CHAPTER 90

### Let Me Entertain You

There was a knock at the door.

"Hello?"

"Are you up?" Danny chirped.

*"I'm sorry, I can't come to the door right now but if you'd like to fuck off and leave me alone, please do so after the tone. BEEEEP."*

"Charming."

"Ugh. What time is it?"

"An hour later than the last time I knocked. Time to get up."

"Nooo," I cried. I could have done with at least another week in bed. "Okay, okay, I'm coming," I said, sitting up and instantly wishing I hadn't.

"I'll put my key under the door so you can have a shower."

*"Nonono! Hang on."* I said, "I'm just coming." I didn't want to risk being locked in again and lunged out of bed. I tried opening the door, it wouldn't budge, and a mild panic started swelling. Then I noticed that I'd obviously Wookiee-proofed the room at some point by sliding the button across on the Yale.

"Oh mate, you look terrible," Danny remarked when I eventually opened the squeaking bedroom door.

"Thanks very much."

"Phew, and you could do with a Tic Tac?" He remarked, wrinkling his nose and waving his hand across his face.

"Anything else?" I asked bluntly.

"Let me think," Danny said cradling his chin. "Er, you look like shit, and you've got breath to match. No, I think that's everything."

"Well, it's been lovely chatting. Thanks for popping by, please don't call again."

"Enjoy yourself last night?" Danny asked, grinning wildly.

"I've no idea. Did we end up in the bar after that curry," I asked hazily, as the vision of a noisy, smoke-filled room appeared.

"Yes," Danny laughed, "seriously, you don't remember anything in the bar? Dancing, breaking furniture, arm-wrestling with Stevie. Ring any bells?" he asked, raising his eyebrows. I began shaking my head, slowly.

"Drinking whisky?" Danny asked.

"Oh God, I didn't?" I always tended to avoid that particular spirit because of several previous, offensive, and rather uncouth incidents. Bourbon was okay but scotch could get me arrested.

"Oh fella, you were amazing," Danny said smiling, with a hint of admiration and pride, preparing to colour in the gaps for the second morning in a row.

"You started guzzling glasses of Famous Grouse like they were going out of fashion. And you obviously weren't happy with our DJ's choice of '*not another bloody song by Texas*' and told your new best friend to '*turn that shit off and put on some proper music,*' while rifling through his collection of vinyl. I asked you what you were doing, and you poked a finger in my face and shouted that you were on a highly classified mission and had to find 'White Lines' by Grandmaster Flash and the Furious Five or we'd lose the war."

"What war?"

"How the hell should I know you loony? Anyway, Stevie was a bit pissed off and physically removed you from his booth and said he'd find it for you. Don't you remember him picking you up and plonking you on a barstool?"

"Nope."

"Then you probably don't remember your request coming on and trying to breakdance."

"Oh God," I said remorsefully, closing my eyes.

"You did, what I'd describe as, an enthusiastic but technically poor caterpillar before you knocked over two tables and broke a chair leg with a half-arsed head spin?"

"Is that it?" I asked, shaking my head.

"*Is that it?* Oh fella," Danny chortled, placing a hand on my shoulder. "We haven't even scratched the surface."

"Go on, then," I groaned, resigning myself to listening to the full gory details.

"After your breakdance masterclass, you challenged the whole bar to have an arm-wrestling competition in which you came last, after losing in the first round to the eventual winner, Stevie. Shortly after that, you vanished."

"Where to?"

"I found you in the loo. You were on the phone to a pizza company, leaning over the urinal with your head against the wall."

"Oh God, why didn't you stop me?"

"Well, you were mid-flow."

"No, you dick, I meant from ordering food."

"Oh, I tried, but before I managed to grab your phone off you, you'd ordered enough for everyone in the bar and, I reckon, most of the houses across the street. Oh, and you peed on my shoes in the process."

"Sorry. Please tell me that's it, I've heard enough." I looked at the floor, grabbing my sweaty forehead in one hand, feeling the blood throbbing across my temples.

"Oh no, there's loads more." *Oh goodie.*

"When the two delivery boys staggered into the bar carrying the EU pizza mountain, you stood on a table, punching the air with both hands, and got a huge round of applause by boldly shouting at the top of your voice that you could *eat any Scotsman under the table.*"

"And did I?"

"Well, you gave it a bloody go. I watched you demolish a whole twelve-inch loaded with jalapenos in about two minutes."

"What? I don't even like jalapenos. That explains the disgusting taste in my mouth though. Please tell me I didn't pay by credit card," I winced.

"Fella…"

"What?" I cringed.

"…you paid by credit card."

"Oh shit," I grimaced, slapping myself on the forehead, immediately wishing I hadn't, "this is getting worse by the second. That's from our joint account and only for emergencies. I don't think clearing out Domino's to feed a room full of drunk Jocks counts, do you? Alice is going to bloody kill me."

"I expect so. Then for your finale, you turned the disco into an impromptu open mic night and managed to get the whole bar swaying and singing with a few classics. After 'Sweet Caroline' and 'Waltzing Matilda,' you launched into your very loud, horribly tuneless but I have to admit extremely passionate, *second* rendition of 'Delilah.' I tried wrestling the microphone from you and told you to go to bed. That's when you took a swing at me."

"I tried to hit you? I'm so sorry," I bleated, lowering my head in shame.

"I say tried but I'm not even sure you could really call it a punch. I couldn't tell if it was supposed to be a slow-motion haymaker, or you were just trying to grab the mic back."

"Was I really that bad?" I asked, cringing.

"*Bad?* You were a bloody star fella. It was like being back in the mess at Lossie. Some people pay good money to watch a performance like that."

"I am never drinking again." *That sounds familiar.* "Oh God, do you think I should apologise to Stevie?"

"Are you joking? He thought you were great. I think he's planning on offering you a residency."

"Is that everything? I'm not going to appear on Crimewatch or get stopped at the airport or anything?"

"No mate, that's it, you bloody legend."

"Ha," I smiled with the faintest flicker of pride. "Right, bugger off then, and let me get my shit together."

## CHAPTER 91

### Comfortably Numb

Sitting on the bed in my damp towel, showered but feeling far from clean, I desperately wanted to be home, back in my own house, in my own bedroom, with windows. However, after last night's frolics, I didn't fancy travelling any further than back to bed. Battered and broken seemed to be a recurring theme this week. If Alice had been here to nurse me through the aftermath of last night, she would have been oozing sympathy, patting my forehead while calling me a poorly little soldier, right before she started banging the bed with the hoover. My head thumped, my stomach ached, and my sorry rear end made me think I'd been violated by a cactus dipped in tabasco. *Dear Arse, clearly dragging you through a thorn bush wasn't bad enough. I thought I'd treat you to a traumatic tour of the entire Scoville scale too. I can only apologise.*

Despite my fuzzy condition, a realisation began emerging through the haze of my crippling hangover. Six months of extreme camping with the Army was going to put me miles away from the daily pressures of controlling at Swanwick and home. Okay, there would be some fallout from Shooting the Gap, but it wouldn't be anywhere near as punitive as if I stayed. More importantly, if I really did have the Medusa Touch it couldn't reach my family from South Central Asia. I'd save a packet too and be eligible for a deployment bonus. Hopefully, even the MoD wouldn't be insensitive enough to make someone redundant while they were being shelled by the Taliban. *Maybe Isaac has done me a huge favour.* Then again, I'd be missing another irreplaceable half a year of being a dad, unable to guide Toby and Jack, take them fishing, kick a ball or just be around and enjoy watching them grow. Not to mention the emotional wrench of being apart from my faithful, loving, devoted girl, and my wife of course.

My watch said 10:25 and breakfast would only be served for another five minutes. Danny said he'd already eaten, but I felt that my stomach could not be trusted to handle solids just yet, not even a slice of burnt toast. Instead, I started sorting my room, as much as my delicate condition would allow, then began packing.

Danny sat waiting on the bottom step and would have heard the slow thud… thud… thud of my suitcase thumping down the stairs, loosely attached to a bald, red-eyed, shuffling corpse. We lugged our bags to the car, before walking back to the bar to find Stevie to check out. He found us first.

"Ah, Tom Jones," Stevie boomed, shouting from the kitchen doorway as I stepped into the bar cum dining room cum cabaret.

I immediately started apologising, spotting the broken chair in the corner of the room and staring in horror at the towering pile of pizza boxes stacked next to it. *Oh, my sweet Lord, just how much did I order last night?* Alice was going to go ballistic when that 'little' transaction appeared on our next statement. I wouldn't be able to intercept the postman either, as I'd probably be gone before it arrived. At least I'd have the protection of 3,500 miles and be in a slightly less hostile environment.

"Thanks, Stevie," I said, handing over the key to my vault and shaking hands, "it's a special place you have here."

"Thanks, but it's gonna be pretty quiet withoot yous two. At least I have a mass to look forward to tomorra."

A small part of me had a burning desire to ask if it would be Catholic or black but the rest of me still felt like it was dying and couldn't wait to get out.

"Thanks for everything Stevie and sorry about the chair," I grimaced. "I hope you won't get in any trouble."

"Nae problem wee man, dinnae fess yerself, the Devil looks after his ain."


## CHAPTER 92

### Take Me Home Country Roads

Thankfully, Danny was feeling well enough to take the wheel for the quiet, event-free drive back to Edinburgh Airport. I reckoned I'd have still been well over the limit and in no fit state to be put in charge of a motor vehicle or even Lego. Drifting in and out of sleep, I kept fidgeting and adjusting the seat of my trousers.

Arriving just before noon, Danny drove us straight to the car hire drop-off.

"Wakey wakey," he chimed.

I opened my eyes, leaning forward gently as Danny stopped reversing and killed the engine.

"Ugh, what time is it?" I asked, yawning loudly.

"Almost twelve. Come on Rip Van Winkle, let's go."

To my relief, my dinner date Holly wasn't at her desk, so we popped the keys in the drop-box before heading to the terminal to check in. I felt like I'd had a minor victory when I didn't encounter any hitches with security after checking in my bags, breezing through without so much as a bleep. It looked like the gods might be smiling down on me for a change, granting me a hassle-free and painless trip home, apart from my ring of fire that continued glowing.

Waiting for our gate to be called, I sat gazing into space, clenching my bum, swaying as I moved uncomfortably from cheek to cheek while dragging my tongue across my teeth, scraping off a layer of sour scum.

"What *are* you doing fella?"

"What?"

"You're sat there gurning and rocking like a complete nutter."

"Sorry, I can't get comfortable. I can't believe I was stupid enough to eat jalapenos on top of a curry, not after what my poor arse went through on Thursday night or rather what I put through my arse," I grimaced. "Not that *anything* happened Thursday night," I growled, turning to look Danny squarely in the eye.

"Nothing did happen on Thursday night though," Danny confirmed.

"That's right, nothing at all," I reiterated icily, "nothing... at... all."

"Alright, message received," he said, backing away, putting his hands up in surrender.

"My mouth tastes like I've been gargling fermented battery acid," I gurned. "I need a coffee, want one?" I asked, getting up and walking towards the Costa stand while clamping my arse cheeks together to stop them from chafing.

"Café latte please, Sweetie."

"Okay."

"...and fella," Danny shouted.

"Yes," I replied, turning back.

*"Walk properly. You're mincing!"*

Danny stood looking up at the information screen when I minced back, coffee in hand.

"Here you go," I said, holding Danny's cup in front of his face. Taking it, his eyes stayed fixed on the monitor.

"Thanks. Our flight's boarding, Gate 9. Come on."

Getting to Gate 9 involved trudging back towards security, and on arrival, we joined the back of a long, snaking line of passengers slowly filtering through.

After securing my rucksack into the overhead locker, without the smuggled carcass of a fruit bat inside, I collapsed into my seat, wincing as I landed. I clicked my lap strap, pulling it tight before leaning back and falling fast asleep before we'd even taxied. An hour later I woke as the aircraft began descending into a wet and grey Southampton Airport.

Touching down just after one o'clock, the wheels of the Dash 8 bumped and screeched onto the damp tarmac, and stretching, I gave a long, deep, and relieved sigh. *Nearly there, almost home.*

Having collected our bags, Danny and I caught the shuttle to the car park, trudging a short distance in the rain to find a parking meter and Danny's waiting BMW. We quickly loaded our wet luggage before climbing in and roaring off.

Fat drops of rain splatted the windscreen and I could feel the car's rear end twitching on the wet and greasy surface, but thankfully Danny eased off the accelerator. Although the roads looked fairly empty, I felt enormously relieved that he wasn't trying to improve his stage time on the return leg, in the wet. Sitting quietly, the euphoria of our boys' trip quickly evaporated, the lulling mood in the car feeling flat and sombre. My mind began tumbling with thoughts of my imminent trip and being parted from my loved ones. As Danny turned off the motorway, retracing the route we'd taken just two days ago, he broke the silence.

"I know it's going to be tough being away again, but don't worry about Ali and the boys. I'm around if there's a problem."

"Thanks, mate, I appreciate that, and thanks again for this. It's been…" I started, struggling for a suitable adjective.

"…memorable?" suggested Danny.

"…emotional," I concluded, twisting in my seat.

Pulling up outside, Danny applied the handbrake but left the engine running, getting out of the car.

"Aren't you coming in?" I asked, more out of politeness than a genuine offer, both of us knowing that I faced a poignant reunion.

"No fella, you need to spend as much quality time as you can with Ali before you go. Just tell her I said hi."

I spotted Alice jumping up from the sofa, her face appearing in the lounge window and the two exchanged a wave.

"Look, I don't know if I'll see you before I fly out. You know what it's like."

"I do, so if I don't see you, take care. Remember, keep low, move fast," Danny winked.

"Cheers Danny," I said with heartfelt thanks and a twinge of sadness. "I love you man," I blubbed, grabbing him in a macho embrace.

"I love you too, you soppy bugger," he said, patting me on the back.

"I won't forget this."

"Me either fella. Me either."

"Er, you'd better forget *it*, you promised," I chuckled. "Thanks again though," I said, releasing him from my man hug with tears trickling down my face.

"You're welcome," he grinned, climbing into his car. "See you later fella."

Raising my hand towards the back of the speeding motor, I stood waving as it disappeared up the road. Grabbing my bags, I started down the steps and along the path to the front door, preparing to be reunited with my girls.


## CHAPTER 93

### Can I Kick It?

Gypsy began pronging and barking excitedly, acting like I'd been missing in the jungles of Borneo for a year as Alice threw her arms around me, dissolving into a flood of tears. I'd only been away for two days but knew her emotional outburst was because we probably only had a couple of weeks together before I headed off for another six-month operational tour. We simply stood in the hallway, me holding her, rocking gently as she wept.

"Hey, it's alright, we've done this before," I said, smoothing her back.

"I know, I know, but we'd made plans and promised to take the boys away. He's messed all that up. I really don't want you to go away again."

"Well, I'm not exactly mad about the idea, but you know how it is."

"We haven't told them yet, either. They're going to be really upset." I didn't want to think about that. While I'd been away, I'd tried putting a lot of thoughts on hold but now that I'd come home, facing them, and explaining this to the boys would be agonising. Toby and Jack had been nine and five the first time I'd been deployed. There had been lots of tears, but they'd had no concept of the real dangers and had adapted to their new routine without me within a few weeks of my departure. Now they were seventeen and thirteen, and Afghanistan wasn't just another name for some strange faraway place that Daddy had to go to as Kosovo and Iraq had been. They watched the news. They knew what could happen.

Cradling the sobbing Alice, my phone started ringing, the sound of Maroon 5's 'Harder to Breathe' filling the hallway.

"Hi, Vlad."

"Hi, Henry, good trip, my friend?" Vlad wheezed, sounding like he was in an exceptionally good mood.

"Yes, mate. Look, can I call you later? It's not really a good time. I literally just walked in the door."

"Sure, I imagine the missus is a bit upset."

"That's an understatement."

"Well, if you've got five minutes this might cheer her up." I put my hand over the mouthpiece.

"It's Vlad, he said he knows something that might cheer you up," I shrugged.

"Okay," Alice mouthed, nodding.

"Go on then," I said, walking into the kitchen, and guiding Alice into a chair before flicking the switch on the kettle.

"So, you remember that 5-a-side game I invited you to?"

"Yes."

"Well, no one was supposed to mention it to Attila the Runt, but somehow he found out."

"He'd probably been sneaking around and overhead someone talking about it, or he's bugged the Crew Room," I suggested.

"Yeah, probably. So, surprise, surprise, there he was, bang on five o'clock, in his junior England strip."

"What a shock. I bet he was about as welcome as a turd in a hot tub."

"You could say that. Anyway, Tony Williams turned up five minutes later and you know how he feels about the boss and what he's like on a sports pitch?"

I did. The stocky, robust flight sergeant and former Pontypridd U-21 loosehead prop could best be described as a thuggish but well-balanced Welshman, having a massive chip on *both* shoulders. Despite his short fuse, I knew Tony to be a competent, professional, and well-respected controller. A few months ago, he had bent my ear after his squadron commander, Isaac, had given him the poorest, most unflattering, and scathing appraisal he'd had in his eighteen years of service. If Isaac had willingly put himself into a sporting arena with that disgruntled Man of Harlech, whose career prospects he'd severely shat on with a damning and unfair annual assessment, he was braver than I thought.

329

"Our resident angry Welshman?"

"The very same. Well, Isaac was doing his best Maradona impression and running with the ball towards the goal in search of glory when Tony came hurtling from the wing like a vendetta-fuelled charging rhino. He obviously forgot what shaped ball we were playing with and converted the little fella over the crossbar."

"Oh, my God. Is Tony's foot okay?"

"Very funny."

"So, was he hurt then?"

"Who?" Alice mouthed. I held up a finger.

"Oh yes," Vlad rasped gleefully, "he came down headfirst, landed awkwardly and his shoulder decided that it no longer wanted to sit in its socket and popped round the back to say hello to his shoulder blade."

"Yowzer. That must have been horrendous."

"Yeah, he was still screaming fifteen minutes later when they put him in the back of the ambulance. Anyway, I thought it was important to do my welfare bit and let everyone know. He's in QA in case you want to send flowers."

"Very noble of you Flight Lieutenant Netsov. I'll let Alice choose a bouquet. Triffids maybe."

"Hah, see you later mate."

"See you."

"Flowers for who?" Alice asked as I put my phone down.

"I'll make us some tea, we'll go into the lounge and when you're sitting comfortably,

I'll begin."

As I relayed the story to Alice, she sat biting her lip, expressionless, until I got to the point where I mentioned the screaming and how long it had taken for the ambulance to arrive. At that point, she started grinning.

"You see, my love, there is a God," I suggested.

"No, if there was a just and caring God, *he* would be going to Afghanistan instead of you."

"I don't think even The Almighty would want to go and spend six months with the Army in Lashkar Gah."

"Very funny," she sighed, "you know what I meant."

"Well, I don't think Isaac will be going anywhere for a while. He couldn't pick up a spud gun at the moment, no matter hold a rifle."

"Sooo, are you going to visit him?"

"In the hospital? Why on earth would I want to do that?"

"*Oh, come on Henry*," Alice chastised, "I think you should pay him a visit." She smirked, her eyes suddenly playful. "I mean, just imagine how pleased *you'd be* if you were lying in a hospital bed in pain and he turned up to see you."

It slowly dawned on me exactly what she meant. *Am I really being presented with the exceptionally rare prospect of getting one up on my old foe?* I started feeling tempted by the idea and extremely grateful that Alice was on my team.

# CHAPTER 94

## Please Forgive Me

I called the Queen Alexandra Hospital in Cosham to find out what ward I had to visit and asked about Isaac's condition. I also checked on the visiting hours, deciding I'd go and see him around four o'clock.

As we sat huddled on the sofa chatting, Gypsy jumped up, squeezing between us. Alice wanted to know about the trip away, so I selectively told her all about it, but obviously not about it all. I explained that we'd flown up and day one had been rained off, so we'd relaxed, had an early night, then played golf on day two, been out for a meal, and flown home this morning. Of course, I knew she wouldn't believe half of the stuff coming out of my fetid mouth and would be thinking that there was a lot more to my story. For starters, my eyes looked like those of someone who'd been sleeping rough for a year, and I had the faint whiff of a distillery about me. God only knows what she was thinking about the way I kept fidgeting; twitching and squirming like I'd been unable to resist the amorous advances of a lonely submariner.

"Right, I suppose I'd better go and sort my gear out," I suggested, climbing off the sofa.

"Okay, just throw your dirty stuff in the basket. I'll sort through it all in the morning."

My heart started beating rapidly. *That could be a problem.* I didn't fancy an interrogation about how I'd got blood spatters and cat DNA on my clothes.

Grabbing my gear, I started lugging it up the stairs. Gypsy followed, watching me throw everything onto the floor of the spare room. I noticed that the funky smell had gone. *Funny that.*

"Hello girl, are you here to help?"

As I opened the suitcase, before I could stop her, Gypsy sprang, diving headfirst into my laundry, tail wagging. Growling as she rooted around, snorting loudly, she suddenly stopped and then began tugging. Walking backwards, she continued snarling, shaking her head, dragging my bloodied golf trousers out from the heap, spitting them out into a black crumpled heap. She sniffed again then sat down and started whining, staring at me accusingly.

"What? Don't look at me like that? It was an accident!" I was just waiting for her to tut and shake her head. Before I had the chance to explain, she walked out, giving me a final backward judgmental look of disgust.

"*It was an accident!*" I whined, as her haughty backside flounced out of the room.

Hearing the sound of Alice padding along the hall, I bent down, grabbing up enough for a load, including the incriminating trousers. I waited, hunched over, on tenterhooks, listening. As she bolted the toilet door, I began creeping downstairs, wincing halfway as one floorboard began creaking before hurrying down the last few steps and rushing into the kitchen. Easing the door open, I started throwing everything plus a liquid tablet into the washing machine, panicking at the sound of the toilet flushing. Slamming the glass door shut, I kept frantically pressing the start button. Clunk. The welcome sound of hissing water started echoing around the kitchen. *Phew.*

"I said I'd do that." I jumped.

"I know but... well, I've been away, and I haven't, you know... been very helpful lately. I thought I'd save you a job."

"Then why do you look like I just caught you rummaging through my knicker draw?" My neck prickled and I suddenly felt like Alice had turned all the radiators up to 'blast furnace.'

"What? Knicker draw? I…what… I'm just a bit, you know, jet lagged."

"*Jet lagged?* You flew from Scotland!"

"I know, I know, tired, tired, I meant tired."

"You're a bit tired. *Oh, you poor thing.* Well, if the washing's on why don't you go and do something about that special odour of yours before you have a nap? You smell like a wino's duffel coat."

I still felt shabby but delighted in being back under a well-behaved shower, loving the comfort and reassurance of the familiar embrace of my own four walls. Refreshed and on the road to something approaching nearly normal, I started clinking through the array of bottles and jars in Alice's emporium, looking for an intimate soothing balm.

Standing with one leg up on the side of the bath, I moaned softly with the blissful sensation of the cold cream cooling my smouldering embers. *Oh yes, that feels so good.* I frowned, disturbed by the feeling that those words seemed horribly familiar.

Stepping out of the bathroom, I sashayed along the landing with my arse feeling like it was chewing a peppermint toffee.

"Aah, hello bed." My head had barely touched the pillow before I started impersonating a Massey Ferguson.

## CHAPTER 95

### Sympathy for the Devil

Dressing slowly, I began mentally preparing myself for the philanthropic hospital visit, deciding that first I needed to nip into town and pick up a couple of things. *I can't just turn up empty-handed now, can I?*

"Okay, I'm off now," I shouted to Alice, nearing the bottom of the stairs.

"Alright, my love. I picked up some nice red meat for dinner," Alice said, popping her head into the hallway.

"Lovely, what are we having?" I asked, looking back with one foot out of the door.

"Well I did think about a rabbit casserole," she chuckled.

"That is never going to be funny. *Ever!*" I blanched.

"Don't panic, bunnykins, I got you a fillet steak. You might need your strength later," she winked.

"I can't wait. See you later," I replied, shutting the door behind me, and breathing deeply to calm my racing heartbeat.

Reversing into the parking space at the back of the hospital, I heard the faint, broken pitter-patter of raindrops on the roof. Jogging the short distance to the nearest ticket machine, I blanched at the exorbitant tariff of charges. For the price of one hour, I thought it would have been cheaper to hire a limo. *If these hospital planners had any sense, they'd put the A&E and Coronary Care wards closer to the ticket machines, so that they were ideally placed to deal with the increased number of cardiac arrests.* I placed the ticket on the dashboard before shutting and locking the car door. Walking towards the entrance, I pulled my jacket over my head, breaking into a sprint as the spitting gave way to a heavy downpour.

The Orthopaedic Ward sat on Level D, two floors above the North entrance that I had slid into moments ago. I asked for directions at the main reception desk and could have sworn that I'd been following them to the letter but still got lost, ending up at the entrance to the Geriatric Ward with its unmistakable musty sweet scent of digestive biscuits, boiled cabbage, and stale wee. Stumbling on a Help terminal in the hallway, I typed 'Orthopaedic.' *Aha, I just need to walk to the end of this corridor and turn left.*

Walking past the open door to the Nurses' Station, a voice rang out. "May I help you?" asked the stern-faced Ward Sister.

"Yes," I replied nervously, clearing the lump in my throat. "I'm here to see Timothy Koch." My palms instantly became clammy.

"He's probably sleeping. You're his first visitor," she replied, getting up from her chair and leading me down the corridor to his bedside. My adversary appeared to be out for the count.

When I'd called earlier, the duty nurse had explained that due to the severe ligament and tendon trauma he'd suffered, Isaac had been put on a high-dose analgesic. She also mentioned that it had taken a long time to finally relocate his shoulder. Even though the doctors had managed to force it back in, the shoulder had repeatedly dislocated, and the slightest hand movement had been enough for the ball joint to pop out of its socket. He wouldn't be writing damning reports, stabbing people in the back, or doing anything else that he did with his dominant hand for a while, and I thought that he did a lot of one thing with it repeatedly.

I stood staring at my sleeping nemesis, who wouldn't have looked out of place in the Children's Ward, noticing his pained expression. I thought my natural instinct would have been to grab a pillow and see how well he could breathe through it but strangely my feelings were far from murderous. What had that nurse said, 'You're his first visitor.' I don't why but I started feeling a twinge of pity in some small part of me, probably a toenail. Placing the card and present on his bedside table, I felt a small yet faintly hollow victorious grin spreading across my face.

Walking out, heading back towards the corridor the sister called after me.

"Excuse me, was it you who phoned earlier?" she asked my retreating back. I stopped.

"Yes, it was," I replied, turning around.

"How was he?"

"I don't know, Sister, he didn't wake up. I think he's a bit spaced out."

"Yes, well, he is on an intravenous opiate, and he'll still be in a lot of pain when he does wake up."

"Could we wake him up then?"

"Sorry?" she replied, shocked by the question.

"So that he can see a friendly face," I explained with what I hoped sounded like sincerity.

"Oh, I see. No, it's probably best to just to let him rest."

"Okay. And he's on strong painkillers and in a lot of pain you say?"

"Yes," the sister confirmed with a sympathetic nod.

"That's good," I grinned.

"Pardon?"

"That he's got a strong painkiller."

"Oh. Yes, I see," the sister replied suspiciously. "So, should I say who called?"

"No, it's fine," I smiled thinly, turning to leave, then stopped. "Actually, yes you can. When he comes round could you tell him that Guy Fawkes popped in?"

Walking back along the hospital corridor, a thought suddenly struck me. It could only have been a few days ago at the most that he'd volunteered me to go to Afghanistan. Signals and paperwork for an Out-of-Area detachment took a certain amount of processing, these things didn't just happen overnight, they had to be confirmed, emails had to be exchanged, phone calls made, etc. If my underhand and scheming boss hadn't got all of his backstabbing ducks in a row and all of the admin finalised before the 5-a-side 'accident', there might still be a slim chance that I wouldn't be going anywhere. *I reckon he'll be in hospital for at least a week, perhaps two, God-willing nine. Maybe he hasn't confirmed my eligibility in time and the RAF hasn't got his rubber stamp of approval. Maybe.*

Walking out of the hospital, I discovered that the rain shower had almost stopped, and stepped into the fresh, crisp air of a brightening Saturday afternoon. Floating as I strode back to the car, I nodded, smiling to myself. The world around me glistened, beams of sunlight began streaming from the heavens as the dark clouds continued breaking up, melting away like the dissolving shroud wrapped around my mind that I could feel sliding, slipping, and fading.

## CHAPTER 96

### I Can See Clearly Now

*Wow, what a week!* Sitting in the car, I gazed vacantly, biting my lower lip, pondering the events of the last seven days. *When had all this madness started? Was it forgetting our anniversary? If Alice had meant to punish me there's no way she could have foreseen the fallout. That whole dressing-up palaver had certainly knocked me off kilter, but was anyone really to blame for what followed?*

As the last few dwindling raindrops bounced off the car roof, I continued staring, lulled into a stupor by the hospital's dull, flat grey walls. In whatever way all of this had come to pass, I certainly couldn't be blamed for putting Isaac in a hospital bed, although plenty would have understood if I had. Neither should I feel guilty about Gypsy. I'd never meant to poison her. That nightmare had been caused by a lapse of concentration and being side-tracked by the door-knocking God Squad. Then of course, there was Alice, but

338

ultimately, I'd performed first aid and saved her. As for Shooting the Gap, I hadn't gone to work last Sunday planning to have a mid-air collision, I'd been traumatised by that bunny girl outfit, distracted by Alice's heaving knockers, and preoccupied with the prospect of hosting the Gerry Adams' Fan Club.

The more I thought about it, the more I realised that Danny was right. I'd never had an incident in all my years of controlling and if I was being honest, I'd always been a bit cocky, arrogant perhaps about my spotless record. *Had that been hubris? Its aftermath had certainly brought me down a peg or two. And as for those poor cats.* I shuddered.

Sitting in the visitor's car park, staring at the dreary facade of the Queen Alexandra Hospital, Cosham, I finally understood. One small event had caused me to trip, then stumble, and fall headfirst. Toppling downhill, gathering momentum, my world had then snowballed with me stuck at the centre of a giant whirling sphere of havoc and chaos, tumbling out of control, not knowing which way was up, as I was carried crashing from one disaster to the next.

*None of this was my fault.* I hadn't been acting like some homicidal lunatic, hellbent on causing death and destruction, I'd simply been a victim of circumstance, and just really, really unlucky. Danny and Vlad had both said it and they'd hit the nail squarely on the head, *shit happens!*

***

# Epilogue

## Everybody Hurts

It had been almost two weeks since I'd visited Squadron Leader Koch in the hospital. Yawning, I stretched from my cramped seat on board the ageing RAF Tristar passenger jet. The seven-hour-long flight from RAF Brize Norton had left me feeling tired, achy, and ever so slightly irritable. Despite my fatigue, I still managed to smile at the thought of Isaac's face on waking up to discover I'd dropped by and left him a get-well card and a gift. I grinned, imagining him picking up the tube of Pringles, trying to pull off the foil lid, and screaming as his dislocated shoulder popped again.

The card read:

*'Sir, I was really sorry to hear that you'd had a minor accident. It's easy to imagine just how much pain you're in, I think about it every day. I speak for everyone when I say that you should take all the time you need before you come back to work. Please enjoy this tube of Pringles as a small token of my appreciation for everything you've ever done for me and remember, "Once you pop you just can't stop."*

*Henry x'*

My thoughts were interrupted by the crackling announcement from the air loadmaster, instructing everyone to check their protective equipment, as the captain was preparing to make a tactical descent to land. Looking across the aisle, peering through the window into the inky blackness beyond, the bright cabin lights went out, replaced with a dim, faintly familiar eerie green glow. The world lurched downwards, as the engines' whine continued climbing, accompanied by the faint thudding pop of anti-missile flares as the aircraft dropped into its steep, final approach profile towards Kabul. Resting my chin on the top of my flak jacket, I felt my Kevlar helmet slip forward thudding against the seat in front. As the cry of the engines rose to a whistling scream, I closed my eyes. Not in prayer, my thoughts travelled home. I knew that being away from my family would be hard, it always was, but an extended break from my double-crossing thundertwat of a boss had its merits. Still, six months away from my loved ones was going to feel like a lifetime and my heart started aching, as I sat thinking about how much I'd miss all of them, Alice, Toby, Jack and of course Gypsy.

*On the other hand, how bad is it going to be? I've heard that Helmand Province is lovely this time of year…*

**APPENDIX**

**CHAPTER**

Song Title - Artist (Year)

**CHAPTER 1**

Stairway to Heaven – Led Zeppelin (1971)

**CHAPTER 2**

Private Dancer - Tina Turner (1984)

**CHAPTER 3**

Joy and Pain – Maze (1980)

**CHAPTER 4**

I Surrender – Rainbow (1981)

**CHAPTER 5**

Fast Car – Tracy Chapman (1988)

**CHAPTER 6**

Welcome to the Jungle – Guns N' Rose (1987)

**CHAPTER 7**

Weak in the Presence of Beauty – Alison Moyet (1987)

**CHAPTER 8**

Embarrassment – Madness (1980)

**CHAPTER 9**

Killer Queen – Queen (1974)

## CHAPTER 10

Walk Like an Egyptian – The Bangles (1986)

## CHAPTER 11

Do You Really Want to Hurt Me - Culture Club (1984)

## CHAPTER 12

Welcome to My Nightmare – Alice Cooper (1975)

## CHAPTER 13

Danger Zone – Kenny Loggins (1986)

## CHAPTER 14

If I Could Turn Back Time – Cher (1989)

## CHAPTER 15

You're the Devil in Disguise – Elvis Presley (1963)

## CHAPTER 16

Don't Worry Be Happy – Bobby McFerrin (1988)

## CHAPTER 17

Cry Me a River – Ella Fitzgerald (1961)

## CHAPTER 18

The Bitterest Pill (I Ever Had to Swallow) – The Jam (1982)

## CHAPTER 19

Smoke on the Water – Deep Purple (1972)

## CHAPTER 20

Burning Down the House – Talking Heads (1983)

**CHAPTER 21**

Daydream – The Lovin' Spoonful (1966)

**CHAPTER 22**

I Don't Like Mondays – Boomtown Rats (1979)

**CHAPTER 23**

Barbie Girl – Aqua (1997)

**CHAPTER 24**

Who Let the Dogs Out – Baha Men (2000)

**CHAPTER 25**

Homeward Bound – Simon & Garfunkel (1964)

**CHAPTER 26**

Wake Up Boo! - Boo Radleys (1995)

**CHAPTER 27**

We Are Family – Sister Sledge (1979)

**CHAPTER 28**

A Little Respect – Erasure (1988)

**CHAPTER 29**

Pull Up to the Bumper – Grace Jones (1981)

**CHAPTER 30**

Free Fallin' - Tom Petty and the Heartbreakers (1989)

**CHAPTER 31**

Missing – Everything but the Girl (1994)

## CHAPTER 32

Beautiful Day – U2 (2000)

## CHAPTER 33

Enola Gay - Orchestral Manoeuvres in the Dark (1980)

## CHAPTER 34

Poison – Alice Cooper (1989)

## CHAPTER 35

So Emotional – Whitney Houston (1987)

## CHAPTER 36

You're My Best Friend – Queen (1976)

## CHAPTER 37

Lean on Me – Bill Withers (1972)

## CHAPTER 38

She Drives Me Crazy – Fine Young Cannibals (1989)

## CHAPTER 39

Money, Money, Money – Abba (1976)

## CHAPTER 40

Sweet Child o' Mine – Guns N' Roses (1987)

## CHAPTER 41

I'm Going Slightly Mad – Queen (1991)

## CHAPTER 42

Little Lies – Fleetwood Mac (1987)

**CHAPTER 43**

Get Lucky – Daft Punk (2013)

**CHAPTER 44**

Escape (The Piña Colada Song) - Rupert Holmes - 1979

**CHAPTER 45**

How You Remind Me – Nickelback (2001)

**CHAPTER 46**

Wicked Game – Chris Isaak (1989)

**CHAPTER 47**

Hanging on the Telephone – Blondie (1978)

**CHAPTER 48**

Suspicious Minds – Elvis Presley (1969)

**CHAPTER 49**

When You Say Nothing at All – Ronan Keating (1999)

**CHAPTER 50**

Cold As Ice – Foreigner (1977)

**CHAPTER 51**

Should I Stay or Should I Go – The Clash (1982)

**CHAPTER 52**

Smells Like Teen Spirit – Nirvana (1991)

**CHAPTER 53**

Land of Confusion – Genesis (1986)

## CHAPTER 54

Don't Stop Believing – Journey (1981)

## CHAPTER 55

Rocket Man – Elton John (1972)

## CHAPTER 56

Wind of Change – Scorpions (1990)

## CHAPTER 57

I'm So Excited – Pointer Sisters (1982)

## CHAPTER 58

Don't You (Forget About Me) – Simple Minds (1985)

## CHAPTER 59

Shut Up and Drive – Rihanna (2007)

## CHAPTER 60

My Ding A Ling – Chuck Berry (1972)

## CHAPTER 61

Up, Up and Away – The 5th Dimension (1972)

## CHAPTER 62

Beautiful Liar – Beyoncé (2006)

## CHAPTER 63

Do You Know Where You're Going To – Diana Ross (1975)

## CHAPTER 64

Ain't That a Kick in the Head – Dean Martin (1960)

**CHAPTER 65**

A View to a Kill – Duran Duran (1985)

**CHAPTER 66**

Don't Fear the Reaper - Blue Öyster Cult (1976)

**CHAPTER 67**

Run to the Hills – Iron Maiden (1982)

**CHAPTER 68**

Red Right Hand – Nick Cave and the Bad Seeds (1994)

**CHAPTER 69**

Stray Cat Strut – Stray Cats (1981)

**CHAPTER 70**

Suicide is Painless – The Ron Hicklin Singers (1970)

**CHAPTER 71**

Highway to Hell – AC/DC (1979)

**CHAPTER 72**

Rat Trap – The Boomtown Rats (1978)

**CHAPTER 73**

Hot N Cold – Katy Perry (2008)

**CHAPTER 74**

I Just Called to Say I Love You – Stevie Wonder (1984)

**CHAPTER 75**

Maneater – Hall & Oates (1982)

## CHAPTER 76

She's a Lady – Tom Jones (1971)

## CHAPTER 77

Show Me the Way to Go Home – Robert Shaw, Richard Dreyfuss, Roy Scheider (1975)

## CHAPTER 78

Getting Jiggy With It – Will Smith (1997)

## CHAPTER 79

What's Going On – Marvin Gaye (1971)

## CHAPTER 80

Girls on Film – Duran Duran (1981)

## CHAPTER 81

Grease – Frankie Valli (1978)

## CHAPTER 82

Green, Green Grass of Home – Tom Jones (1967)

## CHAPTER 83

Shake, Rattle and Roll – Big Joe Turner (1954)

## CHAPTER 84

Feeling Good – Nina Simone (1965)

## CHAPTER 85

Size of a Cow – The Wonder Stuff (1991)

## CHAPTER 86

Spice Up Your Life – Spice Girls (1997)

**CHAPTER 87**

Cigarettes and Alcohol – Oasis (1994)

**CHAPTER 88**

Rag Doll - Aerosmith (1987)

**CHAPTER 89**

Wake Me Up When September Ends – Green Day (2004)

**CHAPTER 90**

Let Me Entertain You – Robbie Williams (1997)

**CHAPTER 91**

Comfortably Numb – Pink Floyd (1979)

**CHAPTER 92**

Take Me Home Country Roads – John Denver (1971)

**CHAPTER 93**

Can I Kick It? – A Tribe Called Quest (1990)

**CHAPTER 94**

Please Forgive Me – Bryan Adams (1993)

**CHAPTER 95**

Sympathy for the Devil – The Rolling Stones (1968)

**CHAPTER 96**

I Can See Clearly Now – Johnny Nash (1972)

**Epilogue**

Everybody Hurts – R.E.M. (1992)

Printed in Great Britain
by Amazon